ORPHANS OF
THE STORM

CELIA IMRIE

With historical research
by Fidelis Morgan

BLOOMSBURY PUBLISHING
LONDON · OXFORD · NEW YORK · NEW DELHI · SYDNEY

BLOOMSBURY PUBLISHING
Bloomsbury Publishing Plc
50 Bedford Square, London, WC1B 3DP, UK
29 Earlsfort Terrace, Dublin 2, Ireland

BLOOMSBURY, BLOOMSBURY PUBLISHING and the Diana logo are trademarks
of Bloomsbury Publishing Plc

First published in Great Britain 2021
Copyright © Celia Imrie, 2021
'Behind the Scenes' copyright © Fidelis Morgan, 2021

Celia Imrie has asserted her right under the Copyright, Designs and Patents Act, 1988,
to be identified as Author of this work

A catalogue record for this book is available from the British Library

ISBN: HB: 978-1-5266-1491-9; TPB: 978-1-5266-1490-2;
SIGNED SPECIAL EDITION: 978-1-5266-4249-3;
EBOOK: 978-1-5266-1489-6; EPDF: 978-1-5266-4527-2

2 4 6 8 10 9 7 5 3 1

Typeset by Integra Software Services Pvt. Ltd.
Printed and bound in Great Britain by CPI Group (UK) Ltd, Croydon CR0 4YY

To find out more about our authors and books visit www.bloomsbury.com
and sign up for our newsletters

ORPHANS OF THE STORM

BY THE SAME AUTHOR

The Happy Hoofer
Not Quite Nice
Nice Work (If You Can Get It)
Sail Away
A Nice Cup Of Tea

Tuesday 9 April 1912, Nice

'They are here with you?' There was a hesitation in Aunt Thérèse's voice that frightened Marcella.

'Who?' Marcella replied. 'Are who with me?'

'The children. Are they here?'

'They should be with you, Aunt Thérèse.' Marcella's mouth went dry. Her knees buckled. 'Why? Why aren't they with you?'

She watched the colour drain from her aunt's face.

'What's happened? Something's happened!' Marcella reached out and grabbed the handle of the front door to steady herself. 'They're not hurt, are they?'

'I'm sure they're fine, Marcella.' Thérèse's voice was level now. She sounded much calmer than she looked.

'So why haven't you brought them?' Marcella felt dizzy – what of a hundred reasons could have prevented her children coming here today?

'I... I...' Aunt Thérèse hunched up her shoulders, lost for words. 'There was nothing I could do.'

Now Marcella was really scared.

'Yesterday Michael took them. He...'

'My god, Aunt Thérèse,' Marcella couldn't stop her voice quivering, 'what have you done?'

Thérèse Magaïl looked down at her feet.

'You let him take them away,' Marcella cried. 'You let him steal my children.'

'We'll find them.'

'No, Aunt Thérèse.' Marcella grabbed her aunt by the elbow and looked straight into her eyes. 'We both know what Michael is capable of. If he has taken them, he will make sure that I never see them again.'

PART ONE

Marcella

September 1911, Nice, France
'Before we continue, I must note down a few details.' Monsieur Nabias unscrewed the lid of his pen and scratched Marcella's name on to a clean sheet of paper. 'This is a mighty step to take, especially for such a young woman.'

Marcella looked into her lap. She was frightened. She had come here on impulse. Just walked in off the street. She had bought the lace for the shop on Avenue de la Gare and was going to buy something for her children, some toys to make them smile, before taking the tram back to work. Then she had seen the golden sign that indicated a lawyer's office. Beneath it, alongside the door, a brass plaque read: C. NABIAS, NOTARY, SOLICITOR. NO APPOINTMENT NECESSARY. So she walked in.

Stepping inside had been an impulse, but it was nonetheless something Marcella had been contemplating night after night as she lay awake beside her sleeping husband. For eighteen months, since the birth of Edmond, her second child, divorcing Michael had been her one overriding thought. Remembering the baby now, with his plump cheeks, his mischievous smile, his head of dark curls, strengthened her resolve.

She mustn't be scared. There was no other way. Monsieur Nabias had welcomed her into his office, after all. He had not laughed in her face, as she feared he might.

She watched him concentrate as he moved his pen across the paper. She was amazed at how young he seemed. He could be only a few years older than her, with his mustard-coloured hair and the slight down on his chin.

He looked up at her.

'Please take a seat, madame.'

Marcella set the packet of lace on the floor and sat down on the other side of the desk. Thanks to the thick layer of dust on the windows, it was shady and cool in the lawyer's office. You could barely see the sun, although, as she'd stepped inside, Marcella had felt it burning through the back of her dress.

'Madame Navratil, what is your date of birth?'

'Thirtieth of January 1890.'

'I see, so you are still only twenty-one. And how long have you been married?'

'Three years, and five months.'

'You have children?'

'Two boys.'

Marcella felt sure that Monsieur Nabias made a slight tutting sound. He disapproved of her being here. It had been a stupid idea. Of course men would stick together. Why should this man be any different? Perhaps he was one of her husband's drinking companions. Why would he take the side of a young woman like her against a businessman like Michael?

She'd made a mistake. She should go. Forget the whole thing. No good could come of it. She stood up, scraping the wooden chair against the tiled floor.

Monsieur Nabias peered at her over his spectacles.

'Madame Navratil? Are you feeling unwell? Would you like me to fetch you a glass of water?'

'No! I mean… No, thank you, I… I shouldn't have come here… I'm sorry, I—' She bent down to pick up her package.

'Please, madame. Don't be afraid. It is very brave of you. Rest assured that everything will be all right. What you tell me here is strictly between us. Inside this room, every word is private. Believe me, Madame Navratil. At first everyone has doubts.' He spoke gently to her. 'You look very pale, madame. Please do sit down. I wouldn't want you to faint.'

It was true. Marcella did feel terrible. She gripped the back of the chair. Why had she come? If Michael knew, then what would happen? How would he punish her? She didn't want to be locked up again.

'Madame Navratil?'

Marcella looked at the man. She felt as though she was in a dream.

'Nothing has happened yet. There will be plenty of time for you to change your mind, if you wish. All we are doing now is having a little chat about your circumstances. To help get things clear in your own head, as much as anything else. And then, I will advise you about what course you can take. Only then need you make a decision as to whether or not to proceed.'

Monsieur Nabias turned and from a shelf behind him produced a jug of water and a glass. He filled the glass and held it out for her.

She took a few sips. She was not convinced. Perhaps Michael was following her. It wouldn't be the first time. He might be outside on the avenue, leaning against a plane tree, puffing on his pipe. How would she explain herself? I was visiting a friend? I was looking for a doctor?

'I need to get back... I...' As she drank the cool water, she noticed a fly crawling across the window. It took off, circled the room, then flew back against the pane, trying desperately to get out into the sunlight and the open air, not understanding that the glass was blocking its way. She could hear it tap-tap-tapping as it collided with the window again and again.

It was just a fly. But even a mere fly knew that, when you really needed to escape, hurting yourself could be worth it, if at the end you gained your freedom. If a fly could do it...

Enough was enough. She had to protect herself. And her children. She had a responsibility to her mother and stepfather too.

Marcella placed the glass on the desk and sat back down, smoothing her long skirt.

'Do you remember when you moved to Nice?' Monsieur Nabias continued, inspecting his notes. 'Which year?'

Outside, a tram went by, rattling the window frames.

'I think I'll open the window. Get us a little air and let out that poor fly.'

Monsieur Nabias rose and went to pull down the sash a few centimetres.

Marcella looked at his profile against the dusty glass.

'1906,' she said. 'The eighth of October, 1906.'

Monsieur Nabias turned and gave her an astonished glance. 'You remember the exact date?'

'Oh yes. I will never forget it. It's the day of the festival of the patron saint of Nice, Saint Réparate.'

'Good lord! You've heard of her?' He smiled at Marcella. 'My wife is fascinated by the lives of the saints. She is forever telling our two boys stories about them.'

He flattened the sheet of paper on which he had written Marcella's name. 'The least we can do is help you. Now... Madame Navratil, when and where did you first encounter your husband?'

'It was at a tailoring class,' Marcella said. 'About four months after I arrived here.'

Monsieur Nabias picked up his pen.

'Go on...'

CHAPTER 2

8 October 1906, Nice

Marcella ran along the beach until she was out of breath. Then she pulled off her buttoned boots and let the tide swill around her feet.

'Hello! I love you, Bay of Angels!' She picked up a pebble and flung it over the shimmering water. The grey stone skimmed two or three times before sinking a few metres away, wrinkling the flat surface with a spreading circle of ripples.

The sea was utterly calm. As the French say, a sea of oil. To Marcella it was a sea of satin, eggshell blue shot through with palest pink. She'd like a dress made of such an evanescent colour.

She lay down on the pebbles, threw back her arms and let the setting sun bathe her face with autumnal warmth. 'Nice! Nice! Nice!'

She was so happy that her mother's cousin, or whatever she was, a distant relation called Aunt Thérèse, had persuaded her mother that life in this city would be better for all of their souls than being stuck up in the hills behind Genoa, in a miserable village where the bus passed through but once a week and from which there seemed no escape.

Here in Nice there were trains, boats and trams going everywhere. There were restaurants and bars and drinks with tantalising names like Mandarinette and Cinzano advertised on great hoarding signs high up on the fronts of buildings. People laughed as they strolled along the wide streets. Men tipped their bowler hats and straw boaters at a pretty girl. At Marcella some of them even winked.

She was sixteen and ready to love this magnificent city, bustling with energy and life.

Marcella remembered too well those months spent alone with her mother, Angela. Years, really, while her mother sobbed, unable to get over the loss of her husband, Marcella's father, and her son,

Marcella's baby brother, both of whom died of a fever. Though only an infant herself, Marcella had felt she had to support her mother. She had felt so alone. Finally, her mother had found happiness again with Antonio. With him, she'd had three more children, between a string of miscarriages, who all died within the space of six years. But that was another story.

Now that she, her mother and Antonio, Ton-ton to Marcella, were here in Nice, scores of relations suddenly materialised. They must have existed all along, but Marcella had had no idea about any of them. That was the thing with Italians. They wandered the earth, spreading out into vast family trees. And most of Marcella's relations appeared to have settled here. Her mother had already told her of at least three relatives in Nice and five more a few kilometres along the coast in Cannes and more in Saint-Raphaël. Now there would always be someone to run to, a shoulder to cry on, someone to laugh with.

But for Marcella, Nice was more than family. It was hope, excitement, possibility. Behind her stood the magnificent opera house. Out on the jetty to her right were the fantastical oriental-looking buildings of the casino, as resplendent as an Indian palace, silhouetted against the orange of the setting sun. Further back into town, in Place Masséna, where all the trams joined up in an almighty spaghetti of iron rails, there was another theatre inside another casino along with hundreds of cafés and bars, where every night singers and musicians entertained a carefree public. In this cosmopolitan city, Marcella imagined audiences of French, Italian, English, Russians, Austrians and Americans pouring out of music halls having seen variety shows, concerts, operas and operettas. She had already read many of the posters plastered on walls along the tree-lined boulevards.

Marcella was sure of one thing: she was going to be a singer. One day her name would be up there on those posters. *Marcella Caretto, grand artiste, chanteuse.* She would wear beautiful clothes and travel in luxurious automobiles. Audiences would worship her, wherever she went. They'd throw bouquets in her path. She would travel to London and New York. Everyone would know her name. She would be famous.

Marcella hummed a few bars of 'La Petite Tonkinoise', then opened her mouth and sang out:

'He calls me his bourgeois p'tite
His Tonki-ki, his Tonki-ki, his Tonkinoise
They make sweet eyes at him
But it's me he likes best.'

She noticed a man who was walking a dog along the water's edge stop, turn his head and glance back at her. She shut her mouth and smiled to herself.

'But it's me he likes best.'

Oh yes! She'd show them.

It was suddenly cold. The scarlet sun was halved by the horizon, the sea blood-red. Marcella shivered and turned back towards the city. She heard a clock strike. Oh no! How had she let herself do this again? Always late. Always late!

Hauling on her boots and slamming her hat on her head, Marcella jammed the pin in so hard it scratched her scalp. She had to hurry. How long would they wait for her? And if she didn't find them, how would she know where to go? She stupidly hadn't written down the address of the new flat or of her Aunt Thérèse's shop or anywhere.

Stumbling on the pebbles, she ran up the beach, her boots slipping down as she hadn't the time to button them. She clambered up the steps leading to the Quai du Midi.

She should have been there half an hour ago. They would wait for her, surely?

She ran into the Ponchettes, across the Cours Saleya and into the dark maze of streets of the Old Town. Here it was cold, damp and gloomy, even on a sunny day. The streets so narrow, the buildings so high. She held her hat as she ran, darting past shops where the owners were packing up the goods and pulling down the shutters, closing for the night.

She felt as though she passed the same corners over and over, then finally she saw some steps leading up into Boulevard Mac-Mahon, where her parents would be waiting, she hoped, in the café on the terrace as arranged.

Ahead she could see a clock tower. She was now an hour and a half late.

She turned another corner and ran helter-skelter, shoving through the crowds.

Thanks be, there was Ton-ton, standing waving.

When she reached him she could barely catch her breath.

'Gigi gave up waiting for you,' he said. 'She's tired, you know. The move is quite an emotional thing.'

Marcella felt rather guilty. She didn't want to give her mother anything else to be anxious about.

'Let's go, then,' she said quietly.

But Antonio turned back into the terrace café and pointed to a corner table.

'First you must meet your Aunt Thérèse.'

Marcella saw a formidable-looking woman in her mid-fifties. Plump and handsome, she looked like someone you wouldn't want to cross. Marcella followed Antonio through the tables.

'Good evening. You're late. But I have got you a job,' said Aunt Thérèse. 'You start tomorrow.'

Marcella couldn't believe her luck. To be starting off right away in the theatre. How quickly her dreams had come true. 'How? Where? Oh, Aunt Thérèse, how wonderful. Where do the rehearsals take place?'

'Rehearsals? What on earth are you talking about?'

Marcella's excitement evaporated.

'In my establishment we start as we mean to go on,' Aunt Thérèse continued. 'You will be beginning, as everyone does, in the work-shop. Evenings you will spend taking classes with me, learning the elements of the craft of tailoring for ladies.'

Marcella felt her mouth go dry. This was not how she had planned things.

'And another thing, Marcella. At work you will not address me as Aunt Thérèse, but as Madame Magaïl. Understood?'

Marcella nodded while Madame Magaïl rooted in her reticule and pulled out a business card.

'9 Rue Garnier,' she said. 'Easy to find. Just off Avenue de la Gare. I'll see you there tomorrow morning. Seven a.m. on the dot.'

She snapped her reticule shut and rose abruptly. 'If you are late you will not be paid for that day, which, nonetheless, you will work through. I do not approve of slackness in young people. This is a hard world and success only comes from working even harder.' She pulled out her watch. 'Too late to go into Old Town now. It's the feast day, you know. Saint Réparate, patron saint of the city. Quite a brouhaha. Welcome to Nice, Marcella. I'll see you in the morning.'

Her aunt vaguely kissed her on one cheek.

'*Buona notte*, Antonio.' She kissed Antonio on both, giving him a slight hug, before moving off. '*A domani!*'

She marched across the street and disappeared into the smartly dressed crowds.

'I'm sorry, Marcella,' Antonio shrugged. 'But you have to understand that it's time to grow up and forget these childish dreams.'

'But I haven't had a chance, I—'

'Your aunt is right.' He cut her off. 'If you are to survive you must learn a trade.'

Marcella was overcome with tiredness, anger and frustration.

'I can't learn a stupid trade,' she cried. 'And I won't.' She tore up her aunt's business card and threw the pieces on to the table. 'I am going to be a singer. I'll be famous, too. Everyone will know my name.'

'Of course, my dear.' Antonio tried to appease her. 'But that will be once you have learned a trade. It's the way the world works. Then you'll always have something to fall back on.'

'I've had enough.' Marcella shoved her way out of the café terrace. She ran back along the boulevard, dodging couples walking arm in arm, and narrowly avoiding the driver of a *calèche* as he jumped down from his perch to open the door for his passengers. Tears flooding her eyes, she dived down the marble steps leading back into Old Town and took off, running blindly into the maze of alleyways. She wasn't sure what she would do now. She had nowhere to go. She didn't know the city at all. But she was not going to work day and night sewing clothes with that horrible woman.

Turning a corner, she ran into a gang of boys pressing towards her. She spun round to find another horde surging forwards, laughing loudly. She squeezed through them, determined to come out of these dark alleyways and back into the open air of the seafront. But whichever direction she took only seemed to thrust her further and further into the crowds.

She came into a square. It was packed with people. They all held burning candles. She pressed into the melee, trying to force her way to the other side. Ahead of her, seemingly in the centre of the orange glow, was a little child of six or seven, dressed in a red velvet cloak. The child, smiling serenely, was held aloft, head and shoulders above the throng. Who could this mysterious child be? Why was she being paraded like this? And how was she keeping so still? The whole scene seemed like a dream.

Then the child appeared to sway. Marcella was alarmed that she might fall and be trampled underfoot. It was then that she saw the little boat. The child stood in a wooden boat packed tight with dark red roses. Six strong men walked solemnly forward, bearing the craft on their shoulders like a coffin. Was this a funeral of some kind?

Near to Marcella's face, a candle flickered. She watched as hot wax splashed on to the cheek of one of the carriers. Instinctively, he put his hand up to the burn. The girl staggered and leant perilously to one side. The boat rocked.

Marcella flung up her arms to save the child, but she was too late.

Toppling from the boat, she sank into the sea of people, then plunged down, down, down.

Marcella felt suddenly faint. She seemed to lose sight and staggered forward, held upright only by the crowd. Slowly she herself slithered to the ground, her head slumped on her chest.

When she opened her eyes, she had no idea where she was. Beside her lay the child in a red velvet gown, scores of hands reaching down to help her up. It was only then that Marcella realised the girl was not a child but a doll, a life-size doll made of wax.

CHAPTER 3

January 1907, Nice

Marcella examined the seam she had just sewn and found it to be practically perfect. Not that her aunt would admit that. Aunt Thérèse could always find fault. But then it was her insistence on perfection that earned her the loyalty of her customers. Marcella had once flipped through the books and seen that the same people came back to Madame Magaïl year in year out. And now that the boutique had moved to the fashionable Place Grimaldi, a leafy square full of cafés and shops, there were scores of foreign customers too. They just walked in and ordered whole sets of dresses, ballgowns, coats and travelling costumes as if they were made of money. Maybe they were. Especially the Americans.

Marcella believed that secretly her aunt was pleased with her progress.

After all, she had worked hard for the last four months. She was good with customers. She could speak Italian, French and a smattering of English – though that needed improving, it was true. She'd earned a fair amount, carefully putting the money aside, collecting as much as she could for the day she'd start her singing career. Sometimes she would sing quietly during the fittings. Some of the ladies had complimented her on her voice.

She tied the final knot and cut the thread with her teeth, humming a few bars of her favourite song.

'He calls me his bourgeois p'tite
His Tonki-ki, his Tonki-ki, his Tonkinoise
They all make sweet eyes at him
But it's me he likes best.'

Her aunt strictly forbade anyone to cut the thread using teeth. In Madame Magaïl's workshop, only scissors were permitted. But Marcella couldn't be bothered to get up and walk over to the wall where all the different types of scissors dangled from their coloured ribbons. She had finally completed the garment she'd been left to finish, but glancing up at the clock she saw that there were still twenty minutes before Aunt Thérèse would come back to lock up. Marcella put her needle back into the pin pad and brushed some loose threads from her skirts.

What next? She didn't want to sit around. She knew that that would make her aunt furious. She had to get on with something, make herself useful. The place was already quite clean, so no point faffing around with a duster, polishing up the parquet or fiddling about with the mannequins which stood in the shop, proudly wearing the latest outfits, like some gay but boring waxwork display.

Marcella decided to surprise her aunt. Why not start work on a new skirt? She would prove that she was ready to move on up to the next level.

She went through to the shop to look at the order book. The details would be in there. She had watched the senior assistant, Anna Piano (a cousin from Saint-Raphaël), do it a hundred times. You opened the order book. Then you matched up the number with a small packet filed on a shelf in the rear workshop, where she was now sitting. That packet was full of pieces of thin tissue-paper with lines on them. These you pinned to the fabric, which would be found in a roll similarly numbered, leaning against the side wall. You rolled the fabric out on to the worktable. You pinned the paper to it. Then you cut along the edges of the tissue, just as she had done as a child making paper clothes for a cardboard doll.

How hard could it be? Anna did it all day long. Snip, snip, pieces of a sleeve. Snip, snip, a cuff. Then those patches were given to Marcella who pinned them and sewed them together. And, hey presto, a sleeve!

As she flipped open the book, Marcella started singing at the top of her voice,

'I'm his little girl
His Anna-na, his Anna-na, his Annamite

She noted the number of the packet and the reference to the fabric, then, still singing, made her way back through the baize curtain to the workshop.

The number: 4819.

She found 4819 on the shelf between 4800 and 5467. Clearly there was some order here, though Marcella didn't quite understand what it was. She laid the packet down, and went to fetch the fabric – a roll of magenta silk brocade. It was heavier than she expected and, unable to support its weight, she dropped it clumsily on to the worktop. Then she squared it along the edge of the table and started to unroll it.

Perfect.

But now where had the pattern gone?

She could make out a slight hump beneath the cloth and realised that she'd unrolled the brocade over the damned pattern. Lifting the edges of the fabric, she put her head underneath to hold it up, like a tent. Then she stretched out her arm. She could touch the packet with her fingertips, but succeeded only in pushing it further away and now it was completely out of reach.

She pulled her head out, folded the cloth back on to the roll and retrieved the pattern. As she flung it on to the chair beside her, the cloth tumbled off the table, unrolling as it went.

Now the fabric lay loosely all over the floor. She would have to wind it back carefully much more tightly on to the spool or it would be impossible to lay out.

This was not going well. There must be a knack. Why hadn't she thought it through before she started this mad escapade?

After about five minutes Marcella managed to get the brocade laid out smooth and flat on the worktop. She pulled the flimsy tissue-paper pieces from the envelope and was placing them precisely on to the fancy silk when a sudden gust from the window sent them flying. She spent the next moments gathering them up from all corners of the room.

Now she needed to have the pins close and in reach, perhaps in her mouth? She fetched her pincushion from the other side of the workshop and placed it on the cloth. Then she began to lay out the tissue pieces again. It didn't take her long to work out that it would be overly ambitious to cut more than two pieces right now, so she folded the other sections of the pattern back in their envelope.

Hanging from a hook beside her were the scissors on their multi-coloured ribbons. There was the tiny pair which she should have used just now to cut that final thread, all the way up to a pair almost the size of garden shears. She decided on the second-biggest.

It was only after she had made the first cut into the brocade that Marcella saw that she had chosen the pinking shears by mistake and now the fabric was cut into a zigzag rather than a straight line. Holding the already-cut cloth down with one hand to prevent it tearing along the seam, she turned round to find a more suitable pair. But then the rest of the roll once again plunged to the floor, this time taking the pincushion and the remaining pieces of tissue pattern with it, ripping along the line she had cut. She spat out the pins held between her lips. A pin spiked the finger which was stuck through the handle of the shears and it started to bleed. Meanwhile, her other hand was somehow still tangled in the ribbons tied to three pairs of scissors hanging on the wall. Managing to wiggle free, Marcella collected everything up and threw it over her head on to the worktable. A drop of blood trickled from her finger on to the fabric. This was terrible! She wetted her handkerchief with spit and stood up, ready to dab the stain away.

But she was not alone.

Aunt Thérèse was standing on the threshold, accompanied by a tall, blonde woman wearing a smart navy-blue suit with a high-collared poplin blouse. She must have been about Marcella's age.

'Good evening, Marcella.' Thérèse Magaïl swept past her to inspect the wreckage on the workshop table and the floor. 'Meet Rosa.'

Marcella hung her head. She dreaded how her aunt would react next.

Snatching the pinking shears from Marcella's hand, Madame Magaïl slung the ribbon back over the wall hook. 'Rosa is my niece. Your cousin. Rosa Bruno.'

A cousin! How could that be? She couldn't look more different. Marcella was dark, olive-skinned, with almost black eyes. As was her aunt, her mother, all her relatives. Who was this blonde Amazon with her mother's maiden name?

'Hello, Rosa.'

'Hello.' Rosa briskly nodded. Marcella stood awkwardly holding the pincushion in one hand, pattern pieces and a corner of the fabric in the other, the rest of it unravelled all over the floor.

Thérèse lurched forward and grabbed the cloth from Marcella's hands. Silently, she folded it back on to the roll.

Marcella could barely breathe. Why did Aunt Thérèse say nothing? She tried to catch Rosa's eye, but Rosa looked away.

'I see you are rather determined to go your own way, Marcella.' Thérèse Magaïl turned back to Rosa. 'Excuse me, Rosa, if you don't mind. I need a quiet word with Marcella. Would you please wait outside the shop for a minute or two?'

Once Rosa was out of sight, Thérèse rounded on Marcella. She spoke very quietly. Marcella thought that this was what it must feel like to be a fish watching a shark about to turn it into its lunch. 'This is one of the most expensive rolls of fabric in the workshop. Sent from London in fact, at enormous cost.'

'I thought—'

'I don't pay you to think, Marcella. I pay you to do what I tell you to do. If I tried anything as stupid as believing that you were capable of thinking on your own, then where would we be? You were as usual off in fairyland, no doubt.'

'Aunt Thérèse—'

'Naturally the money for the spoiled fabric will be withheld from your wages.'

'I'm so sorry.' Marcella tried to quell the tears which pricked her eyes. 'It won't happen again.'

'You're right. It won't happen again.' Thérèse snatched the pincushion from Marcella's hand. 'Because you won't be coming back.'

'But I… I have to… My mother—'

'Your mother won't be in the slightest bit surprised. She also thinks you're an impulsive little dreamer. Why do you think she sent you to me? To try and put some direction into your aimless life.'

That wasn't fair. She didn't live an aimless life. It was just that she didn't want to do what they all wanted her to do. She had her own aspirations and ambitions.

Marcella tried to help her aunt gather up the pattern pieces, but Thérèse flicked her away with her hand. 'No thank you, mademoiselle. You've done quite enough damage for one day.'

'What *can* I do?'

'Nothing. I had brought Rosa here to improve your English. She is fluent. I was even going to give you the money to take her out for dinner. But…' Thérèse threw up her hands and shook her head. 'No thank you, Marcella.'

'What do I do now?'

'A good idea would be to get out of my sight.'

'But I—'

Thérèse Magaïl stepped into the front room of the shop, holding the heavy green baize curtain to one side so that Marcella could follow her through.

'Rosa!' she called out. 'A wasted journey, I'm afraid. Your cousin no longer has need of your services.'

Madame Magaïl walked over to the doorway, ushering the two young women out of the premises. She locked the street door behind them, then swept off across the road, narrowly avoiding a horse dragging a *calèche*. The driver shook his fist and shouted out an obscenity. Thérèse Magaïl replied in kind. When she reached the other side of the square she stepped up on to the pavement and called across: 'Goodnight, Rosa. Goodbye, Marcella.'

They stood in silence watching their aunt disappear into the busy Rue de la Buffa. Then Rosa caught Marcella's eye and shrugged, before turning. 'Come along. Follow me.'

Rosa set off at some speed in the direction of the town centre.

'Where are we going?' Utterly depressed, Marcella trudged along behind her.

'Away from here. Keep up!'

Marcella obeyed. It wasn't like she had any better ideas. The streets were busy. Some people were leaving work and going home, while others, finely dressed, were heading out to dine. Marcella wove her way through them, Rosa always a few steps ahead. A tram clattered past.

'What will I tell my mother?' Marcella had tried to keep it in, but finally she burst with one long sob. 'She'll be so disappointed. Do you think, if I go back tomorrow morning and apologise, Aunt Thérèse might change her mind?'

'Oh no, no, no!' Rosa sucked her breath in through her teeth. 'I wouldn't try anything like that. Aunt Thérèse can be very harsh.'

'She's a vile old dragon!' Marcella spat out the words. 'And I hate her.'

Rosa held up her hand. Marcella was struck by the elegant length of her fingers.

'No, no. Don't get Aunt Thérèse wrong. My mother told me she's the way she is because she's had a bad time of it. She married the wrong man. Her daughter died and shortly afterwards her husband too. Then she came to Nice and started out all over again and made herself the success she is today.'

'She can't blame me for her unhappiness…'

Rosa looked Marcella in the eye. She spoke intensely. 'I don't think that's what she was doing, Marcella. It's just that she doesn't want you to make the same mistakes she did and not be able to support yourself. She is fierce in everything she does. She makes an awful enemy, that's true. But she'd fight like a lion for people close to her. She simply has no middle way.'

Marcella thought about her aunt. She couldn't imagine her as a wife or a mother. But she felt terrible about her daughter dying. It was unimaginable. To lose a child. No wonder she was fierce sometimes.

The two had arrived on the platform at the tram stop. Marcella wanted to change the subject. She pointed to a book poking out of her cousin's bag.

'What's that?'

'Poetry. It's what I'm teaching at the institute at the moment.'

Poetry! How boring, Marcella thought, her eye caught by the sight of a sophisticated lady in a yellow suit pulled by a saluki dog straining at the end of a jewel-studded leash.

'I love Nice,' muttered Marcella, her eyes following the woman as she stopped to greet a man in a straw boater, wearing a striped jacket and sporting a monocle. 'Where else can you see so many beautiful people?'

'You are so strange.' Rosa gave Marcella a sideways glance. 'We're chalk and cheese.'

'What do you mean?'

'You like it here. All I want to do is leave.'

'I can't go home, Rosa.' With a sudden sob Marcella burst into real tears, which tumbled down her cheeks in a long stream. 'Don't make me. My mother will be so disappointed in me.'

A tram rattled to a stop in front of them. Offering a handkerchief to Marcella, Rosa climbed on to the wooden step and with the other hand hauled her up into the carriage. 'Come on, coz. We'll get you sorted out before you have to face the music.'

'Where are we going?' asked Marcella, digging into her reticule for coins to pay the fare. 'When she told you to wait outside, you just obeyed her. Are you scared of her too?'

'Not scared. But I recognise that she is a formidable woman. It wouldn't be wise to cross her.'

'She was right, though, wasn't she, Rosa? I deserved to be sacked,' Marcella said quietly. 'I was being too ambitious.'

The driver clanged the bell and the tram rolled forwards.

Rosa looked hard at Marcella. Marcella couldn't believe the paleness of her eyes, an icy shade of blue. Cold as a glacier.

'Get this straight.' Rosa pulled up Marcella's damp chin and said firmly, 'You can *never* be too ambitious, my girl. And don't *ever* let anyone tell you that you can.'

The tram lurched across the points, jerking the two women apart. Marcella reached out and grabbed a swinging leather strap. But her cousin didn't stop speaking. 'Be as ambitious as you like. Head only where you really want to go. Make all your preparations first. Think it through. Then go there.'

'Where are you going, Rosa?'

'America!' Rosa spoke as though there was no other possible reply. 'It's where all the money is. I am already making plans, saving for my boat passage across the Atlantic, sounding out work there. But first I need to be a little more qualified. I need to start in America at the top. And you?'

'Actually, I really meant where are you going now? Tonight?'

A little child pushed past, fumbling her way through the long skirts, following her father towards the back of the tram.

'Well, let's see.' Rosa smoothed her dress. 'I think I'm taking you to dinner.'

The tram rounded a sharp corner, sweeping them into Place Masséna. Rosa lost her grip and fell backwards, almost landing in an old man's lap. She bowed low in apology. 'I am so sorry, monsieur.'

Gathering herself together, she winked conspiratorially at Marcella.

'So, cousin, tell me. Where in Nice have you always wanted to eat?'

Marcella didn't need to think about it. 'The Grand Café Pomel.'

'In that case we must get off now,' cried Rosa, grabbing Marcella's hand and heading for the rear platform. A few moments later they were both striding through the arcades of the Municipal Casino.

'Why did you choose this place?' asked Rosa as they walked through the revolving door into the café and were met by a bustle of waiters. Bright lights reflected from mirrored walls and jolly rhythms of an accordion band filled the place.

'For the music,' replied Marcella. 'I'm going to be a singer.'

'How interesting. Tell me, Marcella, how are you going about it?'

'Umm…' Marcella had no plan, only a dream. 'I hadn't really thought about that.'

'And there is your problem in a nutshell.' Rosa raised her hand and attracted a waiter who led them to a table not far from the stage. 'You have no direction, no grasp on reality. Keep your dreams, of course, but in order to follow them you'll need to be able to support yourself. It's either that or marry a rich man.'

'Who knows?' Marcella laughed. 'I might be lucky!'

'Never wait for luck. She can be very elusive.' Rosa took off her coat and laid it on the banquette beside her. 'And you can't depend on a man to keep you. It's so much safer to depend on yourself. Look!' She picked up the menu, laughed, and waved it over towards the other side of the dining room. 'My baby brother, Raphaël.'

Marcella looked across to see a handsome, dark young man. 'Yet another cousin for me. He looks fun.'

'He's a painter and decorator.' Rosa went back to the menu. 'A bit of a Jack the lad, in fact, but he's all right, really. Do you have brothers and sisters?'

Marcella shook her head. It was too difficult to speak about the fact that she had lost so many infant siblings. She scanned the menu, searching for the cheapest thing there.

'I suggest you take a leaf out of Aunt Thérèse's book,' Rosa continued, speaking from behind her menu. 'Sign up for the tailoring course at the college where I teach. It starts next week. Once you can cut and sew a ladies' suit you need never be out of funds. Especially in a town like this.'

Marcella felt gloom descend. No pay this week and all her savings, no doubt, about to go up in smoke on dinner and then in fees for a stupid tailoring course. Why was everyone doing this to her? She didn't want to be a tailor. Nothing could bore her more. Why would she want to spend her days hunched over scraps of material, beading, sewing hems and linings? And, anyway, hadn't she learned all she needed to know about that tedious world from her aunt?

'If you were serious about being a singer, Marcella, it would be rather useful, don't you think, to be able to sew. To make your own costumes, et cetera.'

'Surely famous singers have other people to make their costumes?' Marcella was grasping for a way out. 'They don't make their own gowns?'

'I know nothing about such fanciful things. But I'm pretty sure that nobody starts out as a *famous* singer. The beginners must have to scrape around a bit, I'd think.' Rosa laid down the menu. 'Anyway, I'm going for the sea bass. How about you?'

CHAPTER 4

30 January 1907, Nice

Both Marcella's mother and stepfather agreed that Marcella should take the course Rosa had suggested and start preparing for real life. They would pay the fees and Marcella would pay them back once she started earning.

A few days later Marcella arrived at the noisy college. She didn't like it. As the day students left and the evening group came in, it was like a stampede. Already she had begun to wish that she was back working with Aunt Thérèse. At least there it was quiet and orderly.

The women teachers seemed jaded, and the men treated all the women as though they were inferior, wasting their precious time. At this school, tailoring seemed to be a male profession, though Marcella knew well from working with her aunt that the big money was in tailoring for women and that it was women who, in the back room, did most of the actual sewing.

She watched the other students around her and felt forlorn. She had had no idea so many girls were this keen to be seamstresses. On top of it all, today was her birthday. True, her parents had prepared a little present for her, a pretty cake with a candle that they gave her over breakfast. But she had just turned seventeen. She should be out celebrating. Though who with? Since she had arrived in Nice she had been so tightly tied to the apron strings, she had made no friends. Unless you counted her cousins Rosa and Anna, though they were both too much on the serious side for Marcella. Always talking about their work and planning for the future.

She looked around and suppressed a yawn. This was certainly not how it was meant to be. Today she was seventeen years old. She was an adult now. She had no idea why everyone kept treating her as though she was a child.

A fellow student, Stefan Kozak, jabbed her in the ribs and whispered, 'Wakey wakey!'

'I wasn't asleep,' snapped Marcella, annoyed that she had been noticed in her daydream.

The boy had a slight accent. German, perhaps, or Austrian. He was very tall and very thin. Like a tent-pole, thought Marcella, a tent-pole with blond straight hair and sly eyes. She and Stefan had exchanged names over the previous evenings. They had one thing in common – they both preferred to sit at the back of the class.

The teacher, a fat man with a bald head, stood on a dais in the distance, scratching at the blackboard. He was using chalk to draw the different kinds of stitches. Stefan slipped her a note. She held it under the desk to read it: *What are you doing after the class?*

Marcella blushed. Was this a proposition? Well, why not? Today was her birthday, after all.

She wrote back: *You're taking me for a drink. Because it is my birthday.*

And after class ended that is exactly what he did. They found a small bar near the college and took a corner table beside a roaring fire. Stefan brought over a bottle of local red wine with two glasses.

'Tomorrow will be better,' he said.

'How can that be?' asked Marcella, who couldn't imagine anything could improve those boring classes.

'Tomorrow we'll be hands-on,' said Stefan with some excitement. 'Didn't you read the notes?'

Marcella shook her head. She hadn't read the notes. She just went along with the class, taking it as it came, floating in and out as though with the waves. She had been swept into this thing against her better instincts. It had not been her plan to learn how to sew.

'You can't carry on like that, Marcella! Where will that get you?' Stefan stared hard at her with his pale, lashless eyes. She looked away. She'd only known him a few days, but it seemed as though Stefan was trying to look into her soul. She found it disturbing. Was this his way of flirting? she wondered.

'Go on. Tell me, what do you really want out of life?'

'I want to be a famous singer.' She had said the same thing so many times in her life, but this time she felt silly. It sounded so childish. Something a five-year-old might say. She felt she had to justify herself.

'This tailoring thing is all too much nonsense. I'm only doing it to please my family. And once I'm trained, I will go off and do what I always really wanted to do. Like being a singer.'

Stefan sipped his wine. 'I wonder whether being a singer is what you really want to do.'

'Of course it is.'

'Who are you training with then?' Stefan persisted. 'Do you have private classes?'

Marcella couldn't answer. She wondered if it was something she had always said and now could not get out of the habit?

'All right. Sing something now.'

Marcella felt herself go red. She knew all the latest songs. But so did lots of people.

'I'm more ambitious than you, Marcella.' Stefan topped up her glass. 'One day I'm going to have my own tailoring business. A shop. I may not even stay here in Nice. I've already come a long way.'

'I was wondering where you are from.' Marcella was happy to be changing the subject. 'With that accent you're not local.'

'You have an accent too! Italian, I would say.'

'Correct. And you?'

'I'm from Presbourg.'

'Where's Presbourg?'

'Hungary. Not too far from Vienna. When I was fifteen I left home and moved there. Then last Christmas I decided to come down here.'

'Why?' Marcella asked.

'At first I was fed up with the cold winters. And I'd heard so many stories of this place. It had that quality of a town where the streets are paved with gold. The world visits. So I thought I'd put a toe in the water, as they say.' Stefan knocked back his wine and sat looking at the empty glass as though it might refill itself if he concentrated hard enough. 'I came down by train, through Italy. I took a look at Milan. But it seemed too staid for me. People come here from everywhere on the earth – Russia, Switzerland, Sweden, Italy, Great Britain, even America. It's fashionable and stylish, and has a hint of danger about it. All those rich people from all those far-flung places. What are they, but potential customers?'

Marcella was watching Stefan, fascinated, as he poured more wine.

'How old are you, Stefan?'

'Seventeen,' he said, matter-of-fact, and Marcella felt embarrassed. She was the same age, and yet she still lived with her parents.

'Anyway, this place isn't a permanent decision,' he continued. 'I'm here to see what chances it offers me and, if it's not enough, I'll move on.'

'Where would you go next?'

'I don't know, really. Paris, London, New York.'

He named all the places Marcella had dreamed of visiting, but her dream had been to travel the world to sing, not to work as a tailor in a back room! But that dream of hers now seemed empty. She had no idea how you even became a singer. Did you sing while walking down the beach, hoping that a passing impresario would give you his card and book you the next day for his hotel or club? Did you bang on the door of the opera house and beg to be part of the chorus, then work your way up through soubrette parts and into the principal roles? She hadn't a clue. She knew no one in the world of the theatre. Perhaps that was the thing. You had to befriend someone already in show business, and hope that they would give you a leg-up.

'I've put by a bit in my savings account,' Stefan went on, dragging her out of her thoughts. 'Next thing, I need to get myself a decent position in a high-class tailor's where I have a good chance of promotion.'

Marcella felt chastened by Stefan's clarity and determination.

'No need to feel ashamed, Marcella.' It was as though he could read her mind. 'It's different for boys.'

She had no response to that. So she took another sip of wine.

———

The next night's class was a shambles. Marcella had drunk far too much with Stefan and felt quite ill when she woke up. Her mother had needed her to run errands during the day and to help her stepfather downstairs in the carpentry workshop. She crawled to college in the afternoon and struggled with the simplest of tasks, feeling that at any moment she would be sick. All the while she could see the men there smirking at her. She told them she had a cold coming, but they were not taken in for a moment.

Today she hated everyone. She hated Nice and hated her family for bringing her here. Life in Italy was slower and she had been free to do what she wanted. Here it was all go and ambition. She had had enough of the place.

A girl who always sat in the front row was busily handing out scissors, paper and rough cotton calico. After her last attempt at cutting, Marcella was not looking forward to this lesson. She thanked the girl for the equipment and laid her head back down on the table. Seeing her slumped at her desk, Stefan laughed.

The new teacher came in and greeted everyone. Marcella didn't bother to look up.

His voice seemed to go right through her, making her head pound. He stood on the podium and asked each student one by one what their ambitions were and what had brought them to this class. Marcella had her answer ready. She was there because, against her will, people had forced her to come and, to be frank, she would rather be anywhere else but here. She continued to rest her eyes, and only opened them because the room had gone quiet. She looked up to find the new teacher standing at her side.

'I'm sorry to disturb you, Sleeping Beauty, but as you have paid for this class you might as well get your money's worth. I could let you sleep through it, but I'm sure you'd find it more useful to open your eyes and pick up the scissors. I will not be repeating anything I say simply because you couldn't be bothered to listen the first time.'

The teacher turned to Stefan and asked him his name and where his family was from. The two men then lapsed into a language Marcella couldn't understand at all. Jabbering away, laughing, practically slapping one another on the back. Marcella felt strangely disgruntled by this cosy fellowship of foreignness, especially as Stefan was meant to be *her* friend.

'Teacher's pet,' she hissed, as the teacher resumed his position in front of the class.

'Proud to be so,' said Stefan. 'He comes from a village about thirty miles away from where I was born. I now intend to work on this connection in order to raise myself to top of the class.'

'Oh lord,' Marcella groaned, shaking out her fabric and laying it flat on the desk. 'I can't compete with that.'

'No.' Stefan picked up his scissors. 'You can't.'

Marcella laid her aching head back down on the fabric. When she lifted it again, no one was there. Silence. She wondered whether she was dreaming. She sat up straight and looked around. The lights were on. But the classroom was empty. She was gripping a strange thing. A freak piece of sewing, a sleeve with the cuff at the wrong end and a sock sewn into the lining. Two eyes and a mouth had been drawn on to the sock.

She shook her head, heart pounding, hoping it was the result of some peculiar double vision, and examined the piece of cloth again. White calico sleeve, perfectly stitched but assembled in absolutely the wrong order. How had she created such a thing? Was this the reason she had been held back after class? She had no memory of it, but maybe that's what drinking so much did. Marcella crammed the wreckage of needlework into her bag, resolving to throw it into the first bin she passed on her way home. Then no one would know about it. Whatever had gone on in tonight's class, she wanted to escape. She would tell her parents that everything had gone very well. They needn't hear about this latest debacle. Who else was going to tell them?

She stood up to leave the room, when she heard an odd rasping noise coming from behind the door. Slightly scared, she pulled it open to find Stefan crouched down, with the teacher standing beside him, gazing at her with an implacable expression.

'*Sollen wir es ihr sagen?*' whispered Stefan, wheezing.

Marcella wondered if he suffered from asthma.

'*Nein. Zuerst werden wir ein bisschen Spaß mit ihr haben.*' The teacher folded his arms. 'So, Mademoiselle Marcella Caretto, can you explain yourself?'

Marcella was overcome with remorse. She begged the teacher to forgive her and not to put it in her notes, or let her parents know. She couldn't even remember making the horrible thing, but she must have done as it was there in place of the pieces of fabric and thread she had had on the table earlier.

Last night she had been celebrating her birthday, she explained, and had a little too much wine… The teacher looked angry.

'Drunkenness is no excuse,' he said sternly. 'You will need to do detention.'

Marcella's heart sank.

'You have wasted fabric and made this monstrosity.' The teacher plunged his hand into her bag and pulled out the piece of strange sewing. 'We are going to the principal's office. He will decide on your future.'

He strode briskly towards the main entrance. She trailed down the corridor behind him trying to exchange looks with Stefan, but Stefan was looking very seriously at his feet.

'Follow me!' the teacher said as he went out into the street. 'It's a few doors along.'

Marcella knew that this was the end. Her parents, already exasperated by her behaviour, would be enraged. Why was the world so unfair?

'Right.' The teacher turned. 'We're going in here.'

'But…?' Marcella looked up to see the entrance to a quiet bar on the corner. Stefan stepped forward and held the door open, while the teacher smiled broadly, exposing perfect white teeth. Until this moment Marcella hadn't noticed how handsome he was, with beautifully aligned features and jet-black hair.

'In you go.' He gently rested his hand in the hollow of her back. 'I'm going to treat you to a little supper.'

'I can't. I—'

'I have to eat myself. I rent a room from an elderly lady and she doesn't allow me to cook. I would prefer some company while I dine, and this one here is too full of himself to be interesting.' He cuffed the back of Stefan's head, making him grin. 'Forgive Stefan. Last night he should have bought you food to go with all that drink he treated you to. And he should definitely not have kept topping up your glass.' He tutted and wagged a finger. 'A gentleman would not have let a lady get drunk.'

Stefan said something in that language again. Was it German? Marcella couldn't understand them at all, but she thought Stefan sounded whiny. The teacher replied firmly, then threw another smile in Marcella's direction.

'Stefan and I are already friends. Now I will get to know you, Marcella. I prefer the more radical students. The run-of-the-mill ones bore me. Stefan here tells me you're going to be a singer. I look forward to hearing you sing. Oh, and by the way, you didn't sew in your sleep, nor do you have amnesia. While you were snoring away, we knocked up the rubbish thing out of remnants to give you a surprise when you woke up.' He led them to a table, then pulled out a chair for her. 'I'm Michael, by the way. Michael Navratil.'

CHAPTER 5

September 1911, Nice

Monsieur Nabias lifted his eyes from his notes.

'He was your teacher? Was he very much older than you?'

'Ten years.'

'And he called himself Michael, not Michel?'

'It was the fashion then among the tailors of Nice. Everything "So-British".'

'Ah yes.' Monsieur Nabias made a few scratches on the paper, then slowly filled his pen from a bottle of ink he kept on the desk. 'You still see that. Advertisements written in English, tailoring shops with names like Buckingham and Windsor displaying the British coat of arms outside. The fashion house of Old England is only a few doors up from the office here.' He glanced up from his notes as though to check that Marcella was all right before resuming his questions. 'And how did this relationship with your teacher lead to marriage?'

Marcella shifted uneasily. Now that she thought back on it, she wondered if she had perhaps led Michael on. Though only four years, it all seemed so long ago. Everything had a misty other-world quality about it.

'I had always thought that it was rather out of bounds,' Monsieur Nabias said carefully. 'For teachers to form relationships of a romantic nature with students.'

'Oh, he had as much enthusiasm for teaching tailoring as I had for learning it.' Marcella knew that this was reason enough to excuse Michael. 'Teaching was only a temporary job. He left the institute shortly after we did. Stefan and me, I mean. Michael had been chief cutter at a long-standing tailor's shop in Old Nice and—'

'Do you know the name of that shop?'

'I don't.' Marcella realised that even to this day she had no idea where the shop had been or why Michael had left his job there as chief cutter to become a part-time teacher at an evening class. 'Well, anyhow, he was only teaching while he tried to set up his own tailoring business.'

'And you took a job with him at this new business, and that is how you became close?'

Marcella put her face in her hands – that was not the correct order of the story.

Michael's shop was still a year off. And by then they were already married.

'While we still attended the evening classes, we met up after school to plan the new business. Me, Stefan, Michael and a man called Hoffman. Louis Hoffman. Stefan and I were to join the business as juniors. Hoffman was a senior tailor, along with Michael. But the shop was Michael's idea, and his name was to go over the door. At first I was simply to be a seamstress, but then... Well, things changed.'

'Changed in what way?'

'Well. I married him.' Marcella hung her head. 'And Stefan, I think, never forgave me.'

'Stefan wanted to marry you?'

'No, no, no. Nothing like that. But he wanted... Oh. It simply didn't turn out the way he wanted. Now that I look back on it, it was maybe all rather unfair on Stefan. Michael had promised him—'

There was a sudden rap on Monsieur Nabias's door. Marcella jumped up.

'Please don't tell him why I came. Say it was about my parents. My mother's new apartment. Anything... Just not this.'

Monsieur Nabias called out, 'Come in!'

The door opened a fraction and a blonde head appeared. 'Sorry to disturb you, dear, but I have to go out now. Is there anything you'd like me to bring back?'

'Thank you, Emilie. I'm fine.'

Marcella slowly sat again. Her heart was racing. Once more she feared that, in coming to a lawyer, she was making a terrible mistake. Knowing Michael, this attempt at freeing herself from the marriage could never work. She was sure he was still following her. Last month she had come into town to look in the shops and had seen his reflection in a window, standing in the crowd behind her. Today he had said he was going to Èze to buy some lining fabric from a shop which was closing down, therefore selling things off cheap, and that he wouldn't be back till late, but why should she believe him? He'd lied about so many other things.

The door closed.

'I'm sorry about that, Madame Navratil. That was my wife.'

'Monsieur Nabias, I really must go.'

'I understand you are afraid, madame.' The lawyer leaned across the desk and looked seriously at Marcella. 'Please, let us cut to the heart of the matter.'

Marcella looked into his eyes and nodded slowly.

'Simply tell me exactly why you came here.'

'He is so jealous of me. He suspects everything I do. He is even jealous of the love I bestow on our own children.' Marcella was afraid she would cry and fumbled in her bag for a handkerchief. 'But at the same time, I believe that he hates me. Intensely. And I simply can't cope with it any longer.'

Monsieur Nabias smoothed the palm of his hand across a fresh sheet of paper.

'Let's go back to the start of his tailoring business. Was this before you married?'

'No. Six months or so afterwards.'

'When you first met did your husband have any kind of premises?'

'No. Only a small bedroom he rented from an old lady at the top of Rue Lépante.'

'But once he started his own business he must have had a shop, no?'

'No, not at first. We did all the fittings in our apartment. Then we found a little shop which did repairs and sold parts for motor cars and bicycles, in Rue de France, not far from La Croix de Marbre.'

'It must have been quite a job, turning a shop repairing cars and bicycles into a tailor's?'

33

'No, no. The bicycle people had been thrown out. The owner of the building, an old gentleman developer, had decided to demolish and rebuild. But then he died suddenly. His daughter inherited everything. And her guardians continued the work on her behalf. The new premises were spotless and bright.'

'And your husband put in an offer?'

'One of my relatives told us about it. We got a very good deal from the young lady and the lease won't expire until 1916.'

'When did your husband's shop open?'

'January the seventh, 1908.'

'And you were married in…?'

'May. It was May, 1907.'

'Here in Nice? Or nearer your family's roots, in Italy, perhaps?'

'No. It wasn't like that either. We married in London. There was no family present. Nor friends. Just two strangers as witnesses, in a registry office. In an area called Soho.'

CHAPTER 6

February 1907, Nice

Once a week, Stefan, Michael and Marcella met up for supper and Michael would outline his plans for his business. Marcella suppressed the wild ideas that had begun to creep into her head. She had found herself day-dreaming about Michael and during class was so overcome with a desire for him to notice her, to give her a smile, or compliment her on her work, that her hands trembled as she sewed. When finally he did speak to her she could barely raise her eyes for fear he might see her admiration in them – or was it love? Certainly her heart beat wildly whenever she was about to meet him. Every time they said goodnight she had to hold back the tears. Then she would climb on to the tram, heading back to her parents' flat down near the port, feeling utterly lost and dejected.

One night Michael suggested that the three of them went to the Nice Carnaval and over the next days they sat together in their spare time and sewed themselves costumes for the masquerade. They decided to go as characters from the *commedia dell'arte*. Stefan and Marcella prepared to go as Pierrot and Pierrette while Michael settled on Harlequin.

Now they strolled along through the crowds, eating paper wraps of *socca*, and curly Carnaval doughnuts flavoured with orange-flower water from a shared bag. All around them was a pleasant cacophony of sounds. Accordion players, violinists and flautists competed with the boom of a marching band, joyous with trombones, tubas and a big bass drum.

Marcella walked arm in arm with the two men, one on either side of her, and thought how lovely it was to be here, with friends, in this magical place at this celebratory time. They showered each other with confetti, while more was thrown at them from passing floats, following the crowd through a swirling gale of coloured paper down to the public gardens by the pier. Musicians played popular tunes up on the bandstand, and people danced nearby in the light of coloured lanterns threaded through the leafy branches. Settling down on a grassy slope under a plane tree, far enough away from the band to be able to hear one another speak, Michael pushed a banknote into Stefan's hand and sent him off to buy a bottle of wine.

His face was lit red and green from the lanterns and, behind the Harlequin half-mask, his eyes sparkled like diamonds in a box. He caught Marcella looking at him and smiled. Instantly, she shut her eyes. She thought she might faint from love.

The band struck up a new song now, 'The Dream of Autumn'. The romantic sound enveloped them.

'Marcella?' Michael picked up the bag of twirly *ganse* doughnuts and held it out for her. Even though she knew she would be unable to swallow even a tiny bite, she took one and nibbled at the edge.

He hadn't taken his eyes off her.

She laid her doughnut, uneaten, on the grass.

Then he leaned forward and, laughing, ran his thumb down her cheek.

'You're covered in icing sugar.'

Though she hardly knew what she was doing, she raised her own hand and pressed it against his, still resting on her cheek. Safe in the darkness, while the music swirled around them, Michael put his lips on hers. Marcella stayed still, letting the waves of passion drift through her. Then suddenly he pulled away. She opened her eyes.

Stefan was only a few yards off, carrying a bottle and a single glass tumbler.

'Pierrot is back, bearing booze!' he cried. 'Here!' He thrust the tumbler into Michael's hands, and pulled the cork from the bottle. 'Could only get one glass. We'll have to share.'

Marcella was thankful that they were sitting in such a shadowy spot. Now neither of the men would be able to see the deep colour which she knew had spread across her cheeks and neck. Had Stefan seen them kiss? From the way he had flopped on to the grass, burbling 'It's only plonk. But it's the best I could find,' she thought he had not. But it was the only thing she could think about.

She took a sip from the glass, and handed it back to Michael. Then she stood up, saying to Stefan, 'Come on, slowcoach. Aren't you going to ask me to dance?' She grabbed Stefan's hand, then swept off, leaving Michael sitting against the tree, alone with the glass and bottle.

The band was playing a lively medley by Offenbach. Marcella whirled wildly in and out of the coloured light with Stefan until she could barely breathe.

When the music stopped, the two collapsed back on to the grass, panting.

'I'll need that.' Stefan grabbed the glass from Michael's hand and gulped down some wine. 'Marcella, you dance like a woman possessed!'

'I think it's my turn next,' said Michael, from the shadows.

'So it is.' Marcella laughed and turned to Stefan. 'Off you go, Stefan. You're such a good dancer that now even Michael wants to dance with you. And listen! They're playing an Austrian waltz. While you two dance you'll be able to reminisce about Old Vienna in that language that you know I don't understand.'

———

April 1907, Nice

'If I train you both up to a certain level, we should only need one more to make it a perfect team,' Michael said.

'But why anyone else?' asked Stefan, knocking back his coffee in one then putting the cup back on to the saucer so vigorously that it rattled. 'We're an excellent combination. I am great at cutting—'

'So modest!' Marcella laughed and took a biscuit from the plate in the middle of the table. A sharp gust of wind blew suddenly through the trees of the square and tablecloths all along the terrace flapped.

'I *am* a great cutter,' said Stefan. 'Now! Because I learned from a master.'

Marcella saw Michael mentally receive Stefan's compliment and bat it away, although she could tell he was pleased.

Stefan went on. 'And you, Marcella, are a marvel with both hand sewing and the machine. And as for your buttonholes—'

'And I could sell elephants to Africa and tea to China.' Michael took out his pipe and crammed it with tobacco. 'I can flatter a woman into buying a dress which frankly doesn't suit her. But, seriously, which of us is any good at the boring stuff, like tax, accounts, logbooks and publicity? Somebody has to handle the books. And hopefully we can find someone who is also a fine tailor.'

Marcella took another sip of her coffee, let her head fall back and closed her eyes. The spring sunshine warmed her face.

'You might be fine at charming the ladies,' said Stefan. 'But how are you going to charm the gentlemen with them? After all, they are the ones who generally pay for the dresses.'

There was no reply.

Marcella sensed the charged silence and lifted her eyelids to see both men turned in their seats, facing her expectantly. She felt a mixture of pride and embarrassment.

'"Oh, sir, your wife looks so pretty in that suit"… flutter flutter…' Michael put on a high voice, presumably as an imitation of her. She wondered if that was really how she came across, as a common flirt. She certainly wasn't aware that she flirted. She had just been encouraged by her mother to be friendly.

'"And surely, while you are buying for your wife, you should treat yourself to a new jacket…"' Stefan joined in the mimicking game, pouting his lips in her direction. She turned and playfully slapped his leg.

'Stop it! Both of you.' She pushed a stray strand of hair from her forehead. 'Unless you'd like me to mock both of *you* and your silliness.'

'Oh, Marcella!' Michael gave that low laugh of his. 'We were marvelling at your charm and grace.'

Once more, Marcella felt the blood rush to her cheeks. Why was it that every time Michael paid her the tiniest compliment she blushed as red and hot as a chilli pepper? He hadn't mentioned their kiss, two long months ago, but she still burned with hope it would happen again, looking for evidence that he felt the same.

'So now...' Michael took out a notebook. 'I think we should aim to open by Christmas, don't you think? November. That would give us around six months to find a business partner, and to build up a list of suppliers and customers. There's nothing to stop us selling suits and dresses privately until we have our own premises.'

Marcella watched Michael as he drew lines on the paper. His hands were delicate but firm; his fingers long and slender, with perfectly manicured nails.

She felt flattered he had chosen her to be part of his new enterprise. Her parents would be so proud. The prospect of working alongside him in his tailoring business was quite a different idea to the scheme that they and Aunt Thérèse had cooked up for her. *This* would be exciting. Michael was bound to make a success of their venture, then she could use the money to fund her singing career. Rosa was right – she needed a plan. Here it was.

'Three glasses of rosé, please.' Michael turned to face them. 'We can't clink coffee cups on this agreement.'

Stefan grinned. 'I love a glass of wine at dusk.'

The trees were throwing long silhouettes, it was true, but the sun was still warm and golden even as it skimmed the terracotta roofs of the wide square.

'Actually, I already know someone who might come in with us,' said Michael, laying down his pencil and leaning his head back thoughtfully. 'Louis Hoffman. I've met him around town. He used to have a tailoring place near Riquier. He would suit us three perfectly. He's a man of lists and columns. Boring but necessary.'

Marcella could see Stefan out of the corner of her eye. He seemed to be making a list of something.

'Stefan!'

Stefan jumped, sliding his papers towards his lap.

'What do you think of London? Would you fancy a trip to ferret out the English modes?' Michael asked.

Stefan sprang up and clapped his hands together. His notes fell to the ground and, caught by the wind, flapped into the square. He ran after them, leaping in the air and whooping.

'And you, Marcella!' Michael's eyes were following Stefan. 'Are you busy tonight? I'd like to take you to dinner.'

'Why, yes, but… we three can—'

'Sshh!' Michael was still not looking at her, his gaze firmly on Stefan. 'I mean you, Marcella. You and me. The two of us. Alone.'

Marcella caught her breath. It was hard to speak. She uttered a low yes.

'Good,' said Michael, tipping back his wine. 'I'll meet you on the Promenade in ten minutes, under the statue of Nike.'

Stefan sat back down, out of breath. 'So, Michael.' He grabbed his glass of water and took a gulp. 'Tell me more about London?'

———

Michael had arranged a window table in a small bistro on a side road off the promenade. The room was quiet and intimate, lit by candlelight and a low gas chandelier. Michael was the first person who hadn't laughed when she talked about her singing ambitions. He understood her. More than that, he encouraged her. They drank more wine with the meal and by the time Michael paid the bill Marcella felt quite tipsy.

'I need to walk a bit before I go home,' she said. 'My parents won't like me staggering into the flat drunk!'

Michael put out his hand to help her down the steep steps leading to the beach. 'I was hoping you would say something like that,' he said. They walked along, their feet crunching the pebbles. The casino on the jetty was still lit up, its colours cast on to the water like a rippling stained-glass window. Sounds of music and laughter sometimes rose above the crash of the waves against the rocks and iron columns of the jetty. The moon was full and trailed a line of white on the distant black water.

'Look at that.' Marcella pointed out towards the sparkling sea. 'Have you noticed that, wherever you stand, that silver path thrown down by the moon always leads to where you are? It's as though the moon was laying down a carpet, preparing to come and visit you.'

'Or to tempt you to walk along it to your death.'

'Oh, don't be morbid, Michael. The moon on the water is gentle and soothing. It's wonderful, beautiful, magical.'

'You're right, of course.' Michael laughed, and slipped his arm around her waist. 'The moon is beautiful. But not nearly as beautiful as you are in its silver light.'

Marcella felt her toes curling with delight inside her boots.

As they walked, arm in arm, Michael told her about his life. He came from a small village in Hungary. He had two brothers and a sister.

'You must be the oldest,' said Marcella. 'You have such authority.'

'No. In fact, I was the second.' Michael stopped, picked up a pebble and threw it into the waves. 'Not the eldest, not the girl and not the youngest – that was Joseph. I'm just the one not quite in the middle. And you?'

Marcella didn't want to go into this. Her own background was too difficult to explain. So she said, 'I'm an only child.'

'I could tell,' said Michael. 'You're obviously very much loved and very, very spoiled.' He chuckled to himself.

'What do you mean?' He was laughing at her! She didn't like that. She was hardly spoiled. She always felt her parents were very hard on her.

'I meant your mother is overprotective of you.'

'She isn't.' Marcella found it difficult to hear this. It hadn't been easy for either of them. And she loved her mother very much. Her mother had done everything for her.

Michael continued, 'If she wasn't so protective, we wouldn't have to arrange surreptitious meetings like this one. I could arrive at your flat and simply take you out. And promise I'd bring you back in one piece. Would your mother disapprove of me taking you to dinner, all alone?'

'I can't see why she would. After all, I am seventeen.'

Michael laughed out loud, startling a seagull that had been picking in the sand at the water's edge. It flapped away into the navy-blue sky.

Marcella looked up at Michael. Suddenly he took a step towards her, pulled her into his arms and kissed her all over her face. Tilting

41

her head back, she moved her lips on to his. They kissed for so long she felt dizzy. Then, his face still so close to hers she could feel his breath, hot against her neck, he said, 'Let's get a room in a hotel.'

'No. I can't.' She pushed him away. How had he ruined such a beautiful moment? 'Not like this. We can't. It would spoil everything. We can't.'

He took a few steps back. 'So, Marcella, you don't feel about me the way I feel about you?'

'No, no.' She stretched out for his hand but he snatched it from her grasp. 'It's not like that. I'd love to go with you, but—'

'But your mother wouldn't like it...' His voice had a cruel, mimicking tone.

'No,' cried Marcella. 'It's me. I wouldn't like it. I mean I would like it – so much. But we're not married, Michael.'

Michael pulled her back into his arms.

'Oh, you little teasing pickle!' he said. 'I keep forgetting you are so young, so innocent.'

Marcella wasn't sure she was happy being called innocent.

They walked further along the beach, ducking under the jetty. Above them the bustling casino, but here in the darkness between the barnacled pillars hunched people who were combing the water's edge, searching the piles of flotsam for mislaid valuables, or gathering shellfish. A few sat patiently at the end of fishing lines.

At the top of the beach, they found a quiet spot and stood for an hour in the lee of the high sea wall, murmuring to each other and kissing. And when Marcella's face felt raw from the scratch of Michael's clean-shaven cheeks, she told him that it was time she went home.

He walked her back along the coast road, braving the wind of Rauba Capeu, past the port, with its bobbing boats chinking together in the harbour, up the side of the church and along Rue Arson, right to her parents' door. Under the dim light of a street lamp Michael kissed her lightly on both cheeks and waited, watching until she had gone inside and closed the door behind her.

The next morning, a bouquet of spring flowers arrived at the flat – mimosa, tulips and carnations – together with a box of chocolates addressed to Marcella's mother, Angela. This of course prompted a lot of questions, which Marcella was not prepared for. Michael had been her secret. Not any longer.

'Go, Ton-ton! Out!' Her mother shooed Antonio out of the house.

'But, Gigi?'

Angela held up her hands and waved him away. 'We need some bread.'

'But we already have—'

'All right. Some apples, then. This is woman talk.'

Ton-ton took his hat off the hook and left. Only when she heard the door downstairs slam shut did Angela sit down with her daughter.

The first thing she wanted to do was arrange a meeting with 'the young man'. Then came the barrage of questions: Perhaps one evening Monsieur Navratil would like to come for an aperitif? Was he handsome? What did he do for a living?

Marcella bubbled with chatter about him, but when it came to that last question she hesitated before replying. Instead of saying, 'He's my teacher,' she chose her words with care: 'We're at the institute together.'

It wasn't exactly a lie.

And so a meeting was set up a few days later.

Michael sat primly in her family living room, sipping a glass of red wine. Seeing him here with her mother and Ton-ton, bashful and on his best behaviour, made her love him even more.

She went to fetch some more savoury biscuits from the kitchen, but when she came back the atmosphere in the room was fully charged. It seemed that in her absence Michael had told Angela that he intended to be engaged to Marcella as soon as possible.

'But, Michael, she's still a child,' Angela was saying. 'Could you not wait until she is twenty?'

Michael sighed, then smiled.

'Even eighteen would be preferable,' added Angela. 'After all, that's only nine months away.'

There followed an awkward pause. Antonio stepped forward from behind Angela's chair.

'There's nothing you're not telling us, is there?' He looked to Marcella, who, realising the implication of what he was saying, blushed purple and stammered, 'No, no, no! Ton-ton! No!'

Michael had not even told her he wanted to get engaged before asking her mother. She wasn't sure whether to feel shocked or excited.

Michael leaned back in his chair, quite relaxed. 'If I must wait for an eternity to win her, I shall,' he said.

'That's good, because you must wait,' Angela made clear, scrutinising Marcella's face. 'Legally, my daughter cannot marry without my permission. Not till her twenty-second birthday.'

'Another four years.' Antonio seemed surprised. 'You agree with that, Gigi?'

'And three months.' Angela looked over at Marcella, who was still blushing and staring at the carpet.

Michael beamed. 'I assure you, by January 1912 my prospects will be impeccable. I will be famous throughout Nice, perhaps Europe and the world. I am setting up my own shop. Did Marcella not tell you? I will be in business as a ladies' tailor.'

'That's very good news.' Angela looked Michael in the eye. 'I'm not saying no forever, you understand. But at the moment Marcella is so very young. Perhaps in a year or so…'

'As long as it takes, I will wait. My prospects are good, Madame Frattini. I have big, big plans. By next January, I promise you, my shop will be open, and four years after that I will be practically the King of Nice. Wait and see.'

CHAPTER 7

September 1911, Nice

'So you eloped, then. To marry Mr Navratil?' Monsieur Nabias held his fingertips together and looked at Marcella from beneath his brow. 'Surely it would have been impossible for you to marry here in Nice? You were seventeen. You had to have your parents' approval. The banns, the publication of intent in the newspapers… Your mother would surely have heard about it and stepped in. And yet you say you married a few weeks after this?'

Marcella shuffled her feet on the floor. Monsieur Nabias's gaze made her feel uncomfortable. She had gone along with the secret marriage, so she had been as responsible as her husband.

'Or did your mother perhaps acquiesce, under a battery of your husband's undeniable charm?'

'He did charm her. You're right, Monsieur Nabias. She was all for me marrying Michael. She just wanted us to wait. Not to prevent us from marrying, but to make sure we were doing the right thing.'

'And yet you went against her will?'

'I knew that it was a mortal sin. I would never have consented to sleeping with him.' She blushed deeply. 'The shame of being an unmarried mother – or worse, walking up the aisle six months pregnant – would not have suited me at all. So I did hold out.'

'But you didn't wait until you were twenty-two. That wouldn't have been until next January! It's quite ironic. You are wanting to divorce him before you would even have married him.'

True. But if she hadn't married him, she wouldn't have had her wonderful children.

'So I imagine your mother was brought round to the idea?'

Marcella bit her lip. Her mother had not known about the marriage. Marcella knew she had been headstrong and brought all her troubles on herself.

'You married in May 1907. Did you perhaps believe yourself to be pregnant?'

'No! No! No! I told you!' Marcella rose from her seat. Why was it so difficult to explain? Again, she became full of doubt. Perhaps she had come to the wrong man for help. 'I resisted him right up to the day we married.'

'I presume that up till that day Michael Navratil put more and more pressure on you? Though, with such a man, I imagine it would have been in a very romantic way, rather than through force?'

Marcella nodded and sat again. How could this stranger know Michael so well, when he had never met him? And she had not even told him the half of what had gone on. She thought back to when they were planning the shop while she was still living at home with her parents. After finishing the course, she had got a job working at a tailor's workshop near the railway station. In those weeks, when she finished work, she would often find Michael just happening to stroll past. There was also the stream of presents that arrived both for her and her mother and the secret liaisons Michael somehow managed to arrange with her right under Stefan's nose without him even noticing.

Talking to Monsieur Nabias made her see how clever Michael had been, the emotional pull he exerted. It was as though he was controlling her, a puppeteer moving her around by tugging on her strings. It wasn't simply that he'd tried to persuade her to sleep with him, but that she had found him irresistible.

'Once I caught Michael crying,' she said. 'It was after I had told him I should not see him quite so frequently. He was sitting in a café, on the street, just down the road from here. I was on my way home from work. I held back, watching. Then he saw me and wiped the tears away. He pretended he had something in his eye. So, you see, I had to go to him. I wondered what was wrong, was his family all right?

'"It must be hard living so far from your mother and brothers and sister," I said. I could not imagine never seeing my mother for months, let alone years. But he said he was crying because of me. He said he couldn't live without me and he thought I was distancing myself because I had stopped loving him.

'Of course I simply laughed at him. I told him not to be so silly. I was longing for the day we married as much as he was. So we arranged another of our secret meetings.

'The next time I saw him he was different. Full of determination and vigour. He had moved out of his lodgings and got a new flat. Well, not really a flat so much as rooms in a boarding house, rather than in a landlady's apartment. The new place was down near the promenade. He asked me to go there with him. But I was afraid that I would find myself in a situation where... well... I might have let myself do things I might subsequently regret.'

'And the marriage took place soon after that incident, and in London, you say?' Monsieur Nabias took a new sheet of paper and refilled his pen. 'Did he take you with him on the working trip with Stefan?'

Marcella shuddered when she recalled what happened next. At the time it had all seemed so exciting, although she had felt guilty about Stefan. If only she had done the honourable thing back then, perhaps everything would have been all right now, and she wouldn't be sitting here with a divorce lawyer.

'Stefan didn't come to London,' she said quietly. 'Michael had only bought two tickets. And only let Stefan know the night before that he would be taking me instead.'

'You were planning to elope and marry, was that it?'

'No. Seeing Paris and staying in London, travelling on that long train journey, taking the ferry, I was overcome with the thrill of it all. I didn't really think.'

Marcella felt an immense grief well up inside her. 'That's my trouble. I don't look far enough ahead. I don't prepare for the worst that could happen. When people say that I am childish, they're right. In a three-year-old, behaviour like mine is excusable. Not so much at twenty-one.'

Monsieur Nabias interrupted her. 'Coming here is not a childish move.'

'That's what frightens me.' Marcella felt that in the few minutes of this interview she had changed. 'I took too long to grow up and, now, all of a sudden, I feel very, very old.'

CHAPTER 8

May 1907, en route to London

Marcella and Michael boarded the ferry at Calais, made their way to the outer deck and leaned over the rails to watch the sailors releasing heavy ropes on the quayside. As the boat pulled out through the grey haze over the harbour, they could see curling white breakers ruffling the waters of the Channel ahead.

'I love the sea,' said Marcella. 'Don't you?'

'I love you more.' Michael put his hands around Marcella's waist. She wriggled away.

'No, Michael! Remember, this is a business trip. We're going to look for the latest London fashions. You promised. I can't. Really I can't.'

'You were safe enough on the train last night, no?'

Marcella pulled a face. She had travelled in an all-female couchette car with another woman, while he had travelled in the next carriage along, with another man.

'You know that I want to. But not until we're married...'

He patted the back of her hand and turned to watch the churning water, as the ferry manoeuvred out into the Channel.

'So now we will find out whether you have sea legs, won't we?' he said.

'You needn't worry about me on a little crossing like this. I've known seas as high as you can imagine.'

'And what would a nice little Catholic girl from the hinterlands of Liguria know of the sea, when all you've seen of it is the turquoise curve of the Bay of Angels?'

'I've seen a lot more of the sea than that.' Marcella was annoyed at the way he was teasing her, assuming she'd never been anywhere.

'So you've also seen the azure curve of the Bay of Genoa, I presume.'

It was a long story, and Marcella didn't want to start it.

'More than that, then?' He gave her a knowing look. 'Don't tell me you took the Corsica ferry?'

He was making her feel stupid.

'I crossed the Atlantic. It took two weeks. But it was years ago. I was a tiny child. I barely remember it.' She turned away from the handrail, looking for a door into the ship. 'Let's go and have a bite of lunch, before we get blown away.'

She didn't want Michael to ask any more about it. It really was best to leave the subject alone.

'You did bring all your papers, didn't you?' he asked as they took a table in the small cafeteria. The boat lurched slightly as it pulled out of the sheltered waters into the main swell. 'I wouldn't want the customs men at Dover stopping you and forcing you to turn back.'

'I have everything – my passport, my birth certificate—'

'Can I see them?'

'Don't you trust me?' Marcella clutched her handbag. He was worrying her. She took out all the papers and handed them over. While he leafed through her documents, she thought back to the day before when Michael had told her he needed her, not Stefan, to accompany him to London. At first she had thought he was joking. Then she became nervous.

'It's very important to have a woman's eye,' he had said. 'Go home and fetch all your papers. I'm not sure what you'll need, so bring everything you have.'

She asked him how Stefan had taken the news, but Michael had simply shrugged. 'He'll get over it,' he said.

That was not good. Stefan had been so excited and well prepared for the trip and, now that she had taken his place, she knew he would not be at all happy with her.

'Born in Buenos Aires!' Michael laughed, looking at her birth certificate. 'So you really have crossed oceans. I thought you might be romancing.'

Trying to ignore the implication that she was making it all up, Marcella changed the subject. 'Where will we stay in London? A hotel?'

Michael wafted his hand as though to say it was all organised and there was no need for any discussion. 'It's a place someone recommended to me a few years back. A young man whose job I took over at a tailor's shop had stayed there.'

Marcella still hoped Michael wasn't about to tell her there had only been one room left and that they would have to share a bed.

Michael looked out at her from behind his hooded eyes. 'Oh, Marcella, I can read you like a book. I'm sleeping in a room full of young gentlemen and you are in a room full of young ladies. We're staying in the heart of the rag-trade area, in the middle of town, above a charming restaurant.' He sipped his coffee and did not look at her for some minutes. All the while he fiddled with the spoon. Eventually he said, 'You do realise that you're going to have to tell me how you happened to get born in South America, then sail back across the Atlantic. You can't keep such an essential story from me.'

'It's really uninteresting.' Marcella put down her cup. 'Nothing to it. My parents emigrated to Argentina—'

'Like so many Italians…'

She nodded. 'They lived for a while in Buenos Aires. As you see – I was born there.'

Michael threw his arms up. 'You are South American! I always felt an affinity with Americans!'

'In a way. I was born there but—'

'I know what happened next. They didn't like it: too hot, too strange, missed home, no spaghetti, wanted to see the family, usual story?'

'No. Not at all. My father had this idea that if we went up to the Amazon forests he could find some rare coloured woods. Woods that would make him famous. He was a cabinetmaker, you see. He specialised in inlay and marquetry—'

'While my father was a mere carpenter.'

'I don't understand?'

'You're implying that my father was a lesser man than yours?'

'No! I didn't mean that.' Now she'd upset him. It looked as though she was crowing about her father, when in fact… She gabbled on quickly. 'So we all went up to Brazil. The whole family: my father, my mother, my brother and me. But instead of finding this rare coloured wood, he caught yellow fever, and then my baby brother succumbed too. Within days they were both dead.'

Michael was silent.

Marcella felt that she had ruined the joyful atmosphere, the thrill of this journey to London.

'What happened next?' Michael asked.

'We buried them both. Out there. Then we came home, just my mother and me. I was very young. To be honest, I don't remember much. Just the vast expanse of dark-grey water, a circle of slate around us, with nothing to see but white crests and occasionally the spout of a passing whale. I remember too the setting sun, all red, like a sea of blood, and, when night had fallen, my old friend the moon with her glittering silver pathway always trailing down to our ship, guiding us home to Italy. And I remember my mother, always crying. Crying for the two men in her life – her husband and her son.'

'I'm so sorry.' Michael gently stroked Marcella's cheek. 'I thought you had just been on some silly trip to Spain, or somewhere. I hate having upset you.'

Marcella pressed her hand on his. They interlocked fingers.

'It's all right. I don't really remember my father. Or my brother. I was only about four. My vivid memories are of the years which followed, with my mother sobbing and tearfully going on and on about what a wonderful father I had had, how she should have encouraged him to stay in Buenos Aires, and damn the stupid rare wood.'

'Stay in Buenos Aires? But that would have been no good at all.' Michael smiled and withdrew his hand from hers. 'Because if you had stayed in Buenos Aires, then you would never have gone back to Genoa, never come to Nice, I would never have met you and we wouldn't be sitting here about to land in England to see the London tweeds and woollen plaids.' He scraped his chair back and stood up. 'Come on. Let's go out on deck again and look for cormorants and seagulls and those famous white cliffs.'

Soho was even busier than Marcella could have imagined. The streets clattered with horse-drawn carts, motor cars and omnibuses, while shabby men wheeled barrows and smart men in dark suits rushed in every direction. The London women were either fat and loud, or slim and sophisticated. Marcella saw so many wonderful skirts and dresses, cut to perfection, and worn with such elegance and style. And the London hats: well, they were exquisite.

There was so much hustle and bustle it was difficult to cross the roads. Draymen rattled over the cobbles, overtaken by jaunty gigs which trotted along carrying smartly dressed couples in the back seats. Marcella imagined them on their way to the theatre or paying visits to dukes and duchesses.

They arrived in Marshall Street, where the owner of the building, a chubby red-faced man, greeted them at the door and announced that his name was Kühne, Paul Kühne. Even though he himself was from colder Germany, he was always entranced, he told Marcella, to welcome guests from sunny Nice, particularly members of the tailoring profession. The ground floor of the establishment was taken up by a restaurant, which was already open and serving supper. Through the large square windows, Marcella could see diners at tables laid with white cloths and clunky ivory-handled cutlery.

Mr Kühne walked along past the front of the restaurant and opened a door on the corner of the street. Inside was a small hall leading to a steep staircase with worn lino treads. He let out a piercing whistle and a gangly boy rushed down and took their bags. As they followed, Mr Kühne and Michael talked quietly in phrases Marcella couldn't understand.

Would it be completely self-obsessed to imagine that they were discussing her?

At the top of the stairs, they passed through a swing door into a narrow corridor painted pine green and cream. It was lined with doors. The boy stopped and held open the first one.

'This is the ladies' room, miss.' He opened the door wide to reveal a cramped space with two sets of bunks. 'Gents' room down the other end, sir, if you'll follow me.'

Marcella was relieved. All was fine. She was sleeping in a room with other women. This really wasn't all a plan to seduce her. It was strange, but now she saw that Michael's intentions had been entirely honourable all along, she felt slightly disappointed.

She kicked her valise under the bed and flopped on to the bottom bunk.

Well! This was an adventure, being here in London, a city she had never visited. More than that, she was here with a man she was crazy about, and she was looking forward to seeing the London fashions. Why wouldn't she be happy?

Only weeks before, the very idea of tailoring had bored her. But Michael had opened up a whole new world of possibilities. Now she loved looking at the edging, the trimmings, the line of ladies' dresses and found herself wondering how they had been put together. She also enjoyed sketching her own ideas for new designs.

She lay back and started humming 'La Petite Tonkinoise'. After a few seconds she sang out loud.

A knock on the door silenced her and made her sit up.

'*Entrez!*' she said, then remembering she was in England she added, 'Hello!'

'May I?' Michael popped his head around the door. 'You must be tired. It's been a long journey.'

'No, no… I—' Marcella swung her legs off the bed and stood up, knocking her head on the top bunk. 'Ouch! I'm too excited. I've never been to England before. Might we see the King?'

'I think we should both take a little nap. Just for an hour or so. Then we can go out and find somewhere cosy for dinner. What do you say?'

'I'd love that.'

'Good! See you later.'

He closed the door behind him. But now Marcella couldn't sleep at all. She lay back on the bed and shut her eyes. What should she wear tonight? She wanted to look her best for Michael. She wanted him to notice her. With her finger she traced a line along the pattern of the wallpaper.

A lovely hobble skirt, with a full blouse, a bolero jacket and a wide hat. If only she had such things with her! She would wear the best things she had: her black Gored skirt and her rose-pink silk blouse, the one with leg-of-mutton sleeves.

Nothing mattered now. Nothing except for Michael to desire her.

The next day was a round of the mercers' companies: stores of Nottingham lace and small warehouses full of Scottish tweeds along the Strand and the alleyways running off it. Michael and Marcella visited various shops, one selling only buttons, another with shelves that bulged with trimmings and braids in every colour and texture.

Michael talked about making orders but Marcella suggested that it would be better to make notes of all the products they had seen and find French merchants selling the same things nearer to home.

'But these fabrics wouldn't be available in Nice.'

'No, but they would be in Paris. When I worked for my aunt, she talked about several shops there where she holds accounts. Beautiful ribbons and trimmings, tweeds, worsteds, and some exquisite shot-satins and silk brocades.'

'Can you remember their names?' Michael took out his notebook.

Marcella reeled them off. Then she daringly suggested that on the way home she and Michael might stop over in Paris for a few hours and take a look.

After walking the length of the Strand, from Trafalgar Square to Ludgate Circus, looking in all the shop windows at the latest ladies' fashions, they decided to ride in an omnibus back up to Regent Street.

'And this is where I leave you… for the moment,' said Michael, raising his hat. 'Oh! And I have booked supper for us tonight at Mr Kühne's restaurant. So all you need to do is come downstairs and meet me at around eight. Is that good?'

Marcella couldn't say what she really thought: that she didn't want him to go off on his own, she wanted him to stay with her, but she smiled and made her way back to the ladies' dormitory, where she lay, fully dressed, on the bunk and dozed.

When she woke, someone else was in the room, clicking the fastenings on her own small valise. The girl then clambered up the ladder to the opposite bunk.

Marcella had no idea what the time was, so, in her best English, she quietly asked.

'It's ten past eight, love,' the girl replied. 'And I'm dog-tired. Come all the way from Birmingham this afternoon.'

Marcella sprang from her bunk and hastily checked her face and hair in a hand mirror before rushing downstairs. Michael was sitting alone at a table facing the door, reading a newspaper. When he saw her, he folded it and thrust it under the table, then rose to greet her.

The dining room was almost full, but the diners talked very softly and the ambience was alarmingly dull. Marcella was aware of every sound: the low hum of conversation at the adjacent tables, a wall clock ticking noisily, the hiss of the gaslights, the brittle clink of knives and forks on china plates.

At times it was so quiet that Marcella was afraid Michael would hear her chewing and swallowing her food. What made it worse was that she couldn't think of anything to say. She wanted to ask him where he had been but knew that was not a good idea. On the contrary, it would make her sound like a policeman or a spy.

Michael seemed to have caught the local atmosphere and remained reserved throughout the meal. She worried that he was regretting having swapped her for Stefan as his travelling companion. Perhaps he had gone off her? The fear nagged at her, turning every mouthful of pudding, a delightful apple pie and custard, to sand in her mouth.

When coffee was served, she plucked up courage to ask him straight out if she was a disappointment to him. In response, he pulled a small box from his inside pocket. 'First, I want you to answer a question,' he said. He held his fingers down on the box and looked her in the eye. 'Your taste is often good. But this time I'm not sure…'

Marcella felt scared. He must have found some new style of button or something and wanted her opinion. From his expression, she knew that this was a test. What if she got the answer wrong?

Michael was looking at her in a very strange way. He seemed distant and threatening.

'Your help on this trip has been useful, Marcella. But I am perturbed by one thing.'

Marcella felt her mouth go dry. She licked her lips and swallowed.

How on earth had she disappointed him? How could he be worried? She had been alert and lively. She had made practical comments on the quality and values of all the goods. She had come up with ideas. For the most part she had agreed with his opinions.

For the most part... Perhaps Michael did not like any contradiction.

'The question remains...' Michael lifted his fingers from the box and flipped open the lid to reveal a beautiful ring. 'Will you marry me?'

Marcella felt such a rush of relief and happiness she couldn't stop herself from jumping up and going to his side to smother his face with kisses.

'Of course I will. You know I've wanted to be your wife right from the start. I adore you.'

'So that's final, then.' He took the ring from the box and slid it on to her finger. 'You will marry me.'

Paul Kühne, who had been hovering in the doorway, walked forward brandishing a bottle of champagne.

Next morning was wet, dark and miserable. The rain drummed against the squared windowpanes of the dormitory. Marcella had a pounding headache. Nonetheless, she was floating on a cloud of happiness. She twirled the engagement ring around and around her finger.

After dressing, checking her face in the mirror to make sure she didn't look as bad as she felt, she realised she had not thought to bring a mackintosh. Her coat was flimsy. It would not keep out the rain. And today the plan was to walk the length of Oxford Street. All she could do was hope that the shower would soon pass.

As she descended the stairs, making her way to breakfast, she felt nervous. She pushed through the side door into the restaurant, her heart racing. It only took a quick glance around the dining room to see that Michael was not there. Her spirits plummeted. Had he perhaps thought better of his rash proposal last night? Maybe he was cowering in the gentlemen's rooms, fearful of coming down to face her and tell her that last night he had been drunk, that it had all been a terrible misunderstanding.

She ate her breakfast quickly. She was so upset she could barely swallow.

Then, just as she was gathering her things to go back upstairs, Mr Kühne came in, panting and waving his arms.

'Oh, Mademoiselle Caretto, that was a close thing! I nearly missed you. Signing for a delivery out the back, you know. I saw your fiancé, Monsieur Navratil, earlier and, well… there's been a slight change of plan for today.'

Marcella's heart sank.

Embarrassed about the mistake of last night, Michael had packed up and gone.

'He says you're to put on the best clothes you have with you,' Mr Kühne continued. 'He has set up an important meeting. I will accompany you to the location where you are to meet. You should bring all your paperwork with you. Contract signing, et cetera. I will meet you at the side door in about fifteen minutes. Does that give you enough time, Mademoiselle Caretto?'

As Marcella changed, under the censorious gaze of the girl from Birmingham, she couldn't stop smiling. She was Michael's fiancée! His fiancée!

While she fixed her hair, she found herself giggling in the mirror.

'Glad someone's got something to laugh about,' said the girl in the bunk. 'I've got to go out in this squall and no flippin' brolly.'

At the bottom of the stairs, Mr Kühne was waiting, looking anxiously at his pocket watch. He pushed open the door to the dining room and called out, 'Walter! Hurry along there!'

One of the waiters burst through, bearing an umbrella, and held open the door on to Marshall Street.

'Oh my lord, Mr Kühne! It's coming down in rods,' he cried. The rain was hitting the pavement and splashing up and in through the open door. He stepped outside and put up the umbrella, making sure that Marcella would be completely sheltered. 'Gawd!' he said. 'Am I glad we don't have far to go.'

Marcella hitched her skirt so that the hem would not get covered in mud.

Paul Kühne scurried along under the umbrella's protection as best he could fit.

'Only two minutes away,' he shouted to Marcella, then a few steps along the street, barked to Walter, 'Turn left!'

They were now pushing through the shoppers in a busy street market. Stalls were laid out with old clothes, others spilled over with flowers and vegetables. The stallholders huddled under the flimsy canvas awnings of the shops that lined the narrow pavement. Water poured over the edges.

When they reached the public house on the corner, Mr Kühne called out to Walter. 'Left again!'

'Gertcha!' A horse-drawn cart rattled past, the driver snapping the reins, shooing the carthorse over the cobbles. Paul Kühne shoved Marcella away from the kerb to avoid the brown splash from one of the cartwheels as it rumbled through a puddle.

'Sharp left again, Walter, and go inside.'

Walter came to a halt, holding the umbrella and helping Marcella through two open doors into a dark-green tile-lined hallway. As they entered the hall, a double door ahead swung open, leading further into the building. Michael was standing on the other side of the doors. He was wearing his smartest suit, holding his hat in his hand.

'Could you two wait out there for a moment, please. I need to talk to Marcella alone.'

Paul Kühne grabbed Walter's elbow and yanked him back as the doors closed.

'What's going on?' This was not a shop of any kind. It was more like a municipal office.

Michael fell to one knee. 'Will you marry me?'

'Have you lost your memory? I said last night I would.' Marcella laughed. 'It was only hours ago.'

'I mean, will you marry me… now?'

'What do you mean "now"?' Marcella looked around.

Was this the English equivalent of the mayor's office?

She felt frightened and excited. Thrilled, yet paralysed with a kind of exhilaration she had never felt before. 'But my mother… my family…'

Michael stood up and pulled her close.

'Don't worry. We can do it all again in France, go to a church even. But why not just marry me now? Get the legal bit over and done with?'

Alternating waves of anticipation and doubt left Marcella unable to reply.

'Then, my darling, when we go back to Nice you can finally come and live with me in Rue Croix de Marbre.'

Marcella saw what a leap into the future this was. If she committed to this, nothing could ever be the same again.

It felt wonderful.

'You know why I moved there, Marcella? To Rue Croix de Marbre?'

Marcella could barely hear him above the thoughts that crowded through her head. Should she take up this mad and marvellous offer?

'…because the room looks out over the park where, under that tree, during the Carnaval, I first kissed you. I love that spot. The place where first I lost my heart and soul to you.'

'I'm too young to marry,' Marcella said, suddenly gripped by fear. 'I'm only seventeen. I can't marry without my parents' permission.'

'That's true in France – not here in England.'

'But the banns…?'

60

'Everything is different here.' Michael cupped her hands between his own. 'We can walk in through that door, say a few words, sign the register and come out Mr and Mrs Navratil. Mr Kühne and Mr Kent can be our witnesses.'

'But my mother...'

'She'll come around to the idea.'

Marcella really meant that her mother would want to be here to see her get married.

Michael was still speaking. 'Remember, your mother wasn't against us marrying, was she?'

Another couple burst out of the registrar's office, loudly followed by a mob of friends and relatives, showering them with confetti.

'Come along, Winnie,' the man said, grabbing her hand. 'You're Mrs Trelawny now.'

The newly named Mrs Trelawny blushed and thrust her face into her husband's jacket. He threw his arm around her shoulder.

'Party's waiting, old girl. No need to blush now, eh? Not now you're my missus.'

The group moved through the double doors and away. The assistant registrar came into the hall.

'Next couple! You can come in now. Mr Navratil and Miss Caretto?'

Michael took Marcella's hand and took a step forward.

'Come on, then.'

'But my clothes...'

'I can't imagine you looking any more beautiful than you do at this moment.' Michael bent forward and kissed her lips, silencing her doubts.

'All right,' Marcella said, pulling away and straightening her blouse. 'Let's do it.'

CHAPTER 9

September 1911, Nice
'And that day in London you went ahead and married Mr Navratil? Do you have the marriage certificate with you?'

Marcella opened her bag and pulled it out.

Monsieur Nabias unfolded and inspected the piece of paper for a minute or two.

'You were married in Westminster, England. And Mr Kühne and his waiter, Walter Kent, were the witnesses to your signatures?'

'That's right.' Marcella remembered the small office, the stooped old registrar presenting the pen with a well-rehearsed smile as she and Michael bent over the book, and how Michael's hand trembled as he signed.

'And you gave as your address, 10 Marshall Street, London W1?'

'10 Marshall Street was the address of Mr Kühne's restaurant and his lodging rooms above. It was where we were staying.'

'But you weren't actually living there; that is, you didn't stay there for more than two weeks?'

'No.'

Marcella noticed that Monsieur Nabias raised his eyebrows at her answer as he took an almost imperceptible breath.

'Technically, then, you made a false statement to the Clerk of the Court. You both committed a form of perjury.' Monsieur Nabias glanced back at his notes. 'I'm interested in this Kühne fellow. Before the wedding, how long had your husband known him?'

'I don't know. I'm not sure that they'd ever met before then.'

'Describe him to me.'

'Plump, loud, always smiling. Personally, I didn't take to him, although I must admit that he was very generous with us.'

'For example?'

'When we got back from the registrar's office, there was a special wedding lunch prepared.' Marcella remembered. The whole day had been full of treats. 'And he gave us a sweet little room on the top floor. It was all ready for us that morning as soon as we returned.'

'Your husband, then, was in no doubt that you would go along with the marriage? I'd also suggest that somebody must have posted the banns in the weeks beforehand. Could Mr Kühne have been in on the plan?'

Marcella had not thought about that. At the time it had all seemed so romantic and spontaneous. Surely it wasn't possible that the whole event had been planned by Michael before they even arrived in London? Or, rather, Michael with the help of Mr Kühne.

She tried to suppress the thought that she had been manipulated. What a mix of feelings! Had she unintentionally led Michael on? Perhaps she had encouraged him by always refusing him. Hadn't she always said they could not go to bed together until they were married? That must have been what made him swap Stefan for her on the London trip. She must have let Michael think… no, more than think, she must have let him *know* that she wanted him as much as he wanted her, and that the moment he asked her she would say yes, and marry him.

'Madame Navratil, you haven't answered my question about Paul Kühne.'

Marcella felt crushed. She didn't want to think that she had been tricked. But, now that Monsieur Nabias had pointed it out, she knew that she had been.

'You know that under English law somebody in London would have had to put up a notice signed by one of the parties, with an address at which one of the parties has lived for more than fifteen days, and that notice has to be filed with the registrar twenty-one days before the wedding?'

Marcella had not known this. She was taken aback. Michael must have been in closer contact with Paul Kühne than she could have believed. In fact, even when Stefan still thought he was going to accompany Michael to London, Michael must have been corresponding with Mr Kühne, making arrangements for their wedding.

'As you were under twenty-one years of age, that formal notice would also have stated that there was no living relative who could have objected to your marriage.'

Marcella felt betrayed and deceived.

'I see that this information has come as a shock. But were you happy, then, Madame Navratil? To marry, I mean.'

'Ecstatically. But…'

'But?'

'There was something… It was only a slight niggle. Something which during the wedding breakfast made me feel uncomfortable.' Now that she was here, she might as well say out loud that thing which had given her misgivings, but which she had never before mentioned to anyone. 'It's always bothered me, ever since. While we were in London and I asked about it directly, people just brushed me off. So I never got to the bottom of it.'

'Tell me…'

She clenched her fists and pressed them down on her thighs. To this day it made her feel uneasy to remember how everyone in the room had been laughing at something. Something shared, but which she hadn't understood.

'During the celebrations, in the restaurant afterwards, when people raised their glasses and toasted us, they kept referring to another couple, also from Nice. They had been there in London five years before us. Tailors, as we were, a young woman and a man who was ten years older than her, exactly like us. But it seemed to me, from all the banter and joking, that something must have happened, or that the marriage had never taken place. Anyhow, something went wrong.'

'Do you remember anything else about them?'

'Only their names. The man had also been a paying guest at Mr Kühne's restaurant.'

'Their names?' Gripping his pen, Monsieur Nabias peered up at her.

'Well, monsieur, I remember only because they were singular names. The man had a name very suitable for a tailor. He was called Jean-Baptiste Sartori. The woman, Sidonie Giraud.'

'Oh, my lord! Jean-Baptiste Sartori!' Monsieur Nabias appeared horrified. He stared back at the paperwork; then, after a second or two, he asked, 'Do you know anything of their story?'

Marcella shook her head. All she remembered was a kind of sniggering among the waiters. She also recalled Paul Kühne's eyes popping with childish malice.

Marcella had taken it for crude post-wedding teasing. When Michael exchanged some sharp words in German with Paul Kühne, she had thought he was asking him to pull it back a bit. But when she asked him about it later, Michael had waved it away, almost as though it embarrassed him.

'"It was something that happened a long time ago," was all he said by way of explanation. It was just a joke in poor taste.'

'Poor taste, indeed.' Monsieur Nabias pursed his lips.

Marcella looked down at her lap. She wished that she had never mentioned it. 'Madame Navratil, I am getting a vivid picture of this marriage. Perhaps now is the time to tell me why you wish to end it.'

It was clear, looking back, that everything had changed after the children were born. When Michel Marcel arrived, Michael was over the moon. But then came the sleepless nights, the teething. Everything seemed to upset him. When she doted on the child, he simmered with jealousy. Then, twenty months later, when Edmond Roger was born, Michael became someone else. When she breastfed he sulked, when she played with the children or talked to them in baby-talk he left the room. He turned into a man she would never have married. He did tell her, over and over, in increasingly anguished tones, how much he loved her, but there were times when Marcella felt Michael hated her.

'Madame Navratil?' Monsieur Nabias was staring at her, waiting for her to tell the rest of the story and explain why she had come to him.

Where to begin?

'After the children were born you continued to work in the shop?'

'He insisted. For a while after the birth of Michel Marcel, I stayed at home, but with Edmond, whenever I took walks with the pushchair, Michael accused me of going out to meet men. So he got me back in the shop.'

'Where he could keep an eye on you. What hours do you spend in the shop, Madame Navratil?'

'I start at seven in the morning and finish when the shop closes, at eight at night.'

Monsieur Nabias made a kind of inward whistle. 'How much does Monsieur Navratil pay you?'

'He doesn't pay me. He says everything is for me anyway. The business. For my family. To keep us all.'

'You never answered my previous question. I asked you to tell me what had finally brought you here.'

Marcella braced herself. It was, after all, the reason she had come, the final straw. 'In front of the customers, and Stefan, and anyone passing by, he raged at me and called me a fishwife, a slut, a whore.' Marcella felt her voice breaking as she suppressed a sob.

Monsieur Nabias raised an eyebrow. 'I can't imagine the ladies in the shop thought much of such language?'

Marcella, trying to recall her own feelings, had a startling realisation. Michael only called her names in front of male customers and friends, or in the workroom. Never in front of female customers.

'When did the name-calling start?'

'Shortly after Edmond was born. March last year.'

'Would your husband have any reason to doubt that Edmond is his own?'

Of course Edmond was his. How could anyone think otherwise?

But now that Monsieur Nabias had suggested it, Marcella wondered if Michael had indeed doubted his paternity.

'Michael was jealous of the doctor,' she said. 'The doctor who came to oversee the pregnancy.'

'But that would have been too late for the conception, madame…'

Monsieur Nabias was right. But there was no logic to Michael's criticisms and accusations.

The lawyer was scribbling notes very fast. He did not look up as he said, 'And I think that there is something else which caused you finally to walk in here today?'

'Yes. It was a few weeks ago. I've been trying to pluck up the courage ever since. I have thought about it often, but today Michael is out of town on business, so I felt I could.'

'You've left the shop empty?'

'Stefan is in charge. He was going to have to shut up in order to fetch some lace from a supplier round the corner. So I offered to get it.' She gestured to the packet at her feet. 'It's a little shop which is often closed. It's run by one young lady, Mademoiselle Adrienne Aude. She often hangs a sign on the door, BACK IN 10 MINUTES, then doesn't return for half an hour, so I thought I could spin a story for Stefan about how long I had been away, sitting on the doorstep waiting for her. We've all had to do it from time to time.'

'Well?' Monsieur Nabias glanced up from his paperwork. 'What was the final straw?'

Marcella gripped her bag.

'He… I don't…'

'Let me rephrase that. What did your husband do to you which made you turn the front-door handle and enter my office?'

Marcella knew that once she had said it out loud, she would no longer be able to pretend it was something that had not happened.

She took a deep breath.

'In front of the children… he threw a plate at me. It smashed against my head, then fell to the parquet and shattered into a hundred pieces.'

When she looked up again, Monsieur Nabias was putting away his pen, stacking his papers and preparing to stand. Now he took her for a silly fool being upset by jokes she had not understood.

'I'm sorry,' she said. 'I shouldn't have wasted your time.'

'On the contrary, madame. I'll take on this divorce,' he said. 'We will meet again in a few weeks in the Palais de Justice.'

The Palais de Justice!

Marcella was once more startled, realising what a huge step she was taking.

'No. I can't go ahead with this, Monsieur Nabias. It's all a mistake. I—'

'Don't worry, Madame Navratil. Nothing is officially decided until after the next stage.' Monsieur Nabias moved around the desk to help Marcella up. 'I advise you to keep your nerve and hold your tongue. Don't tell anyone. Not even your mother. First, we must meet the President of the Court in his chambers. He will listen to your case, which I will prepare between now and our meeting. If the president decides to proceed, as I believe he will, he will arrange a date for the next stage. Then, and I repeat, only then, if the president so decides, an order will be sent to your husband summoning him to attend a first hearing before the court. After the second hearing the judges will pronounce their ruling on your case, and you will be officially separated. I would estimate that would happen around the end of November or early December. Four months after that, around April, the divorce will be made final and you will be free.'

Marcella still wanted to change her mind, to stop everything.

Perceiving her anxiety, Monsieur Nabias said, 'If you fear for yourself or for your children, you should have somewhere else where you can take refuge. Some emergency escape route. A friend or relative.'

'I could go to my parents.'

'Good.' Monsieur Nabias held open the office door. 'Before you go, Madame Navratil, may I ask you one more question?'

'Of course.'

'What would you hope to get out of this divorce? A share of the business? The apartment where you now live? Money?'

'Only my freedom,' she replied. 'And the safety and happiness of my children.'

Marcella returned to the shop with the lace. Stefan said nothing about the time she had taken. She worked until he excused her for the evening. By the time she went around the corner and upstairs to their flat, it was dark. She thanked Dolinda, the nurse she had borrowed from her mother to look after the children this afternoon, and sent her home.

Marcella went into the children's room and stared at them, both asleep in their cots. Lolo's dark lashes were flickering, in the middle of a dream. He was clutching the wooden boat Ton-ton had made for him. Lolo loved to float it in the shallows down at the beach. Even in his sleep he would not let go of it, his little hand resting on the counterpane, the tiny fingers tightly wrapped around the blue-painted hull. In the other bed, the baby, Edmond, was lightly snoring, his damp curls stuck to his forehead in the fine sweat of sleep. Crushed against his chest was his favourite cuddly white rabbit.

Shafts of moonlight spilled through the shutters, casting diagonal lines across the floor. Marcella knelt down, laying a hand on the bed of each sleeping child, and quietly sang to herself:

'Good evening, Madame Moon.
What are you doing here tonight?
I'm ripening the prunes
With my silvery light.'

The clock on the church up the road struck nine. Michael would surely be back any minute. She must make him some supper.

When it was all laid out on the table, ready to eat, she crept back to the children's room once more and stood there gazing at their beautiful sleeping faces. It was after half-past nine now. She wondered if Michael was going to stay out all night, as he had done before, memorably last Christmas and on New Year's Eve.

Something in her hoped that he would.

Perhaps he was drinking in a bar with that awful American barber? Was there maybe some woman he went to see, one of the lady customers, staying in a luxurious room in one of the grand hotels down on the Promenade? Or did he just walk the streets, alone, wanting to be anywhere but here with her?

She prayed that he had not been following her today and seen her coming out of the lawyer's office. Was he staying out now to punish her for that?

A key turned in the apartment door. It had to be him. Feeling like a traitor, Marcella went out into the corridor to welcome him.

'I left you some dinner in the kitchen.'

'You shouldn't have bothered.' Yanking off his necktie, Michael pushed past her and disappeared into the bedroom. 'I've already eaten.'

She followed him to the doorway. He kept his back to her.

'I should never have married you,' he said, climbing into bed and turning off the light. 'You're not good enough for me.'

Marcella was finally sure that she was doing the right thing.

There are some occupations which give you time to think, and sewing was one of them. If she had stuck to her guns and tried to find work as a singer, she wouldn't have spent so much time thinking, not while she was busy remembering the words of the songs, concentrating on the tune, listening to the band, feeling for the spirit of the audience. All of that kept your head too full for anything else.

But sewing… While your fingers were busy, your mind could wander, strolling down dark alleyways of the past, raising spectres from the future, imagining possibilities and things that might have been. Now, as she sat in the back room of the shop, stitching the lace she had bought yesterday from Mademoiselle Aude, Marcella realised how alone she was. So many people in her life had gone. There was her cousin, Rosa, who was now working in America in some grand mansion. Georgian Terrace, Elkins Park, Philadelphia, PA! What an address!

There was no chance of meeting Rosa tonight or ever, no hope of a chat or a drink together at the Grand Café Pomel. Marcella could write her a letter, but it would take weeks to get there and weeks to get a reply. Besides, writing a letter meant committing her thoughts to paper, and that was something Marcella dared not do.

Louis Hoffman was gone too. Quiet, sensible Louis who, as Michael's right-hand man, had managed the business with such straightforward calmness. She would like to talk to Louis. But he was now installed in Paris, a thousand kilometres away, running a tailoring shop on the swanky Chaussée-d'Antin.

Her mind wandered back to yesterday's meeting with Monsieur Nabias.

Why had he seemed so shocked by the names Jean-Baptiste Sartori and Sidonie Giraud? Who were they? What had happened to them? But there was nobody she could ask.

She tied a knot in the thread, stuck her needle into the pincushion and held out the cloak to inspect her work. One side was now complete. She pulled a length of thread long enough to attach braid to the other edge.

For the first time in her life, Marcella knew that, from being a young girl who could go anywhere and do anything, she was now stuck here, all alone. There was no one that she could turn to. How had that happened without her even noticing? Since marrying Michael she had lost the companionship of everybody. One by one. It was so imperceptible she hadn't realised they had gone Only her mother and Antonio stayed in touch with her, but she saw them rarely since they had moved out of the flat they all shared above the shop and into their own place on the other side of town. They'd gone in the height of summer, the dog days of August, when temperatures and tempers were running high.

Marcella wondered if they had deliberately chosen an area so far away from her and Michael, an area where they were highly unlikely to bump into them in a shop or at the market.

Marcella tied another tiny knot. She could hear Michael's voice through the baize curtain, in the shop. He was flattering a lady customer into buying one of the dresses displayed on a mannequin in the window.

She knew that in a few minutes Michael had an appointment at the barber's. She'd seen it marked down in the shop's work journal. Marcella dreaded every haircut Michael had. He always came back from Charles Kirchmann's American barbershop a little harder and a lot more abusive.

The boy apprentice, Cyril, coughed and Marcella remembered that she was not alone in the workshop. Cyril sat at the other table, hand-stitching a hem. She wondered if she had made some kind of noise. Maybe she had groaned aloud at the very thought of the smug Charles Kirchmann and his sanctimonious wife, Alice.

The curtain into the shop was pulled back and Michael stood on the threshold. 'Off to the barber's now, Cyril. I'll be back in around an hour,' he said. 'Stefan's in charge. I'll see you later.'

Then he swiped the curtain shut.

Even though she was his wife, he had not addressed her. He had not even looked at her. It was as though she was simply an empty chair. Marcella felt her face redden. It was humiliating. Cyril knew that Marcella was married to Michael, knew too that she was the mother of his two children.

She tried to concentrate on creating a buttonhole. She dug in, pressing the scissors through, narrowly avoiding cutting herself.

How had it come to this? When she first met Michael they had been so happy. Hadn't they?

Chapter 10

May 1907, Nice

After a lavish dinner at Le Train Bleu restaurant, Marcella and Michael, now Madame and Monsieur Navratil, boarded the sleeper train at the Gare de Lyon. Now that they had a marriage certificate, they were allowed to exchange their separate sleepers for a married couple's compartment.

They had spent a day in Paris where Michael was happy to go along with Marcella's suggestion of looking out the suppliers her aunt used. Marcella felt elated being in such a close partnership with Michael while nursing the wonderful secret of their new union.

It was only in the early-morning hours, lying awake in her husband's arms as the train followed the Mediterranean coastline, snaking between the red rocks of the Esterel and the turquoise sea, that she started to acknowledge the reality. Being away had been like a mysterious dream, nothing real about it at all, but soon the train would pull in at Saint-Raphaël, then Cannes, Antibes and finally Nice – home… and her family.

She wondered whether she might persuade Michael to keep the whole wedding episode a secret from them. She started to imagine how upset her mother would be, and how disapproving her aunt. Would Ton-ton get into fisticuffs with Michael? She knew that there would be quarrels and tears, and she couldn't bear it. She was so happy.

Instinctively, she withdrew from Michael's body. He sensed her reaction and pulled her tighter, whispering in her ear, 'Stop fretting, my darling Shadow. It will be just fine. I will make it so.'

Why had he called her Shadow? Marcella wondered.

So she asked.

'Isn't it obvious?' he replied. 'Because you are beautiful, with your black hair and dark eyes, and because now, wherever I go, I want you always to be there, and wherever you go I will be.' He kissed her forehead. 'We are two different people, but, at the same time, we are one. You are my Shadow.'

This made Marcella feel strangely conspiratorial. Now they were one. Her fights were his fights. Michael would help her explain everything.

———

When they got off the train, just after eight o'clock, Michael put Marcella in a taxi with their suitcases.

'Here's the key to my rooms in Rue Croix de Marbre,' he said. 'Just drop the cases off and I will see you outside your mother's apartment in an hour. I'm going to walk down there, via the bank.' He clicked the taxi door shut and leaned through the window to kiss her. 'This will be our first separation, Madame Navratil. How will I last a whole hour?'

As the taxi pulled out, Marcella watched through the rear window. Michael stood waving until it turned a corner and she could no longer see him. One hour later she arrived at her mother's street, but Michael was nowhere to be seen. She started to panic. What if he didn't come and she had to face them alone? She didn't think she could bear it. She leaned against a tree and looked up at the windows. The sun was reflecting against the glass. She raised her hand to shield her eyes.

There he was! He was standing near the window, inside her mother's flat, beckoning her, calling her up to join them. But hadn't he said they would meet outside?

She ran up the stairs, dreading what was to come once she reached the top, but Ton-ton was standing on the landing with a wide grin on his face. She found quite a crowd waiting in the living room. Her two cousins, Rosa and Raphaël Bruno, leaned against the fireplace, looking like the dark and pale version of the same person. They too were smiling. And in the centre of the room sat Michael, teetering on a tiny velvet footstool at her mother's feet. He sprang up, holding out his hand to lead her to a chair.

Her mother's flat was usually so neat and almost spartan, yet today there was an enormous bouquet of flowers crammed into a small vase on the table; next to it, a box of chocolates, already opened and some gone.

Ton-ton rubbed his hands together and said, 'Michael, would you like me to bring in that tray now?'

Michael nodded and Antonio vanished into the kitchen.

'Gigi has just been telling me some wonderful stories of you as a child, Marcella.'

Michael was calling her mother by her nickname already!

'You must have been as enchanting then as you are now, my darling Marcella. I wish I could have seen you in those days, leaping up, dancing for everyone, holding your skirts out, skipping like a little fairy.'

Everyone laughed and looked to Marcella. She realised her fingers were gripping the sides of her chair, her knuckles white with tension. Everything seemed so real and yet so strange. How had this come about? Did her mother know that she and Michael were married and that they were coming here to take her things away so that she could live with him? She had expected a scene of wrath and tears; instead there was this grinning troupe all focusing on her. Her mother didn't appear angry, not even upset. Quite the opposite. She was laughing and smiling, patting Michael fondly on the shoulder as though they had known one another forever.

'It's very good timing, Marcella. You see your cousin Raphaël needs a place to stay, and now he can take your room.'

Raphaël was nodding, beaming at her.

'While I'm staying here, I'm going to repaint your mother's flat,' he said. 'As a special thank you.'

Marcella was brought out of her trance-like state by a loud pop, emanating from the kitchen. Michael ran over to open the door for Ton-ton, who entered bearing a tray of six glasses and a bottle of champagne.

'And now that the most important person is here,' Michael turned and bowed to Angela, 'well, not exactly the most important, for that would be you, dear Gigi, but, let's say, now that my beloved wife is here, we must drink to all our lives and to Love.'

Everyone in the room stood and raised a glass.

'To Love!'

And Marcella was so happy she thought she must be dreaming.

Shortly after the wedding, Michael's old friend Louis Hoffman came onboard with the firm. Tall, slim, dark, also sporting that fashionable moustache, Louis was exceptional at two things: sketching ideas for new lines and doing the accounts.

Once a week all three members of Michael's team – Marcella, Stefan and Louis – would meet up with Michael to discuss how the plan was going, adding clients' names to the list, presenting all receipts for fabric, threads and braids to Louis, who then shared out the orders so that they could each make the garments in their own homes. They advertised as couturières. Because, as yet, they had no shop, and more importantly no shop window.

Michael and Marcella took turns at the sewing machine, their first capital purchase, in the flat. Customers came to the living room for fittings; Marcella measured the ladies, Michael the gentlemen.

Marcella confided in Michael that, since they had married, Stefan seemed not very happy. Michael laughed and told her not to be so silly. 'I was hardly going to marry Stefan, now, was I?'

But whenever Stefan was around there was a *froideur*. Marcella could see that Michael had listened to her and was trying to smooth things over by giving Stefan special tasks, to bolster him up. For example, putting him in charge of the search for new premises so that they could start up a proper tailor's shop.

It was simply bad timing that the very day Stefan arrived at the flat, in some excitement, to tell them about a small place he had found, they were having a family party to announce the news that Marcella was pregnant with their first child, due the following June.

The room was full. Angela and Antonio were there, as well as Rosa, Raphaël and Aunt Thérèse.

Stefan proudly told them he had found a little tailor's shop in Old Town where the elderly gentleman was hoping to retire. The premises should be available in a few months' time.

'Old Town?' enquired Thérèse Magaïl. 'Whereabouts? Which street?'

'Rue Saint-Vincent.' Stefan gave her a beaming grin. 'Smack between the prefecture and the cathedral.'

Marcella noticed her aunt's eyes swivel to Michael. She also saw her husband give a fleeting glance back at Thérèse before saying casually to Stefan, 'I don't think that one's for us. Not Old Town. I was looking more to open up somewhere around here.' Michael put his arm around Marcella's shoulder. 'My wife needs premises at the fashionable end of town.'

As Stefan crumpled, Aunt Thérèse's lips tightened. She stared fiercely down into the bubbles of her champagne and didn't say another word.

Michael moved across the room and slapped Stefan on the back. 'I should have said. We're the New Guard, we don't want to be in the Old Town.'

Stefan joshed Michael and the two men started laughing. The moment passed.

It might have seemed like nothing. But Marcella felt that she had fleetingly been in the middle of an important incident. She had no idea what it meant but knew instinctively not to ask.

Soon afterwards, Thérèse Magaïl kissed Angela on each cheek and announced that she needed to get back to her shop or chaos would reign. As she went through the door she gently stroked Marcella's forearm, whispering, 'Look after yourself, child. I should have given you this earlier.' She passed her a scrap of paper on which was written *To Let: 26 Rue de France, proprietor Mlle Alice Baquis, 15–17 Rue Rossini, phone 7–9 1*, adding brusquely, 'She's a mere girl, protected by an army of lawyers. About your own age. See if you can talk to her personally. Use your irresistible charm.'

MONSIEUR MICHAEL NAVRATIL, TAILOR TO LADIES; ENGLISH AND GERMAN SPOKEN; ENGLISH STYLES A SPECIALITY opened at 26 Rue de France, Nice, in January 1908. Michael paid Mademoiselle Baquis the perfectly reasonable sum of 1,250 francs a year, in two half-yearly instalments, due on the first day of October and the first day of April. With finished dresses selling at fifty to 300 francs each, depending on the detail and the fabric, coats for even more than that, the rental would easily be covered.

Once installed in the new shop, the whole team worked very hard. In Marcella's eyes, Louis was a strange fellow. Cool and slow, he was always a gentleman, and very quiet. He seemed to have no emotions whatsoever. He was never happier than when standing behind the desk noting down and adding up sales figures and receipts in the ledger's long white columns, always in his neat black handwriting. She wondered how he lived. Did he go home to an empty flat? Did he have a wife, or a lover? Did he live with his mother? Nobody knew. Not even Michael. Marcella tried to lead Louis into talking about his life outside the shop, but, whichever way she phrased it, he always evaded answering. He treated her with exactly the same coolness with which he treated Stefan and Michael, or indeed one of the wooden mannequins in the shop.

Marcella found working beside Stefan difficult. She tried to revive the conspiratorial alliance that had first brought them together, but now that she was Madame Navratil, it was gone, replaced with a cold disdain on Stefan's part which no amount of kindness or humour could break through. When Marcella attempted a joke, Stefan ignored her, treating her as though she was an annoying child. He brightened only when Michael entered the workshop. Then he would make comments in German and laugh together with Michael, until Michael disappeared back through the curtain, when he became aloof once more.

Working in silence, at the next table, Marcella eventually gave up trying. She could only think that Stefan needed to be Michael's favourite puppy-dog, his playful, obedient, faithful sidekick, and that by being Michael's wife she was somehow in the way. Every time Michael called her into the shop, Marcella felt the prickle of Stefan's discontent.

But, once the baize fell behind her, it didn't matter any more. For Michael stood there, beaming, as she stepped towards him. He wanted to show her off to important customers. To ladies he would say, 'My beautiful wife will take you into the cubicle to be measured,' and to their waiting husbands he would add, 'I am so lucky. I married the most beautiful woman in Nice.'

Exactly six months after the opening of the shop, when everything was going very well with the business, in their rooms overlooking that park in which Michael had first kissed her, Marcella gave birth to their first child, a boy with dark eyes and a head of black curls. In a heady mix of love, pride and vanity, they named him equally after themselves: Michel Marcel Navratil.

While Stefan and Louis were left to run the shop for a week, the besotted parents stayed at home, where they leaned over the baby's cot, cooing in turn, 'He has your eyes', 'He is so perfect', 'Look at his tiny fingers', 'He has your smile', 'He has your laugh', 'See how he curls his lip when he cries', 'Have you ever seen anything so beautiful?' and all the other sweet platitudes which every parent whispers over the cradle of their firstborn.

But Marcella was not prepared for what happened next. When she looked into the eyes of her new baby she realised that she had never known love like it – not for her mother, not for her stepfather... nor for Michael. There was no romance in this love for her baby, just an all-consuming passion – passion for a creature whom she knew she would willingly defend with her life. It was love beyond reason.

And with the growth of this love came a weakening of her love for Michael. It wasn't that she didn't love him as much as she had before, but the power of the new feelings totally eclipsed it.

Her baby was now the real love of her life.

The proud parents brought the child, wrapped in a soft blanket, lying in his blue carrycot, to work each day. Marcella sat beside the baby, stitching, occasionally wandering over to the machine for a quick burst on the treadle.

Every other minute she would glance into the cot.

Whenever there was a lull in the shop, Michael would come through the baize curtain and join her. They would sit, holding hands, gazing at their son.

Stefan repeatedly commented on how much the baby resembled Michael.

Marcella knew that this was meant as a swipe at her, but she didn't mind at all.

The baby did have the dark looks of his handsome father.

It was one thing that Louis Hoffman never paid Marcella herself a compliment, but she was very put out that, unlike everyone else, he appeared to have no desire at all to bend over the carrycot and make baby noises. In fact, the only time he ever acknowledged the child was when Michel Marcel cried. Then he would lift his head dolefully from the books and murmur tartly, 'I believe the child is hungry.'

When Louis muttered to himself in German, Marcella felt even worse. She felt sure that he was talking about her, criticising her mothering. After all, she was the only person in the shop who did not understand what he was saying.

One day, when business was slow and Marcella had put the final stitches to a pale-orange silk summer suit, she took it into the cubicle and tried it on. So proud was she of her own handiwork on this beautiful outfit that she strolled through the shop wearing it.

'I couldn't resist,' she cried to Michael who was in the corner, talking to an elderly lady.

'I don't think...' he said, almost imperceptibly shaking his head at her. 'That's my wife,' he explained. 'She's very impulsive.'

It was then that Marcella first noticed a portly young gentleman sitting on the central banquette, his back to her.

He turned, saw her and said brightly, 'I say!' Jumping to his feet, he grinned at Marcella. 'No, no, Monsieur Navratil. You should make your wife put on your creations every day. Don't you think,

Mother? Doesn't she make the dress look fabulous? Look, Monsieur Navratil, instead of a bunch of old fabric the dress has come to life. Like a moving work of art. I'd buy it just on the sight of your wife wearing it.' The man looked over at his mother. 'It would suit you too, Mama, don't you think?' Turning to Marcella with a sly wink, he asked, 'Might she try it on? After you've taken it off, of course?'

'Oh, I could never look as beautiful in it as she does.' The lady walked over to Marcella and stroked her cheek. 'You are quite lovely, my dear. Your husband is a very lucky man.'

'Contessa Formia!' Marcella curtseyed, suddenly recognising her as one of the foremost visitors to Nice this season. 'I would be only too glad to help you try the dress on.'

The contessa turned to her son and said in Italian, '*Di' alla cara ragazza di non disturbarsi.*'

Before the young man could reply, Marcella said, '*Nessun disturbo, signora. Le porterò subito il vestito.*'

'*Quindi lei è italiana?*'

The man stepped forward and kissed Marcella's hand.

'*Dove altro si può trovare tale perfezione?*'

She blushed and rushed into the other room to remove the dress and bring it back for the contessa to try.

But Michael followed her into the workroom, grabbing her wrist as the curtain fell behind them.

'What did that man just say to you?'

'Nothing.' Marcella laughed. 'Really. Just repeating silly compliments from his mother.'

'You're lying.' Michael pulled her close so that she could feel his breath on her cheek. 'I know when you're telling me lies. You were mocking me, weren't you?'

'No. I…' Marcella was shocked. She was only trying to sell one of their most expensive dresses.

'You are not to speak Italian in this shop any more.' Michael flung her away. 'In my own workplace at all times I need to know what is going on.'

'But you, Louis and Stefan talk German together, and I don't know what you—'

81

'Remember that while you are in this building, you are my employee—'

The curtain opened and shut. Louis Hoffman stood on the threshold.

'Leave her alone.' He stepped forward and pushed Michael away from Marcella. 'She was doing wonderfully out there. She had practically sold the highest-priced dress here, and before we even had time to put it on a hanger.'

Then, without lightening his tone, he swung round to Marcella. 'Now take the dress off. And get it through to the contessa.'

That night, back at their rooms, Marcella cooked the supper as usual, while Michael sang German and Hungarian lullabies to the baby.

When she came through to the living room with the plates, she found Michael slumped in an armchair, head in hands. He was sobbing. Hastily she put the tray down on the table and rushed to his side.

'My darling, what's wrong?'

He turned and clung to her, face buried in the folds of her skirts. 'I'm sorry, I'm sorry, I'm sorry. How could I have been so cruel to you today? To hurt my darling Shadow is to wound myself. You are my soul. Don't you know how much I love you and need you? You are my world, my light, my everything.'

Marcella felt tears pricking her own eyes.

She stroked his hair, then sat on his lap. They clung to one another for several minutes.

'I need you so much, my Shadow. Please don't desert me. If you left me, I would be lost. Promise me you'll never leave me. Never, never, never.'

'I promise,' said Marcella.

When Michel Marcel's first birthday came around, while everyone, including family, friends and special customers, gathered round the cot at the back of the workshop to drink a toast to the child, Louis

Hoffman chose to stay in the shop, saying that someone had to, to make sure that they didn't lose any custom.

After the episode with the contessa and her son, Marcella had believed that Louis was softening towards her. But his avoidance of the birthday party made her think again. She decided that he was just one of those aloof types, always concentrating on work, scribbling out orders for fabrics from Paris and braids from Lyon or Bordeaux, noting in capitals short advertisements to insert in the local paper, the *Petit Niçois*.

After drinking the health of the baby, Antonio took the opportunity to make an announcement. Clinking his glass, he looked to Angela. As soon as he had their attention he said, 'We have taken a lease on one of the flats here, above the shop.'

Angela linked her arm with his and continued, 'Now, you see, we can help out and be there whenever you need us, to look after this little fellow.'

Marcella was thrilled at this news, but when she turned to share her happiness with Michael he was not smiling. She tried to catch his eye. Silently, avoiding her, he looked away, picked up the bottle and refilled everyone's glass, then went through the curtain to the shop.

He came back with Louis.

'I'm sorry if I'm treading on your toes, Gigi and Ton-ton, as you are such wonderful grandparents to Michel Marcel, but I too have something special to say. Mine is a present for my darling wife, Marcella, who is everything to me. My wife and I both realise that we cannot live in furnished rooms forever, and, as the shop is doing so well, I have taken out a lease on the magnificent Villa Gastaud in Avenue Shakespeare.'

Marcella was speechless. She wasn't sure whether to be happy or not. She had discussed no such thing with her husband.

But she couldn't fail to notice the fleeting expression which passed across the face of Louis Hoffman – a slight tightening of the lips, and the briefest indication of an eye-roll. It was clear that he disapproved of the move.

Nevertheless, a few weeks later the Navratil family moved into their new house.

It was in a quiet residential area, quite a walk to and from the shop in Rue de France. There were steep hills at either end and Marcella wondered how she would be able to get to work, especially with the carrycot. Michel Marcel was growing heavier each day.

'That's the thing, my darling,' Michael said. 'You won't need to come to work. You can stay here with the little man. Stay home and be a lady of leisure.'

Marcella didn't want to be alone all day, wandering around the echoing rooms. She would prefer to be at the shop, to have company, the customers, even Louis and Stefan. But it was what Michael wanted.

She bought a pushchair and every day wheeled the child the long way down to the beach, where they sat on the pebbles with a *pan bagnat*, watching ships slip in and out of the harbour. Every now and then a plane buzzed past, flying from the aerodrome at the far end of town.

Each night Michael came home with some new piece of furniture – a sofa, magnificent throws, paintings for the walls, a leather armchair on which he would sit and smoke his pipe, staring at her in the glow of firelight.

Michel Marcel started crawling on the new Turkish mat, playing with the painted wooden cat made for him by Ton-ton.

Then, one cosy night, Marcella proudly gave Michael the news that a new baby was on the way, a brother or sister for Michel Marcel. She was due to give birth the following March.

'The middle of Lent!' said Michael. 'Carnaval time! That will certainly give us an Easter to celebrate!'

He leaped up and held Marcella tightly. Suddenly he started crying. 'You don't realise how happy you make me, Marcella. My own, my darling Shadow.'

She was lonely, it was true. Her parents dropped in from time to time, but no other friends or family ever came. Ironic, really, that now her parents were living above the shop and she was stuck out here, banging around in a huge house, alone. She missed Rosa, with whom she had fallen out so disastrously just a few days after she and Michael came back from London.

While Michael had taken Stefan to Monte Carlo, in an attempt to compensate him for the abandoned London trip, Marcella had arranged to have dinner with her cousin at the Grand Café Pomel. In the blindness of new love, she asked Rosa what she thought of her wonderful new husband. Rosa tutted. Shaking her head, she put her tongue on the roof of her mouth and made a loud noise of disapproval. There followed a long silence, in which Marcella was aware of the sound of her own chewing, the pumping of blood in her ears.

After what felt like hours, but must only have been a minute, Rosa asked, 'Why did you agree to it?'

Marcella hadn't the words for how she felt about Michael, how much she adored him, she told Rosa.

'That's all very well, but why did you rush into this, Marcella? Everything in this world needs thought and preparation. Especially if it's something you will be doing for a lifetime.'

'It was an easy decision.' Marcella shrugged. 'I simply knew I wanted to be with him.'

Rosa looked about the room, pulling a music-hall comic expression, eyes popping, mouth agape.

'Well, I love him,' Marcella said. 'When he arranged the wedding as a surprise for me, it was such a romantic gesture. How could I refuse him?'

'I don't believe this.' Rosa shook her head. 'A *surprise* wedding? You didn't say that before.'

'No.' Marcella wished she hadn't mentioned it. She felt guilty too, as she had used Rosa to help persuade her parents to let her go to London in the first place.

'What did Stefan make of you going ahead with a surprise wedding? Did he not advise you to think first?'

Marcella felt the heat of a blush burning her face.

'I'm sorry, Rosa, I lied. Stefan didn't come to London.'

Marcella watched as Rosa took a deep breath.

'There's a reason you lied to me, Marcella, and there's a reason you didn't admit to anyone that Michael *surprised* you with a wedding. And that's because, somewhere deep in your soul, you knew it wasn't right.' Rosa folded her napkin and looked down as she spoke. 'You are not only a liar but, worse, you are a fool. Michael made a life-changing decision without you. That is no basis for a trusting partnership.'

Marcella couldn't let Michael take all the blame. 'I wanted the marriage as much as he did,' she protested.

Rosa looked Marcella in the eye. 'Really? Go on, Marcella. Swear to me that it was an entirely mutual decision.'

'I love him. He loves me.' Marcella started to panic. She could remember it all and knew that she hadn't driven any of the events. She had simply gone along with it. But she wanted Rosa to know that that was a good thing. 'It will be good for both of us. We are going into business as well.'

'Oh dear,' Rosa sighed. 'Worse and worse.'

Marcella's skin prickled. Why should she listen to this? Michael was experienced. Rosa was obviously jealous of her because she had no man to take care of her and love her. She was just castigating Marcella for her happiness.

'You're welcome to a life like that.' Rosa dug furiously into her dessert. 'Don't say I didn't warn you. You may not see it, Marcella, but you are worth more than this.'

Marcella blurted out, 'You're just jealous because I have a handsome husband and you are dried up and unwanted by anybody.'

Rosa put down her spoon, then she rose and, throwing a large-denomination franc note on to the table, left without another word.

After this, neither of them had bothered to keep in touch. So, when one morning the doorbell at Avenue Shakespeare rang and Marcella found Rosa standing on the threshold, it was with mixed feelings that she ushered her inside and through to the front room.

It was the end of January 1910. Apart from exchanging pleasantries at family events, they had barely spoken for nearly three years. Marcella was eight weeks away from giving birth to her second child.

A fire roared in the grate. Michel Marcel was walking now and had gained a nickname. The two parents, so proud to have named their child after themselves, had soon realised that, once he was of an age where he could run around, he had to be called, and calling out their own names led to too much confusion. So Michel Marcel was now addressed by everyone as Lolo, one of his first words.

Seeing a stranger coming into the room, Lolo rushed to Marcella and clung to her skirts.

'Lolo! This is your Aunt Rosa!'

Rosa bent down level with the child and said, 'Hello, Lolo. How are you? What a handsome young man you are.'

Lolo smiled and, in a grown-up way, offered his hand, which Rosa shook.

Marcella watched with a pang of sadness. She wished that she had not excluded Rosa from her child's life.

'Would you like a coffee, Rosa? We have a very modern kitchen here.'

'No thank you, Marcella.' Rosa took off her coat, hat and gloves and laid them on Michael's chair. 'You are looking radiant, cousin. Married life suits you well.'

Marcella couldn't bear to tell her how lonely she was.

They sat either side of the fire. Lolo, playing with a wooden car on the rug between them, every now and then gazed up inquisitively at Rosa.

'So, Marcella, you'll be wondering why I've come here. Well, it's to tell you that I am going away.'

'Away?'

'To America. Finally. I have found myself a job there, working for a family in upstate New York.'

'Where is that, upstate New York?'

'To be truthful, I am not sure myself. All I know is that after a week crossing the Atlantic, I disembark in the city of New York, take a train ride for the best part of a day and finally arrive at my destination – a town called Saratoga Springs.'

'There's a name for you!'

'I know. I am told it is a very genteel place, with a spa and a racecourse. The family is very distinguished. They own a whole stable of racehorses! And I will be in charge of teaching their children: Martin, Reina, Matilda and George.'

Although Marcella had spent so long being angry with Rosa, now that she discovered Rosa was going away she felt desolate. 'When do you leave?' she asked.

'I am seeing the American family again in a few weeks. They're here touring Europe, at present, and we will all cross the Atlantic together.'

'But when?' Marcella asked again.

'The ship sails from Genoa on the thirty-first of March.'

'This year?'

Rosa smiled and nodded. 'Isn't it exciting?'

'That's around the time when this one is due.' Marcella patted her round belly. 'When will you be coming back to Nice?'

'That's the thing, Marcella. I don't think I will be coming back. I am going to live in America.'

Rosa must have seen her disappointment for she quickly added, 'Perhaps, Marcella, you might come and visit me. When your children are a little older, maybe.'

Marcella felt a tumble of sadness fall through her. She knew that that would never happen. Her life was here in Nice with her family. Rosa was going away and, when all of them went along to Genoa to wave her off on the big ship, that would be it. Marcella would never see her again.

'Do you have many visitors living up here?' Rosa asked.

The answer was no. But Marcella didn't want to paint a picture of her life as anything but perfect.

'My mother comes often. The doctor, of course. And now you.'

'I noticed that the paint is flaking.' Rosa gestured towards the door. 'I'll send that big kid, my brother, over tomorrow. He can make it look as good as new.'

Perhaps Rosa had sensed how lonely she was and was trying to help. Marcella had no words.

Lolo, feeling safe now in Rosa's presence, dropped his car, toddled over and stretched his arms out to her. She understood and lifted him up on to her lap. 'Michel Marcel! Well now, aren't you a big strong handsome fellow?'

'Tanty!' he replied, touching Rosa's blonde hair. 'Tanty!'

'That's right, Tanty Rosa.' She bent forward and kissed the crown of Lolo's head. 'He's a very bright boy.'

'What happens if you're not happy when you go to this Saratoga Springs place?' Marcella asked. 'Will you come home?'

'No, no, no. I shall move on. America is a huge country, full of opportunity. There are so many families there with so much money and they all want people like me to teach their children. Qualified people are in great demand.' Rosa watched Marcella's face crumple. She changed the subject and said brightly, 'Do you know that America is so big that the train journey takes five days from one coast to the other? Imagine that!'

Lolo started playing with the buttons down the front of Rosa's jacket. She smiled at him. 'I'm very lucky. I can work pretty much anywhere from California to New York, and always at the top end of the market.'

Rosa put Lolo back on to the floor but he stayed close to her and laid his head on her lap, saying over and over, 'Tanty, Tanty!'

Marcella saw her own life through Rosa's eyes. Her real life, not the romantic dream she had once had, but the day after day spent all alone in this big echoing house. A wave of despair engulfed her. What had happened to the sparky young girl of a few years ago? Where was the bright young thing who had dreamed of being a famous singer, of standing on the stage in the casino theatre or the Grand Café Pomel?

It was as though Rosa knew what she was thinking. She leaned forward and said softly, 'Look, Marcella, I didn't mean to upset you by coming here. I just thought I should let you know that I was going away. Like the day you sent that note asking me to bring Raphaël straight away to your mother's place, and when we got there we all discovered that you had secretly got married. You didn't want to leave us out of the moment.'

Marcella was baffled. She had sent no note to Rosa or to anyone else.

Thinking back now, she remembered what a surprise it had been to find the whole family gathered in her parents' apartment.

'Marcella, I really do have to go now.' Rosa stood and pulled a piece of paper from her pocket. 'But if you want to come and wave me off from Genoa – here are the details of the ship's departure. I know you've had your differences with her too, but Aunt Thérèse will be there. Perhaps you could come through with us on the train. And bring little Michel Marcel. Small boys always enjoy all the noise of the wheels turning and the steam puffing from a train, I find. Perhaps he would like to see a huge ship too.' She moved towards the door and as she went out said, 'I'll ask Raphaël to visit you soon and take a look at that paintwork.'

Closing the door behind her, Marcella started to cry, breaking into long sobs. She was so alone.

Little Michel Marcel ran to her side, clinging to her skirts, holding her tight.

———

When Michael got in from the shop, it was dark. A cold wind swept through the house as he slammed the door after him.

He came straight into the front room, flopped into his armchair and lit his pipe.

'Someone has been here,' he said immediately. 'You've had visitors?'

'Just Rosa,' Marcella said nervously.

'Really? I thought you two didn't talk?' He looked her squarely in the eye. 'You've not been fluttering your eyelashes at that doctor of yours again, have you?'

'He hasn't been this week.' Marcella hated mentioning the doctor. The subject always seemed to upset Michael. 'He's due again on Friday afternoon.'

Michael glanced beadily around the room but said nothing more.

Later, as they sat down to eat dinner, Michael shook out his napkin and announced casually, 'I have exciting news, Marcella. I have decided to change the name of this villa. Since our name is Navratil, and I am at the helm of one of the foremost tailoring firms in Nice, why are we living in a house which bears the name of the Gastaud family? Villa Gastaud, indeed! I am therefore planning to change it to something altogether prettier and more appropriate to a family of our distinction. Something which would suit a beauty like you, my wife.'

Marcella wasn't sure what he meant. Ever since he'd come in, he had seemed so cool, she was scared she might have upset him in some way.

'What do you want to call the house? Do you have any ideas?' she asked.

'As a matter of fact, my darling, I've been thinking about it all day. And I have come up with the perfect name. We're going to call it Villa of the Palms. We have palm trees in the front garden, so why not? In any case, on the way home I called in on a signwriter and by now he will be busily at work on a sign bearing the new name. I paid him extra to have it done by tomorrow.'

Marcella was puzzled. Why would Michael be so overjoyed by something as ridiculous as this? The house wasn't exactly Versailles. It was an ordinary house in an ordinary street, just like all the others. What did the name of a house really matter, anyway, except to the postman?

'And what did that cousin of yours want?' Michael picked an olive from the aperitif bowl in the centre of the table and popped it into his mouth. 'You didn't say.'

'She came to tell me that she's moving to America.'

Michael made a scoffing noise. 'I'll believe that when I see it.'

'She has a job teaching the children of a wealthy family in New York.'

'New York?'

'Somewhere called Saratoga Springs.'

'That's hardly New York. It must be some backwater.' Michael picked up another olive. 'As I said, I'll believe it when I see it.'

'She's got her boat ticket and everything.'

'Well, she's welcome to it. She'll be back here with her tail between her legs, soon enough, just mark my words. She's too earnest for Americans. They like a bit of flair.'

'How do you know that? You've never been to America, have you? You don't even know any Americans, apart from the odd customer.'

'On the contrary, Marcella. I have two new friends who hail from that great country. Charles and Alice Kirchmann. They're from New Jersey, just the other side of the river from New York City. As a matter of fact, I'm thinking of inviting them to dinner. That would be nice, wouldn't it? Once you get to know her, perhaps you and Madame Kirchmann might spend your afternoons taking walks together and that sort of thing.'

Marcella thought it might be good to have a friend, someone to talk to... maybe.

'She's what I think of as a very feminine type of woman. Unlike your cousin Rosa.' Michael wiped his mouth with his napkin. 'How about tomorrow? Once the signwriter has come you could go to the market.' Michael reached into his pocket, took out a bundle of banknotes and tossed it on to the table. 'There you go. Buy only the best. We want to show the Kirchmanns that we are people of substance. Some caviar, to start, perhaps. Maybe some foie gras, lobster... You know the kind of thing.'

The following morning, after the signwriter had fitted the new name plaque on the front gate, Marcella got ready to go to the shops. She picked Lolo up to put him in his jacket, but he wouldn't let go of his wooden car. He had been happy playing and didn't want to go out. As she put him in the pushchair, he wailed and kept trying to clamber out, his legs thrust dangling over the edge of the basket, and screaming so loudly she was afraid the neighbours would think she was hurting him.

She ran to the kitchen and brought back a segment of mandarin, hoping that would quieten him, but he just squashed it in his little hand and flung it at her. She knew it had caught in her hair, but while she was using both hands trying to fasten him in and get him outside, there was nothing she could do about that.

It was a long walk to the market, through the tunnel beneath the railway line and then mostly uphill, Michel Marcel shaking his legs and shrieking the while, but she managed to buy enough things for them to eat that evening – some good-quality fish, potatoes and carrots, fruit, a selection of cheese and bread. A jar of foie gras and a bottle of wine too.

On the way home she was hampered by the two large shopping baskets, brimming with her purchases. Every few metres she had to stop and put the baskets down. Then, just as she reached the mouth of the tunnel, she heard footsteps coming up fast behind her.

Her heart thundering, she picked up her baskets and tried to speed up, tripping over her skirts, holding her hand out to steady the rolling pushchair. As the footsteps, echoing in the tunnel, grew nearer and louder, she looked up to see a man running in her direction. She was ambushed.

She started to run, stepping into the road, the baskets of food spilling and fruit and vegetables rolling into the gutter. But then something strange happened.

The footsteps behind her stopped and turned away. The thin, tall man who had been running towards her slowed down and started smiling. He guided her back on to the pavement, holding up his hand to stop a motor car which had turned into the tunnel.

'That could have been nasty, madame.' He picked up the fruit and packages from the pavement and gathered them into the baskets. Marcella saw how very tall he was.

'It was lucky I was coming along. I saw you there, with those two thugs in pursuit, and tried to do the gallant thing. Quite unlike me, really.'

Marcella's heart was still thundering. She thought she would swoon. She staggered slightly and leaned against the damp, filthy wall of the tunnel.

A train rattled overhead. Michel Marcel started up howling again.

The man put out an elbow. 'Lean on me. I will carry the shopping and wheel the pushchair, until you feel better.'

'I really don't want to take up your time, monsieur.' Marcella felt so grateful, but she didn't want to inconvenience him. 'You were heading in the other direction.'

'I've been down at the church lighting a few candles in memory of my dear mother,' he said. 'Today is the anniversary of her death.'

'I'm so sorry.' Marcella now felt even worse for troubling this man who had come to her rescue. 'It must be a terrible thing to lose your mother.'

'It's funny, madame,' he said, 'but you are the spitting image of the paintings of my mother's name saint, Olga of Kiev. I think that she sent you to me.'

'You're Russian? You sound Italian.'

The man laughed. 'I am Italian. My father is, anyhow, and I grew up in Italy.' He looked ahead at a fork in the road. 'Which way now?'

Marcella indicated with a nod.

'Look!' He leaned over the pushchair and adjusted the blanket. 'Your pretty little boy has fallen asleep. That's good. You have had a nasty shock, madame. When you get in you must promise me to make yourself a strong cup of coffee and sit down.'

They reached the top of Avenue Shakespeare, but Marcella stopped. She didn't want to lead him up to the front door.

'You've been very kind, monsieur. Thank you.'

'It's nothing, madame.' With a smile, the man lifted his hat. 'Take care of yourself.'

He turned and was gone.

Marcella rolled the pushchair down the hill to the house. Before going inside she looked at the garish new sign screwed to the gatepost – Villa des Palms.

CHAPTER 12

When Michael arrived back that night, he presented Marcella with a new suit, straight from the workshop.

'I had Stefan finish it today so that you could model it. After all,' he said, pulling on a smart new pair of black trousers, 'we are our own shop window.'

'I'd better put Lolo to bed first.' Marcella moved towards the child's bedroom, but Michael tugged her arm.

'No, Marcella! I have a better idea. Dress Lolo up too; then, once the guests arrive, he can make a sweet little goodnight, and *then* you put him to bed.'

'But he's very tired…'

'And what difference will half an hour make to that? Eh? He'll sleep all the sounder.'

'But why?'

'Because with Lolo with us, they'll also see the wonderful children's clothing we make.'

'Do these people have children of their own?'

'No, but they are our age, so…'

He turned to Marcella. 'You look like a frump. What's that sticky mess in your hair? Come on, girl, I know there's a great beauty lurking inside there. She's been missing lately. Let's see her again tonight, eh?'

Marcella felt crushed. She knew well enough that she must look terrible. After all, she *felt* terrible!

Why couldn't Michael understand? Seven months pregnant and feeling it. On top of all that, after the endless walk to the market on a day when the January sun had decided to be as hot as it was in June, she had narrowly avoided being robbed. Shopping had been an exercise in exasperation itself. Lolo kept climbing out of the pushchair and running away from her, grabbing fruit from the displays, picking up strips of dusty discarded meat from the gutters and trying to eat it. The boy was nearly two. It was famous how at that age children have the energy of an athlete.

Then she had come home, prepared a three-course dinner and set the table. Now she wanted nothing more than to lie down and close her eyes.

The doorbell rang.

Michael called up from the kitchen. 'Marcella! Our guests have arrived.'

Fastening her necklace, she stepped out on to the landing.

Michael, resplendent in his evening suit, looked up at her. He held Lolo's hand. The child was impeccably dressed in a pageboy style, with a lacy collar and knickerbockers. Seeing them both so splendid, she wished they could be alone together and enjoy one another's company.

'You look beautiful!' Michael said. 'Come on down so that we can greet them together, my darling.'

The family of three stood in the hallway.

'Welcome to the Villa des Palms,' said Michael, opening the door. 'Come on in.'

Charles Kirchmann clapped his hands at the sight of little Lolo in his new clothes.

'Attaboy!' he said, laughing. 'Just look at that, Alice! Little Lord Fauntleroy in the flesh.'

Charles then turned and stooped low to kiss Marcella's hand. 'And you must be the beautiful Marcella, of whom I've heard so much. Meet my wife, Alice.'

As they all shook hands, Marcella was taken aback by the contrast between the couples. It was as though they were playing a game of Light and Dark, the Navratils, with their black hair, dark eyes and bronzed skin, meeting the Kirchmanns, silver-blondes, with light eyebrows and pale lashes. The Kirchmanns both had piercing blue-grey eyes and skin so white it was as though they had never seen the sun.

'We have wallpaper just like this back home in New Jersey,' said Charles. 'Don't we, darling?'

'Ours is embossed.' Alice stroked the wall. 'I find French work-manship quite substandard, don't you, Marcella?' She ruffled Lolo's curls. 'One day, young man, I will bring you some German pastries. Best in the world.'

'Come on through.' Michael ushered the couple into the front room for an aperitif, while Marcella took Lolo up to bed. In her new hobble skirt she found it very difficult getting up the stairs, and with Lolo in her arms it was almost impossible. She gripped the banister tight with her free hand. She had to take each step in turn, lifting her feet one after the other, as though she was injured.

Curse on the new skirt. What a fashion! It practically disabled you.

When she came back down again, she found Michael talking animatedly to their guests in German. She should have guessed from their name that they would have German connections.

'Shall we go through?' she said, leading the way to the dining room. The three of them continued talking excitedly in German while they ate the first course and, muttering that she had things to do in the kitchen, Marcella excused herself.

She leaned against the oven. It gave out a comforting warmth. A guffaw of laughter came from the dining room. She bent to take out the fish and, as she laid the platter on a tray ready to bring in, she felt the baby kicking.

'Hello, in there!' she said, then looked up to see Michael standing in the doorway.

'Talking to the fish?'

'No. To the baby. It's kicking. Come. Feel.'

Michael laid his hand beside hers on her belly. He wrapped his arms around her and whispered in her ear, 'I adore you.'

'Come on, we can't ignore our guests,' she said.

'I wish I hadn't invited them,' said Michael, not letting go. 'We could have had a lovely dinner, just us two.'

Too late now.

'You take the fish,' she said. 'And I will bring in the vegetables.' She kissed the end of his nose. 'And one day soon we will have another dinner, just the two of us. It would be lovely.'

During the main course the four of them talked pleasantries about the weather, the traffic and the Nice Carnaval which would start next week. But when Marcella brought in dessert – individual fruit tarts, with a cheese board – they were off gabbling in German again.

Marcella carefully spread Camembert on to a biscuit which she didn't really want, just to have something to do.

They could have spoken French, or even English, and everything would have been all right for everyone at the table. But this felt almost as though they had chosen to exclude her.

After what seemed like an eternity, Alice got up from her seat, whispered something to her husband and swapped places with him.

'I'm so sorry, Marcella. We're being awfully rude, leaving you out like that. But it's so nice being able to chat together in German. You must feel the same way when you're with fellow Italians, I suppose.' She laughed. Marcella laughed politely in return.

Alice leaned in closer. 'It was you I saw today, wasn't it? When we came in, I knew I had seen your very striking face before. Then I remembered where. You were with a very tall gentleman who was wheeling the pushchair. Am I right?'

Marcella thought back to that morning. She couldn't remember seeing anyone else on the pavement watching her.

'He was a knight in shining armour. I had just had a nasty moment under the railway bridge—'

Alice tutted.

'No need to make excuses to me, my dear.'

'No. You're wrong.' What game was this woman playing? 'That's what really happened… These two thugs—'

'I was in a passing hansom cab. I saw what "really happened",' she insinuated.

'But…' This woman seemed set on causing trouble. 'It wasn't like that… Really.'

Michael stopped talking to Charles and leaned forward.

'What are you girls chattering about?'

'Nothing…' Alice said innocently. 'Nothing at all, Michael.' She turned back and beamed at Marcella. 'Just girly chat.'

Marcella felt her stomach lurch. This wasn't 'girly chat'.

After the Kirchmanns had left and Michael and Marcella were doing the dishes, Michael asked what Alice had been so interested in. Marcella couldn't explain. She knew that Michael wouldn't understand. She said, 'I don't like her.'

'Whyever not? I was thinking it would be so nice for you to have a female friend, other than your whiny mother and those pushy Italian cousins and aunts of yours.'

Marcella took a tea towel and dried her hands. 'I mean I don't trust her.'

'Don't be so silly, darling.' Michael laughed and kissed Marcella's cheek. 'They're a charming couple. Go-ahead types, like us.'

Marcella lay awake that night. She knew that this matter would not end here. She knew too that the pale, blonde, harmless-looking Alice had no good feelings towards her.

The clock struck midnight.

Marcella rolled over.

30 January 1910. It was her birthday. Today she was twenty.

Marcella didn't see Charles and Alice again until the following week when she took Lolo down to the Promenade des Anglais to watch the Battle of Flowers.

Lolo loved the cacophony of music from marching bands and musicians on floats which were decorated as ships, cars and planes. He danced, jumping up and down, waving his tiny hands above his head. A pretty lady on a passing float showered them with sprigs of mimosa and pinks. Then suddenly he stretched out his hand and said, 'Boat! Boat!' Marcella felt so proud that he had recognised this garish melange of roses, carnations, lilies and tulips wrapped around the shell of a motor car as being a representation of a boat.

A small group of musicians dressed as tramps, wearing brash face make-up and their hair greased into shiny green spikes, played the final notes of 'La Valse Brune' and immediately struck up 'La Petite Tonkinoise'. As though he knew it was her favourite song, Lolo whirled like a dervish, spinning and leaping. She strode along behind him, always keeping close enough to grab him if necessary.

And she started to sing.

'He calls me his bourgeois p'tite
His Tonki-ki, his Tonki-ki, his Tonkinoise
They all make sweet eyes at him
But it's me he likes best.'

She took his hand and together they danced, kicking out their legs, laughing. The warm February sun beat down on them, the turquoise sea shimmered in the bay. Marcella felt totally happy.

'Should you be throwing yourself about like that in your condition?'

It was Charles Kirchmann.

Behind him she saw Alice, deep in conversation with Michael. Lolo was now tugging at her hand, using both of his own to get more leverage. 'Clowns!' he cried. 'Clowns!'

Charles took a step towards her and said quietly, 'No gentleman friend to help you out today?'

For a moment Marcella thought he meant her husband; then, seeing the glint in his eyes, realised her mistake.

'It's all right, madame. I can keep a secret. I do know the ways of Mediterranean women. That's why I made sure not to marry one myself.'

Marcella heard Michael calling her: 'I bought you some *ganses*.' He was running towards her with a paper cone of Carnaval doughnuts. 'I want to see the little man's expression when he tastes his first one.'

He bent low and offered Lolo a piece, but the child thrust his father's hand away. Darkly aware of the closeness of Charles, Marcella knelt down next to her husband. She noticed Charles exchange a flickering glance with his wife. She took a *ganse*, tore a little off and handed it to the child, who licked it suspiciously and then, seeing his mother take a bite, gobbled it up, holding his hand out for more.

Michael helped her back up. 'You should get home now, and rest.' He dug into his pocket and handed her a franc note. 'Take a cab, chérie. It's too far to walk.'

He strolled with his arm around Marcella to the nearby taxi rank.

'They're a little weird, I know,' he said, as he helped her into the open carriage, Lolo pulling away, trying to get near the horse to stroke it. 'But it's nice to have a couple of friends of our age, isn't it?'

From the carriage, Marcella watched Michael's figure dwindle into the distance. She felt an overwhelming premonition that this was the end.

———

One night, a few weeks later, Michael came home after midnight. He had not warned her, as he usually did, and she had put the child to bed, sung him lullabies until he was snoring, prepared supper and made herself look decent, and still he had not arrived.

Finally, she heard the key in the lock and rushed into the hall to welcome him home. When she saw him, she burst out laughing. He looked like someone else. His moustache was not curled in its customary way, but each end was turned up in stiff right angles, like pipe-cleaners. His hair, glossy with pomade and black as obsidian, was curled over on top, as though he had a liquorice brioche on top of his head.

He stood staring at her.

'Is it for the Carnaval?' she asked. 'It's very funny. Quite the circus villain!'

'As a matter of fact, Marcella, Charles did it for me. It's the latest style.' Michael shoved past her. He was glowering. 'Little you would know about anything like that. Look at the state of you.'

Marcella still imagined he was joking. How could it be otherwise? She followed him into the kitchen.

'Is it mine?'

'Is what yours?'

He turned, his face now mauve with rage.

'The baby, of course.'

She ran to him. 'Of course it's yours.'

'You have men here.'

'I do not.'

'I can smell them. Men have been here.'

'The only two men who have ever come into this house when you're not here are Antonio, with my mother, and Raphaël who came to paint the door. Remember, I told you.'

'I'm not talking about Raphaël. I'm talking about the others. Your boyfriends.'

'There are no other men who enter this house except you, Michael. Unless you count Michel Marcel.'

'And…?'

'Well… the doctor.'

'That's one of them.' Michael looked her in the eye. 'You're in love with him, aren't you?'

'The doctor? Of course I'm not.'

'You talk about him enough whenever he comes round.'

'What else do I have to talk about, Michael? My only life here is looking after Lolo and preparing for the new baby.'

'You're having an affair with the doctor. I know it.'

'He makes me laugh and I like him. But he's just my doctor, checking up on our child.'

'Really? And how intimate is that?' Michael had one eyebrow raised. 'Are you kissing him on the side, leading him on, like you did me?'

'No. I don't. And I'm not.' Marcella was frightened now. How can you prove a negative?

'Stop being coy with me.' Michael strode around the kitchen, sniffing. 'I can smell cologne. Someone has been here.'

Marcella reached out to take Michael's arm. He flung her away. She lost her balance and tumbled back on to the tiled floor, where she lay sobbing.

'Turn off the waterworks,' Michael snarled. 'You can't fool me with your cheap theatrics.'

A sharp pain flooded Marcella's belly. She pressed herself back against the cupboard door.

'Enough!' Michael strode out of the room. 'Keep your amateur dramatics to yourself.'

Marcella tried to call after him, but the pain was too fierce. However much she attempted to raise her voice, the sound came out in tiny mews.

The baby was on the way.

She slid her hands across the tiles, desperate to get some grip. Then, rolling on to her hands and knees, she pulled herself up using the handle on the oven door. Leaning over the counter she took some deep breaths. Then she howled from the depths of her soul.

Michael came back in, ready with the next barb, but, seeing what was happening, he rushed across the room and clung to her, crying into her shoulder.

'I'm sorry,' he sobbed. 'I'm sorry, Marcella. I'm sorry. It's only that I love you. I can't bear to think of you with anyone else. I could never ever live without you, mother of my children, my beloved Shadow.'

CHAPTER 13

March 1910, Nice

Baby Edmond Roger's baptism was held a week after his birth, in order to catch Rosa before she left for America.

On their way to the church, the postman handed Michael a letter. He crammed it hastily into the inside pocket of his suit before giving Marcella a hand up into the waiting hansom cab. Lolo clambered in behind her and snuggled up close. 'Aren't you going to open it?' Marcella asked as the carriage started off. Michael ignored her.

'This bloody cab isn't going to make it up the hill,' he muttered under his breath.

When they arrived, the whole of Marcella's family was gathered around the font: Angela and Antonio, Thérèse Magaïl, Rosa and Raphaël. Marcella felt how sad it was that Michael was represented here only by Louis and Stefan. She had asked him again and again to invite his family down from Szered. Hungary was only a train ride away. But despite being married to Michael for three years and having given birth to two of his children, Marcella had never met any of them. Occasionally, she had suggested that they went to visit, but Michael always said he couldn't spare the time. They had other things to think about.

She had begun to wonder if he was ashamed of her.

Lolo was quiet and stood attentively holding Marcella's hand. And as Michael held the baby in his arms and presented him to the priest for the ritual holy water, Marcella thought he had never looked more handsome.

At the moment that the splash of water woke the sleeping baby, raising a wail, Marcella looked up to see Charles and Alice sneaking into the church together with another man, a plump stranger, at their side.

Marcella was not happy to see them. What were they doing at a family christening? But the next moment she felt sorry for thinking that. After all, Michael had no one here but his two employees; why shouldn't he invite his friends?

At the party afterwards in a room beside the church, Antonio presented her with a cuddly toy rabbit for the baby, and a beautifully carved and painted boat for Lolo. Marcella was relieved they had already left the church or the boy would be running over to try and sail it in the font! She looked over at him now, where Raphaël had him jumping from chair to chair.

Rosa was huddled in the corner with a tall man, his back turned to the room.

Raphaël came forward and stood on a table to raise a toast to his 'twin brother', Michael.

In a quiet moment, Aunt Thérèse approached Marcella and handed her two envelopes, marked *Master Michel Marcel* and *Master Edmond Roger*. 'It's just a little money for each of them. I'd like you to put it in a bank so that right from the start they'll have independent savings.'

Marcella felt her eyes pricking. For months she'd seen nothing of her Aunt Thérèse, who she felt was a termagant. But now Rosa's words haunted her: *An awful enemy, who fights like a lion for those close to her.* To hold back the tears, she asked her aunt who was the gentleman with Rosa. 'Oh, that's Henry Rey di Villarey. He's rather a charming fellow. She taught his sister's children for a while. He's giving us all a lift home afterwards.'

'I suppose he'll miss Rosa when she's gone,' Marcella said.

'Oh, no, no,' Aunt Thérèse laughed. 'It's nothing like that. They're just friends. I think she was hoping he might keep an eye on Raphaël. Up till now she's been his sobering influence. At heart he's still a big kid.'

Marcella glanced across the room. Raphaël was running around, acting the goat as usual, pulling faces with Lolo.

'As you see, it's not working yet. Your mother is looking fragile again.' Thérèse Magaïl took Marcella by the arm and whispered in her ear. 'She has to give up this obsession with trying to have children to replace your brother. How many miscarriages and infant deaths has she had now? Six?' She gave a sad shake of the head. 'There are some things which are not meant to be.'

Marcella thought she was being hard, but then she remembered that Aunt Thérèse had lost her own daughter at the age of two, and a few years later her husband had also died.

She reached out her hand and touched her aunt's arm.

'Thank you for your help, dear aunt. I don't deserve it.'

'No. You don't, dear.' Thérèse gently shook her arm away. 'Now, if I were you, I'd go and rescue that sweet son of yours before Raphaël convinces him to run off and join the circus.'

Marcella tried to persuade Lolo to eat some of her food. Michael broke away from his conversation with Charles Kirchmann's little group and joined her. 'Come and talk to my friends. You've snubbed them so far.'

'I've been trying to make everyone happy.'

'Isn't that the problem? You think only of your own people, never of mine?'

Marcella ignored the barb. 'Who is the stout gentleman with them?' she asked.

'You're in no position to call anyone stout. Look at you. You're the size of a house. But the "stout" gentleman, as you call him, is a *flic*. Our local beat policeman – well, a bit better than that, the commissaire, but—'

Marcella was horrified. 'Why have they brought a stranger – worse, a policeman – to our child's baptism? It seems a very bad omen.'

'Oh, you dramatic Italians and your witchy old superstitions. I think it's a very good idea to keep in with the local police, don't you? He is the boss of our district. You never know when a bigwig like that might come in handy.'

Marcella couldn't think why. Unless you were up to no good, the police would always help you. Wouldn't they?

Lolo was dragging at her arm, trying to get away. He had seen Raphaël throwing pieces of cake into the air and elaborately catching them with his open mouth.

'Let the poor kid go free, for God's sake, Marcella. Raphaël's my kind of chap. And we're brothers, too – you know we share the same birthday?'

Michael made this joke almost every time the name Raphaël came up.

'Off you go, Lolo.' She watched the child run to Raphaël.

Michael sighed. 'Why do you feel you have to trap everyone?'

Marcella could not respond. She had never had a desire to trap anybody.

'Anyway,' Michael continued. 'What did the old hag want?'

Marcella deliberately did not answer.

'Come on – the Evil Godmother, Magaïl, or should we call her Carabosse? She didn't bring a rosy red apple, did she, by any chance, or a spinning wheel with a shiny needle?'

'No.'

'Well, what did she bring? I saw her slipping something in your pocket. What was that?'

'She was being very kind, actually, Michael. It was some cash for the boys, so that we can start them a savings account.'

'Commissaire Guillaume.' Michael swerved away to greet the portly man as he moved across the room with Charles and Alice. 'May I introduce my wife, Marcella.'

'Madame Navratil!' The commissaire bowed low and kissed her hand. His obsequiousness made her feel slightly queasy. 'As everyone has told me, a genuine beauty!'

Out of the corner of her eye, Marcella caught Alice nudging her husband.

She wondered what that meant. Nothing good, of that she was sure.

'Edmond Roger!' said Alice, stepping forward. 'Are they family names?'

'Just names that we liked,' Marcella replied. 'We discovered too late with Michel Marcel that his name was pretty impossible as neither of us could tell whether we were talking to him or each other!' She laughed.

Charles and Alice assumed wan smiles.

'That's why we call him Lolo. For no better reason than it was one of the first words he repeated. "Lolo! Lolo!"'

Michael had moved off, leaving her with this strange group of people who she felt really did not like her. She watched him approaching her mother, now standing chatting with Aunt Thérèse.

'Gigi!' she heard him calling across the room. 'Aunt Thérèse!'

Her aunt was right. Her mother did not look at all well. Michael drew closer and lowered his voice. Whatever he was saying to them was obviously upsetting. Aunt Thérèse suddenly took up quite a confrontational stance. Her mother looked on the verge of tears.

'…Don't you think, Marcella?'

Charles Kirchmann was speaking, but Marcella had no idea what his question had been.

'I'm sorry, I was…'

Alice leaned in and whispered, 'Looking for your gentleman friend?'

'Yes,' said Marcella, understanding her to mean Michael. 'Excuse me,' she smiled at the couple and the police commissioner, 'I just need to go over and see my mother. She is looking rather unwell.'

As she moved away she caught sight of another nudge between the Kirchmanns.

Ton-ton was lying on the floor beside her mother, holding Lolo up, while Raphaël tickled him. Rosa and her friend Henry looked on. Lolo was laughing and crying, 'Stop, stop,' although he really wanted them to continue.

'Boys will be boys!' said Rosa.

'I'm feeling quite left out,' said Henry. 'I rather fancy rolling around on the floor being tickled.' He held out a hand. 'Hello again, Madame Navratil! Or should I say Saint Olga of Kiev?'

Marcella took in the impeccably cut suit and recognised him: it was the tall man who had helped her that day when she had narrowly missed being robbed by two ruffians under the railway bridge. She recognised his aquiline profile.

'I hope you don't mind me turning up,' he said. 'I was only meant to be driving them here and back but, rather than sitting outside in the motor car all the afternoon, they insisted on me coming in. I met your cousin once before,' he said, turning to Rosa, who was watching Michael and Aunt Thérèse.

'Henry. Henry Rey di Villarey. Here's my card. If ever I can help you, you need only ask.'

Marcella slipped the business card into her pocket.

'Michael, only a few metres away, was arguing animatedly with Aunt Thérèse. 'Excuse me, Henry.' Rosa walked away, leaving Marcella alone with him. It was awkward. She wanted to listen, to know what her husband was doing, but Henry continued talking.

Marcella heard Rosa say, 'No, Michael, the point of family is to cling together, not push people out, especially those who only mean you well.'

Marcella watched as Angela touched Thérèse's arm, but her aunt tore it away. 'Whatever you say, I *do* care about Marcella and your children. I care for you too, Michael, for you are joined together as one, by marriage. By giving your children money, I wasn't in any way trying to undermine your position as head of the family. Why would I? How could that help anybody?'

'I don't need your patronising help,' said Michael. 'You only interfere in my life because you know that your little two-bit shop is nothing on mine. Look at you! Your clientele is deserting you, day by day, to come to me. Rats leaping from a sinking ship.'

'Oh dear!' Thérèse Magaïl laughed. 'Now you describe your customers as rats?'

'I'm sorry, Henry.' Marcella could take no more. 'I have to—'

'—be the peacemaker,' said Henry, as Marcella moved away.

'Please, everybody, let's not fight,' she cried, stepping into the row. 'Not today. Please!'

Thérèse pursed her lips and said nothing.

Marcella pointed across to the tiny crib where Edmond was sleeping.

'This day is not about you and your shop, Aunt Thérèse. It's about Edmond Roger. A new soul joining us.'

'So there! Dear Aunty T, your beloved niece has spoken...' Michael said. 'So now you can get out. Go on. Run off with your witch's tail between your bandy legs. Old Fairy Carabosse was never welcome at anyone's baptism.'

Rosa opened her mouth to interject but then Michael rounded on her. 'And as for you! You talk of family, but you're a hypocrite. What does goody-two-shoes Rosa make of her family? Anyone? The answer is: nothing at all. She despises you all so much that she's shoving off to live in America and damn the lot of you.'

Marcella reached out for Michael's hand, whispering, 'Please, Michael. Please stop.'

Rosa took her chance to respond, and she grabbed it.

'Dear Monsieur Navratil,' she looked around the room, 'where is your sanctified mother, your loyal brothers, your perfectly feminine sister? I don't see any of your family here today.' She took a protective step in front of her aunt and stood face to face with Michael, like a boxer squaring up for a fight.

Marcella noticed for the first time that Rosa was slightly taller than him.

Rosa continued: 'Didn't you "shove off" and leave your family back in Presbourg or some backwater not far from there? I know you have a mother in Hungary, and brothers and a sister, maybe nephews and nieces. Yet here you are, with us, in Nice. When did you last see any of them? Eight years ago? Nine?'

Marcella wished that her cousin would stop, but on she went.

'Don't they want you, Michael? Did they wash their hands of you, perhaps? Couldn't wait to see the back of you? Maybe that's why you are here in France. Maybe you're not welcome back in Hungary. Is that it? Have I hit a nerve?'

For one second Marcella thought that Michael was going to hit Rosa, but instead he turned on his heels. 'I'm not wasting my breath on a know-all like you.' He pushed Marcella out of his path and went back to the Kirchmanns.

Marcella span round to face her cousin and aunt. 'Look what you've both done now. Why did you incite him? You've ruined the day. My child's one and only christening.'

Aunt Thérèse was going to speak, but Marcella talked over her. 'Shut up! I hate you both. Hate you! I'd be perfectly happy if I never saw either of you again.'

Thérèse grabbed a glass of champagne from the table, downed it in one, and took Gigi's elbow. 'Come on, cousin, dear. I'm not staying where I'm not wanted.'

'But I—' Gigi muttered.

'You're not looking too well, darling. I'm taking you home.'

'But Ton-ton…?'

'Oh, Ton-ton is quite sensible enough to get home on his own. Anyway, little Lolo wouldn't be happy, would he, losing one of his playmates? Come along, Rosa.'

With a polite nod of the head, Thérèse Magaïl said goodbye to Marcella and left the party. Rosa and Gigi went ahead of her.

Henry discreetly followed them all out, glancing back at Marcella.

———

The evening after the baptism, Michael arrived home from work with a gramophone. He installed it in the front room, its great green horn pointing towards the fireplace.

'I know you get bored, my darling,' he said as he pulled a record from its sleeve and inspected it. 'So, I thought you could have this. Then you don't need to feel lonely here. You can sing and dance to your heart's desire.'

After yesterday's debacle Marcella was not inclined to see her family anytime soon. They knew that she loved Michael, so why had they gone out of their way to upset him? When they got home he had been so distressed he had cried till his eyes were scarlet. On the very day that they had baptised their second child, why would her own family want everything to go wrong for her? She understood Michael. He was insecure and vulnerable. She realised that Rosa had clearly opened a wound from his youth, a hurt that he had kept hidden. She watched him plonk the record on to the turntable.

'It must have cost a fortune,' said Marcella, touched that he had thought of her today.

'It's worth it to keep my Shadow happy,' he said, rushing across the room and kissing her on the cheek.

As the music started to play, he took her by the hand and they danced.

'*He calls me his bourgeois p'tite*
His Tonki-ki, his Tonki-ki, his Tonkinoise
They all make sweet eyes at him
But it's me he likes best.'

'There we are,' he whispered into her ear. 'Just like the old days, eh?'

They danced on for a verse, both singing along with the song. Marcella knew then that, if she had to make a choice between Michael and her family, he would win. She would be his solace.

'Do you know the earliest words for this?' Michael asked, still not letting go of her waist. 'Originally it was written as a sailors' song.

'I am not a big actor,
I am navi, navi, navi, navigator
I know America well
As well as Africa, I know many more
But from these happy countries
It's France that I like best.

'You see!'

'I prefer our version,' said Marcella, as the chorus came round again.

The couple swirled about the room, bumping into furniture.

For the first time since the move to Avenue Shakespeare, Marcella again felt really happy. And the happiness stayed with her until next morning, when she went to her coat pocket to get the envelopes of cash that Aunt Thérèse had given her for the children and found that the money was gone.

CHAPTER 14

March 1910, Nice

That night, Marcella waited by the stove for Michael to join her with the usual cursory kiss.

'What have you been up to today?' he asked.

Marcella noticed that his hair had been trimmed again and was now ultra-shiny. His moustache too had been preened and waxed into an angular shape.

She told him that she had taken the children to Fabron.

'What on earth is there to see at Fabron?'

'It was for a ride on a tram, really. But I did see something interesting. A huge house, with magnificent gardens.'

'And…' Michael leaned over the stove, took the lid from a pot and sniffed the stew she had made.

'It was called Villa Gastaud.'

'Everywhere is called Villa Gastaud. That's why I changed the name of our house.' He took off his jacket, hanging it on the back of a chair.

'There was a sign on the gates. And guess what, Michael. It's also now the Villa des Palms. How about that?'

Instead of astonishment, Michael turned angrily. 'What is your point? Are you calling me a liar?'

'No.' Marcella started ladling the stew into two bowls. 'I was just pointing out the strange coincidence.'

'You've always hated me being ambitious, haven't you? You'd prefer it if we all went back to live in Hungary where I could work as a clerk in a bicycle factory, while you continue to loll about all day, doing nothing.'

She had no idea what had caused this outburst, so moved forward to calm him. He shoved her away, grabbed one of the bowls and stormed through into the dining room.

She had planned to challenge him about the missing money. But now that he was in this mood she could not. She followed him, determined to make everything all right again. But before she got through the doorway he shouted, 'I want to eat alone, if I may be allowed. After all, this is my house.'

From upstairs came the plaintive wail of a hungry baby.

'Go on. Don't just stand there, preening yourself. Go and do your job.'

About a quarter of an hour later, when she had got the children off to sleep again, as Lolo too had been disturbed by his father's angry tones, Marcella crept down to find Michael sitting in the dining room, puffing on his pipe and gazing into space, his unfinished stew in front of him.

'Another thing, now that you are gracing me with your presence. It's not hard to see you are bored here. I presume that's what caused your ridiculous crush on the doctor. So, I've decided that you are coming back to work in the shop. I want you beside me…'

Marcella felt fleetingly flattered, but he went on.

'Then I can keep an eye on you and see what you're up to at all times.'

'What about…?'

'Yes. The children. You see, Marcella, I really can read your mind. I knew you'd come up with an excuse. On that account I have already spoken to Ton-ton and he agrees that, during the time we're both in the shop, it would be lovely if Gigi could play with the little man and take care of the baby.'

'But—'

'No buts, Marcella. Ton-ton has a nurse who cares for your mother while he is at work. So now she can earn her money and look after the children at the same time.'

'But I—'

'Come on, Marcella. They live over the shop. The door is a few metres away, just round the corner. It's a two-minute walk. If you need to breastfeed, you can always pop up during the lunch break. What do you think?'

Marcella didn't really know what to think. Yes, she did want to be back among people, where she could talk and laugh, but at the same time she did not want to be apart from little Lolo or to burden her mother with a three-week-old baby, so soon after her last miscarriage.

On top of all that, Marcella was exhausted.

'Marcella!' Michael slid his hand across the table and rested his palm on the back of her hand. 'I miss you. I need to be near you all the time, Marcella.' He raised his eyebrows and pulled that little-boy-lost face, which always tugged a heartstring. 'I've been missing you, my Shadow. I fear that these days you only have eyes for the babies. Don't you love your old Michael any more? And after all, what is a man without his own darling? I need you with me.'

That did it. She agreed.

'That's good.' Michael emptied his pipe into the ashtray and picked up his spoon and fork. 'So that's a deal, then. No more moping around at home for you. No more welcoming strange men into my house. I'll have you right under my gaze all day long.' He dug his fork into a potato and swilled it around the gravy before popping it into his mouth and chewing insouciantly. 'But, as for now, chérie… You'd better get the washing-up done, as first thing in the morning we'll all be off to work.'

Marcella got up slowly and stood near the door, speechless.

He clapped his hands at her. She suddenly felt as though she was his dog. Perceiving her unease, he burst into a broad smile.

'Congratulations, Madame Navratil,' he said. 'You've got the job. You start tomorrow.'

Marcella knew that, since the children had come along, it was as though he was jealous. Jealous of her love for them. She looked forward to working again, to being with adults during the day. But not being forced away from her children like this. She felt a dull fear growing. She didn't have to put up with Michael treating her this way. She wondered whether she should leave this lonely house and go back to live with her mother? Live once again in a world where there was laughter. But her mother lived above their shop anyway. It would hardly be an escape.

Then she thought of the children. They were his children as much as they were hers. They loved it when he sang to them as they lay in bed, and all the rough and tumble, making them giggle until they could barely breathe. She knew that, even if she wanted to, she could not leave him.

———

Working all day in the shop was not anything like the situation Michael had promised. Kept all day in the back room, she saw no one but Stefan, who treated her like some new recruit who knew little of the business. Cyril, the part-time worker, having not known her before, also treated her as though she was a novice. After all, in his eyes, that is exactly what she was.

Stefan answered only to Michael himself. But Marcella had to answer to Stefan.

Michael would go off to business meetings, first popping his head through the curtain and saying, 'Don't worry, Stefan, true to my name, I will be back.'

Marcella wondered what he was talking about. *True to my name.* It couldn't be anything to do with Saint Michael and the dragon, so presumably it was his surname...

She asked Stefan.

'Could you fill me in on that? "True to my name"?'

'It's a joke in Corat. Navratil. Navrat, in our old language, means just that – I will come back.'

'And your name, Kozak. What does that mean?'

'It means stop trying to find ways to wiggle out of work and get that machine going again. All right?'

Stefan knew his place. He also knew hers.

While she turned the handle of the machine, Marcella spent hours thinking of her children in the flat upstairs, imagining them playing with the nurse, Dolinda, or sleeping, clasping their toys, the light flutter of their eyelids, so delicately lined with magnificent dark lashes.

When Marcella arrived each evening to pick them up and take them home to Avenue Shakespeare, tired out from sewing all day, hair unkempt, she could live without the pitying look Dolinda gave her.

One night towards the end of March, after Stefan and Louis had already left, Michael asked Marcella to wait in the street while he double-checked something in the workroom.

'I won't be more than a few minutes,' he said. 'Go ahead to fetch the children.'

It was drizzling – the kind of rain which soaks right through you. As Marcella ran around the corner into Rue Dalpozzo, she banged into Louis, holding his briefcase over his head.

'Left my umbrella behind,' he said. 'It was fine when I left. Marcella, I have two umbrellas in there. You should take one.'

Marcella followed Louis into the shop. He went through the curtain into the back room.

Waiting by the front door, she overheard the whole row.

'Michael? What in God's name are you doing?'

'I rather think that's up to me, don't you?'

'How much have you taken? A couple of hundred?'

There was a scuffle.

Then Louis spoke again.

'You've left no note, Michael. No record. Were you just going to steal it?'

'It's to pay Rodot in Rue Paradis. You know how they've been going on about the bill for their ruddy lace.'

'I paid them yesterday. If you'd bothered to check the ledgers, you'd have seen that.'

'Oh, bugger off, Louis. Whose name is above the door? Yours or mine?'

'I believed that I was due to get a share of the profit. How will that happen if you're pilfering from your own safe?'

'You said it. My safe! If you don't like it, you can walk. We're doing very well, thank you.'

'Actually, I have been asked by a shop in Paris—'

'Of course you have, Louis. You never stop telling me how you know how to run a business. Well, I know how to run a business too. It's my name on the label and my name on the door. So, Mr Hoffman, tailor superior, with all the advertisements and fancy plans, just run off and stick your stupid ledgers up your pontificating backside.'

'I think you'll find, Michael, that a successful business is based on keeping good accounts. And certainly not stealing from the safe.'

'Really? I thought that a successful business was based on having a bit of flair. So off you go to Paris. Count your numbers till the cows come home, Jewboy.'

Before Louis left the shop, Marcella managed to get back out on to the street and run around the corner.

Whatever happened next between Louis and Michael she couldn't say because she was racing up the stairs to get the children. She did not want Michael to suspect she had overheard.

Next morning Louis did not arrive for work.

While she was sitting in the corner, hand-stitching a hem to an overcoat, she heard Michael tell Stefan that he had sacked Louis for fiddling the accounts.

Marcella would not see Louis Hoffman again for two years.

October 1910, Nice
Edmond Roger was six months old.

Marcella would nurse him in the morning before work and then run upstairs to her parents' flat to feed him at lunchtime and again mid-afternoon.

One crisp autumn day when she arrived back in the shop after lunch, Michael was attending a beautiful red-haired lady who was trying on a turquoise silk suit that Stefan had made a fortnight ago. She was smoothing down the front, tilting her head each way while she gazed at herself in the cheval glass. Michael was staring intently at her.

Marcella spoke to the woman's husband, a nervous-looking chap with ruffled light-brown hair and a matching beard. 'You really should buy her that dress, monsieur. I've never seen anyone else who could carry it so finely.'

The man swung round and looked at her, puzzled. 'Do you really think so? That colour?'

'It's a beautiful colour. Quite rare in fabric. And sets off her hair magnificently. Truly, monsieur, believe me.'

The auburn beauty stopped preening herself in the mirror and swung round to face Marcella. 'And who are you, some skivvy who cleans the back room? Yet that doesn't stop you flirting with my husband.'

Michael signalled Marcella to pass through into the workroom with great speed.

'I am so sorry, madame. Forgive her impudence. She's only a part-time worker. I will reprimand her afterwards.'

The woman's husband stepped forward. 'It's rather ungallant of you, Monsieur Navratil, to talk like that about one of your own employees. She may be a servant, but she is a beautiful woman. I feel sure if she could afford such a dress for herself she would buy it in a flash, and look lovely in it too. And she did have a point, Camille. You look simply splendid in it. The fabric goes so well with your wonderful colouring.'

As Marcella pulled the baize curtain across, she heard the woman say, 'Well, it's no thanks to the cleaner, but I will take the dress, Monsieur Navratil.'

'You're late,' snapped Stefan, as Marcella, humiliated, took her place at the machine.

'Only five minutes.'

'You can do quite a lot of work in five minutes.'

Michael put his head through the curtain.

'Stefan! Please take over the shop. I am going to escort these customers to the Promenade. They're new to the area. And wrap the turquoise. It needs to be delivered to an address in Èze.'

The curtain swiped shut again.

Stefan dusted himself down, ran his long bony fingers across his hair and vanished into the shop.

'Don't worry, dear.' Cyril was threading a needle, preparing to start fitting a garnet-red satin lining to a jacket. 'At least the day after tomorrow it'll be Sunday. Though I suppose Sundays might be even worse for you.'

Cyril normally never spoke. Perhaps that was something to do with Stefan's presence. He gave her a wan smile and looked back to his stitching. Marcella felt humiliated. Even silent Cyril recognised that Michael now despised her.

But what if Michael had asked Cyril to say provocative things like that in order to find out what she said about him behind his back? She made the decision not to engage.

About half an hour later, Michael returned to the shop in a frenzy of anger. He pulled back the baize curtain so forcefully that the rail came away and the curtain slumped to the floor. He strode through and grabbed Marcella by the arm, dragging her to her feet.

'You're a slut,' he screamed. His face was so close to hers that she was showered in his spittle. 'Look at you! Fat frump. Did I marry a dirty tramp from the streets?'

Cyril stood up and tapped Michael on the shoulder.

'Sorry, sir, but I don't think you should talk to a lady—'

Michael spun to face him. 'You're sacked, Cyril, is it? Get out.'

'You can't sack him just for defending me! Sack me! Go on!' Marcella took a step towards Michael.

'Whore!' He slapped her face.

'Pig!' She slapped him back.

In the fraction of a second of shock which overtook him, Marcella slipped past, ran through the shop and out into the street.

She kept on running along Rue de France, aware that people were staring at her. She ran and ran until she could barely catch her breath, then she turned the corner into Rue Grimaldi.

She had no idea where she was heading.

Who could she turn to?

She had alienated everyone.

She limped along, now regretting that she had not gone straight up the steps to her parents' apartment to fetch the children before running away. But where would she take them?

And why drag them into a row that she was having with their father?

Realising that if she continued along this street she would have to pass her aunt's shop, she doubled back along Rue de la Buffa.

By the time she reached the park in front of the English Church, she felt too agitated to run any further.

She collapsed on to a bench, put her face into her hands and sobbed.

'I don't like to see a lady in such grave distress in public.' It was a man's voice, gentle and soft. 'Especially when she is a cousin of a friend.'

She could only see his shoes, stylish, with grey spats, and an elegant ebony cane.

Marcella looked up. She couldn't remember the man's name. Rosa's friend.

'Oddly enough, Madame Navratil, I've just come away from your aunt's shop. I brought her a letter from Rosa, who is enjoying herself immensely. She has a new position in Philadelphia.' He stooped to talk into her ear. 'I think, perhaps, Marcella, we should go inside the church. Even though we might not be of their persuasion, surely they would not mind.' He put out his elbow to help Marcella up to her feet.

Inside the church it was dark and cool. They sat together on a pew at the back of the nave. No one else was there bar a woman sweeping the stone floor around the altar.

Gradually the waves of emotion receded, and Marcella was filled with a dull emptiness.

'I think my husband hates me.'

Henry didn't reply straight away, but after a minute or so he said, 'There are times when a man's problems become too much for him. Inevitably, he would take it out on the person closest. That is why he has upset you. He knows you will put up with it, because you love him. You do love him, don't you?'

Marcella did still love Michael. The problem was she knew he no longer loved her.

'I want us to be a family again,' she said. 'Like we were before.'

Henry took his time before responding. 'The one problem with having such a wish is that in life things can never be like they were *before*. Not in any situation. Times could be good for you again, perhaps, but it would always have to be in a new way. Never as it had once been. There is no going back. We live day to day, doing the best we can, rolling inexorably to our inevitable end. Nostalgia can never be a way forward. If I may be so bold, I think the important thing now is for you to take care of yourself. In the end that will make your children happy too.'

Marcella could see that he was right. How could she and Michael go back to how it was? For a start, she would never again be young and innocent. Now she had children. She was a working woman, not just a silly young thing with nothing to think about but the latest popular song. And Michael, rather than being fired by ambition to have a business, was now full of the cares and stresses of actually running that business. For both of them the dreaming days were over. She was a mother. He was a father. They could never be a romantic couple in the same way that they had been during that first year of marriage. There were two other darling precious souls to think about. Two beautiful sons who depended on them both not only for money, food and shelter, but for love and happiness.

A group of children filed into the church, all laughter and bustle.

'We'd better go.' Henry put out a gloved hand to help Marcella up. 'Remember, Madame Navratil. There are people like your parents, your aunt and me. You are not alone.'

Drenched now with that strange disembodied calm which follows a storm, Marcella resolved to go to her parents' flat above the shop and wait there for Michael to come to find her, as he must if he wanted to see their children.

Then, together with him, Lolo and Edmond, she would try to restart their life together.

It wasn't too late.

Michael's mood with Marcella swung back and forth between desolate love, raging fury, grovelling pleas for forgiveness and sweet generosity.

She continued to work in the back room next to Stefan.

She and her mother had great plans for Christmas that year, Edmond's first. Late in the afternoon of Christmas Eve, Ton-ton brought Gigi and Raphaël up to the house and set up the tree. Then they all worked together, preparing the traditional Christmas Eve feast of seven fishes, and sweet fritters followed by a chocolate log, which Lolo helped Raphaël to decorate with pieces of holly.

Though it was Christmas Eve, Michael was working late in the shop. Last-minute orders for Christmas presents, he said.

As the children were starting to droop, they began dinner without him.

But when by eleven thirty he still hadn't arrived, Marcella decided the family should go on to church for midnight Mass anyway.

No doubt he would know to head there himself, so that they could all come home together.

But he was neither in the church nor at home when they all got back.

Late next morning he staggered in just in time for Christmas lunch, looking ruffled and smelling of smoke and stale alcohol.

When Marcella asked him where he had been, he accused her of being a boring old nag.

A week later her parents were back in the house again, this time to celebrate the feast day of Saint Sylvester, and the welcoming in of the New Year.

Once more, all their preparation for jollity and desire for rapprochement was ruined by Michael. Once more he didn't let them know and stayed out all night.

The following week he was all sweetness, as though nothing had happened.

It continued in this way for a few months until one night when they were leaving the shop after business and Marcella was about to go up the stairs to fetch the children.

Michael took her hand.

'Not tonight. Tonight we're going home without them.'

'But...?'

She was filled with joy. Michael wanted to be alone with her again! Michael wanted to have a romantic evening with her!

As they entered the house, Michael switched on the lights. Marcella took his hand.

'What are you doing?'

'I thought...'

'Thought what?'

She kissed him tenderly on the cheek.

'Get off,' he said, stepping away from her. 'We have a lot of work to do.'

Marcella didn't understand. How could they work here? They had no machines or—

'We're moving out, Marcella. It costs way too much. And I never see the place anyway. A total waste of money.'

Marcella had never been that fond of the house, but now it seemed absurd to be leaving.

'When are we moving?'

'Tonight.'

It was 31 March. The date resonated and Marcella suddenly remembered that it was a year to the day since Rosa sailed away.

At midnight it would be 1 April.

This had to be some elaborate April Fool.

'This is a joke, no? An April Fish?'

'Of course it's not a bloody joke.' Having raised his voice, Michael lowered it again. He seemed very cool about the subject. 'I didn't like to worry you earlier.' Michael shoved open the door to the front room. 'But, without my noticing, the lease ran out today. We have till midnight to remove all our things.'

'Can't we just renew?'

Michael turned and yelled into her face. 'NO! WE! CAN'T! Don't just stand there gaping at me like an old cod! Get on with it. I have ordered a taxi to come in an hour from now. Stefan will be joining us…'

A knock on the door.

'That will be him.'

'But where will we go? Are we to sleep on the street?'

'Stop being such a drama queen.' Michael pushed past her into the hall. 'We're going to stay in your parents' flat. I've already spoken to them. Now get on with it!'

Marcella started emptying the cabinet drawers, trying to imagine the flat above the shop, and everyone living crammed inside it.

'Do my parents…?'

'You're Italian, for God's sake. Don't Italians love the idea of the whole family being together?' He flung his jacket on to his armchair and rolled up his sleeves. 'It will be easier for everyone. Now go upstairs and start packing up your things, and the children's, and leave down here to Stefan and me.'

CHAPTER 15

Mid-November 1911, Palais de Justice, Nice

Marcella had hurried across the town for the meeting with Monsieur Nabias. As she rushed up the steps, she glanced at the clock on the church across the way. She had a minute to get inside and find him.

She had left the children with her mother, who, ignorant of what Marcella was doing, had arrived late at the flat above the shop.

Two weeks before, with no warning, Dolinda the nurse had left, never to return. Marcella had no idea why or where she had gone. But not having someone there to look after the children was, in a way, useful as it meant that Marcella could slip away without Michael knowing.

With Dolinda out of the picture, Michael had ordered Marcella to take her work upstairs to the flat. He and Stefan had lugged up the sewing machine, a tailor's mannequin, an iron, rolls of fabric and boxes of braid, and installed it all to the side of the living room.

Marcella had a little worktable, under the central lamp.

While trying to entertain two boisterous children, she had been working on a gentleman's coat in pale-grey wool, lined in jade-green satin. It was a particular order for a VIP client. It had special safety pockets, with flaps to prevent pickpockets.

As she hurried across the marble hall of the law court, she saw Monsieur Nabias sitting on a stone bench going through the contents of his briefcase.

He saw her, stood up and beckoned.

'No need to rush, Madame Navratil. I've left us an hour before our appointment.'

Marcella sat down. Lawyers bustled past, clutching folders tied in ribbon and large books from which protruded many sheets of paper.

Everyone here was dead-set on their business. It might have been a busy place, but they were as good as alone.

'You are aware that this next step is the most serious one.' Monsieur Nabias took out a pencil and pad of paper.

Marcella tried to drag her thoughts away from the children at home with her mother, and concentrate.

'I need to write down a few names. Any witnesses to the charges you bring against your husband? The persons present at any of those occasions?'

There had been people there when Michael called her abusive names, people who had once stood up for her, but one by one they had vanished from the scene, or declared themselves too disturbed or upset to be able to talk about it, people who refused to listen to her once the subject was Michael Navratil.

Stefan, Louis and Cyril had all seen Michael insulting her. But would they stand against him? No. Louis was gone. Cyril could probably be found somewhere in Nice, but why would he want to drag himself back into the fray? Michael had sacked him when he'd stood up for her. And Stefan was in Michael's pocket. There had been customers there too, but how on earth would she find them?

Rosa knew. But Rosa was in America.

Marcella thought back to how, on that January day when Rosa had come to say goodbye, her cousin had said nothing and yet made Marcella see the misery of her married life. She knew that she had brought the whole trouble upon her own head.

Then there were her parents. They must have overheard some of the cruel things Michael had said when they all lived squashed up against each other in the flat above the shop. Marcella knew in her bones that that was the main reason they had moved away, feeling that they were to blame, for suffocating the couple. Her mother and stepfather would always take her side, but how would their opinions count? Whose mother would not stand up for her own daughter?

There was no one to defend her.

'What if I can't produce witnesses?'

'Then you will have a weak case.'

Marcella's heart sank.

'So you can't give me the names of anybody who might have seen or heard any of the things you have laid down in evidence? Who was there the day he called you all those names, for instance. You weren't alone in the shop.'

Knowing it was pointless, Marcella reeled them off: 'Louis Hoffman, Cyril the apprentice, Stefan Kozak and some customers, but I don't know their names.'

Monsieur Nabias wrote on his pad.

'But Louis Hoffman has since ceased to be part of the business?'

'He's been in Paris for over a year now. My mother heard from my aunt that he runs a very successful shop in the most chic area of the city. I believe his mother still lives down here. He may visit her from time to time. But obviously he never calls on us.'

'After Monsieur Hoffman left, did anything change regarding the shop?'

'I'm not sure what you mean?'

'Did your husband bring in an accountant or does he manage the accounts himself?'

Marcella had no idea. Why had she not taken more interest in such things? She'd had too much else to think about. The children, her marriage, work...

'There was one thing,' she said. 'Not long after Louis left, a man came into the shop. I only caught the end of the episode. But Michael started raising his voice to this man, so my ears pricked up. He ended up shouting, "There's no point pursuing me. I am not Michael Navratil. I am Louis Hoffman."'

Monsieur Nabias raised his eyebrows. 'Why would he say that?'

'I wondered if it was some jealous husband, come to chase him. By now, you see, I felt sure Michael was having an affair.'

'What made you think that?'

'Many things. He became more and more furious with me. It was as though my very presence prevented him living the life he really wanted. I could only presume that this was a woman. Oh, and another thing: he bought a new record, "Amoureuse". Before that we only had the two, "La Petite Tonkinoise" and "The Dream of Autumn", which we both loved. "La Petite Tonkinoise" was for jolly dancing, but on romantic nights we would waltz in the dark to "The

Dream of Autumn". Then along came "Amoureuse". He only ever played that when he was alone. He would go into the living room, shut the door in such a way I knew not to disturb him, and he would stay inside and play it over and over on that damned gramophone.'

Marcella sang quietly.

Letting the words come out of her mouth still broke her heart.

'*My senses are soothed by your kiss*
You are my crazy drunkenness
You make me alive, you make me suffer
And, if you want, you can make me die
To die under your caresses.

'It hurt me. Because I knew that when he played it, it wasn't my kiss causing this crazy drunkenness, it wasn't the lack of my caresses that made him suffer so.'

'Do you know the identity of this woman?'

'I often wondered whether the object of his affection was a redhead I once saw in the shop. I remember the turquoise silk dress she was trying on. She was married to a fidgety little fellow with a wispy beard, who bought the dress for her and asked for it to be delivered to an address in Èze.'

'Do you remember their name?'

'No. It was a year or so ago. But I think he might have called her Camille.'

'Aah, perhaps her very unavailability might provoke Michael's pursuit of her,' said Monsieur Nabias. 'It would not be the first time I have seen a love affair grow very much bigger due to simple frustration.'

'It was when meeting that woman that he first abused me in public. And things were never the same after that. He became distant, his head elsewhere. I knew in my heart something was going on. But I could never be sure.' Marcella hesitated before telling him the next part. She knew it would show her in a bad light. 'I went searching in the waste-paper basket when he popped out of the shop.'

'Why did you do that?'

'Looking for signs, anything. I had seen him crumpling up pieces of paper and throwing them out. I imagined I would find love letters from her.'

'And did you?'

Marcella shook her head.

'I simply found lots of bills. I think he must have known I had looked. Perhaps Stefan told on me. Because after that I noticed he stopped putting anything into the waste-paper basket.'

'On those nights when your husband didn't come home might he have gone to her? Do you think?'

'I asked Michael where he had been and his response was simply "out". But whenever it happened, when I took his shirt to wash it next day, it smelled of perfume.'

Marcella felt desolate. How desperate must she appear to this young man?

Monsieur Nabias took out his watch. 'We still have a few minutes left. Once the president has agreed that you have a case – and the more you tell me, the more I am convinced that you have – you will need to be prepared for the eventualities which may arise once your husband is told of your action and is summoned to court.'

'What kind of things do you mean?'

'Well, for one thing, will your husband have any charges to bring against you?'

Monsieur Nabias pulled a pile of papers wrapped in a pink ribbon from his briefcase and placed them on his lap. Marcella saw her name written on the front and a flash of terror shot through her. Again she wondered if she was doing the right thing. It wasn't too late to stop the whole procedure.

'Might you have anyone, someone of substance here in the city, who would provide a character reference should your husband throw mud at you?'

The only person Marcella was certain had an excellent reputation around Nice was her Aunt Thérèse.

The last Marcella had seen of her aunt was her back as she walked out of the christening party.

If only Marcella had gone with them to Genoa to wave Rosa off and let Lolo see the great big ship, she could have tried to make amends.

But she knew that it would have upset Michael.

'Once we have laid all your grievances before the president, he will decide on the next date, by which time your husband will be informed of the charges you are bringing against him. He will be given a week or so to provide a rebuttal.'

'What does that mean?'

'He and his lawyer will provide a case against you.'

'Monsieur Charles Nabias. Room 15, please. President's Chamber.' An usher walked through the hall, his voice echoing up into the high ceiling.

Marcella was paralysed with apprehension. It was as though her legs would not obey and help her to stand up. In a panic she was racing through her memories, trying to think of the things of which Michael could accuse her. Flirting with customers? Not preparing his dinner to his liking? Not getting on with his friends, the Kirchmanns?

'Come along, Madame Navratil.' Monsieur Nabias gathered his things together and straightened his stiff white collar and bands. As he took a step forward, Marcella grabbed his arm.

'I need to tell you something.'

'Quickly, before we go inside?'

Until now, Marcella had hesitated. But she knew that she must tell him what had happened last night. Something which made her feel at the same time very worried about taking forward this divorce, yet certain she must do it, both for her own safety and the protection of her children.

'Yes?'

'I found… in his coat pocket.'

'Yes…?'

The usher repeated his call. 'Monsieur Charles Nabias – President's Chamber, immediately.'

'What did you find?'

Marcella spat it out.

'I found a loaded gun.'

Once they had registered the case and the Clerk of the Court had dismissed them, Monsieur Nabias whispered in her ear.

'There is a café opposite. We are going there now, into the privacy of the back room, to talk further.'

Marcella hesitated. She really should not be late relieving her mother.

'It won't take long, Madame Navratil. But I have something to tell you.'

'I know all that – Michael will now be told what I have said to the court against him…'

'Not that. No.' Monsieur Nabias pressed harder. 'It's some information I should have given you much earlier.'

As they crossed the square and moved past the tables on the terrace into the gloomy interior of the café, Marcella considered running away. Leaving town altogether. Could things get any worse? But her children. She had to stay for them. She had to protect them.

Monsieur Nabias took a table in the darkest corner, near the door to the kitchen and ordered two coffees.

'This is important.' He spoke in a sombre tone. 'Within hours your husband will receive the letter from the court, laying out your evidence and advising him to take legal advice.'

Marcella felt her heart lurch. Michael would certainly see this as being shown up in public. And she was the person to blame.

'When you talked about your wedding in London, you mentioned to me two names: Sidonie Giraud and Jean-Baptiste Sartori. I recall you stating that people referred to them in a jovial manner during your wedding breakfast. Am I correct?'

Marcella nodded.

'I must tell you now that those names were associated with a scandalous case which took place back in 1902. The event was reported by newspapers throughout the world, from the United States of America to New Zealand. But nowhere did it stir so much interest as here in Nice, because the drama started mere steps from where we now sit.'

Before continuing, Monsieur Nabias took a sip of coffee.

'On Rue Saint-Vincent, André Giraud and his wife Baptiste ran a tailoring shop with their five children. In 1899 they employed a male cutter by the name Jean-Baptiste Sartori. Monsieur Sartori fell in love with Sidonie, one of their daughters, a girl ten years his junior. They proceeded to have a secret affair. One day, Sidonie discovered that Monsieur Sartori was in fact married, and called a halt to their liaison. But Jean-Baptiste Sartori would not take no for an answer and continued to shadow Sidonie, blaming her for everything, threatening to expose her to her very religious parents as a marriage-breaker. So poor Sidonie took the sensible way out. She left Nice, following her brother Jean, who had recently taken a tailoring job in London. Soho, actually.'

Marcella feared what Monsieur Nabias would tell her next.

'Jean-Baptiste Sartori was not finished with Sidonie Giraud. He would not leave her to start anew, and before she'd been there a couple of weeks he followed her. He spent much of his time at a restaurant in Marshall Street run by a certain Paul Kühne. At the very same address where your husband took you, on your trip to London.'

Marcella's thoughts reeled back to the knowing smiles of the waiters at her wedding.

'Did they marry there as well?' she asked. 'Did Paul Kühne arrange that too?'

Avoiding her question, Monsieur Nabias continued.

'Once in London, Jean-Baptiste Sartori persuaded Sidonie Giraud to meet him – just to talk, he said. But despite his protestations of love, Sidonie stayed firm, telling Monsieur Sartori that she wanted nothing further to do with him.'

Monsieur Nabias placed his cup back in the saucer.

'Had it ended there, everything would have been fine. But on a bright Sunday morning two days later, knowing that she would be alone in the flat, Sartori arrived on Sidonie's brother's doorstep.

'At first she refused to let him in. He had come only to say goodbye, he told her. But the goodbye he intended was altogether more sinister than she could have imagined. For in his pocket Monsieur Sartori had a loaded gun. Once inside, he held it up to Mademoiselle Giraud's face, demanding that she write her signature at the bottom of a note which he would not let her read. It was a suicide note. She refused to sign. So he grabbed her hand and guided it across the paper, using her lip-rouge.' Monsieur Nabias paused. 'Then Jean-Baptiste Sartori shot Sidonie Giraud. The bullet grazed her face. Bleeding profusely, she turned to break away from him. He fired at her again, twice. One bullet entered her neck. The third bullet rested in her hair. Screaming for help, she staggered to her brother's bedroom, managing to shut the door. Then she heard another shot.'

Shattered, Marcella asked, 'I presume he killed himself?'

Monsieur Nabias laughed. 'Not at all. Not him. He tried to make it *look* as though he had *attempted* to commit suicide. Luckily for her, at this moment, Sidonie's brother, Jean, entered the flat, with the police, who had been summoned by the neighbours. Monsieur Sartori and Mademoiselle Giraud were taken to hospital, where he was charged with attempted murder. He is currently eight years into his prison sentence. He has almost as many years yet to serve.'

'And Sidonie?'

'Amazingly, she survived the attack. I believe once she recovered she came home to her family. As far as I know, they're all still there, down in Rue Saint-Vincent.'

While Marcella tried to take all this in, Monsieur Nabias ran his slender fingers across the table, making invisible patterns.

'I only tell you this sanguine saga, Madame Navratil, for two reasons. The first is that Paul Kühne, the man who signed your marriage certificate, was a character witness at the Old Bailey trial of Jean-Baptiste Sartori. He knew Sartori, he entertained him, he put him up. Having been in Nice in 1902, working in the tailoring business, Michael Navratil must have heard about this terrible episode. It was the talk of the town. I think it is quite possible that your husband knew Sartori. They were both cutters. Sartori left his position a little after your husband started to work in the town, so their time here certainly overlapped.' Even though his coffee cup was empty, Monsieur Nabias raised it to his lips and tipped it back. 'Presumably he also knew something of Paul Kühne's involvement. Monsieur Kühne does not advertise his rooms to let. Yet your husband knew about them. How else would he have arranged a room for you there, why else choose his restaurant as a venue for your wedding breakfast and ask for his signature on your wedding certificate? From what you tell me, it seems much too much of a coincidence that there was no connection. And now that you say your husband possesses a gun, that worries me. Do you know where he got it?'

Marcella shook her head.

'What sort of gun is it?'

'It's a hand pistol,' she replied.

'They're not so easy to get hold of.' As Monsieur Nabias stood up, his face darkened. 'I implore you, Madame Navratil, take care of yourself.'

CHAPTER 16

Mid-November 1911, Nice

When Marcella arrived back at the flat it was just after two; her mother was there looking after the children. She said that around noon some-one had arrived with an official-looking letter, which she had signed for. Minutes later, during the lunch break, Michael had come in.

Angela had handed him the letter. Michael had read it. He then went straight to the bedroom and, without a further word to Angela or the children, immediately left.

So the die was cast. Michael now knew she had brought a case for divorce.

There was no turning back.

It was time to tell her mother.

Of course, when Marcella told her what she was doing, Gigi burst into floods of tears. 'If Michael had died, like your father, that would be one thing, Marcella. But divorce! That is something too terrible. It's against God. You cannot...'

Marcella held her tongue. She couldn't believe that her mother would stand by the teachings of the Church over the warnings of her real life. Gigi had seen him insult Aunt Thérèse and Rosa. Did she really think that she, his wife, would be immune from his temper?

She might be alone, but she was not turning back now.

It was too late anyway.

Michael knew.

Simply receiving the news would have made Michael incandes-cent with rage. If she withdrew the case now nothing could ever wipe out the fact she had done it.

Marcella went through into the bedroom, opened the wardrobe and plunged her hand into the pocket of Michael's coat.

The gun was gone.

She quickly fumbled through every pocket in every jacket and waistcoat hanging there. Her blood ran cold.

Michael had taken the gun away. Presumably he was out looking for her.

Marcella ran back into the living room.

'Mama, please can you take the children to sleep with you tonight. Or perhaps take them to Raphaël's place. What do you think? Michael is… I just think the atmosphere… I want them to be safe. I will call you a taxi, so that you can travel up to your place in comfort.'

As she dressed the children, Marcella smiled and cajoled them. 'You're going on a trip with Grandma, to see Uncle Raphaël and Ton-ton.'

Lolo jumped up and down. He loved to play with the two men. As though he could feel Marcella's fear, Edmond grabbed hold of her leg and squeezed himself into her skirt.

Tonight she would have to face Michael and it was better if she was alone.

As darkness fell, while she waited and waited, the story of Sidonie Giraud and Jean-Baptiste Sartori went round and round in her head, along with the memories of herself, Paul Kühne, Michael and their wedding on that wet London morning.

Just after nine, a key turned in the door.

Marcella braced herself.

Michael came into the living room, calmly walked over to Marcella and kissed her on the cheek.

'Good evening, darling,' he said. It was the first time he had called her 'darling' since Edmond had been born. 'Are the children in bed?'

'They've gone off to stay with Gigi and Ton-ton for the night.'

'Ah!' Michael raised an eyebrow. 'What's for dinner?'

So this was how he would play it.

The battle had begun.

Rue Saint-Vincent was narrow. Too narrow for a cart, but men wheeled barrows along and women shoved past Marcella, pushing prams, dragging children. Marcella wondered whether she was doing the right thing. She was about to turn back when she came face to face with a small statue of the Virgin Mary, standing in a niche cut into the corner wall, smiling down on her. That made up her mind.

An old man inside a cobbler's workshop was banging at the sole of a large brown boot. Two dogs fought over a bone, which they must have stolen from the butcher's shop on the corner.

Then Marcella saw rolls of fabric and swathes of cloth hanging from upstairs windows, rails of ready-to-wear clothing lined up outside the door.

This had to be the place.

A dark-haired woman a few years older than Marcella was sitting on a stool outside, embroidering a shawl. As Marcella stopped, she looked up.

'Can I help you?'

'I'm looking for Giraud's tailoring shop.'

The woman put down her embroidery and stood up. 'Are you looking for a coat or a suit or…?'

'No. No. I was looking for Sidonie Giraud. I don't even know whether she works here or…'

'Follow me.' The woman turned and walked into the shop. 'I'm her little sister, by the way. Joséphine.'

Marcella followed Joséphine into the cave-like interior of the shop. Drawers and boxes, interspersed with rows of different-coloured fabrics, lined the walls.

'Sidonie!' Joséphine pulled open the green baize curtain. 'A lady to see you.'

The back room was very dark. Sidonie was working at a small desk in a corner by the light of a brass lamp, which shone down on a dazzling piece of satin beaded with tiny pearls. It took a few seconds before Marcella's eyes adjusted.

Sidonie had risen and edged her way around the table.

She and Marcella stood face to face.

Sidonie's left jaw was gone, blown away, and on that side her eye drooped down. Her head bowed towards one shoulder. Part of her ear was missing.

Involuntarily, Marcella took a step back.

'Are you all right, madame? You look very pale.'

'I'm fine… I…'

'Let me get you a chair.' Sidonie turned and pulled out her own seat from the worktable.

'No, no. I won't be long. I don't want…' Despite herself, Marcella sank on to the chair. 'In London…'

Sidonie flinched.

'…there is a man called Paul Kühne. He runs an establishment which is advertised as a restaurant, but upstairs he has a kind of flophouse.' Marcella chose her words carefully. She didn't want Sidonie to think that Mr Kühne was any friend of *hers*.

Sidonie stood rooted to the spot, like a tailor's dummy.

Marcella felt overcome with guilt. What good was it coming here, troubling an already troubled woman? 'I'm sorry, Mademoiselle Giraud.' Marcella rose. 'I don't know why I came. I have wasted your time.'

'Really… It was so long ago. I don't mind talking about it now. Nine years. How time flies.' Sidonie touched Marcella's arm and smiled. 'If you were thinking of booking one of his rooms, I wouldn't—'

'It's not that…'

'So how can I help you, Madame… Madame…?'

'Navratil,' said Marcella automatically.

It was now Sidonie's turn to reel back. Marcella had not expected such a strong reaction.

'So you *did* know my husband?'

'I can't say anything, madame. If you are his wife, then—'

'I am divorcing him… He has a gun.' To her own surprise, in the dim light of the Giraud workshop, Marcella burst into tears.

'Sidonie?' Joséphine popped her head through the curtain. 'Are you all right?'

'I'm fine, Joséphine.' Sidonie strode past Marcella and whispered to her sister. 'Bring some brandy. Two glasses.' She turned back to Marcella. 'If you want information about him, I am afraid I can only tell you that your husband was not popular in this family. I would also ask please if you would try not to mention your surname in front of my sisters or my father. He is very old now. I wouldn't like him to have any nasty shocks.'

'How do you know Michael?'

'I don't. But there was a vacancy here after I left, rather hurriedly, to go to London. Your husband came to the door, young, wet behind the ears. Only that morning, he said, he had arrived in Nice. He was wearing cheap, tatty clothing. He had no references, no papers at all, he told my father. He'd been robbed on the train. They'd taken everything. His money, his passport. Naturally my father felt sorry for him, gave him the job. And in no time he made himself indispensable, cosying up to both my father and mother. At first my little sister fell under his spell. But then... those things happened to me, and after my... bad experience... she felt sufficiently warned and so resisted him.' Sidonie leaned back against the edge of the worktable and folded her arms. 'He used quite a line with her, called her his Shadow.'

Had not the curtain been pulled open and Joséphine entered bearing a bottle of cognac and two glasses, Marcella would have vomited.

After Joséphine came and went, Sidonie continued.

'By the time I recovered from my injuries and was well enough to come back from London, your man had gone.' Sidonie poured two glasses and handed one to Marcella. 'A few years later we discovered that, even though he had had very little experience in the trade, he had wangled himself a job teaching at that technical school. His reference had apparently come from my father. But my father would never have given him a reference. *Never.*'

'Because of your sister?' Marcella took a gulp of cognac and felt the heat hit the back of her throat.

'Oh, no. My father may have been extremely distressed by what had happened to me, and concerned for my sister too, but he had picked up the discrepancies in the accounts.'

'Michael was dismissed? For stealing?'

'It was more of a conjuring trick than plain theft. Money went out of the till, but the invoices attached to the debit notes had not been paid. Those kinds of things don't show up for a while. Not until the supplier comes calling, asking after what they're owed.'

'I know.' Marcella thought about her visits to Mademoiselle Aude and how she always expected cash before handing over her lace and braids. As Sidonie continued, with a shudder she recalled that day when Louis had found Michael taking money from the safe.

'He denied everything, of course. Accused the suppliers of pocketing the money. He was an impressive liar. We also discovered later that he did have papers – and a perfectly good passport – as he frequently went over to Italy to meet one of our customers.'

141

Marcella thought once more of the red-headed woman. She realised with a sinking feeling that, though she had thought for the last three years that Michael had changed and that it was somehow her fault, he must always have been the same.

'My poor old father. All of that happening at the same time as... Well, it aged him. A couple of years ago we tried to talk him into retiring, we even put the place up for sale, but... he would have none of it. As you see, we're still here.'

Sidonie knocked back the brandy, placed the glass on the tray and continued.

'Even in those days, your husband had a gun. From his time in the army, he told everyone. He flashed it around like a trophy. My father is convinced that the... wretch... who did this to me only got himself a gun before he followed me to London because he was inspired to do so by your husband.'

'They knew each other?'

'They crossed over, working here, for a few days. Your husband came in at the bottom – cutter's apprentice and general dogsbody. Taking my place, really. As soon as my father realised the cause of my running away to London, he sacked Monsieur Sartori, and your husband was bumped up from floor sweeper to cutter.'

Instinctively, Sidonie ran the backs of her fingers down the side of her scarred cheek. 'So, no. I never knew your husband, but by repute.'

'There are times when I wish I had never known him either. Except that, without him, I wouldn't have my darling children.'

'How many?'

'Two boys. One and a half and three.'

'I envy you. It will never happen for me now.'

Marcella looked at Sidonie's shattered face, her tilted head, her crooked neck. She tried to think of something reassuring to say, but realised there were no words.

For some moments the two women sat in silence.

'But Madame... I won't say the name... I wish you good luck. However you continue.'

'Thank you.' Marcella stood, bent over and kissed Sidonie's ravaged cheek.

CHAPTER 17

Mid-November 1911, Nice

'Where have you been? Whining more lies about me to your feeble lawyer?'

Marcella was surprised to find Michael not in the shop, but sitting in his armchair, reading the newspaper.

After visiting the Giraud shop, Marcella had walked home along the Promenade, thinking, the setting sun ahead of her. Her mind was still churning with all this new information.

'I thought you'd be at work.' She glanced at the clock. It was around six.

'After that bombshell?'

She turned to hang her coat on the rack, then stood facing him.

'Actually, Michael, I've been visiting your old haunts.'

'Madame du Camp's brothel? Looking for work, I suppose.'

Marcella let his snide remark bounce off. 'I know you have a gun,' she said.

'Oh, darling, I had a gun long before I met you.'

'I know that too.' Marcella let the words, her fears, spill out of her mouth. 'You have to get rid of it. It's not safe to have a gun around the flat when we have such young children.'

'It's not "around the flat".' Michael pulled the gun out and held it up, pointing it towards her.

Marcella stood very still. He couldn't really just shoot her, here in their living room. Could he?

'Out of interest, where *are* the children?'

'With my mother.' Marcella could not disguise the quiver of terror in her voice.

'There's a surprise!' Michael casually slid the pistol back into his suit pocket and rubbed his hands together. 'So, tell me. What's for dinner? I'm starving.'

Marcella moved towards the kitchen.

'Who have you been talking to about me?'

Marcella was about to tell him everything, but then feared that he might go down into Old Town and upset the Giraud family again. Best to keep the information to herself.

'Does it matter?'

'Not really. Not now.'

After a week of this quiet but threatening harmony, with Lolo and Edmond back with them, one morning Michael said calmly to Marcella over breakfast, 'I suggest you send the children to your mother again. This time for a few nights. They won't want to witness the events which are going to happen here.'

He laid the newspaper down on the table, and stretched out to tousle the hair of the two boys, sitting either side of him.

'Your mother would surely oblige, or perhaps one of your innumerable cousins. There's no need to tell anyone about it, except that, in the light of recent sly and malicious manoeuvres taken by you against me, we need a little "alone" time.'

He smiled, wiped his mouth with a napkin, rose and stretched.

'Fancy that! After all I've done for you, Marcella. After everything I have sacrificed for you, yet you see only bad in me.'

'You haven't been very kind to me lately.' Marcella reached across to spread butter on a piece of brioche for Edmond, who could now utter a few words including Monmon, meaning himself. She tried to keep the tremble from her fingers. 'I keep hoping that the husband who I married will come back.'

Michael took his jacket from the back of his chair and put it on.

'Why would he come back to a fat slut of a fishwife?'

'I am neither of those things and you know it.'

As though she had not spoken, Michael popped his hat on his head.

'No rest for the wicked, eh, Shadow?' He laughed to himself. 'Whoever heard of a shadow attacking its owner? Anyway...' He patted his jacket pocket. 'Nothing like a little target practice to keep a woman on her toes.'

Marcella felt hot with anxiety. Had he been down to Rue Saint-Vincent? What was he planning to do to her?

Michael kissed her on the cheek and the two children on the crowns of their heads.

'Make sure that the little darlings aren't here by the time I get home, won't you. Understood?' He picked up his briefcase and held open the front door to the flat. 'I wouldn't want them seeing anything upsetting. These things can scar you for life.'

After he left, Marcella gave the children some crayons to play with while she tried to work at the sewing machine, her mind constantly drawn back to Michael's threat. Surely he wasn't planning to come back here to murder her?

But then, maybe he was.

She was frightened. But would be more so if the children were here. Lolo was fierce in his protection of her. If Michael laid a finger on her, the child would step in and she didn't want him to get hurt.

After lunch she took them both up to her mother's place and asked if she could please look after them for a couple of days. Things at home were too stressful, she explained.

Gigi raised her eyebrows, as though to say, 'And whose fault is that?'

Depressed, scared and lonely, Marcella trudged back across town to the flat alone. She spent the rest of the afternoon working on the grey coat, full of dread at what her husband had in store.

When it became too dark to see the small stitches, she put the coat away. As she moved from the worktable, she could hear the clatter of dishes and the conversations of diners coming up from the brasserie over the road.

Should she cook dinner for him? If she did and he didn't come home it would be a waste, but if she didn't there would be a row and more name-calling. She decided on a small salad, which she left on the table with bread and cheese.

Then she waited.

The sounds from the brasserie died down; she heard the rattle as the waiters pulled down the shutters and locked up the bar.

Still Michael did not return.

Marcella pulled an armchair over to the door, and watched the handle, fearful of sleep in case he came in catching her unawares.

She was still awake when the pink sun rose over the rooftops, and the clatter of trams and carts resumed.

The brasserie opened up.

Marcella went to the window and watched the waiters in their white aprons, bearing trays laden with coffee jugs and glasses of freshly squeezed orange juice.

Then she saw Michael, sitting at a small sunny table, sipping his morning coffee, contentedly reading the newspaper.

She pulled away from the window.

She didn't want him to see her looking out. Had he sat there watching the flat all night? she wondered. If not, where had he slept? She didn't think it could be the shop floor as he looked as neat and fresh as ever, perfectly turned out for a busy day running a fashionable ladies' tailor's.

She glanced into the mirror. Her hair was a mess, her eyes bleary with lack of sleep. She considered going next door to the bedroom, flinging herself on to the bed and sleeping. But what if he came in once she was asleep? He had made it clear he had some plan.

She crossed back to her armchair near the front door and sat there.

Would he come up here before opening the shop? Would he take one of those 'Hold the fort for me, Stefan, I need to pop out for a while' breaks of his?

She wondered if there was any way she could get a message to Monsieur Nabias. Maybe he might be able to do something? Her mother would certainly not come, that was sure, as she would have that romantic idea that they were here alone together, making up, lovebirds going back to how a marriage is before children come along.

The only other person she could think of to contact was Raphaël, but he seemed to have developed such a buddy, birthday-sharing brotherly relationship with Michael that she wasn't sure she would trust him. Aunt Thérèse lived in the flat next to him. She would probably advise him against coming anyway.

Then she thought of Rosa's friend, Henry. She searched the flat and found his card, not in one of her pockets where she thought she had left it, but propped up on the dressing table. He was calm and impartial. He would advise her. Surely he would know what she should do.

She hastily wrote a note.

Dear Henry, you told me that if I ever needed you I only had to call. I need you now. My marriage is over. I am alone. When my husband called me a whore and struck my face, it was you who comforted me. I need that solace now. Please come. Yours, Marcella.

She rooted around in the drawers for an envelope, wrote his address on it, then shoved the letter inside, carefully sealing it.

She ran up and down the stairs, knocking on the doors to the other apartments, until she found someone who might deliver it for her.

On the first floor an old lady told Marcella that her nephew came in daily with her food and necessities. She would ask him. Marcella gave her a five-franc note which should easily cover any travel expenses.

Then she went back to the flat and took up her position again.

She tried to remember exactly what Michael had said at the wedding breakfast when everyone joked about Sidonie Giraud – joked! How could anyone joke about an episode like that? Especially when he had known her family, when he could well have goaded Sartori to such actions. It made her feel sick to recall.

Surely Michael wouldn't come here and shoot her. If he did, he would be caught and arrested, like Jean-Baptiste Sartori. Then he would be locked up in prison for years. Michael couldn't put up with that.

Marcella got up and moved over to the window. Hiding behind the curtain, she peered out.

There were other people sitting at the café tables now. Michael would be in the shop downstairs, charming some beautiful woman from Monte Carlo or New Mexico. Did he have the gun with him?

Where was the gun?

Perhaps she was going mad.

Maybe the gun was still here, hidden in the flat.

She wanted to sleep. Then a thought shook her awake. Of course Michael wouldn't do the dirty work himself. But what would stop some paid thugs coming in to attack her... maybe kill her? That was it! She would be dead, and then Michael could be free in every way. She would be gone. And he wouldn't be to blame. Why hadn't she thought of that before? While she stayed here she was a sitting duck. She had to get out of the flat.

Downstairs the street door slammed.

She didn't know where to turn.

Footsteps on the stairs.

Was this the hired ruffian, come to see her off?

She pressed her ear to the door.

The clack of feet moved past this landing and went on climbing, getting slower the higher they went.

For a moment she rested her head against the architrave and closed her eyes in relief.

She was tired, tired, tired.

Dragging the work stool nearer to the window, she lowered herself so that she could watch the road below.

How had it come to this?

Twenty-one years old and terrified of every sound, every movement.

Why had she brought this divorce? Surely she could have put up with his insults? Anything would be better than this fear.

She went through to the kitchen and put on some coffee. Slumping down on to one of the wooden chairs, she sat by the stove and watched the blue flame flutter.

She mustn't shut her eyes.

Suddenly the percolator was hissing and popping.

She must have dozed for a few minutes.

The coffee had boiled away to almost nothing. She poured the syrupy remains into a small cup and carried it back to the front room.

Michael would have to punish her for bringing the divorce, for making him look stupid. She should have never done it. Men like Michael didn't like being shown up.

Over the road the lunchtime rush had started.

Wait!

Was that Stefan sitting at a pavement table with his head turned away? Marcella withdrew quickly.

Was she going mad?

Michael did hate her.

Didn't he? Had he ever loved her? she wondered.

And when he married her, he had known about Sidonie and he had joked about her.

She ducked low and crawled across the floor so that no one would see her, should they look up.

She couldn't stay here.

She had to go to the children.

But what if he followed her and ended up hurting them?

No. No.

He would never do that. Not them. They were his own flesh and blood.

It was Marcella Michael wanted to punish, not them.

She would go to Monsieur Nabias's office and ask him to withdraw the divorce petition. But what was the point?

The damage was done. Even if she withdrew, there would be no hope of escape. Never ever. Just an eternal limbo of hatred.

But she could go and ask Monsieur Nabias what she should do, where she could go... He must have an answer.

She went to the bedroom to fetch a wrap. She didn't know how long she would be out. And although it was sunny now, once the shadows started to fall and evening turned to night, it got very cold.

Once in the bedroom, she forgot what she had come for. She sat on the end of the bed. All she wanted was to lie down, to sleep...

She realised she hadn't slept for thirty-six hours.

Before going out Marcella stood at the front door and listened. As soon as she was sure that no one was there, she opened up and peered out through the crack.

No one on the landing or the staircase.

She was about to click the door shut, then discovered that she hadn't brought the keys so ran back inside to fetch them.

If only she might lie down, just for a moment, and sleep…

But she knew she couldn't. She slipped the keys in her pocket and slowly, silently, started the steep descent, clinging to the handrail.

When she reached the bottom step, she opened the street door and looked out.

The spindly fair-haired boy she had thought was Stefan had gone now, and the table was occupied by four ladies in big hats, happily chattering.

Marcella straightened down her clothes and pinned on her own hat. She must look normal. She didn't want people to notice her.

Turning sharply left, she marched away from the tailoring shop.

Her head was spinning.

At the next crossroads she couldn't remember which direction to take. Where was she going? Why was she out in the street? The shadows were growing long. It would be dark soon.

Footsteps behind her.

Someone was following.

She ran out into the road, squeezing behind a horse and carriage. But still the footsteps came after. The person must be following her, why else would they cross here?

She walked faster.

The footsteps also gained pace.

Treading on to the pavement opposite, Marcella started to run.

The footsteps were still there, gaining on her.

Why had she left the flat?

She had been safe in there.

Her breath was giving out now.

How could she keep going?

A hand grabbed her shoulder.

She cringed and turned.

'Marcella?'

It was Henry.

'I got your note. I came at once and saw you leave the flat.' He held out a gloved hand. 'Are you feeling all right? Sorry to be ungallant, but you look awful. Are you unwell?'

Marcella collapsed to the ground, sobbing.

'I'm sorry. I'm sorry. I'm sorry.'

'Here.' Henry helped her to her feet. 'Take my arm. Let me take you home.'

'I'm frightened, Henry. Frightened.'

'It's all right. Your aunt told me that you are going through a difficult time.'

My aunt? thought Marcella. Which aunt? Nobody else knows what is happening. How would Aunt Thérèse know anything?

In silence, Henry walked Marcella back to the front door and asked her to unlock it.

'Don't leave me alone, Henry. They are coming to kill me.'

Taking the keys from her, Henry opened up, never letting go of her. He guided her up the steep stairs and opened the door to the flat.

'Now, let's get you inside.' He looked from side to side. 'Where is the bedroom? I think you must sleep.'

He helped her through.

'You should get undressed now.'

'No! No!' she whimpered. 'Don't leave me. My husband. He's going to kill me.'

'No one is going to kill you. Not while I am sitting through there.'

'Michael has a gun. I saw it. I'm divorcing him. He'll kill me.'

'I promise, Marcella, that I will stay here until you wake up and after that we can talk about what will come next, all right? Now sleep.'

Henry left the bedroom, went into the living room and, after slipping the bolt across the front door, took a book from the shelf and read.

Marcella's dreams were a tumble of images. The leering faces at the wedding breakfast, the little wax girl falling from the boat, then running along a street full of Pierrots and Harlequins, each bearing a tailor's dummy. Then came her dead father, working on a piece of maggoty wood, banging and banging, Ton-ton beside him, wielding his own hammer, nailing down a little wooden boat.

Marcella opened her eyes.

Henry stood at the bedroom door.

Marcella had no idea where she was, or why Henry was there.

'What's happening?' She raised herself on one elbow. The banging continued, even though she was awake.

'I took the liberty of bolting the door as I didn't want any surprises. It appears that, as you feared, your husband has come home very angry, and wants admittance. Should I let him in?'

'Yes. Yes. Let him in, of course. Let him in. Oh my God.' Marcella sat up. 'But don't leave me alone with him. Please, Henry. Please.'

Henry went back through to the living room. Marcella heard him slide the bolt on the door. And she heard Michael, his voice raised in anger.

Before she could pull on her stockings, Michael was standing in the room, with a man behind him. Marcella remembered him well. It was Monsieur Guillaume, Michael's pet police commissaire.

Michael swung back to Monsieur Guillaume.

'As I told you, commissaire, and now you can see for yourself. My wife is a common slut.'

CHAPTER 18

Late November 1911, Palais de Justice, Nice
Marcella glanced across the courtroom at Michael. He was avoiding
her gaze, smiling and chatting with an elderly man with snow-white
hair and a pince-nez.

'He has engaged Maître Pointurier,' Monsieur Nabias whispered
into her ear. 'He will be a formidable opponent. But don't be put off.
Remember, you are very young and your case is very strong. I fancy
you will win a handsome settlement.'

Marcella looked at Monsieur Nabias. His fingers were quivering.
Was he frightened too?

She glanced around the chamber, which was small but imposing,
with marble columns up the walls. It was like a church, thought
Marcella, without the smell of incense or the feeling of benevolence.
They sat on long seats, like pews; facing them, where the altar would
be, a wide wooden bench for the judges.

From the desultory chit-chat in the courtroom, Marcella realised
there were other people sitting behind them. She wondered who
they might be. Members of the public perhaps, journalists from the
local paper, junior law students, swotting up? But before she had
time to ask Monsieur Nabias, a rustle went around the room, a side
door opened and the two lawyers indicated to their clients that they
must stand.

Three judges and the President of the Court took their seats on
the bench.

'Good morning, lady and gentlemen.' The president looked
ahead at the two lawyers. 'Today we meet so that both parties can
lay all their evidence before the court – and by evidence, I mean
giving me the reasons that you…' he broke off and glanced down at

his papers, '…Madame… Navratil… that *you* are bringing this case to end your marriage to Monsieur Navratil. Once we have heard your case, Monsieur Navratil will put forward any grievances he has against you. My fellow judges and I will then take this information away and discuss it all. We will meet again on December the thirteenth to give our initial verdict. Four months after that, towards the end of April 1912, will be the time for the finalisation of the divorce. Do you understand?'

The two sets of lawyers exchanged papers and, in silence, read them through.

Marcella glanced across the aisle. Michael was staring at her. Their eyes locked. It felt to Marcella as though Michael was a child playing a game of who could stare for the longest. Instinctively she submitted, lowering her eyelids, looking down at her skirts.

After what seemed an interminable fifteen minutes during which the two solicitors read out legal statements concerning addresses and identities, the Clerk of the Court called Monsieur Nabias to rise and present his case.

One by one he gave the reasons why Marcella wanted to end her marriage, just as she had told him. The insults, the violence, the staying out all night, the hours Michael kept her working when she had only just given birth, the times he refused to eat with the rest of the family. How he had ruined both Christmas and New Year, and finally how he had thrown a plate at her, which smashed against her head.

After Monsieur Nabias finished, Marcella caught the almost imperceptible exchange of glances between the judges.

They saw her point. She knew it. They understood that her husband had been unreasonable.

As he rose, Monsieur Pointurier's heel scraped noisily on the marble floor. He paused, waiting for the full attention of the room, flicked some dust from his gown and cleared his throat. Only then did he speak.

'I am sure, my lords, that you will all appreciate the "terrible" things Madame Navratil has had to suffer while being kept in luxury by my client.'

Michael's lawyer, his white hair sleeked back, his elegant demeanour and his smooth, oily way of addressing the court, sounded utterly in control. As he flicked through his papers with a scornful sneer, she felt belittled by him. He was the kind of man, Marcella knew, who, if he bumped into you in the street, would blame you and reply, 'Little girl, you are in my way.'

Marcella was scared of him.

'My client, Michael Navratil, is the breadwinner, while Marcella Navratil sits at home, as indeed many wives do, twiddling her fingers. But for her to accuse my client of such trivial indiscretions is ridiculous. This is especially true as she herself is a known adulterer, and has been so ever since the start of the marriage, a marriage which she presumably endured only in order to enjoy the fruits of my client's labour. And while she can provide not one single witness to the alleged incidents she brings against him, my client will now bring forth a man of impeccable character, the Commissaire of Police of the 4th Arrondissement of Nice, no less. Commissaire Guillaume will attest that he himself was there on the evening when poor Monsieur Navratil caught his wife *in flagrante delicto* with a certain Monsieur X.'

Marcella heard gasps from the benches behind her. She glanced across at Michael. He smiled back and gave a little wink.

She could not be sure, but she thought she heard Monsieur Nabias groan.

Michael had taken control of the proceedings. She may have brought this action against him, but he had made the divorce his own. His words at Edmond's baptism party rang in her head: *It's a very good idea to keep in with the local police. You never know when a bigwig like that might come in handy.*

Suddenly Marcella could see what was going to happen next. Michael was going for custody of the children. She grabbed a pencil and sheet of paper from the desk and wrote: *I don't care if I get nothing whatsoever from this divorce but my freedom. I don't want alimony. I don't want ANYTHING. There is only one thing he cannot take from me. My children.*

She slid the note to Monsieur Nabias, who nodded and wrote back: *It's a rare judge who doesn't grant custody to the mother.*

Nonetheless, when the court met again two weeks later to present its judgement, the president announced that the panel had decided that, in the circumstances, and until both parties could provide more concrete proof of their accusations, the two children, Michel Marcel Navratil and Edmond Roger Navratil, would be immediately taken from the parents and placed into care.

The parents must pay the cost of this carer, who would be appointed by the court. Any other costs must also be covered. These would include food and any travel expenses. Until the court ruled again, both parents would, within reason, have equal rights of visitation.

This state of affairs would continue until one parent or other could strengthen their case. If not, it would remain in place until the court announced the final divorce decree, in the third week of April 1912.

Marcella was distraught. They couldn't take her children away! How would the poor babies survive, living with total strangers? Lolo was only three and Edmond one and a half years old. Marcella turned to Monsieur Nabias.

'Help me,' she whispered. 'Help me!'

Monsieur Nabias bit his lip.

The judges rose and turned to leave the court.

'No!' Marcella stood up. 'Come back! They're just infants. They should be with their mother—'

Monsieur Nabias grabbed her arm, pulling her down.

'No!' she shouted again. 'I cannot allow this! No! No! No! Wait! Come back! I will give up the divorce. I will do anything, if you will only let me have my children.'

But the three judges were gone.

The clerks and ushers gathered at a desk in front of the tribunal's bench, signing and stamping papers which would finalise the procedure.

Marcella continued shouting at the empty bench.

Then footsteps clattered down the marble-floored aisle.

Madame Thérèse Magaïl walked past her and up the step to the clerks' desk.

Marcella was shocked to see her here.

As though in a dream, she watched her Aunt Thérèse whispering urgently with the Clerks of the Court. One of them rose and silently ushered her through the door into which the judges had just disappeared.

Five minutes later the president returned to the court. He declared the session once again open, and then announced that, until the divorce was settled, the guardianship, care and protection of the two Navratil children was to be awarded to Madame Thérèse Magaïl, couturière, of 11 Rue de l'Hôtel des Postes, Nice.

CHAPTER 19

January–April 1912, Nice

Michael railed against the court's choice, but it was too late. Dissatisfied and suspicious that Madame Magaïl was favouring Marcella and letting her see more of the boys, on 2 January Michael went back to court, claiming that Marcella's family was a great Italian mafia who disliked him, and that, unfairly, the children spent much more time with their mother than with him. He was particularly aggrieved that Marcella had had them for Christmas Day.

He worked during the day, it was true, and by order of the court the children had to be with Madame Magaïl from dusk to dawn, but Michael failed to mention that most of the days when he let Marcella have the children were the occasions when he had other, more pressing engagements.

In purple ink, the Clerk of the Court noted Michael's grievance in the margins of the case file and sent a stiff letter to Madame Magaïl. After that, Thérèse took great care to make sure that Michael would never again have the slightest reason to feel hard done by.

When he came to her flat to pick up Lolo and Monmon, she sympathised with him and chatted about the troubles and tribulations of working in the world of fashion. Michael was a busy man with so many pressures, she agreed. It was obviously much harder for the boss of a tailoring shop to take time off when he pleased. Marcella, Thérèse felt sure, would be quite content to have the children only on days when Michael had decided that it was impossible for him.

More importantly, after the letter from the court, Madame Magaïl made a point of giving Michael first choice on every birthday or holiday.

Shortly after the New Year's court episode, Marcella heard that the Kirchmanns had returned to America. Aunt Thérèse told her that Michael seemed happier in himself, and the children appeared keener to spend time with him.

After a day with him, they would frequently arrive back at Madame Magaïl's dressed up in newly tailored suits.

'After all,' Michael joked with her, 'if my own children can't be my shop window, who can?'

This state of affairs would not last forever.

Sunday 7 April 1912, Nice

April arrived, in a whirl of orange blossom and sunshine.

When it came to Easter, Madame Magaïl grovelled. 'I have made sure that Lolo and Monmon will be spending a joyful Easter Day in your company, Monsieur Navratil.'

Michael blushed and told her that in fact he didn't want to have the children for the big day (which had been his bone of contention over Christmas), but he would rather take them out on the day after Easter – Monday.

Madame Magaïl knew that it was only a matter of two weeks now until the divorce would be finalised.

Because of her responsibilities of guardianship, she needed to be in touch with the court at all times. She made sure always to ask the clerks pertinent questions, trying to weasel out how the case was moving within the privacy of the judges' chambers.

For all his status and experience, she heard that Michael's lawyer, Monsieur Pointurier, had been unable to persuade the Commissaire of Police to sign the document he had prepared, confirming that he had caught the couple 'Monsieur X' and Madame Navratil *in flagrante delicto*.

Commissaire Guillaume would only say that he had seen them 'together in the flat', that 'Monsieur X' was fully clothed and Madame Navratil was in bed.

Without this evidence being presented to the court as a sworn affidavit, the president believed it reduced its value. It was too flimsy a charge to bring against Marcella.

The clerks whispered to Madame Magaïl that they believed by 23 April the judges were very likely to grant a decree absolute with a full settlement and Marcella winning custody of the children. Michael would of course have visitation rights. Naturally, Madame Magaïl said nothing to him.

As a result, Easter Sunday was a wonderful day.

It was sunny and warm. Everything felt perfect.

As the church bells rang out over Nice, Madame Magaïl, driven by Raphaël, arrived early with the children to spend the day with Marcella and were shortly followed by Gigi, Ton-ton and Edouard Bruno, another nephew who had recently moved to Nice from Saint-Raphaël.

After attending Mass in the local church, the family gathered in the garden behind the apartment house, under the shadow of the railway viaduct. After the court hearing in November, Marcella had moved out of the flat in Rue Dalpozzo and found a small set of rooms near her mother on the other side of town. The great benefit for Marcella was not only the feeling of safety but the fact that there was a small communal garden in which her sons could play.

While the children searched for hidden eggs, dropped behind bushes by Raphaël and Edouard, Marcella spread a tablecloth on the grass. In the shade of an umbrella pine tree, they laid out a magnificent picnic of charcuterie, cheese and gateaux from the best patisseries in Nice.

Antonio had been busy in the workshop with young Edouard, his new apprentice. They had made a surprise toy for the children – an Easter chicken. Prettily painted in pink and yellow, it was a wooden bird unlike any other, with a clockwork feathered tail, which, when you pushed it down, opened a trapdoor in the chicken's belly. From the trapdoor dropped small chocolate eggs.

'Cock-a-doodle-doo!' crowed Edouard as he put the chicken down in the centre of the cloth. 'Cock-a-doodle-doo!'

'You sound just like the real thing!' Marcella laughed and lay back on the grass, staring up at wisps of cloud floating across the cerulean-blue sky. The sun warmed her face. She had not felt this content for years. Finally, she could allow herself to hope that the worst might soon be behind her and a happy new life on the horizon.

'Cock-a-doodle-doo!'

Every time Edouard crowed, the children screamed with laughter. They spent a good half hour pressing the bird's tail, giggling as the eggs dropped. Lolo soon grasped the concept that the eggs needed to be replenished. He took the job of refilling the chicken very seriously indeed. At almost four years old, Lolo had a magisterial air. Edmond, now two years and one month, staggered about like a sailor, lurching from one lap to the next, attempting strings of nonsense words which he pronounced with defiant glee.

'Maman', he could say, and 'Papa' too, although, in present company, that was not quite so welcome a sound. His favourite phrases were 'Monmon hungry' and 'Monmon tired'. Monmon had tried hard at saying 'Lolo'. The nearest he could manage was a solid 'Lump'. He also used the word 'Lump' to mean anything of importance.

The presence of the magic chicken, though creating nothing but elation, posed a new problem. 'Chicken' was way beyond the limits of his linguistic prowess. So from now on the word 'Lump' was used for Antonio, Edouard and the wooden chicken.

Occasionally Marcella hugged her darlings, but they wriggled away, wanting nothing more than to play roughly with Edouard and Raphaël, who teased them, spinning them round, swinging them high in the air, treating them as though they were little chimpanzees rather than boys. Their delighted laughter rang around the garden.

Everything in the world was perfect.

But no day lasts forever, and, as shadows began to fall, the garden took on a slight chill.

Madame Magaïl tapped her watch.

'We don't want to ruin things at this late hour, Marcella. Not when everything is going so well,' she said. 'Let's go now, boys. Kiss your mama goodnight.'

Raphaël got up, took his leave and went out to fetch the painters' wagon to take Madame Magaïl and the children back down to Rue de l'Hôtel des Postes.

Edouard and Antonio helped Angela bring everything inside, piling plates up in Marcella's kitchen, while Madame Magaïl took Marcella into the hall and spoke briefly with her.

'That husband of yours seems to have cheered up quite a lot. Tomorrow he's taking the children up to lunch with Louis.'

'Louis who?'

'Louis Hoffman! He's back in Nice, staying with his mother up in Cimiez. Louis was always a good influence on your husband.'

Marcella thought back to the last time she had seen Louis, that rainy evening in the shop. 'To be frank, Aunt Thérèse, after the way they parted I'm surprised Louis can bear to speak to Michael at all.'

'Louis has money now.' Madame Magaïl gave a shrug. 'I think he wants a foot in Nice. His mother is not getting any younger. Perhaps he wants to do some kind of deal with Michael.'

'Ah well,' said Marcella, wondering if some good might come from this rapprochement.

'Cock-a-doodle-doo!' Edouard was still larking around with the boys. 'Cock-a-doodle-doo!'

'Mama, Mama, Mama, Mama?' Lolo was jumping up and down, pulling at Marcella's skirt. 'Can we take the chicken with us, to show Papa?'

'No, darling. We're going to leave it here.' Marcella walked out to the front of the house and sat on the step with the children. 'Don't worry, sweetheart. You'll see it again soon enough.'

'When will we come back to see you?' asked Lolo, fiddling with a stray curl of Marcella's which had fallen on to her shoulder.

'Tuesday,' she replied, kissing his cheek.

'When's Tuesday?'

'You go now and sleep tonight. Then tomorrow you see Papa. Then you sleep again. And when you wake up, you're coming back to see me.'

'And the chicken!' cried Lolo.

'Cock-a-doodle-doo!' Edouard hollered.

'Yes,' Marcella laughed. 'And the chicken!'

'Lump!' added Edmond.

Marcella hugged them both close.

CHAPTER 20

Tuesday 9 April 1912, Nice

On Easter Monday, Marcella had busied herself tidying up after the party. She had had a skirt to sew. She was working on commission for her aunt now, in order to have enough money to treat the children, to keep herself in food and pay the rent.

When she'd finished the work, she baked a cake, ready for the return of the boys.

Tuesday morning arrived.

Upon hearing the gate click and footsteps coming up the front path, Marcella ran downstairs from the kitchen to open the front door.

Her aunt stood on the doorstep, brandishing an Easter brioche, dotted with sparkling crystals of sugar and little brightly coloured eggs.

'I thought the boys might like this.'

Marcella glanced down the path and around the sunny front garden, hoping to see the children jump out from behind a flowerpot.

There was a short pause.

Then Thérèse asked brightly, 'They are here with you, Marcella?'

There was a hesitation in her aunt's voice that frightened her.

'Who?' she replied. 'Are who with me?'

'The children. Are they here?'

'They should be with you, Aunt Thérèse.' Marcella's mouth went dry. Her knees buckled. 'Why? Why aren't they?'

Marcella watched the colour drain from her aunt's face.

'What's happened? Oh no. Something's happened!' Marcella reached out and grabbed the handle of the front door to steady herself. 'They're not hurt, are they?'

'No, no, I'm sure they're fine, Marcella.' Thérèse's voice was level now. She sounded much calmer than she looked.

'So why haven't you brought them?' Marcella felt dizzy – what of a hundred reasons could have prevented her children coming here today?

'I… I…' Aunt Thérèse hunched up her shoulders, lost for words. 'There was nothing I could do, Marcella.'

Now Marcella was really scared.

'Yesterday Michael took them. He…'

Marcella knew all this. Yesterday was her husband's day with the children.

'So… If they are not here with you, then he still has them.'

Aunt Thérèse put her face in her hands.

A new type of fear flooded Marcella.

'But Michael was due to bring them back to you last night. He did bring them back, Aunt Thérèse? Didn't he?'

Aunt Thérèse remained silent.

'Tell me!' Marcella stepped down on to the path.

Thérèse moved back and threw her hands up.

'No. No, he didn't. But—'

'Then why didn't you report them missing last night?' Marcella yelled so loud that a passer-by, out in the street, beyond the fence, turned to look. 'You should have reported him to the police. Why wait till now?'

'No, no. When Michael collected them – it was his day, after all… Well, as he lifted them into the taxi, he told me that at the end of the afternoon he would drop them with you. A special Easter treat, to let you have them overnight.'

'But you know that's not allowed. They're not allowed to stay with either of us overnight. It was a ploy.'

'I didn't think.' Thérèse had started shaking. 'I had no reason to doubt him. After all, Cimiez is only up the way from here and…' She raised her hand, pointing first to the hill behind Marcella's garden, then placing it across her mouth, as though stopping the words would make the reality untrue.

'He said he'd bumped into Ton-ton and that Ton-ton had suggested it.' To Marcella this whole thing sounded like a lie. A typical Michael lie. Convincing at the time, no doubt delivered with his flashing handsome smile, but a lie, nonetheless.

'I couldn't stop him taking them, Marcella. He was always going to have them on Monday and you on Tuesday. And the boys were so excited to be going to a party with their father. When he didn't come back last night, I just thought he had done what he said he was going to do… And that he'd brought them to you.'

Marcella ran her fingers through her hair. What to do next?

'What time yesterday did he come to you?'

'Right after breakfast,' Thérèse replied quietly. 'Around nine thirty, ten…'

Marcella's heart was thumping. She had to calm down, to think clearly.

'It was only when I was getting up this morning that I started to wonder if it wasn't a little strange…' As Thérèse blundered on, high up, on the viaduct behind the house, a train puffed past, heading towards Monte Carlo, Menton, Italy. Thérèse had to raise her voice to be heard. '…Michael's change of character, his softening towards you. So I got Raphaël to give me a lift up here…'

Marcella glanced over her aunt's shoulder and saw her cousin out on the road, perched on the driver's seat of his painter's wagon, waiting. A motor car went past, blaring its horn, startling Raphaël's old horse.

'I just needed to make sure that they were here.'

'But they're not here, Aunt Thérèse,' Marcella was shouting now. 'Michael didn't come here *at all* yesterday. I haven't seen him since January, when we were last in court.'

The church clock up the road struck nine. Michael had had the boys for almost twenty-four hours! You can travel a long, long way in a day.

'My God, Aunt Thérèse,' Marcella couldn't stop her voice quivering, 'what have you done?'

Thérèse Magaïl looked down at her feet.

'You let him take them away,' Marcella cried. 'You let him steal my children.'

'We'll find them, Marcella. Come on. Raphaël will help us. Perhaps Michael simply overslept—'

'No, Aunt Thérèse.' Marcella grabbed her aunt by the elbow and looked straight into her eyes. 'We both know what Michael is capable of. He has taken them. He will make sure that I never see them again.'

Michael

CHAPTER 21

Tuesday 9 April 1912, Calais

As Michael climbed off the train at Calais Gare Maritime, the wind was whipping up. For the whole journey he had been looking forward to the fresh air, especially after Monmon had had a nasty accident in his pants when they didn't manage to reach the WC at the end of the carriage in time. Michael had spent the best part of the Lille to Calais hour wiping Monmon's bottom. But out in the open air, Michael felt vulnerable. It had felt safe enough in the sleeper cabin with the curtains drawn, but not now, looking along a crowded platform. There were so many people getting off the train. His fellow travellers were concerned with their luggage, finding porters, pulling out their tickets and papers for the boat – surely they were too busy to notice him and the children. In this throng they would be safely hidden in plain view.

'I'm tired, Papa,' cried Lolo, as Michael, case in one hand, traipsed along the platform.

'You still like boats, don't you?'

'Boats,' said Edmond as Lolo shrugged.

'Well, we're going on a boat.'

'Now?'

'Now!'

Lolo jumped up and down, and Edmond as usual copied what Lolo did.

Michael had been slow getting off. It appeared that their carriage was the wrong end of the train too, as they now found themselves towards the back of a very long queue. The people ahead trundled forward, disappearing slowly into the small embarkation building.

While they were waiting, Michael checked all his pockets for things he would need today. He had the passport. He had a voucher for English money, which he knew he had to pick up at the Thomas Cook office when he got the ongoing tickets. Ludgate Circus. Michael wondered why it was called Circus. Would he be able to promise the children clowns as well? Anything to keep them quiet.

In his trouser pocket he found Saturday's damned letter and that got his blood boiling again. Well. He had evaded all that now. It was behind him. He tore the letter into little pieces and dropped it into a waste bin as they all shuffled forward.

Just as Michael got within metres of the entrance, with no warning, Monmon flung himself down and sprawled out on the dusty grey platform.

'Get up!' Michael muttered. 'Get up!'

Having travelled more than 1,200 kilometres without once attracting attention, he didn't want to start now.

'I'm tired, Papa,' wailed Edmond.

'Don't be silly, Monmon. You've been sitting down for hours. You can walk this short way.'

'You need to get the pushchair out, Papa.' Lolo looked up at Michael as though he could produce a pushchair from thin air.

'We don't have it.'

'You should have brought one,' said Lolo, as if it was the most obvious thing in the world. And truly, Michael wondered why hadn't he got a damned pushchair? It would have made his life so much easier. He had thought ahead well enough when he and Stefan had sat up all night on Saturday creating a collection of outfits for the boys. For weeks he'd also told the new apprentice, Raymond, to run up a set of children's clothes, telling him that working in miniature would hone his skill.

Michael laughed at his accidental ingenuity. Raymond's tiny suits were only meant for when Lolo and Monmon were seen out with him, but...

'Porter, monsieur?' A rough-looking fellow, prowling the platform for custom, porter's cap tilted to one side, stood before them wielding a barrow.

Michael hesitated. It would be more noticeable to refuse. Especially now that Monmon had decided to make a drama of himself.

'Please,' he said, shaking his head and rolling his eyes for sympathy. 'Two-year-olds!'

'It's that age, monsieur, you're right.' Throwing the case on to his barrow, the porter pushed his cap back and walked towards the embarkation hall.

'Lots of white horses on show this afternoon, eh, monsieur? Your crossing might be a little on the rocky side.'

Michael didn't want to get drawn into a conversation, even if it just was small talk about the weather, so said nothing.

'Will there be horses on the boat?' asked Lolo.

'There we go, sir. Figures of speech.' The porter threw Lolo a glance and laughed. 'Explain that one away!'

They arrived inside the main embarkation hall.

Now came the customs and passport moment.

The officer scratched a chalk mark on the suitcase then waved the porter to take it on ahead, while the dock official asked for Michael's tickets and papers.

Tickets first.

All in order.

Michael pulled the passport from his pocket and handed it over.

Realising that he was holding his breath and that it must look suspicious, he gently patted Lolo on the head and said, 'We'll be onboard any minute, little man. Don't worry.' He glanced at the customs officer. 'He's a bit overexcited. It'll be his first time on a boat.'

The man looked down at Lolo and smiled. 'Wow! I remember my first voyage. Watch out for seagulls, young man! Bon voyage, boys!' He handed the tickets and papers back to Michael. 'And bon voyage to you too, Monsieur Hoffman.'

Michael was starving. He had been really looking forward to lunch.

But the moment the ferry left the harbour, for all his professed love of boats, Lolo had started being violently sick.

After the first eruption, Michael took both children out of the comfortable warm passenger lounge and up on to the cold outer deck.

It was drizzling and the wind whipped their hair.

Misery.

One set of Lolo's clothing was now totally ruined. Michael's own trousers needed a good wash too. He knew he'd have to spend the whole train journey from Dover to London bent over the basin in the WC, washing the jacket and shorts and sponging down his own clothes. He couldn't arrive at the hotel looking like this. It would be totally memorable to any desk clerk.

Once the children were settled, he planned to dry everything out tonight on the hotel radiators. According to the brochure, the place boasted all luxuries, including central heating, so there had to be radiators somewhere.

Now everything they were wearing smelled horrible.

What an impression he'd make! A stinking man with vomit-flecked trousers.

Lolo wasn't the only person onboard who was being seasick. Many adults were up on deck, green-faced, heaving into buckets. It was far from a charming place to be.

'Where's Mama?' groaned Lolo. 'I want Mama.'

The child started to cry. Then, as soon as Monmon saw Lolo crying, of course he echoed him, only much louder.

'Mamaaaaaa!' Monmon wailed. 'Mamaaaaaa! I want my mamaaaaaa!'

Michael put his hand to his brow.

Now everyone was looking at them.

A woman bustled over. 'Could I be of any assistance, sir?'

Michael would like to have told her to get lost, but now that she was here he knew he had to say something. He stood and whispered into her ear. 'So sad. Their poor mother died a few days ago. Tuberculosis. I am taking them to their aunt in Liverpool.'

'Mamaaaaaa!' It was as though Monmon knew how to play the part to perfection. 'Maaaaaaaaaaaaamaaaaaaaaaaaaaaaa!'

The woman gazed down sympathetically at Monmon, utterly anguished by Michael's invented saga.

'Poor little mites. So young for such a terrible—'

Michael put his finger to his lips.

'Want food, Papa!' Monmon looked up pitifully at the woman while still clinging to Michael's leg. 'Hungry Monmon. Monmon hungry.'

He wasn't the only one, thought Michael. Monmon might be baying for lunch but so was his own stomach, which growled fiercely.

'The one thing I might ask you, madam, if you could be so kind. We were due to take lunch aboard but... obviously...' He indicated Lolo. 'I wonder whether you might see if it's possible for someone to bring us a sandwich or a bar of chocolate. Anything we could eat out here.'

'Oh why, of course,' said the woman. Michael plunged his hand into his inside pocket, pulled out his wallet and gave her a note.

As she rushed off, he looked towards the prow of the boat. Michael realised that this was the longest time he had ever spent alone with the boys.

It was all right for Marcella. She liked baby-talk and seemed to revel in their company. But it was different for a man. Michael felt utterly exhausted and further wearied by the banality of the conversations he was forced to have – not only with the children, it seemed, but even with total strangers.

At last. Through the mist he could see the white cliffs of Dover. No more *flics*.

England! From now on it would only be British coppers he had to be wary of and, with them, he could always play the dumb foreigner with no communication skills.

Lolo retched again. But now his stomach was empty. A long string of dribble, caught in the wind, flung itself across Michael's new grey coat. It had even stained the flap of jade-green lining.

Oh hell!

———

An hour later the ferry was tied up and the passengers started disembarking.

'Mama has got a chicken,' said Monmon out of nowhere as they joined the crowd tottering down the steep gangplank.

'We're going to see it today,' said Lolo. 'Are you taking us there?'

Michael pressed his coat pocket to check for the passport.

Louis Michel Hoffman. Louis Michel Hoffman.

Same age, same colour hair, moustache, not much difference in height. Though Michael knew that he was handsome, while Louis… Well, best not go to *that*.

Fancy, though! Fancy old Louis Hoffman turning up on the scene, and inviting him to Easter lunch! What a miracle of timing. It couldn't have worked out better.

What serendipity. Saturday morning, 6 April, minutes after he had read that bloody letter telling him he was about to be declared bankrupt, out of the blue, Louis arrived at the shop, saying that it was time they made up their quarrel and would Michael come to lunch at his mother's house on Monday.

Rather than laughing in his face, Michael had had one of those inspired moments. Out of the darkness he saw a clear path opening before him.

With the bankruptcy set for 23 April, and the final divorce hearing to be held the same week, he didn't have much time.

After Hoffman had bustled off, looking all important and Parisian, Michael had put Stefan in charge and gone to see Camille, as planned, in Monte Carlo. Her husband was on business in Italy for the weekend. Some meeting in San Remo, she'd said. So they decided on meeting up at the Hôtel de Paris, a nice place, and impersonal.

They took a table in the American Bar and ordered some drinks. He blurted out some of his problems to her, mainly the visitation and divorce stuff with Marcella. Nothing about the bankruptcy, of course. Women didn't like to hear about failure. However, he knew that women always love to hear how awful the last woman had been.

He was really enjoying her company, and wondering whether he dared suggest getting a room for the afternoon, when suddenly some loud woman, reeking of perfume and indiscretion, came rushing over to their table.

'My darling Camille!' she exclaimed. 'Fancy bumping into you in here, of all places!' She bent low and whispered into Camille's ear.

Michael dreaded what she might be saying.

'No, no, no!' Camille hurriedly stood up. 'Nothing like that, Bernice! I just saw my tailor sitting all alone over here and thought it would be rude to ignore him. Poor fellow.' She looked pityingly down at Michael, who knew to play the role as she described it. 'He's been stood up, poor man. Thought he was here to snare a rich American customer, and make his fortune creating haute couture models for him to take back to Appalachia or Arizona or somewhere, but alas, the sly American has already moved on to Cannes and pastures new, leaving him nothing but a message with the bellboy!' She turned and held out her hand for Michael to kiss it in a suitably obsequious tailorly way. 'Good luck, monsieur. I hope all goes well for the rest of the day after your wasted journey.'

Michael liked the way she had thought *not* to use his name. He also enjoyed the way that, as she walked away with Bernice, Camille put her hand behind her back and crossed her fingers.

And then, just as the waiter arrived at the table with their two drinks, she was gone.

Now Michael was utterly depressed.

Wasted his time and his money too. Lucky he hadn't splashed out on that hotel room. That would really have added insult to injury.

After knocking back both glasses of Martini, Michael left the bar.

He stood aimlessly for a moment in the hotel foyer. What to do now? He had so little time to act.

He had to get away. But where to go?

Opposite the bar, lining the other side of the hotel foyer, stood a row of shops – jewellers and specialists in travel goods. Smack in the middle of them, was a small agency with a huge painted banner across the front window: COOK'S TOURS – VOYAGES TO ALL PARTS OF THE WORLD. The lower panel of the door read: SALOON AND EMIGRANT TICKETS SOLD AT TARIFF RATES. Whatever that meant.

International tickets! Even better, this shop was not in France, therefore not under the jurisdiction of the French police. He was in Monaco now. A shop, inside a hotel, inside another country. What could be more perfect?

He entered the travel agent's and asked if they had any bargains.

The clerk suggested a destination.

'Would that be for two adults, sir?'

'Just the one.' Michael's mind raced. Perhaps… Why not? That would show her! And, after all, they were the fruit of his loins. He'd be bringing his own two boys with him, to inherit his new business, and then, as they grew up, they could work alongside him in the shop.

'Oh – and two children. We can share the same compartment.'

'All the way?'

'How much would that cost?'

'First or Second Class?'

'Second.'

One adult, two children. That would be twenty-six pounds.' The clerk ran his fingers over a desktop adding machine. 'I'll just convert that into francs for you, sir.' He scribbled down a figure.

It was as easy as that.

Cheap at the price, thought Michael, handing over the money.

'Name…?'

Michael hesitated.

Then out it came: 'Louis Hoffman.'

The clerk behind the desk stamped the paperwork and presented him with an envelope containing his order.

'Once you're in London, Monsieur Hoffman, you'll pick up the actual tickets from our central office. While you're here, would you like to arrange some foreign currency?'

Why not be prepared? he thought. Then the money could be waiting for him in London and no eyebrows raised.

'Don't forget to bring your passport with you, will you, Monsieur Hoffman.'

Oh God!

What an idea!

This plan was getting better and better.

Now he simply had to arrange things with Stefan and, above all, get that passport.

When Michael got back to Nice he went straight to the shop to tell Stefan his plan. They sat at a pavement table in the café on the corner.

'We work together now, Stefan. This is our secret, yours and mine. You'll move immediately into the flat upstairs, and, when no one's looking, get as much of the valuable stuff up there as you can manage. Make it seem normal in the shop, but rescue the pricey stuff from the grasping hands of the bailiffs. I'll keep in touch all along the way. Then, when things are right, you follow me. There's just one little thing I need you to do… On Monday. Up at Hoffman's place.'

Michael laughed to himself at the memory of Stefan's face as he emerged from a supposed trip to the bathroom in Hoffman's mother's flat; seeing him tap his pocket – the sign that he had found the passport and had it safely stowed.

Louis Hoffman wouldn't miss it, that was sure. Why should he? He'd said he'd be down in Nice for the rest of the spring and summer, staying with his mother. And anyway, you didn't need a passport to travel between Nice and Paris, and where else was he thinking of heading?

He'd stay there in so-very-polite Cimiez, where Queen Victoria had always holidayed, high up above the heat and clamour of Nice. According to the local papers, the council was about to erect a statue of both the fat little English queen and her playboy son in celebration of the *entente cordiale* between France and England.

The children had spent the afternoon bouncing about the old-lady Hoffman's apartment, totally bored. They had provided an excellent smokescreen for Stefan while he went on the search. Louis and his mother had been so busy saving crystal candelabra and Sèvres porcelain figures from toppling off the lace-clothed tables, and rescuing the poor ancient cat from the toddler's sticky grip, that no one noticed quite how long Stefan had spent in the toilet.

Once Michael knew Stefan had got the passport, it was all systems go.

They took their leave of the Hoffmans, mother and gullible son.

In the hall, after sealing a deal in which Louis bought a fifty per cent share of the business in Rue de France for a mere one hundred francs, cash, he and Michael shook hands.

What business?

All hot air, really!

One hundred francs for nothing!

Michael's business was done for.

Even that old bat Magaïl was struggling to survive, he'd heard. Closing up the shop in Place Grimaldi and going to work from home in some dingy flat on the other side of town. Even old Giraud had finally pulled down the shutters, and none of the silly daughters had put up a fight to save the family business.

But now he, Michael Navratil, had almost one hundred extra francs in his pocket and something to look forward to.

England beckoned.

And, with England, the dream of a bright and positive future for himself and his two sons.

Michael and his boys were finally on the quayside. But ahead of them the customs queue was long and slow. Michael hoped they wouldn't ask to look inside the case. If they found the gun they'd probably be suspicious, and if they found the money as well...

The immigration officer glanced casually at the passport, stamped it and waved them through.

Behind the oak inspection table, further officers stood in line, weighing people up. As Michael filed slowly past them, in an attempt to seem nonchalant, he talked constantly to the children.

'Mr Hoffman?'

Michael was asking Lolo if he was feeling a little better now that he was off the ferry.

'Mr Hoffman!'

Hoffman! Oh no! That was him! Michael had forgotten that he should respond to that name as though it was his own.

He turned. 'I'm so sorry... yes?' His heart was thumping.

'Mr Hoffman...'

Michael nodded.

'I wonder whether you would follow me through to the back room?'

Oh God.

They'd rumbled him.

How?

How?

The officer took the suitcase and walked ahead.

'Come on, boys.' Michael strolled along trying to look casual.

If they had anything on him he'd claim mistaken identity.

After all, he was Louis Michel Hoffman, wasn't he? Who was Michael Navratil?

'That's right, kids. Follow the nice gentleman.'

Closing the door, the officer turned to face Michael.

'I was looking for you as you passed through customs.'

Michael blinked.

Don't react.

Don't say anything.

Just play it out.

Stay calm.

Let them make all the running.

'I noticed that your clothes—'

They were dressed too smartly. That was it. They'd know that only a tailor would care so much—

'You hadn't probably planned for all this, I suspect.'

No.

He hadn't.

Michael smiled and tried to look innocent but puzzled.

'Well, sir, I don't suppose you'd be thinking you would be stopped here, at all, did you?'

Michael shook his head.

What to say now?

Put his hands up and admit it?

No. He couldn't do that.

Not with all the money he'd taken, and the bankruptcy hounds baying for his blood.

He had to bluff it through.

'I don't think you want to carry on like this, do you? You see, I know all about the little ones.'

Oh God!

The bitch had got him this soon.

How could she have managed it?

Michael knew the game was up.

'All right, I… But it wasn't—'

'It must be hard, Mr Hoffman. Especially for a widower like yourself. My wife was onboard the ferry with you, you see. She whispered to me that she'd done her best to help you cope with a bouncing two-year-old and a very seasick lad. So I was looking out for you. Took one look and I thought to myself, Reggie, if you yourself were in such a sorry state of dress, would you want to board the train looking like that? No, Reggie. You would not.'

Michael wasn't sure if the man was trying to be funny.

He was smiling, though, so Michael smiled back.

'So, anyway, Mr Hoffman, I thought you'd like a little help. Now, would you like to use the sink in here to clean up a little before the onward journey?' He fished a watch from his top pocket. 'You have a good ten minutes till she pulls out.'

CHAPTER 22

Wednesday 10 April 1912, London
As Michael stepped down from the cab he heard the crack of a flashgun. At first he imagined it was something that had gone wrong with Waterloo station's electric lighting, but then he saw the man under his cloak, holding up the flash.

Photographers!

That was not something Michael had been expecting.

This particular one was photographing a woman, who posed before him beside a large cabin trunk (and wearing rather a stunning blue fox-collared travelling coat). In her arms she was cradling a Pekingese.

Naturally, both children wanted to play with the dog.

It must not happen. He didn't want some photograph of them going into a newspaper. Things could spread very quickly, and then all this effort and expense would be in vain... It wasn't worth thinking about.

Gripping Lolo's hand, Michael scooped Edmond up into his other arm. But how to carry the luggage too? It was another of those moments when a porter was called for. Lucky for him one ran forward with his trolley and grabbed Michael's suitcase.

'Boat train, sir?'

Michael nodded.

'Platform 12.'

The little group walked through the station entrance as quickly as possible, Michael hiding his face behind Monmon's body. But as they came into the main concourse, the child reached back over his shoulder towards the dog and started bawling.

Did children do nothing but vomit and squawk?

There were far more people here than he was expecting. Ahead of them, a huge crowd was pressing forward.

'Sorry about this, sir, but we have to fight our way through this lot. Number 12 is right over there.'

The porter nodded his head in the direction of the platform – as though Michael couldn't guess simply by looking towards the area with the most commotion.

'You're lucky to be on this early train, sir. It's going to get much worse. There's two hours before all the First Class celebrities arrive. This rowdy bunch is just warming up for the big moment.'

A deafening clamour of conversation echoed around the vaulted glass roof. Michael could see that very few among the assembly were intending to take the train. No. They were here to *look* at the people who were boarding.

As Michael got nearer the platform, he was relieved to see an unofficial pathway cut through the crowd.

Beautiful women draped in fabulous furs, accompanied by cigar-smoking men in Savile Row suits, were strolling along that route.

And all along the way cameras were popping, and journalists, notepads in hand, shouted out questions, grabbing people at random to ask them how excited they were.

Some of those voyagers were actually stopping to pose. A plump woman in an unsuitably large feathered hat stood chatting to some hack, while, behind her, her husband leaned patiently on his silver-topped ebony cane. So many potential customers! Michael felt sorry he hadn't had the time or the idea to have business cards printed. He envied the man having that silver cane. He'd get himself one soon. How distinguished it would make him look.

'Who are these people, Papa? Is it the Carnaval?'

Ahead, a blockage of passengers shoved towards the barriers.

'Ticket holders only, please,' cried a bearded man in uniform. 'All ticket holders this way!'

Michael felt oncoming cramp from holding his forearm wrapped around Monmon in the same position too long.

'Give me the tickets, sir,' said the porter. 'We'll get through faster.'

Michael had to move Monmon on to the other arm to reach into his pocket for the tickets. And that involved letting go of Lolo for an instant.

That tiny moment was all Lolo needed to be able to run off, attracted by the same stupid woman in her fur-collared coat, and her Pekingese.

Michael stumbled forward, trying to catch the child. But there was too much of a crush and Lolo was small enough to scamper through people's legs.

Monmon knew his cue and started shrieking.

Michael didn't want to yell Lolo's name. Chances were it could be just that, which somehow got mentioned in the newspapers.

The porter shouted, 'Give me the nipper, sir.'

Michael had no idea what he was talking about, but handed him Monmon and ran forward.

Lolo was in the middle of a scrum of people.

To reach his son and grab him, the only way left was brute force. The hat woman rounded on him.

'Pardon me, my man, but we're all in a hurry. Perhaps you might learn some manners.'

'I'm sorry, madam. But my little boy, who is not even four years old, just ran through and I'm trying to reach him before I lose him absolutely.'

'Foreigners! All the same. Brutes!' The woman gave Michael a contemptuous sneer and let him pass.

———

The porter stepped aboard the train with the suitcase while the carriage guard stopped Michael to examine the tickets. 'Madam not travelling with you, sir?'

Michael was startled by this remark, until he worked out that travelling alone with two children was in itself something out of the ordinary.

'She's gone on ahead,' he said, in English, safe in the knowledge that the boys wouldn't understand. 'With the dogs.'

The guard nodded, understanding.

'Is Mama on the train?' asked Lolo, straining forward. 'I wonder if she brought the chicken.'

'Stop going on about that bloody chicken.' The words had spilled out of his mouth before he knew it.

The guard gave him a look, registering Michael's tone, if not the meaning of his words.

Michael hurried on, and climbed aboard the train. The porter was inside, in the corridor, pointing in towards a compartment with three empty seats.

'Stowed the case up there, sir.' He indicated a net over the passengers' heads. While Michael paid him, Lolo went in and climbed on to one of the seats.

'Awfully sorry about that.' A languid man in spectacles removed his satchel from the place beside him. 'Today is quite a thing, isn't it?'

It was decision time. Everyone who was travelling on this train was heading in the same direction. What's more, as this was the Second Class train, all the passengers onboard would be travelling in the same section of the ship as himself and the children: the Second Class. If he got drawn in by anyone now, he really would be stuck in their orbit for a whole week. From his time in Vienna and in his own shop, Michael knew that the British were obsessed with small talk. They could spend hours blabbering on about absolutely nothing. His best plan was to pretend not to understand English.

But which language would it be best for him to adopt?

What the hell was Hoffman? From the accent, he thought German. But he was not going to pull out the passport to check.

'Where's Mama?' said Edmond in French.

Well, that was it, then. Despite being Austro-Hungarian by birth, and German by passport, for the next week Michael would be French.

'*Ah! Comprends!*' said the man. '*Français!*' He stopped there.

Michael hoped the fellow wasn't going to get any further practising his language skills.

And he was in luck.

Fortuitously a lady opposite started up a conversation with the spectacled man and Michael enjoyed listening in.

'I'm a teacher, actually,' said the man. 'Heading off to see my brother in Toronto. Just luck that I got tickets for this one.'

'What do you teach?'

'Science,' he replied. 'At Dulwich College.'

'Oh, Dulwich! That's a lovely part of London. Country, and yet town, all in one. I'm on D deck. How about you?'

'D also.'

'D for Dulwich!'

Michael was glad to hear this, as he was pretty sure he and the boys were on F.

'Papa? Why are these people talking funny?'

'They're English.' Michael laughed. 'It's a different kind of person and they speak differently to us.'

'Looks as though the weather is going to be good,' said the teacher.

'Yes. It's cloudy. But there's no wind forecast. Nor rain.'

'Now, boys,' said Michael. 'Let's look out of the window. And when one of you sees a cow, you can shout out "cow!". How about that?'

While the children pressed their faces against the glass, Michael sat back and closed his eyes. It was time to take a brief nap.

They were almost there.

If the crush at Waterloo station had been bad, it was nothing compared to the frenzy at Southampton. People had got into the train individually. But they all got off at once. And meanwhile, simultaneously, other trains, coaches and cars were spilling people out on to the forecourt of the Southampton dock building.

By the time Michael had woken the children, got the suitcases from the overhead rack and stepped down from the train, a huge crowd was already pressing into the embarkation hall.

Gripping Edmond's hand and ordering Lolo to stand close, he joined the throng, eventually squeezing through the main doors and getting in line with the others.

At this point it was obligatory to stay with your luggage. Michael lugged it up on to the long mahogany customs bench and slid it forward.

Around him gaggles of people, all dressed in very smart clothing, huddled together, chatting gaily.

The sound of laughter reverberated throughout the elegant hall.

As though to make things feel even better, a nearby band struck up, playing jolly tunes.

Another chalk mark was scratched on to his suitcase, and Michael was waved to the end of the line. A porter stepped forward and loaded the case on to his trolley.

'I can take it straight to your cabin, Mr Hoffman.'

He lingered. Michael took the cue and handed him some money.

The porter pocketed the cash and moved briskly away.

Michael noticed that there were policemen everywhere, dotted among the well-wishers, journalists and voyagers.

He prayed that they weren't going to jump him before he got aboard.

Holding his head down, Michael moved on, marching through the embarkation hall and out on to the quay.

It was only when he looked up that he saw for himself what all the fuss was about.

The ship before him was magnificent.

A giant of the seas.

He stooped to whisper into Lolo's ear. 'If you like ships, Lolo, this is the one to see. There's never been a steamer as great as this, never, ever before.'

Lolo looked puzzled. 'I can't see a ship, Papa,' he said. 'I can only see a big black wall.'

Michael laughed.

He supposed that, from Lolo's point of view, that is all you'd be able to see. A huge black wall pierced with a thousand little round windows. Above, white railings and four yellow funnels.

'That's because it's so big you can't see it all at once.'

Michael, however, took a good look, and drank in the sight. The ship was a vast, elegant piece of perfection.

A whistle blew near his ear, and a man started bellowing through a megaphone. 'Second Class passengers, please make your way up the gangways immediately. If you don't want to get left on the quay-side, please make your way onboard. We sail at noon.'

Monmon was again pointing excitedly, this time six various dogs at the end of straining leashes attached to a young bellboy. The poor lad was struggling to keep control because each dog was pulling in a different direction.

'Doggies!' cried Monmon.

Someone tapped Michael on the shoulder.

He dug into his pocket and spun round, fearful that the police were going to grab him at this late moment. He was prepared to fight them off.

'*Incroyable, n'est pas?*'

It was only the English science teacher.

Michael let go of the gun.

'Once we're inside we'll never see it like this again, because we'll be inside it, and it will simply seem like a grand hotel, what?' The man put his hand to his mouth. 'Oh, *pardonez moi*, monsieur. I had forgotten – *oubliez* – *mon français. Oui!*' He stooped to address the children. '*Bonjour, mes élèves!*' Then back to Michael. '*Bon bateau!*' he said, pointing to the ship. '*Très, très bon!*'

Michael smiled inanely in what he hoped would be perceived as a French way.

'See you aboard… *en bateau!*' The teacher tipped his hat, and took his leave. '*Au revoir, tous les trois!*'

If only it really was goodbye, thought Michael, but the likelihood was that he would be forever bumping into this infuriating British nincompoop.

Michael watched the man stride up the ramp and disappear into the steamer.

'Right, boys. The time has come.' Michael gripped each child by the hand. 'Let's go!'

Now to leave Europe. Once he crossed that strip of water, that was it. Next stop New York!

'No, Papa!' Monmon was pulling away, dragging himself on the floor, refusing to budge, heels in, like a donkey. Michael tugged but the child just slid across the dusty paving stones. 'Nooooooo! Papaaaaaaa! Monmon wants to see doggies!'

Michael stooped down and hauled the screaming child up into one arm.

'I promise you, Monmon, we'll see plenty of doggies. The doggies are going onboard too. They'll all be taking their daily promenade on the decks. Come on!' That stupid Englishman was right about the ship, he thought.

'Drink in this wondrous sight, boys. Stamp it into your memory. We are about to go onboard the greatest ship in the whole wide world.' He kissed Monmon's cheek and patted Lolo's shoulder.

'Carry me too!' Lolo yanked Michael's jacket.

Michael placed Monmon back on the ground, then let Lolo climb up on his shoulders. Now, taking Monmon again in his arms, Michael stepped forward and started his long walk up the wooden gangway.

As he reached the point between the dockside and the ship, he glanced at the water.

It was so far down.

'Here we go, boys. The start of a brand-new life.' One more step and they were aboard.

Two rows of uniformed crew and stewards lined the hallway.

'Good morning, Mister Hoffman.' One of the men tipped his hat. 'Welcome aboard the greatest steamship afloat. Welcome to RMS *Titanic*.'

CHAPTER 23

Wednesday 10 April 1912, onboard RMS Titanic

Their cabin was nice enough. A sturdy set of mahogany bunks, a washbasin with running water and a comfortable sofa in a floral moquette.

Michael felt that he'd be quite happy, hiding away in here for a week.

He was glad there was a writing desk and chair. He had lots of letters to write and he needed to write them today so that he could get them posted when the steamer called at Cherbourg, later this afternoon. Michael checked his watch: 11.43 a.m. Only a quarter of an hour and the ship would be upping anchor, pulling in the lines and navigating into the Channel, and away from England.

He chuckled to himself. If anyone had thought that he was heading to New York and beyond, they would be expecting him to board the ship in Cherbourg. If the alarm had been sounded, the ticket and customs control at Cherbourg would now be buzzing with people looking out for him and the two boys arriving from one of the boat trains from Gare Saint-Lazare. Their reasoning was obvious. Why would a man in a hurry make a huge detour to Calais, Dover, London and Southampton when he could have gone from Nice to Paris then on to Cherbourg to catch the ship? Michael reckoned that if they'd worked out that he was heading for America, there would be a line of gendarmes looking for him on the dockside of Cherbourg.

He could watch them from the upper deck.

The joke was, that he hadn't really thought it out as a plan. When he was in Monte Carlo buying the tickets, the young lad had simply presumed he'd want to board at the start of the voyage.

But now the complexity of the journey seemed genius.

He looked at the brochure. They were to dock at Cherbourg this evening at six thirty. That gave him quite enough time to write to his mother and to telegraph Stefan.

He wondered whether Stefan would have got all the valuable things out of the shop and upstairs by now. He trusted him to leave just enough rubbish downstairs so that the shop looked normal when the bailiffs arrived. Meanwhile, he hoped he'd whipped all the expensive stuff – riding coats, evening dresses, mannequins, the upholstered chairs, irons, sewing machines – and piled it up in the flat. He giggled to himself, thinking how he and Stefan, a pair of Hungarian renegades, would have the last laugh on all of them.

'Is this another train, Papa?' Lolo sounded as bored as hell. 'We've had enough trains today.'

'No, Lolo. This is a ship. And once we've settled into our room here, we'll go and explore. How about that? There'll be lots to discover.'

Lolo shrugged. He was not convinced.

'I'm hungry, Papa. Can we have lunch soon, please?'

Michael looked at the boy. Was letting him eat now a good idea? Might he be seasick for the whole six-day voyage? Michael had barely coped during a trip of a little over an hour, even with unsolicited but indispensable help. How would he cope on his own for the best part of a week? He glanced down at the floor. Thank God it was linoleum.

Michael heard the sonorous boom of the ship's whistle. He could certainly feel slight movement and the shuddering hum of the engines had got stronger. Yes, a definite, though almost imperceptible, rocking. Everyone must be aboard, the gangways up. The steamer had started its long voyage to… well… to the future.

To Freedom and a New Start!

A knock on the door.

Suddenly, once again, Michael was all nerves.

He called out, 'Who is it?' As though the police would announce themselves – when would he ever learn?

'Your steward, Mr Hoffman.'

Michael opened up.

'Just wondering if you or the children needed anything.'

'Very kind, but no.'

'The bathrooms are at the end of the corridor. If you need me at all you'll find me around the place all day and at night my colleague will be walking the corridors.'

'Thank you.' Michael was unsure whether this was another moment when he was supposed to tip. But he couldn't go on tipping every time someone opened their mouth or came knocking unsummoned at his door. 'Where are the public rooms?'

'Up a couple of decks you'll find the library, which is the main saloon here in Second Class; along from that, the dining room. There is also a smoking room – for gentlemen only, of course. That's right up top.'

'Thank you.'

The man lingered still.

Reluctantly Michael pulled some coins from his pocket and pressed them into the steward's hand. The man smiled and walked away.

Michael closed the door.

'Who was that, Papa?' Lolo stood, hands on hips, indignant.

'That's the steward, Lolo. He's here to fetch us things and help us.'

Lolo gave a shrug of indifference.

Meanwhile, Monmon had crawled up on to the lower bunk. 'My bed,' he announced.

'No, Monmon!' Lolo turned, irate. 'It's *my* bed!' He too got on to the bed and stood up, his head scraping the bottom of the bunk above.

'It's a bed for both of you. One each end. Or side by side. Whichever you fancy.'

The engines were running high. Things on surfaces – pens, toiletries – started to quiver from the vibration. Michael imagined the ship surging forward out of its berth, pulling out into the deep water.

They really were moving now, moving towards a bright new future!

Michael threw himself on to the lower bunk with the boys and tickled both children until they were breathless with excitement.

Then he lay back on the bunk with a child snuggled into each arm.

Suddenly there was a slight jar.

The engines stopped.

Everything was still.

Surely they couldn't be more than a few yards from the dockside.

Why had they stopped?

It was the police, wasn't it?

At the last minute, they were coming onboard. But they'd chosen to do it now that the ship was away from the shore, so no one could get off.

Michael got up, flipped open the case and slipped his revolver into his trouser pocket. He opened the door a crack and peered out.

A teenaged boy was running along, full of excitement.

'Hey there!' Michael tried to appear insouciant, merely mildly interested. 'What's going on? Any idea?'

'Yes,' the boy panted. 'Thrilling! This steamer was only a few yards out when the suction pulled at all the other boats along the dockside. The *Oceanic* swung out, then the *New York* broke its cables, or whatever they're called. There was almost the most almighty smash-up.'

'Did anyone come aboard?'

'How could they? We were already on the go. But it was a near disaster.'

'I see!' Not now, thought Michael. Not when things were running so smoothly. 'Will we have to turn back?'

'No, no. We're sailing on out of it, leaving chaos behind us.' The boy was straining to move on. 'I'm going to get my big brother to come up and watch too.'

As the boy ran away, Michael gently closed the cabin door and got his breath back.

Another false alarm.

It was time to stop worrying and start enjoying the day.

He put the gun back into the suitcase and clapped his hands.

'Right, boys! Who fancies lunch and an explore?'

Both children clambered off the bunk and jumped up and down on the spot crying, 'Me! Me! Me!'

'Then what are you waiting for...?' Michael straightened his jacket and flung wide the cabin door, ready to explore this wonderful ship and all she had to offer.

That kid in the corridor was right, he thought to himself: We're sailing on out of it, leaving chaos behind us.

———

As Michael and the two boys got out of the lift taking them up to the outer decks after lunch, Lolo asked, 'Is this a hotel, Papa?'

'I know it looks like a hotel, Lolo, but it's a steamer. A really big ship.'

'So where is the sea? Mama takes me to see the sea and ships go by. You have to have sea for it to be a ship.'

Michael pushed open a door at the side of the landing.

'Here you are.' They walked out on to the deck. Most of the other passengers had got bored by now, as Michael knew they would. They had all enjoyed the deck first thing, as the ship pulled out of Southampton, then had gone inside to lunch.

There were still a few people about, but the crowds were inside gorging themselves.

The sea was slate. The wind whipped Michael's hair about his face. Looking back, he could just see the Isle of Wight disappearing into the misty grey horizon. Next stop Cherbourg.

While the two boys had fun running up and down the deck, Michael sat on a bench and gazed out to sea, his eyes towards France.

He remembered what a relief it was the first time he had arrived in that country.

Strange that now it was such a relief to have left it.

He had been on the run that time too.

Aged twenty, he had been called up to do his national service. Michael went, as every healthy male was obliged to.

But he didn't like army life. He hated everything about it: the food, the clothes, the other men, the dirt, the stink, the brutality. He hated being a cog in a machine, an anonymous face standing in a line, a skittle lined up to be knocked down. He was better than that.

That said, he knew he looked pretty splendid in the dress uniform. It had been a very easy way to attract women: leaning against the bar in the local beerhouse, uniform pristine, regulation cap slightly askew. All the women wanted to straighten it for him.

But being shouted at by huge common thugs while crawling around in the mud wasn't a pleasure at all. He managed to get through almost two years, then one day he simply decided he'd had enough.

So, rather than stick out the final year, he had bolted.

It was December; they were on manoeuvres, suppressing some rioting anarchists or socialists in some godforsaken alpine market town kilometres from Vienna.

It was all too cold, too noisy, too bloody and too dirty. His clothes were filthy and soaking wet. He saw several of his fellow squaddies being carried back from skirmishes on stretchers, some with their heads covered. Dead.

Michael decided that he had no intention of joining them.

Next morning he and his fellow troopers were due to be moving on to somewhere decidedly more dangerous. Most of the blokes in his regiment seemed rather excited about that. Not Michael. He'd been a little too near sufficient danger already, thank you.

He'd saved a bit of money. He slipped it into his pocket. Then, late one night, while his comrades were all drinking and chatting up wenches in a smoky beerhall, Michael simply slipped away.

Darting in and out of doorways, he ran along to the nearby railway station and got on the first train heading out of town. He wanted to cross the border before the guards discovered that he had gone, came running after him and dragged him back.

Next morning, at some sleepy little town, he hastily bought some clothes and changed out of his uniform, which he dumped in a bin up an alley behind the shop.

He returned then to the station, no longer in uniform, and took another train, then another, all the while getting further and further away from his regiment and nearer to freedom.

By the end of the day, he'd crossed the Italian border. Next thing he knew, he'd arrived in Turin, where he planned to start a new life.

Before he got the hateful call-up papers, he'd been an apprentice in a tailor's shop. He thought it would be easy to work his way back into the trade.

But not here in Turin. All the Italians in the clothing business had very snooty ideas about themselves, looking down on a foreigner like him. And he didn't have the language. He could speak German and Hungarian fluently and had sufficient French and English to get by.

So within a few days of arriving in Turin, he'd had enough of the place.

Thus it was that in February 1902, he climbed aboard another small train, this one winding down through a snowy mountainous valley arriving eventually at Nice...

A seagull swooped low, crying loudly, shocking him out of his daydream.

He jumped to his feet.

Where were the bloody children?

He ran along the deck. No sight of them.

He turned back and ran the other way. Racing around the corner, he saw them, in the distance, sitting on a bench chatting with some bellboy who was taking a couple of toy dogs for their afternoon airing.

Trying to disguise his obvious panic, Michael slowed down and strolled to sit on the bench a few metres along from theirs.

For the moment he'd leave them playing with the dogs.

That was them happy for a while.

Once Michael's heartbeat had returned to its normal rate, he looked back towards the horizon.

He wondered if his mother and brothers still appeared the same, ten years on. He knew that his sister had changed a bit, got much fatter. She'd sent him a photographic snap, posing with her fiancé, George, a plump-looking roly-poly with a lot of unkempt facial hair.

He would have liked to have seen his mother again. His brothers too.

But of course, by deserting the Austro-Hungarian army, he was now on a wanted list. He *couldn't* go back home. The moment he crossed the border into Austria he'd be pulled out of line, bundled off and thrown into prison. He wondered whether they'd also make him do that army year which he'd skipped.

Still, there was no point worrying about that.

It was never going to happen.

As much as he missed his old mother, no one was worth that indignity.

He chuckled to himself thinking about wily old Stefan. What a clever boy! He'd managed to leave the country before the wretched call-up papers arrived. So he'd escaped the hell, but without the ignominy of becoming a criminal.

It was funny how, at Monmon's baptism, Marcella's Amazonian cousin Rosa had so nearly got it right. *Maybe you're not welcome back there in Hungary*, she'd crowed. *Is that it? Have I hit a nerve?* The blonde giant. Michael wondered if somehow she knew the truth. Or had she just taken a shot in the dark, a shot which had been right on target.

He glanced up. Lolo had moved on from the dogs and was sitting down on the boards of the deck playing with some little girl of his own age. Monmon, still perched beside the bellboy, was looking on.

Michael jumped to his feet and ran along to join them. He didn't want them chattering away to strangers, maybe spilling the beans.

'Come on, boys, let's explore the rest of the ship.'

It was only then that he saw that the little girl was being guarded by a woman, presumably her mother, seated on a bench around the corner, near the lifeboats.

'Let them play,' she said to Michael in English. 'It's good to make friends.'

Michael shook his head as though he'd not understood her. She promptly went into a mime, accompanied by shouting in English, 'Good to make friends!'

Michael tipped his hat at the bellowing woman, took his children by the hand then backed away, talking to them busily in French.

He didn't want to get close to anyone, let alone making friends with them. Walls have ears.

And women and children like to talk.

Back in the cabin, he found that Monmon now possessed a painted wooden toy soldier. Damn. Now he'd have to find that wretched woman with the little girl and return it to her before they came after him. But not right at this moment.

He left the children playing among themselves on the sofa while he got down to the important business of writing letters.

First to Stefan Kozak (alias Etienne Stefan, c/o Poste Restante, Central Post Office, Nice) to let him know that everything had gone to plan so far and that he hoped Stefan had cleared the shop. When the bailiffs came, he wrote, act dumb: 'I'm just a poor employee. Haven't been paid' et cetera.

Then he scratched a letter to his mother back in Presbourg, telling her that he was safe and travelling, but, above all, warning her that if Marcella contacted her she was to ignore it, and, whatever she was told about him, she must NOT reply to Marcella in any way. He would explain all in a few days' time in a further, longer letter.

He daren't say anything else to her quite yet. Not till they were past Ireland, and preferably just after they pulled into New York. Just to be sure. At this stage you couldn't be too careful.

All the time he was writing, Lolo kept crying out that he was bored. Then, when Lolo stopped playing with him, Monmon kept attempting to climb up on to Michael's lap to snatch the pen out of his hand.

With this constant jabbering, it was impossible to concentrate.

And it was imperative that he worded these letters precisely.

He grabbed some notepaper from a drawer, folded it into darts and threw them. That at least diverted the boys while he carefully sealed and addressed the letters. He double- and triple-checked the addresses – he didn't want to find he had accidentally put in the shop address, or sent them to Marcella! Once satisfied that they were correct, Michael stood up and told the boys that they were all going for another look around the ship.

He glanced at his watch. He had to get to the purser's office before they sealed the box which would take the mail ashore at Cherbourg.

The boys didn't move. They were still crawling over the floor, playing with the paper darts.

'Anyone for a walk?' He tried to sound bright and breezy, but the truth was he was dead tired. 'Come on, boys!'

Monmon now disappeared under the bed, only his legs sticking out. Playing hide and seek.

'I don't want to go,' whined Lolo.

'Fine!' Michael turned and opened the door. 'I'm going off to get some hot chocolate. Maybe you don't want any?'

That got them to their feet quickly enough.

Having persuaded them to follow him, Michael hoped he would find somewhere which served hot chocolate at this time of day. He didn't want any tantrums in public.

Michael was starting to wonder if it had been such a good idea bringing the children with him. Their constant attention-grabbing and disobedience was grating on him. And there was still so far to go.

At the back of his mind a thought kept niggling. Did he really want to live with the children, so much as to remove them from Marcella's grasp? He certainly wasn't cut out to be a nanny. Mind you, now they were good as gold, following like sheep. Michael led them up the flights of stairs rather than taking the lift. He hoped it would be a good way of tiring them out.

While looking around he'd passed inviting lounges, full of men like himself, sitting cradling drinks, puffing on their cigars and pipes.

But he knew that he couldn't go in with children in tow.

Only once the kids were tucked up in bed and asleep would he be able to make the most of this marvellous steamer, wander around, drink in the bars.

It had cost him enough to buy the tickets. Surely by now he should be allowed to relax and celebrate.

———

Michael took the boys up on to the top deck to watch their arrival at Cherbourg. He hadn't realised that the ship didn't actually dock there. He thought he could watch the quayside for any gangs of *flics* boarding, but the passengers were all being brought onboard by two little boats almost the size of the Channel ferry, and being loaded through gangways in the side of the big ship.

There was no way for Michael to tell whether he was safe yet.

Even though it was drizzling, he considered it best to sit out here till the ship pulled away.

'Good evening, Mr Hoffman!'

It was his room steward passing by, on some errand.

Mr Hoffman!

Then it dawned on Michael. If the police in Cherbourg *were* after him, they'd be looking for Monsieur Navratil.

Why would they be looking for Hoffman? Even Hoffman didn't know Michael was now called Hoffman!

Only Stefan knew, and he had very good reason not to tell.

Monsieur Hoffman. He'd had all his papers and tickets checked, and the only man aboard of his description with two kids was Monsieur Hoffman.

Monsieur Navratil didn't exist and wouldn't exist for days. Not until he'd arrived safely in Chicago.

'Come on, boys,' Michael shouted to the children, who were huddled together, sheltering under the lee of the funnel, shivering. 'Let's go inside.'

'Aren't we getting off now?' asked Lolo. 'I thought we were out here cos we were getting off. I'd like to get off now.'

'Get inside!' Michael grabbed the child by the shoulders and thrust him through the door.

They took the lift down to the cabin and took their coats off, Michael drying their hair with a fluffy new towel. He dabbed at his own, afraid that he would now look extremely scruffy.

'Shall we see if anyone is taking dinner yet?'

'I want to play,' Lolo wheedled. 'Aren't there any toys in this hotel, Papa?'

'It's a ship, Lolo.'

As they climbed the steps back up to the dining room, Michael noticed a sign with a hand pointing towards THE BARBER SHOP. Good. After three days on the run, his hair and moustache were a mess.

He wondered whether the Kirchmanns would meet the ship? He'd have to send a telegram to them, asking them to come.

'Is Mama inside there?' Lolo was tugging at Michael's hand, trying to get into the lounge saloon.

And when Michael tore himself out of his thoughts, he realised why Lolo had asked.

A small band was playing. And of all the tunes in the world they had picked hers – 'La Tonkinoise'.

'He calls me his bourgeois p'tite
His Tonki-ki, his Tonki-ki, his Tonkinoise
They all make sweet eyes at him
But it's me he likes best.'

Lolo managed to break away and make a dash for it, bursting through the doors, chasing the music. When Monmon saw Lolo gone, he set up an almighty row, shrieking as though he was being murdered, or, at the least, manhandled.

Michael hovered near the door, unable to control Monmon, but afraid of bringing him inside.

The common little ditty seemed to go on and on, with Lolo running around the room, staring into the faces of all the women gathered there, searching for Marcella.

Margaret

CHAPTER 24

Wednesday 10 April 1912, Cherbourg

'Excited?' said Gilbert Tucker, standing at Margaret's side on the outer deck of the White Star's tender, SS *Nomadic*, as it pulled out of Cherbourg harbour.

'Very,' replied Margaret. The creamy sun was sinking towards the grey horizon. Ahead, beyond the breakwater, she could see the black silhouette of the big ship lying at anchor. She glanced over her shoulder. Inside, beyond those sparkling brightly lit windows, practically all the famous millionaires in the world were sitting chatting, sipping tea.

Soon they would all be together onboard.

Margaret Hays had been away from home now for more than four whole months. But, finally, today things were looking up.

It had all come about like this: When Margaret's old schoolfriend, Olive (Mrs Olive Earnshaw, née Miss Olive Potter), had first proposed a trip around Europe, she had described it to Margaret as 'an adventure'.

Later Margaret's parents said she couldn't refuse going as it sounded so exciting and full of promise. 'Sensational' was the word her mother had used.

And it was true. The trip had *sounded* amazing.

Margaret's father, Frank Kissam Hays, however, had not accepted Olive's mother's offer to pay his daughter's way. He was a proud man – quite well off, as it happens ('comfortable' was the word they used within the family). More importantly, he did not want anyone to think he couldn't *afford* to pay. What on earth would that have looked like to the neighbours in West End Avenue?

But for Margaret the *idea* of visiting all those wonderfully thrilling places was rather badly balanced against the dullness of people she was travelling with.

Olive Potter had never exactly been the life and soul of the classroom.

Then, soon after graduating, to everyone's astonishment, Olive had impulsively married. It had taken Olive three miserable years to recognise that her frightful husband, Boulton Earnshaw (what a name!), coal dealer (what a profession!), was a ghastly womaniser and that her marriage to him had been a terrible mistake. She started divorce proceedings.

At the news of a divorce in the family, and its depressive effect on Olive, the redoubtable Mrs Lillian Potter, Olive's mother, had proposed that 'in order to take the poor dear's mind off *things*' (the 'things', naturally, being 1. the gossip of their neighbours; 2. the mud-slinging that would be expected from the New York lawyers; and 3. the prettiness of her husband's new paramour) she and her daughter would be doing the celebrated Grand Tour of Europe.

But Lillian Potter was no fool. She understood that it would be no use dragging her daughter abroad if all she was going to do for six months was mope around on her own, thinking about the nasty coal merchant and his chocolate-box new lady-friend. She knew her miserable, regretful daughter quite well enough to know that that would certainly be the case... unless... well, unless the girl invited some fun-loving gay companion along, someone guaranteed to liven up proceedings and take Olive's mind off what was going on back home.

And who better to provide that element of exuberance than West End Avenue's own bubbly little debutante, Margaret Bechstein Hays?

Thus it was that, to her delight, Margaret had been picked to be Olive's 'merry companion'.

Margaret's parents had been very keen for her to join the trip. Perhaps a little too keen, Margaret now thought. They had told her often enough that she was frittering away her life, and they believed travelling broadened the mind.

Margaret wondered whether perhaps for a few months they were also glad to be rid of her.

But, back then, in December, when the three of them – Olive, Lillian and Margaret – had set off from New York, on a steamer across the Atlantic, the idea of exploring all these famous places sounded utterly wonderful. After all, it was an itinerary to die for: firstly, France – gay Paree, to be exact – then down through all those vineyards and things, to the Mediterranean coast (or 'the Côte d'Azur', as Margaret now preferred to call it). The party of three passed through the merchant city of Marseille, and through the red rocks of the Esterel to Cannes, Antibes and Nice, which had been very pretty. Next, their journey took them along the Ligurian coast of Italy, across to Venice with its smelly canals and garish churches. After that they headed down the long leg of Italy, to Rome, where, if it could be believed, the churches were even more garish than the Venetian ones. As members of the American Episcopalian Church, Lillian, Olive and Margaret were used to churches with plain cream walls, white ceilings and unshaded hanging wooden lamps.

However, while Olive and Mrs Potter tutted at the baroque splendour – the ornate walls, bright with coloured marble and gold ormolu, and all those dangling naked painted bodies sprawled across the ceilings of the Gesù and Saint Ignatius in Rome – Margaret almost burst with awe and secret exhilaration.

Walking out in the streets of Rome, when Margaret passed, Italian men called aloud and wolf-whistled. Coquettishly twiddling her parasol, Margaret pretended to be appalled (obviously) while slyly determining that one day she would come back, next time without the Praetorian Guard provided by Mrs Potter and daughter. Next time she would really make the most of it.

From Rome they had taken a very uncomfortable train down to Naples, where they spent a tedious day walking through cobbled streets lined with abandoned houses – the ruins of Pompeii. Lily Potter had declared this the highlight of the tour so far.

And in a way it really was that for Margaret because it was while poking over Pompeii that she had encountered Gilbert Milligan Tucker, Junior.

She and the Potters had been standing in one of the thousands of derelict houses. Tall, with collar-length sandy hair, wearing a floppy linen suit and straw boater, Gilbert had caught Margaret's attention when he had popped his monocle out of his eye in feigned horror at a mural of a naked priapic faun, playing a lyre.

She turned away to stifle a laugh, only to find Olive, looking down, admiring the dusty remnants of the mosaic floor.

'Quite a lot of bother over nothing,' said Gilbert loudly to his party.

'Oh, I agree with you, young man,' replied Lily Potter. 'And, believe me, I know about flooring. My late husband was very big in linoleum.'

Margaret exploded with laughter and had to hang her head and feign a coughing fit.

'Am I the only one in this Pompey place who's bored out of his wits?' asked Gilbert (but obviously aiming the question at Margaret). 'It seems to me, you see one hollowed-out house – you've seen 'em all.'

Later, while they all paused at a little café by the exit to refresh themselves with a light iced drink, Gilbert told the Potter group that he was due to return to America with his family in a couple of days. But, giving Margaret a discreet wink, he suggested to them that three women travelling alone really needed a male escort to guard them from the horrors of European brutishness, and that he himself was more than willing to provide it.

Lily Potter, not yet recovered from the pornographic ceilings and wolf-whistles which she had endured while in Rome, immediately agreed to taking on Gilbert's services as guardian and chaperon.

That evening Olive confided in Margaret that she thought Gilbert had taken a fancy to her, adding that, when they all returned to Philadelphia, it would be very good for her to be seen with another man on her arm. That would certainly show her beastly ex-husband Boulton Earnshaw that two could play at that game.

Margaret knew that on this point Olive was absolutely delusional. Olive had something too earnest about her. She could never be seen as a beauty or in the slightest bit attractive to a high-spirited type like Gilbert.

Her horn-rimmed spectacles didn't help.

Anyway, Margaret knew for a fact that it was she whom Gilbert fancied.

And that was a good thing.

The important thing was that although Margaret felt no such reciprocal feelings for Gilbert, she knew that when men buzzed about one, it always attracted more!

That evening the four of them ate pizza on a dockside terrace overlooking a wide bay overshadowed by the dormant lopsided volcano, Vesuvius.

'Wouldn't it be fun if it went off,' said Margaret.

'No,' said Olive and Lily in unison.

'Rather!' said Gilbert at the same moment.

Margaret knew they were going to be great friends.

On the quayside, as they walked back towards the hotel, a female beggar held up a sign saying, PLEASE TAKE MY DOG!

Margaret threw down some coins and returned to her hotel room the proud owner of a Pomeranian puppy, christened Bébé, which, as she kept telling everyone, was French for Baby.

Margaret was very proud of the French phrases she had picked up while travelling. '*Ça ne fait rien*,' she would say. '*Je voudrais une glace au vanille et une tasse du thé, s'il vous plaît.*' '*Merci beaucoup, vous êtes très gentil*' and '*Où se trouve les toilettes?*'

She knew so many jolly useful phrases like that. No good in Italy, obviously, but French sounded so *soigné* and sophisticated that Margaret decided to stick with it.

From Naples on, Margaret started enjoying herself. Bébé and Gilbert would at least provide her with playful company. There was absolutely nothing playful whatsoever to be had from either Lily or Olive.

Gilbert was a very welcome hoot. He could even make Olive laugh aloud, and that was saying something.

From Italy the little group ventured onwards, boarding a rather rusty-looking ferry to cross the Adriatic Sea, heading for Greece.

'We're taking our lives in our hands,' said Lily as they flopped down in rickety deckchairs on the top deck. 'We'll be lucky if we make it to the Land of the Gods across the wine-dark sea.'

Margaret couldn't understand what Lily was going on about. The sea was blue not red. Perhaps she needed an eye test.

'Talking of wine,' whispered Gilbert. 'I could just fancy a bumper of burgundy.'

'Ah, the joys of Dionysus the pig-plucker,' said Lily. 'Deity of wine and ecstasy.'

'Jumping jingo!' said Gilbert. 'Steady on, Mrs Potter.'

'It would be a shame if we were to stop now,' said Olive. 'The best is yet to come.'

For the rest of their trip was to be dedicated to admiring what was left of the Marvels of the Ancient World.

Even from the photographs in the brochure Margaret could see that by that they meant piles of dusty old stones.

They made it to Greece and, after visiting the Acropolis (a few pillars and a lot of dusty old stones), they boarded another, even rustier ferry onward to Turkey.

Mrs Potter enthusiastically read aloud the brochure which promised 'a mysterious taste of the glorious remains of the Ottoman Empire'. But Turkey turned out to be even more frightful than Rome for provocative men, though Margaret privately reflected that these leering Lotharios weren't nearly as handsome or well dressed as the ones in Rome.

To this were added the horrors of peculiar-tasting food and stinking streets full of dung (which could well have been human).

And then there were the flies.

Flies, flies, flies.

It was like being thrust into the insect cage at the New York Menagerie.

Despite the torrid heat and disagreeable conditions of Turkey, the Potter party agreed that it was essential they visit the Temple of Diana at Ephesus. It was, after all, one of the two remaining Seven Wonders of the World (the other being the Great Pyramid of Giza).

In order to achieve this goal it was necessary to take a fifty-mile trip out of the city and, to accomplish that, they had to utilise the service of a dilapidated motor car with a seedy local chauffeur dressed in a grey linen suit and dark glasses.

The car couldn't manage more than about fifteen miles per hour, the road was rocky and during the entire journey they were scared out of their wits that they would be attacked by brigands, who the driver nonchalantly told them operated along the route.

When finally Margaret and her friends reached the said Wonder of the World, they found only a bare scruffy field surrounded by low hills, around the edges of which stood a few small whitish stones.

In Margaret's opinion it was like travelling all day to look at a bankrupt builder's yard in Hoboken, New Jersey.

Included in the excursion, to refresh them before the ghastly ordeal of the journey back, the driver took them to a local café for coffee and sherbets.

A hawker was flogging last week's English newspapers.

Lily bought one, more to use as a shield against the sun, than to read.

But later, while fanning out the pages, Margaret found an article about the brand-new luxury steamer of the White Star Line. It was due to set sail in a week's time, carrying a collection of the most celebrated rich people in the world from Southampton and Cherbourg to New York – home.

It was going to be the social occasion of the year.

Within seconds Margaret formed a plan.

During the hellish road trip, she asked if everyone was enjoying themselves. Naturally no one replied yes.

She asked whether they yearned for a little comfort.

Then, when everyone was at their most miserable, swatting away a plague of flies, Margaret read out parts of the article and suggested that if they changed their tickets and booked a crossing on this White Star steamer they could soon be enjoying the luxury they all craved.

'But it would mean we arrive home a few weeks earlier than planned,' said Olive, firmly slapping a mosquito which was guzzling on her forearm.

In Margaret's eyes, of course, this was yet another advantage.

So, after much cajoling by Margaret (and Gilbert, who would do whatever Margaret asked), by the time they took to their beds that night in the slightly grimy hotel in Smyrna, the whole party had decided that it would be utterly thrilling to race back across the continent by express trains to Paris, and, once there, to take the boat train up to Cherbourg and, along with every American celebrity and millionaire you could think of, board the most famous ship in the world.

Next morning Mrs Lily Potter visited the Smyrna offices of Thomas Cook and, for the grand price of eighty-three pounds, two shillings and two pence, bought two cabins in the First Class.

And that is how Margaret now found herself, the wind whipping loose strands of hair around her face, standing on the deck of this tender, clutching the dog she had rescued.

As the little ship left the shelter of the harbour, a fishing boat sailed past, heading back into the port of Cherbourg, leaving a wake.

The decks of the tender rose up and plunged down again.

'Oooo-eerrrr!' Gilbert grabbed the railing and winced. 'I hope that won't be what lies ahead.'

'Don't be so silly.' Margaret threw her head back and laughed. 'That majestic black shadow out there is the most luxurious palace afloat. Don't you see, Gilbert? Forget Paris, obliterate all your memories of Rome, Naples and Athens. We're about to go on the biggest adventure of our lives.'

Michael

CHAPTER 25

Thursday 11 April 1912, onboard RMS Titanic
Cock-a-doodle-doo! Cock-a-doodle-doo!

Michael awoke as though still in a dream. He had no idea where he was. He was facing a white wall – then remembered that it was the ceiling and he was on the top bunk.

Yet the cock kept on crowing.

The children were very quiet, he hoped still asleep.

He leaned down to check.

Their bed was empty.

He sat up fast, banging his head, slithered down the ladder and hastily threw on some clothes.

Cock-a-doodle-doo! Cock-a-doodle-doo!

What the hell was going on?

He left the cabin still barefoot. His boots would take too long to pull on.

Instinctively, he followed the sound of the cockerel's crow.

After rounding two bends in the corridor, he bumped into one of the stewards, bustling along behind a cart laden with clean linen.

'My children have gone missing!'

'They're yours, are they? One of my colleagues caught them wandering about half naked, wrapped them in a blanket and took them along to the purser's office.'

Michael had had enough. All he wanted to do was sleep. Runaway children were the last thing he needed.

Cock-a-doodle-doo!

'And what is that racket? We're in the middle of the sea, so how are we able to hear cocks crowing?'

'That'll be coming from a shipment of live poultry bound for New York. They're stowed along the way.'

'Oh God.' Michael ran his hand across his forehead. 'Are they going to make that din every morning?'

'I don't see how we can stop them, sir. You can't muzzle a cockerel.'

'And my children. What do I do now?'

'If I were you, sir, I'd run along to the purser's office on E deck.'

At the wood-panelled office he was told that, as no one spoke their 'lingo', they hadn't been sure how to place them, and so the lift boy had taken them into his care. Michael had merely to wait by the lift until it arrived and they should be inside.

A tune on a bugle from the outer deck drowned out the last piece of advice.

'What the hell is that?'

'That, Mr Hoffman, is the First Class call to breakfast.'

At the same moment, a few metres away, a gong clanged deafeningly.

'And that, sir, is the Second Class call.'

'Being on this ship is worse than being in the bloody army,' growled Michael under his breath, heading for the lifts.

He found the boys, happy as larks, giggling with the lift boy, who seemed little older than a child himself. Must have been fourteen at the most.

Thanking the lift boy, Michael asked him to take them all down to F deck, slipping him another tip.

Once back in the cabin, Michael shouted at the children, 'You're not to run away again.'

'We didn't run away,' Lolo shouted back. 'We heard the chicken, so we went looking for it. Mama promised us we'd see the chicken after one sleep but we've already had two sleeps.'

That bloody chicken.

'Look. I'm going to get you some crayons and then we can sit quietly somewhere and draw. Hey?'

'You're mean and horrible and I hate you.'

'You like drawing—'

'I don't want to draw.' Lolo stamped his foot. 'I want to see Mama.'

'Well, Mama isn't on the ship, so you can't.'

Monmon started to howl.

'I hate this hotel,' said Lolo. 'And I hate you and I want to go home.'

'How many times?' Michael gritted his teeth. 'It's a ship.'

He had paid through the nose to take his children on the most famous steamer in the world and they weren't in the least grateful. He'd never felt so worn out. When would he be allowed to have some fun?

'Why don't we all go up and have breakfast?' he said, placatory. 'You must be hungry. I am.'

Monmon held out his hand. 'I'm hungry,' he said.

Lolo grunted and dragged reluctantly behind.

The ship stopped again, late in the morning, and anchored just south of Ireland. Various tenders embarked more passengers.

But by now Michael felt confident. He doubted police would come aboard to look for him here.

So, if he could only keep the children quiet, he might finally be able to relax a little, start enjoying the voyage.

After lunch he lured them into the library-saloon, the only public room apart from the dining room that he was allowed to take them. He gave them paper and pencils. He set them an exercise: to draw a dog. The winner would get ice cream for dinner.

As it happened, he had already seen that ice cream was on the menu, so they could really have it if they wanted.

There weren't that many people in there. A few old dears, chatting in a gaggle in the corner. A couple of chaps taking a quiet smoke; others reading books they'd picked up from the library end of the room. A youngish man, sat at a desk in the corner writing a letter. Michael wondered when that would get posted. They were hardly going to send them by pigeon post. So presumably it wouldn't go off till they reached New York.

Michael was glad he'd got his first letters off yesterday at Cherbourg. They'd be well on the way by now.

He hoped if Marcella and her family approached his mother for help she would manage to keep quiet.

Michael sat back in an armchair near the window, lit his pipe and closed his eyes.

It was lovely listening to the small band playing, even though the sound was muffled by passing through the panelling, behind which was First Class. Haunting music. None of that French tripe now. This afternoon it was waltzes by Strauss and Hungarian dances by Brahms and Liszt.

Would he ever go home again, to Nice?

No. But with any luck, after the brouhaha of the bankruptcy had died down, Stefan could sell what was left and come over and join him in Chicago.

He hoped also that maybe Camille would run away from her wiry goat of a husband. If not, there were plenty of women who would do. It shouldn't be too hard to find a new wife in the USA. Let Marcella get her precious divorce at the end of the month. It would leave him free to start a totally new life.

He imagined that American women would be nicer than Italians, less temperamental, better at housework, not so hoity-toity.

Marcella was an ungrateful cow. Whine, whine, whine about the move to Avenue Shakespeare. Michael had thought she would enjoy being a cut above her own family, living in a nice place, not just a rented set of rooms above shops, as they all did. But no. Avenue Shakespeare might be in a really good area, but it was 'too hilly', 'too far from the market', 'too far from the shops', 'too lonely' for her.

Not too far for constant visits from doting doctors, though, or for romantic strolls in the street with that solicitous beanpole, Henry Rey di Villarey. Stupid supercilious twit. Why couldn't he have a single surname like everyone else?

Michael paused, remembering, with a skipped heartbeat, the threatening letters from the landlord at Avenue Shakespeare.

That final reminder, which arrived just as they were leaving for Edmond's baptism, telling him, in no uncertain terms, that he was already in arrears and if he hadn't paid the outstanding debt along with the next six months' rent, *in advance*, by midnight on 31 March, bailiffs would arrive, they'd be flung out on to the street and he would be taken to court. He'd held out as long as he could. But he had known that the Avenue Shakespeare lot meant business. They even warned that their next step would be to take his shop from him. It wasn't worth losing the shop just to stay in some stupid fancy house that his selfish wife couldn't even stand. Although that house had suited his own personality perfectly. Especially with the new name. It made him seem like a gentleman. A squire. Lord of the manor. A somebody.

He looked around the library-saloon of RMS *Titanic*, with its white pillars and classical woodwork. If only Marcella knew! Now he really *was* a somebody. He was travelling in great style on the most famous ship to ever set sail. Himself, Michael Navratil, along with every important businessman and millionaire in the world. They were all onboard. They might have been travelling in First Class, while he was in Second. But so what? They were all in the same boat! They were just through the wall, where the sound of music came from. All those railway and retail magnates. The richest men on planet Earth. And him. Michael Navratil.

What's more, he had lots of money in his suitcase and he was going to set up such a stylish and wonderful business in Chicago. Who knows, maybe one day he'd be as big as those Strauses? They owned Macy's department store. That was clever of them. He should have chosen another name for his shop, rather than his own surname. Using your own name made you more vulnerable to vultures. If only he'd thought of that when he opened up in Nice, before they all came after him.

Michael had already chosen the name of his new shop, in Chicago. Edelweiss. How about that! The national flower of his homeland. He'd patched together a kind of British coat of arms for the labels. After all, everyone wanted English styles. Look at this very room, with its coffered ceiling and oh-so-British decor!

But the new shop would certainly not be called Navratil. That name turned him into a sitting duck. If anyone came after him now, they'd have a job finding him. He laughed to himself, remembering that first time someone had arrived in the shop with a legal summons for some final demand and he'd pretended to be Hoffman. His first narrow escape.

Navratil was too noticeable and it wasn't very American. He didn't want to start out as though he was some foreigner. Some immigrant.

He wanted to belong.

And with a name like Edelweiss…

Magnificent.

'Calling Mr Hoffman… please! Mr Louis Hoffman!'

Michael looked around him, then suddenly remembered that, whatever this was, it would be for him.

What could it be?

The children were still safely crawling about the floor with their paper and pencils.

Why was he being paged?

'Mr Hoffman… please!'

Had police got onboard at Ireland, after all? But then why had they waited till the ship was well on its way before searching him out?

Did they have a prison onboard?

He glanced at the bellboy's face, then towards the door. It didn't look like a trap.

'Mr Hoffman… please!'

Maybe someone had died. His mother, perhaps. Or a brother. Or Stefan.

He raised a hand, signalling to the lad.

'I'm Hoffman,' he said.

'Telegram, sir!'

The boy handed over the cable.

As he took it, Michael saw that his own hands were shaking. He dug into his pocket for another coin to slip him.

'If you want to send a reply, sir, I can take it now.'

'No. That's fine. Thank you.'

Before tearing open the envelope, Michael waited for the boy to leave the saloon. Then, heart thumping, mouth dry, he pulled out the message.

CARABOSSE COME GONE. ALL WELL. BON VOYAGE. ETIENNE.

He couldn't help laughing aloud.

Stefan, the wonder boy!

He'd telegraph him straight back. Congratulate him. He would use the code they'd invented. A simple word-replacement system. As basic as anything. But in Hungarian. If anyone intercepted that, it would take them forever to decode what it said. Any telegram had to be indecipherable, they agreed, except by them.

Michael spent a good half hour coding his reply and then reducing it to ten words.

He had just about finished when something hit him on the head. He looked around, then at the children. Instead of drawing a dog, Lolo had managed to work out how to make darts from the sheets of paper and was now throwing them around the library.

Shaking the dart from his shoulder, Michael straightened his hair. Lolo simply didn't associate these darts with aeroplanes. Just as he couldn't understand that they were in a ship and not a hotel.

The child adored ships but hated aeroplanes.

Lolo's terror for planes, Michael had hoped, might have swung the divorce judges in his favour. It was all her fault. Marcella had taken the children down to the beach, as she always did. She'd taken him there too, at the beginning. It was obviously her preferred location for winning people over. He remembered bitterly how she'd lured him down there to seduce him.

A few weeks ago, Marcella had made one of those picnics she was so fond of whipping up. She took the boys to see some aeronautical display put on by the flying club based in the west of the bay at Californie. They were always having events like this in Nice. There was even a special aviation section in the newspapers, as though it was some kind of sport. Only that day – in March, it had been – something happened. And the next day Michael had had the children.

Michael asked Lolo how he was and the kid went into fits of hysterics about something his mother had done to him.

Michael felt that it was his duty to wheedle it out.

It seemed that while on the beach Lolo had witnessed a terrible accident. Well, what did the woman expect? Taking children to watch something as dangerous and experimental as men in flying machines! If God had wanted man to fly, we'd have all been born with wings.

On that day some plane took off from the aerodrome and flew over the bay, towards Cap Ferrat. A few minutes later, the pilot fell out of the cockpit, just metres away from the boy, and the plane came crashing down into the water behind him. Everyone on the beach was in a terrible state, rushing forward, trying to get through the waves to save the pilot.

The poor child had been highly affected by the event. Traumatised.

Michael's lawyers thought it would be very much in his favour if Michael complained about this – citing the fact that Marcella was responsible for organising the afternoon.

But it had never come to that, thanks to the announcement of his imminent bankruptcy.

He laughed.

He hadn't needed any blame to throw at her.

He'd got full and total custody anyway!

Everything had worked out all right for him.

Hadn't it?

CHAPTER 26

Sunday 14 April 1912, onboard RMS Titanic

The children were driving Michael out of his mind.

In fact, everything was driving him out of his mind.

He was bored of the endless grey circle of sea, the low clouds, the constant throb of the engines. He was bored of dressing for dinner and being polite all day, and music playing everywhere he went. He was bored of his own company.

Even if a seagull flew past, it might make things a bit more interesting. But it seemed that even seagulls didn't venture this far out.

Last night had been the final straw.

Both boys seemed to have found some demoniacal energy and simply would not go to sleep. He tried reading and singing, and all the usual things, but no. They screamed and shouted and leaped about until the wretched Spaniard or Mexican (or whatever he was) from the next cabin came knocking again to ask if he could kindly control his children.

Finally Michael just gave up and, while they shrieked and jumped up and down, he sat at the cabin desk, put bits of cotton wool in his ears and wrote a letter to his mother.

He asked whether she or one of his brothers could please take the boys to live with them. Michael couldn't possibly set up a new shop and start a new life with children in tow. They seemed to want attention twenty-four hours a day.

All those times Marcella wept because he kept her working in the shop while she wanted to be with them. She must be mad. What sane person wouldn't prefer working in a shop to goo-gooing about, making baby-talk?

It would be much nicer for Lolo and Monmon, he wrote to his mother, to live in a family home, a family home like his brother's, rather than go through the trials of his own American experiment.

Johannes, married two years to his lovely wife, Anna – a perfect wife. Wouldn't it be good for them and for their own baby, Francis, to have a pair of older cousins to play with? Anna had another kid on the way too. So by the time Lolo and Monmon arrived in Austria she'd be used to caring for children. And it meant that his mother could finally get to meet her grandchildren. She could see them all the time, in fact.

It was a perfect solution for everyone.

If that wasn't convenient, Michael added, perhaps his sister, Maria, and her husband, George, might take them.

He sealed the letter and slipped it into the pocket of his new grey coat.

Then he ripped it open again and added a postscript: DO NOT LET MARCELLA KNOW OF MY WHEREABOUTS OR THE WHEREABOUTS OF THE CHILDREN.

He found a clean envelope and put the letter inside, addressing it to his mother.

He then worried that if the police arrived at his mother's place, as they surely would, they might search her house. So he folded the letter in half and put it into another envelope, and addressed that one to his porky brother-in-law George, with a short explanatory note.

If he still felt the same in two days' time, and there was no reason to think he wouldn't, he would post it from New York, before he caught the train to Chicago.

He now wished he'd thought of this idea before getting this far into the journey. If only he'd come up with the plan in Paris, it would have been so easy to put the children, care of the guard, on a train bound for Vienna. Even if he'd worked it out in London, it wouldn't have been too late. One of his brothers could easily have got to London in a day or two, and till then he could have paid some nanny to keep them at the hotel.

He thought of telegraphing his brother, but he'd had enough trouble sending the telegram to Stefan. On Thursday he had finished working it down to ten coded words, including his name 'M'. It had to be like that because any more than ten words cost a lot more money. He had to let Stefan know to inform Mademoiselle Baquis to change the name on the apartment lease. Michael did not want her bloodhounds of lawyers pursuing him to the USA, and, unlike Marcella, they had the funds to do just that.

After putting the children to bed on Thursday, Michael had taken the carefully worded and coded cable down to the telegraph office to have it sent. He had arrived there to find the door closed and a notice up: TELEGRAPH SERVICE DOWN.

When he came back the next day, they told him that the ship had a massive backlog, there were hundreds of telegrams in the queue before his and to leave it with them – if he was lucky it might go off on Sunday night.

Michael hadn't wanted to leave the telegram sitting there, especially when the Marconi boys had nothing better to do than lounge about reading them. What if one of them was a keen code-breaker who enjoyed working things out and, by chance, spoke Hungarian? Unlikely, of course, but best not take extra risks. Michael had shoved it into his coat pocket, alongside the letter for his mother, where it remained.

'Bang! Bang! You're dead, Papa!'

Michael had not seen Lolo wake and climb out of bed. He was standing near the open suitcase. He was holding Michael's gun, pointing it at him.

'No, no, Lolo.' Michael raised his hands and edged himself towards the boy. He wondered why his hearing was so muffled then remembered he had put lumps of cotton wool in his ears. 'Put the gun down.'

Lolo shut one eye and aimed, his tiny fingers reaching across the trigger.

Michael threw himself forward, smashing his son to the floor, lying on top of him, immobilising him. Lolo started bawling.

Wrenching the gun from the child's hand and slamming it on top of the desk, Michael got on to his knees.

Behind him Monmon had woken, and began to howl.

'Shut up, Monmon!'

Both children screamed, full-voiced. Michael was aware of the proximity of the next cabin.

'You must promise Papa never to touch the gun,' he hissed into Lolo's crumpled teary face. 'You understand? It is not a toy.' He tried a more conciliatory tone, while stroking Lolo's tear-stained cheek. 'It's very dangerous, you see, Lolo. It's for Papa's work.'

Michael had used that reasoning with him before, in the shop with the hot irons and scissors, and it had done the trick.

As both children sobbed dramatically, Michael stood up and brushed himself down.

A rap on the door. Michael grabbed the gun and tossed it into the suitcase, flinging a neatly folded shirt on top. Another rap, this one louder and more insistent.

Michael opened the door a crack.

It was the wretched Mexican again, standing on the threshold in his pyjamas, flinging his arms around and hollering about getting a night's sleep.

'I'm sorry, monsieur…' Michael employed the pious tone which had worked so well on the cross-Channel ferry.

The man went on ranting in English. Michael decided to pretend he didn't understand him.

'I don't speak English,' Michael said quietly in French.

To Michael's shock, the Mexican now started the rant again, this time in broken French.

Apart from pretending to be Chinese, there was little escape. Michael stepped forward and whispered, 'They've recently lost their poor mother, you see. It's a tragic story.'

'But a story which is of no interest to me, monsieur,' snapped the Mexican. 'If it carries on like this, I shall complain to the captain.'

'Thank you for your understanding,' Michael replied, making no attempt to disguise his sarcasm as he clicked the door shut. When he turned back into the cabin, both boys were standing silently looking up at him with doe eyes.

'Is Mama lost?' asked Lolo, quietly.

'I want to see Mama.'

'Not today.' Michael lowered himself to their eye level. 'Into bed with you. I'll sing you a lullaby.'

He had to get them off the subject of their mother. Especially while they were trapped on this floating palace surrounded by all the nosy parkers aboard it.

He wanted to get off now.

Dining was bad enough. He didn't trust the people at his table at all, so used the children as an excuse for eating rather earlier or later than everyone else. Mostly he wanted to avoid the English schoolteacher. The man was always asking questions. Mind your own business, Mr Teacher!

Michael had got into the practice of swerving the dining room till Mr-Smart-Alec left.

Then yesterday, he was happily tucking into a nice dish of curried chicken and rice when some wretched pest of a girl called (typically) Bertha, real peasant type, joined the table. She told everyone proudly that she had confined herself to her cabin since she'd come on board at Cherbourg and hadn't been at table because she had been so, so very sick. As though people sitting eating dinner wanted to hear about her gruesome episodes of vomiting!

In one of the moments when she wasn't gabbling about her stomach contents, she must have overheard Michael speaking French with the boys and, as a result, later on, lolloped across the saloon to suggest she might look after his children for a while. Of course she did the usual wheedling act, trying to prise information from him. 'Oh, Monsieur Hoffman, it must be so difficult… without a wife… to care for the little ones' and 'Oh, Monsieur Hoffman, it's a pity you didn't bring a nanny with you…' That kind of thing.

In the end, without giving her any personal details, Michael saw there might be advantages to taking up her offer, so he relented and let her take the children off for the afternoon.

Michael made the most of the time out by joining a group of fellow travellers in a hot-poker game in the smoking room.

He'd already played a few hands, on Friday night, when the children were asleep. He'd taken a wad of cash from his roll, gone up to the bar, had a few drinks and joined a game. It had been fun. But he'd lost rather badly, and he was determined to make the money up, while those players were still around.

It had suddenly turned very cold. Michael wished he'd packed a few more warm clothes. But stewards were dashing around turning on heaters and drawing curtains over doors, working up a bit of a fug.

The sea was so calm, as well. Too calm, really. It meant everyone was rushing about in the public spaces all the time, as no one was seasick any more. There had been a very good thirty-six hours after Cherbourg during which the public rooms had been almost deserted, but of course that was when Michael was spending every waking moment chasing about after the lawless children.

He had to thank his lucky stars that Lolo wasn't finding this ship vomit-inducing, as he had the ferry.

Thinking about it, Michael did wonder whether, if he'd come aboard on his own, he might by now have found a nice lady-friend? There were a few good-looking single young women around, making moon eyes at him.

He'd had a strange moment during the poker game the other night, when the players started taking out their wallets and showing photographs of their wives. Michael had felt sorry that he didn't have a picture of Marcella to show them, as she was much more beautiful than any of their frightful specimens.

He would certainly have won that round – the 'who's got the prettiest wife' contest. The thought of her laugh had made him smile, then he felt angry with himself for having done so. Louis always said how much he admired Marcella's spontaneity and high spirits, but, as Charles Kirchmann had pointed out, there was a fine line between artlessness and cunning.

Why had Marcella changed so towards him?

It was the children.

That was it.

He should have left them with her. They were going to hold him back.

Michael had heard a saying: 'Romance always ends at marriage.'

In their case it had lasted a little longer than that.

Her family hadn't helped. Always gathering around her, advising.

She belonged to him, not them.

She was married to him.

She was his consort, his mate.

She was his.

But she changed from a ravishing, laughing beauty into a solid, dull brood-mare, fussing about the children, too tired to please him.

It wasn't fair.

He didn't want to think about her.

How dare she humiliate him?

How dare she?

———

Dinner on Sunday night was a miserable affair. The oak-panelled dining room was so cold, and the refectory-style tables too depressing. To make matters worse, the food was grim. A tasteless consommé, followed by turkey, boiled potatoes and puree of turnips – on the menu, the waiter told him, as it was 'very popular in America'. Well! If this was the preferred cuisine of the country which was henceforth to be his home, Michael had to admit that it gave him slight concerns about moving there. What a flavourless concoction, a plateful of beige.

At least Lolo and Monmon were happy. They had had their favourite dessert, ice cream, strawberry and vanilla, while he settled for the safer choice of cheese and biscuits. Even then, the cheeses served were hardly Roquefort or Époisses de Bourgogne, but some rubbery stuff with little flavour and an unpleasant texture.

People sat at the table huddled up on their bentwood chairs, in coats and scarves. Michael laughed to himself. It was like being back in a railway waiting room in Hungary on a miserable December night. Not unlike the night he escaped from the army.

That lumpish girl, Bertha, kept nodding in his direction and grinning. Did she think she was in with a chance to be the next Mrs Navratil – oops, sorry, Hoffman – he wondered?

But when he retired from the table and took the children down to the cabin, it was a great surprise when they willingly climbed into the bunk and were both fast asleep within minutes, snoring softly like puppies. Whatever the girl had done with them all afternoon had exhausted them. Which was all to the good.

For half an hour Michael hung around the cabin, just in case they woke.

He had the rest of the night to himself.

He shoved a wad of English and American money into his inside jacket pocket, and very quietly let himself out of the cabin. Taking the lift up, he went straight to the smoking room, looking for a group of men likely to fancy a game of cards.

The smoking room was perishing and deserted. One lone steward wearing gloves, a scarf tied around his neck, advised him that most of the passengers had gone to their cabins, and all the gentlemen looking for 'a little entertainment' had moved down to the library-saloon where it was warmer.

Michael left the smoking room and walked out on to the deck. The night was black.

Nothing to see except for the odd yellow flash in a ripple, reflections from the brightly lit portholes on the ship.

There was no moon tonight.

No sparkling pathway always leading back to Marcella.

In the distance, up in First Class, Michael could hear the band playing.

A slow waltz.

One of his favourites.

'The Dream of Autumn'.

Haunting and majestic.

The one piece of music that he and Marcella agreed on and loved.

But who could hear it and not believe that it was beautiful?

For a minute or two he stood still, listening. The only other sounds were laughter coming from somewhere upstairs, the constant hum of the engines, and the hiss of the prow cutting through the ocean, speeding him to America and a new life.

He was about to take out his pipe, but his hands were too cold to get the tobacco rolled and to light the match.

Anyway, no point staying out here getting maudlin and sorry for himself.

He stepped back into the companionway. Even inside, the temperature had dropped so low he was able to see his breath billowing from his mouth in a long white cloud.

He trotted down the stairs, trying to get warmer.

The library-saloon wasn't very busy, but at least it was cosy.

In a corner a group of six men were furtively playing poker.

Michael had gathered that, among many passengers and the company itself, playing cards on a Sunday was frowned upon.

He pulled up a chair and threw down some cash.

He was dealt in.

His first hand was rubbish and he knew it. But in a way that was good. Better to start off looking like a loser cos then, when you had a dazzling deal, you could catch the others off-guard.

One by one the other passengers in the lounge, who had been sitting around chatting and drinking, many in evening dress – not adequate for tonight's temperatures – quit the room to retire to the warmer space of their cabin.

Finally there was only the merry little band of card-players left. Now they could raise their voices.

'Anyone know where we are?' A hearty man with a handlebar moustache and a blue blazer scooped up the winnings and waited for the next deal.

'The Second Class saloon,' replied a wiry little man with slicked-back blond hair and a green tweed suit.

'No, I mean where the ship is.'

'Middle of the Atlantic, of course,' a rotund man with rosy cheeks guffawed. 'Where else do you think we'd be? South China Seas?'

'My cabin steward told me we're somewhere called the Devil's Hole.'

'No need to be indecent, old boy.' Rosy Cheeks laughed again, brushing a bit of fluff from his worn black tuxedo. 'There are ladies present.'

'Oh, no there aren't!'

Everyone laughed.

Everyone except Michael, who was still losing.

He had a two and a four. The flop was all picture cards. He folded.

Two days ago he had had almost eighty pounds – all that was left out of the money he'd got from Thomas Cook in London. Since start of play tonight, he was now down to twenty-five.

But *nil desperandum*.

You couldn't lose forever.

The next deal went down as Blue Blazer continued, 'The Devil's Hole is this part of the ocean where many accidents have happened.'

'Superstition. A load of fiddle-faddle.'

Michael's next hand was shaping up. He had three jacks.

He raised.

Two players folded.

He doubled again, but Green Suit, the only remaining player, raised the kitty so high that Michael was scared off, and folded.

He cursed himself when the man lay down three tens.

If only he'd stuck it out.

The dealer dealt again.

Michael glanced at his cards. Two aces.

The flop went down.

Two aces and the four of clubs.

'It's all devils today,' said Rosy Cheeks, pointing at the four. 'That card's known as the Devil's Bedpost. You can see it if you look. It's a devilish night, to be sure.'

Michael wished the stupid man would shut up so that he could concentrate. He had four aces! Who could beat that?

There was a sudden crunch and the ship lurched.

The pack of cards slid off the table and floated down, littering the carpet.

'What the hell was that?' asked Green Suit.

'Big wave, I should think,' said Blue Blazer.

'No,' replied Green Suit. 'I think we hit something.'

'It'll just be a great big wave.' Rosy Cheeks knelt down and started gathering the upturned cards from the floor.

'Or a whale,' said Green Suit.

They all laughed.

A loud scraping noise like the jangling of a chair or gravel under wooden cartwheels continued as they talked.

'Of course we'll have to deal again now,' said Rosy Cheeks. 'We've all seen what cards are left.'

Michael tried to suppress a gasp.

How could that bloody wave have timed itself worse?

He threw his aces face down into the pile of cards, which the rosy-cheeked man had dumped on the table.

'Do you know, I really do think we've hit something!' Rosy Cheeks ambled across to the window. 'Oh by jingo! Look. It's all bright-white out there. What in heaven's name is going on?'

'Look at that!' Green Suit had run to the doorway and was peering out into the darkness. 'It's an iceberg!' He stepped out on to the deck, shouting back, 'It's enormous!'

A low vibrating rattling noise, like marbles running down a tin tube, silenced all talk.

Then the engines stopped.

The man in the green suit came back in bearing a handful of lumps of ice.

'Any of you chaps for rum on the rocks?'

The next deal went down. Green Suit hastily sat, flinging the ice into a nearby pot plant.

This time Michael had the Jack of Diamonds and Queen of Spades. Not too bad a hand. But... the aces. He pulled himself together. No point wishing to go back in time.

The flop went down: Nine of Diamonds, King of Spades, Knave of Clubs.

Michael had a pair. With an eight and a ten he'd have a straight.

He put down a sufficient amount – a lot of money but not enough to give away too much confidence in his hand.

The turn: Five of Clubs.

Damn.

But Michael decided to put a little more money down on this round. Perhaps a Queen would come up in the river and he'd have two pair. Or another Knave and he'd have three of a kind.

He looked at the men around the table.

No one had that glint in their eye.

Rosy Cheeks folded.

'Evening, gentlemen! Sorry to be a spoilsport, but...'

The steward had entered, muffled up against the cold. 'Well... I've turned a blind eye to your little poker game, but it's a quarter to midnight now, so just to warn you that I'll be back in around ten minutes to turn off the lights. And, by then, you'll all be gone, won't you?'

'What just happened?' asked Blue Blazer. 'Any idea?'

'Nothing much.' The steward shivered. 'We hit an iceberg. Don't worry. Nothing serious.'

He went back out into the cold and left the men to finish the game.

The river went down: the Queen of Hearts!

Michael had two pair. High ones.

He laid down the rest of his money.

Two men folded.

It was only him and the man in the green suit, the one who'd brought in the ice, left in the game now.

Green Suit met Michael's challenge.

They both laid down their hands

Michael looked at the other man's cards: Six of Spades, Ten of Hearts.

Why was the other man grinning so? Surely Michael's hand had won?

'Straight, old chum.' Green Suit scooped up all the money from the table.

Michael had been cleared out.

All he had left now was the roll of French francs. No US or English money for tipping or getting a taxi to the station in New York. Or for food on the train.

He wondered whether he had any time to find an exchange in New York before the train left for Chicago.

He'd have to. He hadn't yet bought the tickets and now didn't even have the money left for that.

As they all rose from the table, Blue Blazer turned to Michael.

'You look as if you've had it, old man.'

'I... I...' Michael didn't know what to say.

'Cleaned out, eh? Here you go!' He flung down some coins.

'You can make back your losses tomorrow.' Green Suit joined him and flung down some more. 'No point having no one left to play with cos you've just won all their money.'

Laughing, he left the room with his friends.

'If you can't spare it, you shouldn't play it, old boy.' Rosy Cheeks gave Michael a look of pity. 'Aren't you the Froggy widower chappie, with two children in tow? Better be more careful next time, eh?'

He went, leaving Michael alone, totally humiliated.

The steward crept in and moved slowly around, turning off the lights. 'I left it a little longer than I said I would so you could finish your game. It's a bit after midnight now. Hope you did well, sir.'

Michael picked up the coins: six sovereigns which he put into his silver coin purse and two shillings which he dropped into his pocket.

What a bloody nerve.

These English bastards really did believe that their pathetic little island ruled the world, didn't they?

He took out his pipe, stuffed it and lit it, before climbing the stairs to the promenade deck.

Pressing himself against the corner rails and looking up on to the First Class above, he could see that quite a few people were out walking, many of them leaning over the side. It was the same down on the Third Class promenade below. More people out than you would expect at midnight. Especially on such a cold night.

But there was no longer any sight of the iceberg, only a coal-black sky pricked with a million stars.

It was strangely silent too.

The engine wasn't running. The ship was no longer cutting its way through the water.

Nothing but silence and the murmur of voices from above and below.

Two women, who had thrown coats over their night attire, suddenly burst through the doors behind him, gasping as the cold air hit them.

'Where is it?'

They were addressing him.

'Where is what?'

'The iceberg. They said there's a huge iceberg out here and that was what that noise was.'

'Oh. That. No. It's gone now. Out here, there is nothing but a tapestry of stars.'

They looked crestfallen.

'Darn it! Pardon my language.' The taller of the two spoke. 'I've always wanted to see an iceberg. It's so unfair.'

'We came up as quickly as we could.'

They both giggled. He noticed the tall one pulling at the other's sleeve.

'Oh well,' said the shorter woman. 'If there are no other ladies up here, we had better retire.'

'Or at least get some more clothing on!'

They disappeared as suddenly as they had come.

Michael pulled deep on his pipe and enjoyed the crisp burning sensation of the tobacco smoke hitting the back of his throat.

CHAPTER 27

Just after midnight, Monday 15 April 1912, onboard RMS Titanic
Back down in the cabin, Michael flopped on to the divan, consumed with anger.

The children were huddled up together in the bunk. They lay so still they looked like wax dolls. Why would a grown man be travelling about with two wax dolls?

Nothing seemed to have a point any more.

He opened the case and took out his wad of French francs, hoping to find an English or American banknote which had accidentally fallen in among them. But no.

How could he have blown £200 on a stupid game? It was their fault. The wax dolls. If he hadn't felt so bored and stuck he would never have thought of joining that pack of cheating wolves. Why had the bloody boat shuddered and hit that iceberg? He'd have won that round. Four aces! Who could have beaten him? How could he have been so stupid? Humiliating himself like this? He was the only one at that table who would feel like a fool tomorrow, because he had lost all his travelling cash.

Michael shoved the money back into the suitcase. At least he still had that. And it was an enormous amount. Enough to set up his shop and live for a while. He'd just have to find a bureau de change in New York to get some cash for the journey. It wasn't the end of the world.

He needed a drink. A brandy or whisky. Something which would burn right down through him, warm him and take away the edge of the self-revulsion.

There must be a bar open somewhere. Or a steward willing to fetch him something to drink. Something strong.

He left the cabin and wandered through the maze of corridors back to the lift. Then he changed his mind and decided to take the stairs. More likely to find someone about that way.

He was amazed by how many people were out of their cabins this late.

'I say! Do look where you're going, old chap.'

He lifted his head.

It was Rosy Cheeks from the poker game.

'Oh lord, old man, are you all right?' he asked. 'You look done in.'

'I am rather.' Michael was so full of self-disgust that even this comical figure would be better company than none. 'I'm trying to find a drink.'

'You'll have trouble at this time of night.' Rosy Cheeks shrugged. 'Actually I'm not quite ready to go up the wooden hill to Bedfordshire myself. Come on, old fella. Let's go find you a drink.' The man switched direction and joined Michael trudging up the stairs. 'Sorry you had such a drubbing tonight. They're a wily pair, those two. I wonder if they're not professionals, you know. Card sharps. Certainly won't be playing with them again myself.'

Michael gritted his teeth. That was it. They were pros. Cheats. Why hadn't he spotted it straight away?

'Perhaps you and I could look around and find some more congenial fellows to chum up with for a game tomorrow, eh? What do you say, old man?'

Michael didn't have anything to say. He wasn't going to risk the little money he had. Those coins that they had flung down at him as though he was some servant.

'Everyone says you were recently widowed, old boy. Sorry about that. It's not a good thing to play for money when you are in grief, you know. Your judgement goes right up the wall.'

Again Michael chose not to reply.

'If those tiddlers of yours are anything to go by, she must have been a darned good-looking woman. Very handsome pair of young'uns you've got there.'

'I've changed my mind.' Michael stopped and turned to go down. He didn't want to spend half an hour hearing this fool's conjectures about Marcella. 'I think I'll go to bed after all.'

'Hey, steward!' Rosy Cheeks called out to a man who was a few steps ahead of them, walking across the landing.

The steward spun around.

'Any chance of a drink, old boy?'

'At one o'clock in the morning?' The steward shook his head as though it was a stupid question.

'Maybe if I slipped you a quid…? What about that? Surely you could lay your hands on something for a pair of gents in distress?'

The steward hesitated.

'My friend here isn't feeling all that great, you see. Needs a little pick-me-up.'

'All right.' The steward looked about him, then beckoned them. 'Come with me.'

Michael and the man followed the steward through a door marked CREW ONLY.

They entered a different world. Once behind the pass door, the polished finish stopped. Everything was basic metal, painted in gloss. No ornate woodwork or fancy carpets in here. This was the bare bones of the ship.

The steward took a key from the chain on his belt and pulled open a cupboard. The shelves inside were lined with bottles of spirits – gin, whisky, brandy.

'Take your pick.'

'A whisky would be nice,' said Michael.

'Ditto,' said Rosy Cheeks.

The steward poured two large whiskies.

Michael knocked his back in one.

'Steady on, old man.' Rosy Cheeks took a gulp and swallowed. 'Funny thing is I feel rather tipsy already. Is the floor giving way under me, or what? Don't you feel it? Strange sensation as though I'm leaning over, or something, and only had one mouthful.'

Now that he mentioned it, Michael was aware of a sensation of being askew.

'I say – look at that!' Rosy Cheeks pointed up at the shelves. 'All the bottles! Look at the levels. What on earth's going on?'

The liquid in each bottle was at an angle of about twenty-five degrees off true.

'The ship's all skew-whiff... What?'

An officer burst through the pass door. He was wearing a life jacket.

'What are you doing hiding in here?'

The steward stood at attention, looking guilty.

'Didn't you receive the captain's orders, Percy? Every member of crew is to gather all the passengers and get them to assemble on boat deck, wearing life preservers.'

'I say, we're not sinking. Are we?' Rosy Cheeks suddenly turned whey-faced.

'At this stage, sir, it's just a precaution. But we are loading passengers on to lifeboats. So, could I please ask you, gentlemen, both to put on a life vest and head upstairs.' He addressed the steward. 'And as for you, Percy, you should be going round the cabins, knocking on doors and rousing people with this information.'

As Michael and Rosy Cheeks came out of the crew-only quarters, they found scores of people trudging up the stairs, most wearing life jackets, some in nightwear, others in evening dress, a few in coats, hats and mufflers.

A passing crewman was struggling up the steps bearing a pile of life jackets. He handed one to each of the men. 'Makes my life easier if you take one,' he said. 'I want to get shot of them.'

When Michael and his new friend reached the boat deck they found people standing in huddles, chattering. Women were fighting with their husbands, struggling to avoid the terrifying ordeal of climbing into a dangling lifeboat and facing the ninety-foot drop that it entailed.

Somewhere in the distance musicians were playing the closing bars of a jaunty tune: 'Alexander's Ragtime Band'.

'Women and children only,' a male voice shouted. 'Hurry along there, please. Come on, ladies. Get in. We can't hang around.'

A hissing noise above them, and all at once the darkness was broken by the dazzling glitter of a flare, soaring above the ship into the black sky.

Michael glanced over the side of the ship. For a few moments the water was brightly lit. He could see that a number of crowded rowing boats were already floating down there in the sea. There were at least four on this side of the ship.

'Old boy? Shouldn't you go down and get your nippers?'

Michael had no idea what the man was talking about.

The band struck up. 'La Petite Tonkinoise'.

'Your two tots. Your boys!'

'I… I…' Michael felt utterly disorientated.

'He calls me his bourgeois p'tite
His Tonki-ki, his Tonki-ki, his Tonkinoise…'

All around him, these bunches of people wearing life jackets, babbling animatedly in voices he could not hear, and the knowledge that all those silent rowing boats were bobbing about, down on the liquorice-black sea…

'They make sweet eyes at him…'

Michael felt panic rising.

He was paralysed to the spot.

'But it's me he likes best.'

He didn't know what to do.

'Come on, Hoffman. Pull yourself together, man.' Rosy Cheeks grabbed Michael's elbow. 'I'll help you, old boy. Can't carry two sleeping children on your own, can you? Only got one pair of arms, eh?'

Once down in the cabin, Michael pulled back the covers and stared at Monmon, who had somehow wriggled out of his night-shirt. Suddenly he looked so tiny, barely more than a baby.

'You'd better put a coat on, old fellow. Me too. Look, I'll be back in a jiffy. My cabin's just along the way.'

And he was gone.

Monmon moaned and Lolo pulled the covers back over himself.

Michael opened the wardrobe and slung on his coat.

The money!

He hastily threw open the suitcase, snatched the great wad of cash and stuffed it into his coat pocket. Then he saw the gun and slid it in next to the money. Then he stooped to shake Lolo.

Rosy Cheeks reappeared at the door, a coat thrown over him and a top hat perched on his head.

'Only head covering I could lay me hands on, old boy. Now hand over the baby.'

Michael bent down, picked up Monmon, still wrapped in the ship's blanket, and passed him across.

Then, grabbing Lolo and cradling him in his arms, he followed Rosy Cheeks out of the cabin.

Instinctively Michael turned towards the lift.

'No, no,' shouted Rosy Cheeks. 'Not with the ship at this angle. It might stick. Then where would we be?'

The two men started the long climb up six staircases to the boat deck.

The stairs and landings were now packed with people, all pressing and shoving, trying, as they were, to reach the top and get into a lifeboat.

The slow walk up felt interminable, and Michael's arms ached with the weight of Lolo.

Out on deck, nothing could be heard above the excruciating hiss of steam being released from pipes on the funnels.

Gripping the children tight, the two men thrust themselves forward, pushing through gaggles of men, some smoking, others fighting, everyone elbowing their way towards the few remaining lifeboats.

Near to them, a gang of sailors were tugging on ropes, and another lifeboat disappeared down the side.

'We need to go the other way, old man!' cried Rosy Cheeks. 'Head towards the prow. There are no more boats back here.'

They both turned. Ahead of them a group of men were hauling a lifeboat down from its position above the officers' quarters.

As he ran Michael sensed that the incline towards the prow was now so steep it felt as though he was running downhill. He was fearful that he would slip on the damp boards, tumble and break the fragile child in his arms.

'STOP!' bellowed Rosy Cheeks as a nearby lifeboat packed with women was about to be lowered. 'We bear children!'

Michael could see that this lifeboat wasn't like the others. It had dark pull-up canvas sides.

Michael stepped up, hoping to climb over the side and get in.

'Get back!' a deckhand shouted. 'No men!'

'But… I'm their father. Their only—'

'Get back! Get back, or I'll shoot! No men!'

Michael wanted to grab his own gun and force the sailor to let him in, but his arms were full with the child.

He glanced across and saw that Monmon was already on the lifeboat, a tiny bundle in a blanket, being handed over everyone's head, from woman to woman.

'RELEASE COLLAPSIBLE D!' cried the officer.

The little boat shuddered as the crew started to unwind the ropes which held it out, suspended over the ocean.

'My mother knows where to…' he whispered into Lolo's ear as he thrust the boy forward, remembering that the letter containing his destination was still in his pocket. 'Your mother will find you. Tell her—'

'LOWER LIFEBOAT D!'

Just as the collapsible disappeared over the side of the ship, Michael threw Lolo from the deck into the descending lifeboat. 'Tell her… Tell her I'm…' he shouted.

But he knew there was no point finishing the sentence.

CHAPTER 28

Two a.m., Monday 15 April 1912
Michael rushed forward, following Rosy Cheeks, still wearing his top hat, to join a group of around fifty men trying to dislodge the last lifeboat from the roof of the officers' quarters. It was another collapsible, with dark canvas sides, just like the one his sons were in.

But the tilt of the ship was against the men. They were attempting to drag the boat uphill, while working with their arms above their heads.

A teenaged boy took a knee-up and clambered up the white metal wall, using the window frames for a foothold. Once on the roof, he started kicking the lifeboat forward towards the men's outstretched arms.

The *Titanic* suddenly lurched, tumbling the boy backwards off the roof, knocking Michael to the floor.

Lying flat on his face, cheeks pressed into the deck, Michael started sliding down towards the encroaching water, already lapping the pine boards.

The wretched band was still playing. A Strauss waltz, reminding him of his mother and his childhood with his family back in Presbourg.

Hauling himself against the incline, Michael saw the lifeboat roll over the side of the roof and slither down on to the deck. Like wild animals diving into their prey, the men around him descended upon it. But the boat was upside down, and the great angle of the deck meant that no one would be able to get it up on to the davits.

Scrambling to his knees, Michael started crawling uphill towards the other men and the upturned boat.

Using their joint strength, they pushed it.

Michael stood up. The water now reached his knees.

A sudden wave knocked him off his feet again and washed the collapsible from the deck into the sea, taking most of the men with it.

Michael watched the others as they leaped off the deck towards the hull of the boat.

That was the way to do it!

He would join them standing on the floating boat's hull.

Using the ship's rails he pulled himself up and, once balanced, launched himself into the air, aiming to hit the centre.

But at the same moment the ship shuddered and the lifeboat bobbed away.

Michael hit the freezing water and was pulled right under.

The shock made him gasp. He took in a mouthful of seawater.

Spluttering, he bobbed back to the surface, and managed to swim towards the inverted lifeboat.

As Michael swam he banged his hand on a broken floating deckchair, which someone had flung overboard. He pulled his fist out of the water. In the light from the portholes, sparkling on the waves, he could see blood flowing down into his sleeve. He grabbed hold of the remains of the wooden deckchair till he regained his equilibrium.

Then he tried to take another few strokes forward.

His coat was too heavy.

It was pulling him down.

Ahead of him he could see that some of the men had managed to climb up on to the boat's hull, others were lying face down across the wooden planks, a few kneeling.

He took another few strokes.

Finally his fingers slid along the canvas sides resting on the surface of the water.

He tried to haul himself up but his coat kept tugging him back, dragging him down.

Another wave swept him away from the upturned boat, and safety.

He tried to swim forward again but his damned coat was preventing him.

It was the gun.

The bloody gun.

Why did he have a loaded gun in his coat? Of course it would pull him down, and at this point what could he do with the stupid thing anyway?

He plunged his injured hand into his pocket and felt for the gun's handle. The revolver was stuck in the pocket flap. He couldn't get it out.

Shoving his hand further down, Michael gripped the hard metal of the barrel, then slid it upwards.

It was no use.

He had to get on the boat!

His fingers were touching it. All he had to do was haul himself up the sloping bottom, then it wouldn't matter that his coat was heavy.

He lifted his arm and thrust it forward towards the wooden slats of the lifeboat.

Then he saw that he had inadvertently pulled all his money out. Floating on the surface all around him were French franc notes.

Thirty thousand worth.

He grabbed out, trying to grasp the banknotes.

Trying to shove handfuls of money back into his pockets.

The band played on.

'The Dream of Autumn'.

He could see himself waltzing around the living room in Avenue Shakespeare. Marcella was in his arms, throwing back her head, laughing.

Then he saw another large wad of banknotes, drifting on a wave. It was only a few metres away.

It wouldn't be too hard to reach.

He let go of the lifeboat and stretched for the money.

At the same moment, a huge explosion threw Michael out of the water and plunged him down, down, down.

He couldn't see.

He couldn't breathe.

Darkness.

Margaret

CHAPTER 29

11.40 p.m., Sunday 14 April 1912, onboard RMS Titanic

When the iceberg struck, Margaret Hays was lying in bed, staring at the ceiling, thinking. She was thinking principally how she was bored to tears and absolutely longing for this eternal journey to be over.

After the horrors of their accommodation in Europe, the ship had provided a welcome level of absolute comfort, it was true.

But Margaret was disappointed.

It appeared to her that all the famous people and millionaires kept well to themselves.

It all started on the *Nomadic*. As the tender neared the big ship, the celebrated names were called to go into the *Titanic* first, while those not in Superior (though still First Class) cabins, like herself, were left right to the end.

Once onboard it was an evening of great excitement, discovering all the cafés and lounges, gawping at the gymnasium and swimming pool and racing Gilbert up and down the grand staircases. She had been longing to chat to Colonel and Mrs John Jacob Astor IV (after all, Mrs Astor and Margaret were practically of an age – give or take five years). She wanted too to get a glimpse of the elderly Isador Strauss, or see the streetcar tycoons, Mr and Mrs George Widener, who didn't live that far from her grandparents in Philadelphia, and were accompanied by their handsome 27-year-old son and heir, Harry... Who knew? Perhaps she and Harry Widener might hit it off and then she too could be a millionairess. She had read that he had a passion for books, so she made sure always to carry one around the ship in case he might pass her and ask what she was reading.

But, despite scouring the promenade decks every day, Margaret had never managed to get near any of them. They were so cliquey, these famous, rich people. They swanned around in their priceless evening gowns, always in the far distance, surrounded by maids and valets, who moved ahead of them like a snow plough on a train, pushing the riff-raff out of their path.

These stars of the social scene never seemed to frequent the public lounges, unless it was at a time when Margaret was elsewhere. Whichever restaurant Mrs Potter chose for the evening, naturally the celebrities were dining in the other one. It seemed to Margaret that they were deliberately avoiding her.

Then, tonight, four days into the voyage, Margaret had finally managed, if only from afar, to watch the Wideners at dinner. They were only one table away, seated in a corner of the *à la carte* restaurant on B deck. It was a slightly special occasion as they were hosting a fancy champagne-swilled party in honour of that pompous bearded windbag, Captain Smith. From where Margaret was sitting, it all looked very gay.

The dinner menu included 'jambon d'York' and 'artichoke bottoms', which, for some reason, she and Gilbert had found hilariously funny and they laughed so loudly that some members of the Widener family had turned to look. Margaret had also attracted the Wideners' attention when she made leery noises at the sight of her gaudy dessert: 'peaches in Chartreuse jelly'.

But apart from that, life at sea was so very, very dull, even with Bébé and Gilbert in tow. And there were three long days ahead.

What could one do, really, onboard ship, but eat, sleep and chat?

Even if *Titanic* was the most famous ship in the world, it was still essentially just a ship, despite all the fuss. There were glorious staircases, dining rooms and salons. The covered walkways were nice and the Café Parisien (named that although it bore no relation to any café Margaret had seen while in Paris) was light and elegant, with its wicker chairs and trellises up the walls. The orchestra was great, so was the food. And having a gymnasium and swimming pool onboard was a terrific novelty, Margaret was told, although neither attracted her to use them. Much too *sportif*! Really, being aboard the *Titanic* was like being in a very posh New York hotel, only you were trapped inside.

So, when, just before midnight on Sunday 14 April, the rumbling shock had quivered through the cabin which she shared with Olive, practically shaking her out of her bed, in Margaret's opinion, it was a very welcome bit of excitement.

After the long crunch – for that is what it was like, a massive sickening crunching sound – Margaret managed to rouse Olive, who had been snoring like a wild hog. Olive denied being asleep at all and claimed she was only 'snug in bed against the frightful cold'.

'That noise wasn't normal, Olive. You must admit.'

'I didn't really hear anything.'

'That's no excuse, Olive. Believe me. Something's up.'

Together, in their dressing gowns, they went along the corridor to talk to Mrs Potter, who was extremely alarmed and ordered them to hurry back to their cabin and put on warm clothing (it was a perishing night, for certain). Then they should go up on deck to find out exactly what was going on.

'You realise the engines have stopped,' shouted Lily Potter after the girls. 'Stopped! In the middle of the Atlantic Ocean! That means there's something very wrong!'

On their way up the stairs, Margaret and Olive encountered many stewards who all told them the same thing: 'Nothing to worry about, ladies, Best go back to bed.'

But Margaret felt sure these men weren't 'in the know', and that, if they went looking, there was more to be found out.

On the outer deck there was some kerfuffle. A bunch of men were throwing lumps of ice about. 'You missed the best bit,' they told Margaret. 'A huge iceberg bashed into us. It was like a great white wall. But it's gone now.'

As the two girls slowly descended the grand staircases, Olive said to Margaret, 'It is all slightly odd, don't you think? I feel as though something is gently pulling me down the stairs. Do you feel the same?'

Now that Olive mentioned it, Margaret did think that there was a disconcerting feeling about the steps, almost as though they were slipping away beneath her feet. Everything seemed out of kilter. It was how she had felt back in Smyrna, after a few glasses of that awful Turkish wine.

They went and banged on Gilbert's door.

He was already fully dressed, pulling on an overcoat.

'What's going on?' he cried. 'Have we run aground? There was the most frightful scraping noise—'

'We know, Gilbert.' Margaret beckoned him. 'The ship hit an iceberg. Come on! There's lots of fun happening up on the outer deck.'

'I think we'd better talk to Mother first.' Olive was, of course, being sensible.

'Right ho, gals!' Gilbert grabbed some gloves, threw on a hat then joined them going round the corner to knock on Mrs Potter's cabin door.

'We're sinking, aren't we?' Mrs Lillian Potter, usually so staid, was now near hysterical. 'Look! We're miles and miles away from land. We're all going to drown.'

'No! No! Nothing like that,' said Margaret, just as a steward appeared at the far end of the corridor.

He was knocking on doors.

'Captain's orders, ladies and gentlemen,' he shouted. 'Life vests on and assemble on boat deck.'

'You see! We are all going to die!' shrieked Lillian, gripping the door handle in a state of near collapse.

'I believe it's simply a precaution, madam,' said the steward. 'To lighten the load on the ship while we straighten her up.'

'Nonsense!' said Mrs Potter under her breath. 'Straighten her up? Whoever heard such a thing?'

'Hurry along, ladies,' said the steward as he moved off. 'But don't be alarmed. No danger, no danger whatsoever. You'll be back onboard for breakfast.'

Margaret noticed that his face was as white as paper.

'"No danger whatsoever"! "Straighten her up"! We're heading to the bottom. We're all going to die!'

'Calm down, Mother.' Olive watched the steward disappear. 'It'll all be fine.'

Margaret heard the quiver in Olive's voice, saw that she too was terrified.

'There are lifeboats on deck,' said Gilbert brightly. 'It's just a matter of getting in them.'

'Quickly, then,' said Mrs Potter. 'Do as the steward says. Grab all your valuables and wrap up warm. Corsets off – they'll hamper us if we need to swim. We'll assemble at the foot of the staircase in two minutes.'

As Margaret ran off with Olive to their cabin, trailed by ever-faithful Gilbert, she wondered why two minutes. If they were in a rush why not one; if they weren't in a rush, then why not five?

'I'll peel off here to fetch my life preserver.' Gilbert disappeared round the corner as the women unlocked the door to their own cabin.

Bébé was curled up asleep on Margaret's pillow. Typical of a dog to make the most of the warmth of the spot where her head had lain minutes earlier. Margaret wrapped her tenderly in one of the ship's blankets.

'What are you doing?' asked Olive.

'Unlike you, Olive, I didn't bring swathes of diamonds and pearls. Bébé's my valuable thing, isn't she? She's all I have in the world. And she does love me so.'

Margaret knew that a dog was a very good way of meeting people. People always talked to dogs; then, if they were polite, they had to talk to you. The steward had said that everyone was to gather up on deck, so surely that meant *everyone*. Perhaps a dog would be the gateway to making the acquaintance of somebody who really *was* someone.

Four minutes later, when they all reached boat deck, Margaret saw ahead, at last, one of the subjects of her cherished desires: huddled with a few others, the Astors were standing under a light outside the gymnasium. Mrs Astor was in a large hat wrapped in a scarf and sporting a long coat.

As Margaret strolled nonchalantly towards the place where the millionaires were sheltering, she also noticed Sir Cosmo and Lady Duff-Gordon sweep past, heading towards the forward part of the deck. Lady D-G, Margaret knew, was the fashion designer Lucile.

She too was wearing a long coat, but hers was made entirely of mink or squirrel. Something lush and luxurious, anyway. It must have cost a fortune. Lucile looked rather fatter than Margaret thought she would be, then she realised she must have on lots of warm clothes underneath.

It was certainly freezing. Margaret now wished she'd thought of putting on a dressing gown and a few more sweaters.

On the water side of the deck a gang of burly sailors were hauling at the tarpaulin cover of a nearby lifeboat, pulling ropes and pushing levers, while someone in uniform was barking orders at them.

'Let's stop here,' said Margaret brightly, swerving inwards to be nearer the Astors.

'Hey there, Hogg!' called the officer to a passing crewman. 'Jump up inside there and check the plugs.'

'I hope somebody has wirelessed ahead for assistance,' muttered Lily Potter. 'You know where we are, don't you? Miles away from anywhere.'

'Don't worry, Mother.' Olive patted Lily's arm. 'Look around. There is no panic. It's more like a drill.'

Seeing Bébé cradled in her arms, a passing passenger stopped in front of Margaret. 'Oh, how darling!' he said. 'I suppose we really ought to put a life preserver on the little doggie too!'

'Oh, everyone's wearing them this season,' Margaret replied with a little bob, which she hoped showed off her figure to advantage. 'They're all the rage in gay Paree, you know.'

She smiled at her own joke and coyly kissed the dog's head.

But when she looked up, the gentleman was gone.

'Start boarding Lifeboat 7!' shouted the officer. He then turned to the gaggle of people on deck. 'Come along, ladies. All aboard. Quick as you can.'

'Why should we go?' called a woman standing behind Margaret. 'There is nothing wrong, is there?'

'It seems more sensible to remain aboard this big ship, J-J,' Margaret heard Madeleine Astor murmur to her husband. 'After all, she is supposedly unsinkable.'

'Better safe than sorry, my darling,' said Astor himself. 'And best, too, I suppose, for us to set an example to the others.'

Another lady nearby was arguing quite loudly with her husband. 'No, no, no, Frederick! What is the use? I don't want to flail around out there in the darkness, bobbing about in a tiny little dinghy while I could be comfortable and safe standing on the solid boards of this ship. Look at the drop, Frederick! Just look at the drop! I'm not a pole-vaulter.' She shuddered and pressed her face into her husband's life vest. 'I couldn't bear it, Freddie. I'm staying here with you.'

At this moment, Captain Smith marched past. 'All aboard Lifeboat 7, ladies and gents! As Officer Murdoch has ordered.'

When no one moved, he clapped his hands in that really annoying jolly spirit of bonhomie he was always employing. Then he put on one of his sickly grins and said, 'Honeymoon couples! Come on! All honeymooners on to Lifeboat 7, please. Let's get going!'

Some couples reluctantly stepped forward and clambered in, followed by a small group of men talking to one another in French.

'Look at the list,' whispered a man passing close by. 'Very disturbing. It's a real slope. We're definitely going down.'

Lily followed the man's gaze along the deck, then said loudly, 'That's it! Come on, girls!' She marched to join the line boarding lifeboat number 7. 'We're getting on that one too.'

'But Mother—' cried Olive.

'Surely we'd be better to wait until things—' Margaret curtailed her sentence when she noticed that among the queue to climb aboard Lifeboat 7 was none other than the Hollywood film star, Dorothy Gibson.

Instantaneously, she observed Colonel Astor pushing his wife forward to join them.

'Yes, Mrs Potter,' said Margaret loudly. 'You are quite right. Come on, Olive! Gilbert! Let's catch this lifeboat...' she raised her voice, hoping it would carry further, '...we really *must* set an example to others.'

Not far away the band struck up. They were giving a lively rendition of one of Margaret's favourites, 'Alexander's Ragtime Band'.

'Let me help you up, Mrs Potter.' She grabbed Lily's arm and shoved her into the boat, then gripping Bébé close to her breast, she

257

clambered after her. While Olive and Gilbert followed, Margaret was very disappointed to see Mrs Astor rush back into her husband's arms.

Just then, when it was too late to get off again, the sailors cried, 'Let her go!' and the lifeboat started its terrifying descent into the ocean. As the ropes were let off it shuddered down, jerk after jerk, for the whole ninety feet to sea level.

All the women shrieked and, Margaret suspected, so did the men, only more quietly.

'Is it meant to go down like this?' asked one of the young ladies.

'I don't know,' replied the boy from the crew who was standing at the end of the lifeboat grasping the rope which suspended them from the davits. 'I've never been in a lifeboat before.'

Well, that was encouraging! Fancy discovering *now* that the people in charge were as much amateurs at this lifeboat business as they were.

If Margaret had known it would be this bloodcurdlingly scary, she might not have been so keen to get in, film star or no film star.

As Lifeboat 7 hit the water with an almighty smack, everyone inside was drenched with ice-cold spray.

Then water started gushing into the bottom of the boat.

'My feet are soaked!' cried a lady sitting in the centre.

'Mine too!' said her neighbour. 'There's water pouring in.'

Margaret shuddered at the thought of the black sea swirling beneath them. This was real, wasn't it? Two of the sailors aboard untied the oars and started rowing.

'The plug will have come out,' yelled crewman Hogg, from the tiller. 'You need to push it back in, pronto.'

Dorothy Gibson bent forward and struggled for a few seconds with something on the floor. 'The stupid thing just keeps popping back out again.'

'Jam it!' shouted Hogg. 'Stamp on it.'

'That doesn't work either.'

'Then use your ingenuity or we'll all drown.'

Drown! He said drown! They really might drown. Margaret tried to swallow but her tongue seemed paralysed.

'I'll use my silk undies,' cried Dorothy. 'But I'll need more than one pair. Anyone?'

Margaret had no intention of drowning now. She had to help. She reached down and, with as much propriety as possible, yanked off her undergarments and passed them forward.

'Thanks, dear lady back there,' cried Dorothy Gibson, receiving Margaret's pants.

Through her fear, Margaret felt a warm glow. She had contributed.

'Any more, anything in silk or cotton. Come on! These plugs are pretty large. And we'll sink for certain if we don't get it to stay in.' Men and women alike pulled off stockings and passed them along to the centre of the boat.

Four men were at the oars now, rowing the boat further and further away from the big ship.

When they were about one hundred yards out, they rested.

Margaret was glad she wasn't sitting near her friends. She didn't want them murmuring things which would frighten her. More than that – she didn't want them to see how scared she was. In the rush to get on they'd all been separated. Gilbert was nearest. She could see him, two laps along the same bench, squashed up against the far side.

While the lifeboat floated gently on the glass-flat sea, Hogg asked a woman sitting just behind Margaret to take over the tiller while he moved across to help the oarsmen.

He then clambered all over her, trampling on her coat, as he made his way to the middle of the lifeboat.

'Come on! Help there! You!' He pointed towards one of the men who was in a languishing position, leaning back on the bench behind him, taking up two seats. 'Take an oar!'

'Absolutely not,' snapped the man. He had an accent – German or Dutch, thought Margaret, not unlike her grandparents'. 'Baron Alfred von Drachstedt does not do manual work.'

'Then could I ask you, sir, to extinguish your cigarette, as I believe it is upsetting the ladies.'

'You can ask me, but I'm certainly not going to put it out.' The indolent man took another long drag, and tapped the ashes into the sea, scattering pale sparks over the water. He then crushed the stub against the side of the boat and tossed the butt away. Margaret was about to applaud, but the man immediately pulled a packet from his coat pocket, stuck another cigarette between his lips and lit up. 'There!'

Margaret decided that she hated him.

Shouts caused everyone to turn their heads.

'Lifeboat 5 here!' Another sailor in a nearby lifeboat called across to them. 'We're overloaded. Can you take a few?'

The two boats moved towards one another until their hulls gently bumped together.

The number 5 sailor strapped ropes across, attaching the two boats, then he and Hogg carefully helped four women and a baby climb over into theirs.

While this went on, the boat rocked so violently that Margaret was scared they'd capsize. She gripped the edge of the wooden seat with one hand, while clutching Bébé with the other.

'We need another male over here. A strong one. To row. We are short of *real* men on this boat.' This was said with a certain weight.

The baron snorted.

A man from Lifeboat 5 scrambled over into number 7 and briskly took up an oar.

The two boats separated, and Hogg ordered them to row as fast as possible.

'Why are we moving away from the ship?' asked a woman whose face Margaret could not see, for the people in between. 'When we were told we would be going back after a while…'

'We don't want to get pulled in by the suction when she goes down,' replied Hogg.

When she goes down. Was that what he'd said? Did this mean that everything they'd been told before was all a lie and they weren't getting back onboard? He had clearly said, *When she goes down!* Heart pounding, Margaret peered back over her shoulder towards the *Titanic*. She could see that the ship was tilting forward quite dramatically. One whole row of windows was practically submerged. She tried to count the decks down from the top. That would mean that E deck was totally flooded. Only two decks beneath their own cabins! Margaret had been down to F deck to see the swimming pool and racquet court. By now they must be full of water, right up past the ceilings. The ship really might sink!

Margaret hugged Bébé closer to her breast. Her warmth made up for the ice cold of Margaret's fingers. She remembered that she had entered her for the dog show tomorrow. She supposed that wouldn't go ahead now. And her fancy-dress costume would now be wasted.

Suddenly a flare shot up into the sky, sounding like a cannon but looking like a beautiful firework, briefly illuminating the ocean in a bright-white sparkle.

She glanced beyond Gilbert's lap and noticed that, since the additional passengers had been brought aboard, their own lifeboat had sunk further.

Was that a good or bad thing?

The light of the flare diminished and was gone. They were again in the dark, lit only by the reflection from the lights on the big ship.

Over the sound of the oars cutting through the water, Margaret could hear the band. They were playing that funny French ditty that had blared out from every café in Paris and was so very popular down on the Côte d'Azur.

'He calls me his bourgeois p'tite
His Tonki-ki, his Tonki-ki, his Tonkinoise...'

Margaret turned her back on the ship. It was too terrible to look at. While she was looking, watching it sink before her very eyes, she had to believe what was happening. But if she diverted her eyes, she could imagine other things. Nice things.

She stared at the gloved hands of the men gripping the oars as they rowed on into the black night. She noticed that one of the Frenchmen wore a monocle while rowing. How stylish to leave it in while tugging at an oar! But that was the French for you. She could also see that his mouth was moving. As he rowed he was singing along with the band.

'D'autres me font les doux yeux
Mais c'est elle que j'aime le mieux.'

At a signal from Hogg, when Lifeboat 7 was a good half mile away from the ship, the men once more stopped rowing, and let the boat drift.

'It's like a glittering palace in a fairy tale,' sighed the other Frenchman. 'It doesn't even look real, does it? More like a piece of scenery… from a Christmas operetta.'

'You're right, Monsieur Chevré.' Dorothy Gibson gave a sob. 'It looks just like that. A curious, painted reproduction.'

'The music they're playing only helps the illusion,' he replied. 'Ah! Listen! One of my favourite tunes. "Songe d'Automne".'

Margaret stared ahead. There was no doubt now that the *Titanic*, so majestic and huge, really was sinking.

For many long minutes every person in Lifeboat 7 gazed at the ship.

No one spoke.

With a crackle, another flare lit the sky and sea. Margaret could make out the silhouettes of five or more lifeboats, like cockleshells, floating in the distance.

As the glow of the flare faded away, she watched one, then another, line of electric lights on *Titanic* snuff out as the decks sank under the water.

Every time this happened Lillian Potter let out a little wail.

Under a tar-black sky, Margaret could see that seawater had now reached *Titanic*'s front funnel.

From that position there was no way any ship could be righted.

Suddenly the funnel broke away and tumbled down with a giant splash.

They were not going back to the *Titanic*, after all.

This wasn't an 'adventure'.

They were stranded in a tiny wooden boat, thousands of miles away from land.

There was no chance that they could row to the shore like she had done as a child with her grandpappy out in the dinghy on Lake Nelson in Piscataway Township, New Jersey.

They were alone, in the middle of an enormous, cruel ocean.

For the first time in her life, Margaret felt real fear.

She gripped Bébé, who, in compensation, licked her face.

Margaret wished she hadn't, as it meant she was now very aware of the cold air on her cheeks. At the moment she started wiping the dog-spit away, the *Titanic* lurched forward.

A loud gasp from everyone on Lifeboat 7 was eclipsed by the much louder roar from the ship, a terrific sound, like thousands of tons of rocks rumbling down a metal chute. The noise growled on for several seconds.

'Dear God!' cried Lily Potter. 'Lord save us!'

Margaret wanted to comfort her. But there were no words.

A burst of red sparks showered up from the ship and descended slowly, a fountain of fire.

It was like some nightmare version of the Fourth of July.

Margaret saw in the glow that every face in the rowing boat bore the same expression of awe and horror.

Two more dull underwater explosions followed, and then the keel of the *Titanic* rose up from the water.

Margaret could see the propellers.

This was it!

Oh God!

All the remaining electric lights on the ship flickered and were extinguished. The *Titanic* seemed to dance in the water, turning slowly on her axis; then, after staying still for about a minute, she slid gracefully down beneath the waves, leaving behind nothing but darkness.

The sounds of the ship were replaced by the deafening roar of hundreds of people floundering in the water, screaming for help.

Up till now Margaret had imagined that everyone had been saved, snug in a lifeboat; that they'd all be out there, floating in little boats, as she was.

But the desperate cries indicated that hundreds and hundreds of people were in the ice-cold sea.

'We must go back,' someone shouted at the other end of the boat. 'We must try to save them.'

'No, no,' replied another. 'We'll be swamped. They'll pull us under. Then we'll all be dead.'

Who was right?

Margaret wished she could be deaf to the screams of those poor people in the water.

She tried to hum to herself.

A man nearby hoarsely whispered, 'My brother is among them.' He covered his face with his hands.

For an hour those wild cries floated over the water, growing fainter and fainter, until finally all was quiet.

CHAPTER 30

Early Monday 15 April 1912, Lifeboat 7

Margaret was roused from a trance of fear and exhaustion by the shattering crack of a gunshot.

Everybody in the lifeboat screamed.

'What are you doing, you idiot?' shouted Hogg.

'I thought if I fired off a shot or two,' said the baron, 'we might attract the attention of a passing ship.'

Hogg held out his arm and pointed into the darkness. 'There is no ship. If you want to do something useful, take off some of your clothing and give it to the ladies around you who are suffering badly from cold.'

The baron made a scoffing sound.

Margaret could hear the Frenchmen talking quietly among themselves. She hoped they were plotting to throw that horrible person overboard.

If this man was an example of what aristocrats were really like, she wanted to have nothing to do with them. It was quite an education.

Margaret looked up. The sky was thick with stars. She had never seen so many in all her life; the glass-black water itself sparkled with their glow.

If only it wasn't in the middle of an ugly nightmare, Margaret thought it must be magnificent.

'Look!' One of the women at the front of the boat tried to rise. 'A ship! A ship! There's the starboard light. A green light! Look!'

'I'm sorry.' Hogg gently helped her back down. 'But that'll be one of the emergency cutters. They have green lights.'

Margaret knew that there were other lifeboats out there, but it was so dark she couldn't see them. She wondered how everyone else was doing. All those people at her dining table, for instance? All the ladies and gentlemen she'd seen taking lunch in the Café Parisien yesterday? All the people who had boarded at Cherbourg on the SS *Nomadic* with her? Were they all nearby, floating in cockleshells too? She hoped so.

Margaret couldn't tell where the sea ended and the sky began. There were so many stars, and some of them were so bright. She hoped they had got it wrong and that one of the stars on the horizon really was a ship.

Her mind kept swinging back to school, to the large poster on the classroom wall showing the whole world, with the USA in the centre. On either side of America was a huge blue patch representing an ocean, each one bigger than the country itself, one of which was the Atlantic. Having only travelled in the tiniest corner of her country herself, she remembered that it took days to travel even half an inch by motor car. And here they were in a tiny rowing boat, in the middle of that huge blue ocean. They wouldn't even be a minuscule dot on that map. With only oar power to move them.

And that was terrifying enough, without imagining the miles of black water stretching beneath them, down into abysmal depths.

They had already been bobbing here for hours.

What if no one ever found them?

A ship might pass two miles away but not be able to see them.

What if no ship came?

Would they all die of thirst?

Would they eat each other, like people in that horrid big painting she had seen in the Louvre Museum in Paris, *The Raft of the Medusa*?

Would the lifeboats drift slowly to shore, and one day, in the far-distant future, someone in Africa or Lapland would find a battered old lifeboat full of skeletons?

Margaret shuddered with fear.

Or was that the cold?

She was bitterly cold.

She'd never known cold like this, even during a New York winter.

But she was lucky. At least she had the warmth of Bébé cuddled up to her abdomen.

Hogg had been so worried about some of the women in the centre of the boat that he had pulled out a sail and stretched it across people's heads. Margaret was glad she wasn't on those seats. She'd hate to be covered by a sail. She liked to be able to see. Even though there was nothing there except blackness and a billion white sparkles, which were really stars.

On the bench in front of her, Margaret could hear Lily and Olive murmuring prayers.

That *really* wasn't helpful.

She tried to focus on the stars.

Perhaps she could try counting them.

That might take her mind off the horrible reality of the situation.

She wondered now how she had ever thought the name 'artichoke bottoms' so funny that it made her cry with laughter.

What time might it be? It felt as though they'd been out here for days. But it was still dark, so it could only be four or five hours.

Would dawn never come?

'Is that a ship?' A woman's voice just in front of Lily and Olive.

'No,' replied a male voice, which Margaret thought was one of the crew aboard. 'It's a star. Venus, maybe; that's usually bright and lies on the horizon in the early morning.'

'Look, though, sailor. It's moving. It can't be a star. It's a light.'

'If it's moving, then it's a shooting star.'

Margaret scanned the darkness for this star which was so bright. But all stars looked much the same to her.

'It's still moving,' muttered the woman. 'Imperceptibly, but moving. It *has* to be a ship.'

Margaret had heard of people lost in deserts, dying of thirst, who saw an oasis ahead of them. But when they reached it found that it was only a figment of their imagination, a mirage. That was probably what the lady had seen. A mirage. Something she wanted to see. Something they all wanted to see.

'Look east,' called a man. 'Is that dawn, finally?'

Now *he* might be right. Margaret really could perceive a faint streak of pale blue behind them. She twisted in her seat and peered towards the horizon. The eerie glimmering glow was spreading, taking on a pink hue.

Thank God, soon, daylight would come.

Surely once the darkness left them they would feel better?

'It is a ship! Please believe me. That light is a ship.'

Margaret tilted her neck forward and peered at the black in the west. She saw it now, the light. Right on the horizon. And the woman was correct. It *was* moving. Surely no shooting star lasted that long, no planet moved that fast?

The dawn light meant that they could at least see the water around them. A cobalt-blue mirror. Not a ripple.

Margaret started to be able to make out other lifeboats.

And lots of ships, tall and white against the glimmering skyline!

She was about to shout with joy, but then she realised that they were not ships that she could see floating around them upon the silver water. They were icebergs, white as swans, gracefully gliding between the dots of lifeboats.

The eastern horizon behind her now bore a radiant red band. The rosy light caught the bergs, turning their peaks to crimson.

'There *is* a ship!' cried Hogg. 'Look there! About four miles off. Now is the time to fire your gun, baron.'

'I've no cartridges left.'

'Row now! Row, everyone,' Hogg shouted. 'Row with all your might!'

A distant green fizz soared into the sky.

'A rocket! They're firing rockets. They're looking for us!'

'Hoorah!' the Frenchmen shouted. 'Hoorah!'

Margaret thought her heart would burst.

The men at the oars were joined now by two women, who tugged and pushed, turning their little boat towards the glowing horizon.

As the dawn's light diffused, and the lifeboat pulled forward, Margaret saw that the sea all around them was alive with wreckage.

She could see chairs, pillows, rugs, benches, tables, green velour cushions, what seemed to be the front of a piano, a large glistening black circle of coffee beans, a fur coat suspended on a piece of wood, a steamer trunk.

'Left on the tiller!'

A piece of a staircase. A door. Huge mahogany splinters, panels of white enamelled wood, a silk-covered couch, a mattress. Lifebelts, and lumps of cork which had slipped out of them.

A man dressed in an evening suit, face down.

A long white satin glove.

'*Pull for the shore, boys, pull for the shore,*' sang the men on the oars.

The lifeboat swayed a little and a wave slapped its side.

Overhead, a gull shrieked.

'There's a breeze coming up,' said Hogg. 'We'd better get a move on. These boats weren't built for high seas.'

'*Pull for the shore, sailor, pull for the shore!*'

A woman's slipper floated past, a dead baby, a top hat.

'*Heed not the rolling waves, but bend to the oar.*'

Margaret stifled a sob.

Marcella

CHAPTER 31

Wednesday 17 April 1912, Nice

After another day of impotent desolation, Marcella went down to the shop in Rue de France to talk to Louis again. It felt as though he was the only person who shared her desperate need to trace Michael.

The children had been gone now for more than a week. Every day Marcella had been to the Commissariat of Police, and every day had got nothing but the same rude shrug and a sighed, 'After all, he *is* their father.' They wouldn't even record the disappearance.

Monsieur Nabias had been equally ineffectual, telling Marcella that it would be best to wait a while before taking out an injunction.

An injunction! A little late for that.

But Louis had a vested interest in finding Michael, since he had been sold a crock – a worthless shop with a bankruptcy notice hanging over it which would take effect less than a week from now.

Marcella believed that if she and Louis worked together they might come up with something. Any small idea might lead to a clue to finding her children. The insignificant could prove meaningful. After all, a tiny pinhole letting in light made a photograph.

When she saw that a customer was with him, Marcella dawdled by the door.

The new boy, Raymond, came over offering his assistance, but Louis gave him a signal to leave her alone.

Marcella crossed the shop-floor, heading for the beautifully upholstered pair of armchairs in the corner, put there for husbands to lounge on while their wives were fitted. But they had been replaced by two plain wicker chairs. Marcella recognised them as having come from their kitchen upstairs.

What a strange decision. Had Louis sold the armchairs to try and avert the bankruptcy?

She settled on a kitchen chair, wondering how long Michael had been planning his departure. If the missing 30,000 francs Louis had quoted her was correct, that would mean Michael had been siphoning off the petty cash long before she had started divorce proceedings.

She looked across the room at Louis holding out samples for the customer to choose and thought about all the tradesmen from whom she had collected fabrics and trimmings. Mademoiselle Adrienne Aude with the BACK IN 10 MINUTES sign; the big fancy shop Bellanger, in Paris; grumpy old Monsieur Rodot in Rue Paradis – all cheated out of their cash.

'Marcella!' Louis swept across the room and took her by the arm. 'Let's go out for a little walk.'

Raymond was now seeing to the customer.

She followed Louis out into the street and started to speak, but he raised a finger to his lips.

They walked on for a few hundred metres in silence.

'If we go to the beach,' he then said, 'we can be sure that we are not overheard. To be honest, I no longer trust anyone.'

'Not this way!' Marcella steered Louis onwards past Rue Meyerbeer. 'His best friend has a place down there. The American barbershop.' Even though she'd heard the Kirchmanns had left in the New Year, who knew whether or not they might be back by now.

After passing Villa Masséna they turned towards the Promenade.

On the corner of Rue de Rivoli and the prom, builders were busily working on a large construction site, clanging and banging, blocking the pavement with pallets of bricks and wheelbarrows.

'They're building a new hotel, which promises to be smarter than the rest of them,' said Louis. 'In the autumn, when that opens, it will make our shop all the more attractive, if I can survive what is about to come.'

As the palm trees thrashed about in the rising wind, Louis and Marcella walked together down the steps to the beach. She noticed that, although it was noon, the day had suddenly grown strangely dark and cold.

'What's going on?' she cried against the gusts which carried her words away.

'It's the eclipse they were talking about in the newspaper.'

'An eclipse! A presage of doom.'

'You don't believe all that stuff, do you, Marcella?'

She wasn't sure whether she did or not. She only knew that, since her children were gone, she felt an emptiness which was beyond description.

The sky turned even darker and waves crashed against the pillars of the Casino Pier.

Only a few people were left on the beach.

They could talk as loud as they liked.

'Michael has stolen so much from us both.'

'So what have you found out, Louis?'

Marcella prayed that it was more than she had.

'Austro-Hungary. That's about it. But every time Michael told me where he came from it was a different place – Szered, Presbourg, Vienna, Újvidék. He talked of brothers, a sister and a mother. But where are they?'

Marcella understood that Louis knew as little about Michael as she did.

'He could have gone back to his family,' added Louis. 'But, do you know what, Marcella? I seriously doubt it.' He kicked a pebble into the sea and watched it splash.

'Why's that, Louis?'

'Firstly, he has never gone back there in all the time I've known him. Have you ever known him to go home to his family?'

It was true. For all his *talk* of family, Michael had never gone back home.

It was another possibility destroyed.

'His family was my only hope,' she said. 'I felt sure that's where he had gone.'

Louis peered up at the lowering sky and shivered. 'It could be a gloomy evening in November. It's like a dream.'

'A nightmare.'

Louis looked Marcella in the eye. 'So do you really not know any more about him than I do?'

'No.' She watched a wave sweep a piece of driftwood to the shore, then sweep it away again. 'Nothing.'

'He's taken everything from me.' Louis threw his hands up and wailed. 'Everything!'

'It's just money, Louis,' Marcella said quietly. 'Money can be replaced.'

Louis turned and hung his head.

A larger wave rolled up to Marcella's feet and she took a few steps back to avoid the hem of her dress being soaked. The driftwood lay at her feet. She kicked it. 'Stefan knows where he is. I'm certain of it.'

'Why do you think that?'

'The way he looks at me every time I come to visit you. A kind of condescension behind his eyes. The play of a smirk across his lips. He is confident in his superior position because *he* knows my husband better than I do.'

'Might that not simply be Stefan's usual look?' Louis picked up the driftwood. 'That boy's always had an air of arrogance about him.'

'It comes from Michael. He's Michael's adoring pet.'

'Well he won't be so adoring when he realises we're going to have to work every hour God sends for the next week if we're to make any progress.' He swung round and grinned. 'That's it! You do realise that once the bankruptcy is officially declared, we'll have the author-ities searching for Michael too. If we wait for the twenty-third, we can—' Louis was about to throw the driftwood into the sea. Marcella caught his arm.

'Don't.' She took the little branch from him.

'Twenty-third of April.' Louis turned his back towards the sea. 'Believe me, that's our best chance.'

'I can't wait till then, Louis.' Marcella strode across the pebbles and laid the driftwood high up on the beach. As she gathered her skirts, Louis offered to help her up the steps.

'Come with me now, then, Marcella. We'll question Stefan.'

'We'll get nothing from him, Louis. He's a wall of ice.'

'Apply heat. Ice melts.'

As Marcella and Louis waited for a horse-drawn carriage to pass, they saw Stefan ahead, disappearing inside the shop.

He was gripping a baguette, a newspaper tucked under his arm.

'Good timing, Marcella. It's his precious lunch hour.'

Together they followed him through the baize curtain.

'We'd like to ask you some questions,' said Louis.

Stefan sat in his usual chair, his feet up on the machinist's table. He took a large bite of his sandwich. 'It's my break.' As he spoke, he spat specks of chewed bread which landed on the fabric, spread out on the worktable.

Marcella suppressed her instinct to rush forward and protect it.

'Nonetheless, Stefan, as your employer—'

'I don't work for you. I work for Monsieur Navratil.'

Louis's lips were tight. 'I think you'll find, Monsieur Kozak, that I am a partner in this shop and that therefore, during Monsieur Navratil's absence, you work for me.'

Stefan pulled an apple from a drawer in his desk and took a loud crunch.

Mouth full, he said, 'Perhaps you could explain to me, Monsieur Hoffman, why we're having this conversation in the presence of Mr Navratil's ex-wife, who has nothing whatsoever to do with the situation here in the shop or with Mr Navratil himself.'

Marcella went to speak, but Louis put his hand out to prevent her.

'We know that you know where Michael is hiding. And frankly, Stefan, it would be better for you if you shared this information with us.'

'Really?' Stefan was still chewing while speaking. 'And why is that, Louis?'

'Because if we do not find Monsieur Navratil this shop is likely to go under and you will lose your job here.'

Stefan wiped his mouth with the back of his hand, took his feet down from the worktop and stood up. With a loud yawn, he stretched, then casually strolled across the workshop to toss the apple core into the waste-paper basket.

'Now, if you're finished with your cross-examination, I'd like to read today's newspaper. If I may.'

He threw the newspaper, front page upwards, on to the worktable and stood looking down at it.

'You care more about your lunch break than your job, it seems.' Louis fingered the small stain on the fabric, caused by Stefan's crumbs. 'I'll be docking your pay for that ruined shot-satin.'

Both Marcella and Louis expected Stefan to come back with another snide remark.

But he was silent. He stood rock still, staring down at the newspaper.

'Well?' said Louis.

Stefan looked up. He blinked. His face drained of all colour. 'What?'

'I said I'll be docking your pay—'

Grabbing the newspaper from the table, Stefan shoved them out of the way and dashed through the baize curtain.

Louis and Marcella followed him into the shop, but Stefan was already out in the street, bent over, vomiting into the gutter.

'His sandwich must have disagreed with him,' said Louis, heading back to the welcome counter. 'We won't get anything out of him while he's in this state. Come back another time, Marcella.'

'Tomorrow?'

'No. I have a man coming to give me legal advice. It's imperative I get that sorted out before the bailiffs descend next week. On Friday, I have meetings all day about the whole mess. I'll have to remain open on Sunday… It's a disaster.'

Marcella left the shop.

The sky was getting brighter and brighter.

The eclipse was over.

Marcella crossed to the tram stop and waited.

She could see Stefan. He was still sick. Marcella watched him stagger back to lean against the wall on the corner of Rue Dalpozzo. He took a few deep breaths, then went back to reading the newspaper.

That didn't make sense.

After about a minute reading, Stefan returned to the edge of the pavement and started retching again.

A tram came and went.

Marcella let it pass by.

Stefan was still bent over, dry-retching.

He looked up and saw Marcella.

For some seconds their eyes locked.

Stefan then brought his hand up to his forehead, as though shielding himself from the sight of her, and he disappeared back into the shop.

At that moment Marcella knew that Stefan's bout of sickness was not brought on by any sandwich.

It was the newspaper.

The *Petit Niçois*.

Clang! Clang!

Another tram was approaching.

Marcella stepped back from the edge of the platform and walked rapidly away from the tram stop.

She had to find a news kiosk. What was the story which had upset Stefan so badly it made him vomit?

Back in the flat, Marcella laid the paper down, just as Stefan had had it on the worktable. Front page upwards.

There were only four headlines: ARTICLE 340, THE ECHO OF THE ANGLO-FRENCH FESTIVAL; INJUSTICE TO BE REPAIRED; and CATASTROPHE OF THE TITANIC.

Right away Marcella dismissed the Anglo-French Festival.

INJUSTICE TO BE REPAIRED was about a soldier from Nice who, while away on manoeuvres, had let his sick wife and two children die of starvation. The *Titanic* was a ship full of millionaires which had sunk in the Atlantic Ocean – the most formidable maritime catastrophe of our times, the paper called it. Article 340 looked more promising: it concerned the lifting of the prohibition under which children were unable to discover their paternity. All over France, fathers of illegitimate children were about to be unmasked. Had Stefan perhaps got himself some bastards who might come after him?

No. That didn't seem enough to make him so sick.

It didn't make sense.

Nothing was enough to cause a cool customer like Stefan to spill his guts on Rue de France. Perhaps Louis was right and it was the sandwich. But she felt it couldn't be.

Marcella sat beside the window with the newspaper.

She decided to go through it all. To read every word.

But nowhere did she find anything which she could link to Stefan or Michael.

As she went to her bed that night, as she had done every night since the children had gone, Marcella felt an increasing sense of doom.

On Saturday morning Marcella decided to go to the cathedral for Mass, and pray to every saint in heaven to bring her children home safely.

She squeezed on to a pew on the extreme edge of the congregation, two-thirds back, and knelt in prayer.

As the congregation sang the Kyrie Eleison, '*Lord, have mercy on us...*', Marcella glanced towards a guttering candle in the side chapel.

'*Christ, have mercy on us...*'

A child in a red velvet cloak.

'*Christ, have mercy on us...*'

Marcella stood up and moved closer.

A child in a red velvet cloak, in a glass case.

'*Lord, have mercy on us...*'

Yes... It was the waxen doll she had collided with on her very first day in Nice.

'*Lord, have mercy on us...*'

Marcella searched for a sign, something which would tell her more. In a frame pinned to a nearby column, she found a small notice.

SAINT RÉPARATE. CHILD MARTYR OF THE THIRD CENTURY AD.

'*...Cleanse my heart and lips, oh Almighty God, who didst cleanse with a burning coal the lips of the prophet Isaiah...*'

THE ROMANS WANTED TO FEED THE CHILD TO THE DOGS, BUT THE FAITHFUL STOLE HER TENDER BODY, PLACED IT INSIDE A SMALL WOODEN BOAT AND FLOATED IT OUT TO SEA. THE BOAT, BLOWN BY THE BREATH OF ANGELS, WASHED UP ON THE BEACH. HER BODY UNCORRUPTED...

'Vouchsafe, oh Lord, to bless me...'

RÉPARATE WAS CARRIED TO SAFETY IN A LITTLE WOODEN BOAT.

'Glory be to thee, oh Lord...'

Staring eye to glass eye with the wax effigy, Marcella felt gripped by a fear so intense that she could not breathe. She staggered back and flopped down into her pew. She sat, doubled up, her face in her hands, praying to God in his mercy to protect her own children and carry them safely home to her.

When Mass was over, having got nothing from the service but a horrible foreboding, Marcella returned to the shop.

'I'm going to talk to Stefan,' she said to Louis.

'He's not here. Still off sick. He did look pretty ropy when he got back on Thursday morning. His hands were shaking so badly I sent him away. I didn't want any accidents with a sewing machine. I've not seen him since.'

'Come with me, then, Louis to visit him in his sickbed.'

'But...'

'He's only next door, after all.'

'He'll come back in his own time.'

'No, Louis.' Marcella made for the door. 'He may have time. The clock is ticking. Every day my children are missing they become harder to trace.'

Marcella climbed the steep stairs to the flat and rapped on the door.

Silence within.

After waiting some minutes she left the building, only to find Stefan on the doorstep about to come inside.

He looked fine. Fully dressed. He was holding a copy of the morning's *Petit Niçois*.

'What do you want, Marcella?'

'I wanted to check that you were all right.'

'I'm not.' Stefan lifted his hand, indicating that he wanted to pass her. 'I need to go back to bed. I'm ill.'

'Quite well enough to get dressed and go out for a newspaper.'

'Indeed. Thank you for your attention, Madame Navratil.'

'Shall I tell Monsieur Hoffman that you are fully recovered. Or will you?'

Stefan held her gaze.

'As a matter of fact, I was just going to tell him myself.'

'Good.' Marcella turned. 'We can walk together.'

Marcella wanted to shake Stefan, to yell: 'Tell me where Michael is gone! Tell me where he has hidden my children!' But she knew that would only close him up tighter.

'Feeling better?' said Louis as they both came into the shop.

Stefan just nodded and walked past him through the baize curtain.

'I can't talk now, Marcella. I have an important customer in there. For a fitting.' Louis indicated the changing room. 'But please wait. I have some ideas.'

Louis handed Marcella his newspaper. *Le Figaro*. A Paris paper.

'Those poor souls,' said Marcella, glancing at the headline: THE TITANIC DISASTER.

She settled on one of the wicker chairs in the corner of the shop and read.

The fitting went on for so long Marcella found herself reading everything: what was playing in the Paris theatres, which teams had won the sporting events; and then she started on the list of those saved and then the casualties from the tragedy in the Atlantic.

Eventually Louis kissed the customer's hand and guided her out.

It was almost noon. Time for Stefan to get the baguette for his lunchtime sandwich.

Marcella looked up. 'You don't have any relatives on board the *Titanic*, do you, Louis?'

'No.' Louis laughed. 'Why?'

Stefan passed through the shop.

'There's a Louis Hoffman on the list of those missing, presumed drowned. Louis Hoffman and two children.'

Stefan stood frozen in the middle of the shop floor.

'No!' he cried, lunging towards Marcella, snatching the newspaper from her hands. 'Where do you see that? Where do you see that?'

Stefan ran his long bony fingers up and down the page.

Marcella knew what he was going to say next.

Feverishly scanning the list, Stefan scrunched up the edges of the newspaper between his fists. He fell to his knees. 'Oh no! Oh no!'

Gripping Marcella's shoes, Stefan howled into the floor. 'Oh Marcella. I'm so sorry. I'm so, so sorry.'

'Raymond!' Louis barked into the other room. 'Take over care of the shop. Now!'

'What have you done?' Marcella pulled at Stefan's hair, trying to see his face. 'Where are my children?'

Stefan was still sobbing. He was shivering all over, as though he knelt in an ice house, not a warm shop on a spring day in Nice.

'It's him.' Stefan pointed at the newspaper on the carpet. 'It's him.'

'It's who?' asked Louis. 'WHO?'

Stefan's reply was little more than a whisper. 'Michael. It's Michael.'

Marcella could no longer breathe. Her heart thundered. She slumped down.

'Louis Hoffman is Michael.' Stefan moaned. 'When he bought the tickets, he used your name. When we came to lunch at Easter, we took your passport.'

Louis took a step forward, face white and drawn.

But Marcella didn't care about any of this. She remembered what the newspaper had actually said in the list of those missing, presumed drowned: 'Louis Hoffman *and* two children.'

CHAPTER 32

Sunday 21 April 1912, Nice

Marcella woke numb, unable to believe that she had slept at all.

Her mother was there and her Aunt Thérèse. She could hear them in the kitchen now, whispering. The clink of china, running water. They must have sat up all night. She remembered them sometime after midnight pouring her glasses of brandy.

Marcella's thoughts darted this way and that.

To Michael – secretly packing a case, going to Monaco to buy tickets to America: a cabin with two berths, one for himself, the other for their two children.

To Stefan – creeping into Louis's bedroom to steal his passport. Stefan stashing Michael's suitcase into Left Luggage. Stefan buying him train tickets to London. Stefan waving off Michael and her children at the railway station. The railway station a five-minute walk from here.

How could they both have conspired to commit such a crime against her?

How could they both have conspired to commit such a crime against those tiny children?

How could they have done that?

How could they?

Her little darlings.

Her pretty, kind, gentle babes.

Marcella turned her face into her pillow. She wanted to cry, but only a dry sob came out of her constricted throat.

'You must eat.' Her mother stood in the doorway with a steaming cup. 'At least have a coffee. Today your aunt is going to help you. She'll take you to a lawyer's office where you can speak to the people who own the ship. She's already got the details, the telephone number, the names—'

'What good is that, Mama? What's the point? What's the point of anything, if my darlings are lost, if they are… if they are…' Unable to finish the phrase for fear it made it all the more real, Marcella stared down at the white sheets. Like a shroud. She whimpered, 'Oh, Mama. What's the point of anything any more?'

'I'm going to prepare you a bath.' Her mother placed the coffee on her bedside table. 'Tell me what you want to do?'

'Nothing.' What Marcella really wanted to say was: 'I want you to turn back time. I want you to take me back to Easter Day when I was last holding my babies, so that I could never let that monster have them for his day. Sod all the courts and sod the law.' What had law ever done to help her?

She thought about Easter, sitting on the doorstep in the setting sun, waiting for Raphaël to come around with the horse and cart, Lolo fiddling with her hair, Monmon clinging to her neck, both of them babbling about the toy chicken.

There was a knock on the front door.

'Who's that?' Marcella dreaded that her mother might have brought round the priest to talk to her.

'Thérèse has a friend coming to advise her. He's going to keep her abreast of the legal stuff.'

Marcella rolled over and faced the wall.

'I don't care about the legal stuff. The law can go to hell.'

Her mother moved silently out of the room.

Marcella felt cornered. All she wanted to do was lie in this bed and vanish, for a void to open up and take her.

But now that her flat was full of people she had to get up and dressed. If she didn't, they'd all crowd into the bedroom to lecture her.

Pulling on her clothing, her skin felt tender, almost as though she'd been burned. Her stomach still felt as though it was sinking; her head throbbed.

She opened the door and walked along the corridor to the kitchen. She felt disembodied, as though she was watching herself move, not *being* at all.

She stood in the open doorway. Her aunt was sitting at the kitchen table with Henry Rey di Villarey. Spider-thin, dressed as usual in a very smart grey suit, he had laid his hat beside him. They were both hunched over a red-bound book.

'We have multiple choices,' he was saying. 'The British or the American embassies, and/or a lawyer. I would suggest that would be the place to start, and I'd recommend Theodore Moriez. He is cool, efficient and nobody messes with him.'

As Marcella came in they both looked up.

Marcella felt now as though she had walked on to a stage, lit by footlights, the audience sitting, waiting for her to perform.

'I'm so sorry, Marcella.' Henry rose. 'Please don't give up hope. At this point none of the news coming in about the wreck is a hundred per cent accurate.'

'I can't talk about it.'

Seeing how pale she looked, Gigi pulled out a chair.

Marcella slumped into it.

'Please, Marcella. Eat something. A spoonful of honey. *Anything*, to give you some energy.'

'I've got a pounding head,' was all Marcella could say.

'Right.' Thérèse stood up. 'Henry and I are going down to this lawyer's office straight away to start proceedings. As it's an exceptional case he's seeing us immediately, despite it being a Sunday. If you have enough energy, Marcella, I strongly advise you to join us.'

Gigi had gone out to the bathroom and returned with a bottle of pills. She unscrewed the lid, put one pill on the table, then placed the bottle on the sideboard.

Thérèse scribbled the lawyer's address on a scrap torn from Henry's morning newspaper and laid it down before Marcella. Then she passed the torn copy of *Le Figaro* back to Henry.

'I don't need it,' he said. 'Let's go!'

Thérèse tossed the paper into the kitchen bin and she and Henry left the flat. As soon as she heard the click of the door, Marcella turned to her mother.

'I really have to be left alone.'

'They're only trying to help, you know.'

Marcella nodded. But really thought: Help what? Help whom? What help could there be? What can anyone do to help when your children are dead, drowned, with a thousand other people?

'I'd like you to go too.'

'But…'

'Please, Mama.'

'If you really mean that…'

'I do.'

Gigi shrugged, and took her jacket from the back of a kitchen chair.

'I love you, Marcella,' she said as she left. 'Come to me when you need me.'

Marcella picked up the children's toys from the top of her dresser, and held them close to her chest as they once had done. She smoothed down the counterpane. She lay where they had lain, gazing at the ceiling, the same ceiling that they must have gazed at.

On the night table was the mechanical chicken which Ton-ton and Edouard had made. The chicken which had given the children such endless delight that last day.

She averted her eyes. She couldn't bear to see it.

One day soon, she realised, she would have to throw all this away.

Paint the room.

Move home.

How could she go on living here, where everything reminded her that they, once so very alive, were now dead, drowned, pulled down into the infinite depths, the dark sunless chasms and abysses of the Atlantic Ocean?

She could not bear to think of Lolo and Monmon gasping for breath.

Dying.

She closed the bedroom door behind her.

Back in the kitchen, Marcella took the bottle of pills from the sideboard.

Opening a cupboard, she pulled out the brandy bottle which Thérèse had brought round last night.

She poured herself a large glass.

She didn't like brandy at all. Especially neat.

But with any luck it would do the job.

Without her children, what was the point of living?

Marcella counted out some tablets.

She took a sip of brandy, followed by two pills.

She intended to continue doing this until she left this place forever.

A thought flashed through her mind. If she was sick or bled, this table would be stained and no doubt the landlord would charge her mother for the damage. Marcella reached down into the bin and pulled out Henry's newspaper. She opened it wide and spread it out across the table.

She couldn't leave mess behind her.

Marcella took another gulp of brandy and laid her head flat upon the newspaper. As the brandy went down, she closed her eyes. She counted to three, then opened them again, to pick out the next pills.

This time she gathered four, sliding them across the newspaper, one by one, with her finger.

She stared at them for a second, before slipping the next one into her mouth.

PART TWO

Margaret

CHAPTER 33

Six days earlier
Monday 15 April 1912, at sea and onboard RMS Carpathia

It took at least an hour for the lifeboat to reach the red-funnelled steamer. Every fifteen minutes different groups took turns at the oars.

Margaret felt sorry she was too far away to join them. She would willingly have had a go.

From all directions lifeboats were converging on the black-hulled ship. There had to be at least four ahead of theirs.

'RMS *Carpathia*,' said one of the men, as they grew close enough to read the ship's name. 'Thank God for you.'

'We have come back to life,' cried the monocled Frenchman. 'We are born anew.'

Sailors were gathered in an open gangway halfway up the ship's side. They manned the ladders and ropes dangling down into the sea.

As Lifeboat 7 pulled in alongside, Hogg called for the women to go first.

Lily Potter refused. 'I can't!' she whimpered. 'My hands and feet are frozen.'

Margaret wished she would just shut up and start climbing into the ship.

The sailors above in *Carpathia* lowered a swing. Everyone on the lifeboat helped Lily climb into it and she was hauled upwards.

After six older ladies had gone, it was Margaret's turn and, though she was quite willing to climb the ladder and get up quickly, since she had Bébé in her arms, she too would have to take the swing.

Clambering into the unwieldy thing, by jerks she was pulled higher and higher up the black side of the ship. At the top, sailors grabbed her and hauled her inside.

'All rescued people this way, please.' She could hear this being repeated above her, over and over like a stuck record. 'All rescued people this way, please.'

Once Margaret's feet hit the deck, she was lifted up by two rugged sailors and carried through to the ship's saloon.

It was warm, warm, warm.

A couple of stewardesses sprang forward and tugged her behind a screen.

'Let me take the dog, madam.'

One of the women was wielding a large pair of scissors.

'Don't hurt her.' Margaret felt terrified that they were going to kill Bébé.

'We're just going to get those wet clothes off you, madam,' said one. 'We can't do that while you're holding the dog.'

As though in a dream, Margaret raised her arms and let them remove her clothing, then towel her down, rubbing very hard to get the circulation going, and finally wrapping her in a warm steamer blanket.

She saw a pile of wet things on the floor.

'Once we have these dried, we will return them to you,' said one stewardess.

'Many of the ladies onboard have donated garments to tide you over.'

They were dressing her in ill-fitting ugly clothes.

Another woman was by the side of the screen holding a clipboard and pencil.

'What is your name?'

'Hays,' said Margaret. 'Margaret Bechstein Hays.'

'We'll try to get you some undergarments.'

Were they criticising her for having no knickers? She tried to explain that she had given them up to save the lifeboat, but her lips didn't seem to be working.

'You don't mind keeping your wet shoes on? I'd advise you, when you find somewhere to sleep, kick them off in front of a heater. Give them a chance to dry out.'

'Now, Miss Hays, come forward, please.' One of the women steered Margaret back into the main room, where a male steward swept her towards a large table laid out with cups and glasses.

A man was beckoning her.

'I am the ship's doctor. I'd like you to drink this,' he said quietly, handing her a glass. 'Knock it back.'

Margaret obeyed. It was brandy. The shock of the alcohol hit the back of her throat and burned all the way down to her stomach.

'Now this.' He gave her a cup of hot coffee. 'There are sandwiches and biscuits on the other table, when you feel ready. And if you are really hungry the restaurant on the deck below is serving soup and bread.'

Margaret looked around for the first time since being hauled onboard.

They were standing in a shabby saloon, with worn chairs and tables.

Women in evening dress huddled on the sofas, cradling steaming cups. A mournful and bedraggled procession queued inside the door, some clad in heavy fur coats over kimonos, evening slippers and silk stockings, others in nightgowns, a blanket and a hat. Blue-lipped and shivering, the motley group stood patiently in line for brandy and a hot drink.

It was difficult to believe that it wasn't all a terrible dream.

Moving towards the centre of the room, Margaret noticed Lily and Olive standing near the door to the stairs, both draped in *Carpathia* steamer blankets.

A man from the crew was talking to them. 'We will find somewhere for you to rest, as soon as possible. As they are waking and hearing the news, our own guests are giving up their cabins so that you can sleep. If you'd like to follow me down, ladies.'

'Come on, Margaret,' called Lily. 'This young man is going to help us.'

Margaret did not move.

'We need to sleep,' added Olive, as though Margaret had not understood the meaning of the word.

But Margaret couldn't face going down into the darkness of a cabin. Not now. She wanted to stay up here in the light.

'You go on ahead,' she said. 'I'm happy here. Besides, Bébé needs a walk.'

She also knew that at this time she wanted cheery company, not the God squad. 'Have you seen Gilbert?'

'He went off, wrapped in a blanket, supporting one of our crewmen from *Titanic*, who was brought onboard near naked and very badly burned.'

'He's taken him down to the ship's hospital, two decks below,' added Olive, as both women moved off with the *Carpathia* steward.

Margaret lowered herself on to a sofa, nestling beside other stunned women, Bébé lying at her feet. She stared bleakly ahead, watching people coming in, being dried down, drinking their brandy. They were all moving like penny automatons at a fairground.

The eerie quiet of the room was suddenly broken by a sailor running in from the deck. A child of around three or four years old was clutched to his chest. The little boy's almost naked body, carelessly wrapped in a blanket, was floppy, his cheeks as pale as chalk.

'Gangway, there!' yelled the sailor. 'I need to get this child to the doctor.'

A steward rushed forward to push the door wide open.

The sailor slammed through, and disappeared.

I must find Gilbert, thought Margaret. If only I could find Gilbert, he might be able to make me laugh again. He could stop this horrid feeling inside me.

Out on deck, more commotion.

Margaret stood up and walked to the door. She stepped out into the cold, this time barely noticing it.

She watched as crewmen hauled what looked like a mail sack over the rails and place it carefully on the wooden planks of the deck. A terrible sound was coming from within. A kind of yowling shriek which curdled her blood. The men bent down and gingerly opened the sack to reveal a child, little more than a baby, emerging like a chick popping out of its shell.

The baby was silent again.

He blinked twice and looked about him. His hand was clutching a wooden soldier doll. He put the head of the toy into his mouth, sucked it, then took it out.

Then he screamed with all the power in his lungs.

'Lolo,' he cried. 'Lolo, Lolo, Lolo!'

A sailor scooped up the baby and carried him into the warmth of the saloon.

Margaret stepped across to the railings and looked over the side, Bébé trotting behind her.

She watched numb-fingered women clambering up the ladders, and a man who had injured his feet being drawn up in the swing.

Shivering human beings, one after another, were pulled up from very death.

'They're saying that this is the last lifeboat.' A female passenger from the *Carpathia* stood further along the rail, leaning over, talking to a friend.

The empty lifeboats were now being hoisted up on to the *Carpathia*'s deck.

'What?'

'There are no more lifeboats from *Titanic* to be found,' she explained. 'They have accounted for every one of them.'

'Oh no!' the other lady replied. 'Then there is no possibility of any more survivors.'

The first lady shook her head.

'How many have we picked up?'

'The crewman over there told me around seven hundred.'

'How many were on the ship?'

'Two thousand more than that.'

Margaret looked out to sea.

The same sea where last night she had drifted for hours, thinking that every moment would be her last.

There was no marker, no spot which announced that only a few hours ago the world's most luxurious steamship, RMS *Titanic*, had been floating, resplendent, everyone on board her laughing, drinking, partying.

There were only icebergs.

The sky, orange, pink and blue, reflected on the glistening peaks, turning them into vast coloured jewels.

The red sun had risen, creating a crimson path across the water.

It was one of the most beautiful sights Margaret had ever seen.

She hoped never to see anything like it again.

She turned away.

Where was Gilbert?

She had to find Gilbert.

She picked up Bébé and cradled her in her arms, kissing his face all over.

'Look at that!' murmured the *Carpathia* woman. 'The woman with the lapdog.'

'I've seen three like her,' replied her companion. 'Clinging to them like babies.'

'Yes, well…' said the first woman. 'In my opinion, it would have been better if they'd found babies to cling to.'

CHAPTER 34

Later that morning, Monday 15 April 1912, onboard RMS Carpathia Margaret awoke, curled up with Bébé on a corner table in the upper-deck dining saloon.

At first she had no idea where she was – the drab brown-and-green-papered walls, the bright light spilling in through multiple windows. Her feet felt damp. It was coming from her shoes. Why was she dressed in these strange clothes? She glanced at a clock on the wall. Twenty-five past eleven.

Suddenly she remembered everything and had to gasp for air.

She had slept for four hours.

All around the room she could see women whom she recognised from the lounges and dining rooms of the *Titanic*, still gaily clad in evening dresses, but now draped in blankets, huddled silently on sofas, staring blindly ahead.

At the other end of the table where she had been sleeping, a group of women from the *Carpathia* were standing, cutting up blankets, others were in chairs, sewing, others knitting, all creating clothing. They were working on scraps of fabric, tablecloths, ship's blankets.

'My room steward says that there are probably two hundred widows aboard,' whispered one. 'Only yesterday they were wives, some of them newly-weds.'

As they clicked their needles and worked their scissors, the whole group let out a communal sigh.

'Not one of them seems able to believe that the last lifeboat means the last hope. They think there is still a chance we'll pick up more survivors.'

'It would be cruel to correct them.'

'The whole business seems incredible.'

Incredible was right. Margaret knew, from the throb of the engines vibrating up through the table, that the *Carpathia* was moving.

'Oh, I know. Did you see the big brown stain on the sea? Oil and rust. They're saying that's where it went down.'

The women shook their heads in unison.

They look like marionettes being controlled from the same invisible sticks and strings, thought Margaret.

'Hard to believe that's all that's left of the largest ship ever built.'

'Hubris!'

'She was speeding, I heard,' whispered another. 'Speeding through all this ice! Can you credit it?'

Margaret didn't want to listen in to any more of this babble. She felt as though they thought somehow she was to blame. Pulling her blanket tight around her, she went back out on to the deck.

It was cold. But the day was bright. On one side of the ship, an immense ice field stretched as far as the eye could see. It was a marvellous sight: a smooth sheet of snowy whiteness, from which here and there rose lofty cones of shimmering ice, like mountains – like Vesuvius, thought Margaret. Their clear-cut outlines glistened against a bright sky.

Feeling a sudden vertigo, she gripped the rails. Nearer the ship's sides, the Prussian-blue water contrasted strongly with the pure white of the ice.

She needed to sit down, but every deckchair was taken. Most had two or more people perched on them. Nearly all women. They looked bewildered rather than sad. All of them had lost husbands, fathers and sons. One or two were silently staring out to sea, as though hoping another magical lifeboat full of men would miraculously appear on the frosty horizon.

Never before had Margaret been in the company of so many broken-hearted people.

She passed a bench on which a bedraggled girl of about eighteen in a brightly coloured fancy-dress costume consoled an older woman wearing a white dress trimmed with lace and covered with jaunty blue cornflowers. An osprey feather jutted from her jewelled bandana. She was wiping away tears with torn silk evening gloves.

It was all wrong, thought Margaret. Mourners wear black, not furs, not evening gowns – certainly not nightdresses and dainty pale-blue satin slippers.

But nothing, it seemed, was right any more.

It was as though she was hovering above life, watching herself and everyone else. She wondered for a moment whether last night she might actually have died. Perhaps she was here only as a ghost, watching over the others.

That's what it felt like. She certainly didn't feel as though she was alive.

Moving off along the promenade deck, Margaret headed towards the prow of the ship. As she stepped round one of the salvaged *Titanic* lifeboats, tucked up in a corner, she saw a large pile of tarpaulins. She couldn't understand why they would be guarded by a sailor. Were tarpaulins so valuable? Who would steal them? Where could they take them? But the guard, sitting on a stool in front of them, glared fiercely at her.

'Sorry, miss.' He put up his hand, warning her away. 'You can't come down here. Didn't you see the sign?'

She hadn't.

But then, it wasn't real. She was walking about in a weird wonderland of horror, seeing only things which were too fantastic to believe.

'The funerals will be this afternoon, miss. Then we'll open the deck again.'

The funerals?

Oh God!

He was guarding dead bodies!

Margaret reeled backwards, turned and ran along the deck until she reached the familiar warm strangeness of the dining saloon.

'Miss Hays?' A woman came towards her. 'We have your clothing, all dry, ready to put on. When you're ready to collect them, could you come to the room marked CREW ONLY, next to Cabin 45 in the Second Class?'

'I wonder,' Margaret asked. 'Have you seen my friend, Gilbert Tucker? I've looked everywhere for him. I need to find him.'

The woman gave her a look of pity, evidently thinking she was talking about somebody who had drowned. She wanted to correct her, to put her right, but the moment came and went.

Suddenly another woman ran across the room towards the pile of blankets near the screens in the corner. She was muttering furiously. The woman stretched out and hauled at some men's shoes which Margaret could see dangling over the edge.

'You big lazy thug,' she shouted. 'Get off there, at once. You're a pig!'

'Oi! I was just getting comfortable.' The man sat up, glaring.

Margaret recognised the obnoxious baron from her lifeboat.

'I will certainly not get off,' he insisted. 'It's warm and cosy here.'

'Oh, yes, you will. People need those blankets until we have enough clothes to cover all these poor shipwrecked souls.'

'I was shipwrecked too—'

'Look! It's him!'

'It's the one who wouldn't row!'

Two more women rushed forward, then two more, and between them they hauled him off, beating him with their fists.

'You big loafer,' shouted one.

'Shamed by women,' cried another.

A third, wearing a shawl, added, 'Now get lost! No one on this ship wants to see you ever again.'

As the indolent baron limped off, grumbling to himself, everyone in the saloon clapped.

It was a weird rebellion, but one which gave Margaret a great deal of satisfaction. She wished now that she had joined in the party ousting him.

'I always thought I wanted to share the company of aristocrats,' said Margaret quietly to a man standing beside her. 'But that horrible type changed my mind.'

'Oh, he is no aristocrat.' The man slipped in his monocle. 'He's just a spoiled, unpleasant parvenu.'

'Oh, it's you, monsieur! Thank you, thank you, thank you...'
She wanted to fall to her knees in gratitude for his strength and

steadfastness, and his rowing last night, but all she did was feebly grab his hand. Then, remembering that he was French, she said, '*Merci pour votre...* rowing.' She mimed pulling the oars. '*Merci, tellement, monsieur. Merci. Merci.*'

'*Bonjour, mademoiselle.*' He held out his hand. '*Pierre Maréchal. Je suis ravi de vous rencontrer.*'

'Margaret Hays,' she replied. 'Isn't it awful, Monsieur Maréchal? How could we be so unlucky?'

'Did you lose any loved person in the shipwreck? A husband, perhaps?'

'I am unmarried,' said Margaret. 'I lost no one.'

'Nor me. So we are not unlucky at all. It is we, Mademoiselle Hays...' He rested his hand gently on her shoulder. 'It is we, the single survivors, who are the *lucky* ones. Don't ever forget that.'

He moved off, leaving her standing alone.

Margaret was flooded with regret. Regret that she had survived. Regret that she was just wandering around, listening and watching.

She had to find Lillian and Olive, who were probably mopping up blood or something down in the hospital ward. She wanted to roll up her sleeves and join them.

That was it. That was the antidote to this feeling. She would be useful.

But when she got to the doors of the makeshift hospital, she was stopped.

'You'd be in the way,' said a stewardess, looking at Margaret with pity. 'We only need experienced people. Best go and rest, madam. You look all in.'

'I have to help. I have to do something.'

'You're in no fit state.'

'I'm fine. Really, I am.'

'You might think you're all right, madam...' the woman reached out a hand and patted Margaret's arm '...but you've gone through a terrible ordeal.'

'But I—'

'Anyway...' The stewardess glanced down, Margaret thought, with a note of scorn. 'We wouldn't allow the dog inside. You'd have to get a bellboy to take him away. Hygiene, you know.'

Scooping up Bébé, Margaret dragged herself back up towards the saloon. On the next landing, she passed a gaggle of *Carpathia* women, gossiping in hushed tones.

'I heard one of them mourning for her jewellery and her handsome Paris gowns. *How can* they talk like that, when others have lost husbands, parents, children?'

'Oh, my dear, there are lots of little children here onboard, some without even a mother or father,' replied another.

'Poor little mites,' said a third.

Grabbing the rail, Margaret was about to traipse on up.

'Excuse us, please!' Male voices from below. 'Gangway ahead! Please could you clear the stairs. We have a heavy load. We need the whole width of the steps. Please clear.'

The *Carpathia* women wandered off along a corridor, still chattering. Margaret simply stepped back off the landing.

'I hope no more of 'em go and die on us,' said one male voice.

'Lucky we've a priest onboard.'

The four men were carrying something heavy, something wrapped in blankets. They stopped on the landing to readjust their grip.

Margaret knew that it was a dead body. Someone who had been pulled up alive from a lifeboat. And then, here, in the safety of the *Carpathia*, had succumbed to their injuries.

As the men passed by, Margaret turned her face away and crossed herself – something she had seen people do when she was walking around all those churches in Rome.

She had thought she was unhappy on that tour. What did she know of unhappiness? She was just an ungrateful, selfish little idiot.

She let out a quiet sob. What was she? Some butterfly, flitting from pretty flower to pretty flower, while everyone else around her was mourning people who had been really important parts of their lives. Some had actually lost their lives. And what had she lost? A few dresses. Some books. A little money.

And what was she contributing to the world?

Nothing.

Margaret still had her parents, her friends and even her stupid dog.

If only she could find Gilbert.

She looked down at the clothing they had put her in. She had to give it back. Someone else might need it more than she did. She decided to make her way to Cabin 45 and retrieve her stuff. She pushed through a door at the end of the corridor and turned towards another staircase, leading down.

'*Allons!*' It was a female voice coming up the stairs this time. '*Petite! Allons manger.*'

A girl of about seventeen, holding the child Margaret had watched emerge from the sack, squeezed past her.

But the baby reached back towards Margaret.

He had seen Bébé.

'*Chien-chien! Chien-chien!*' Despite a tear-stained face, the child smiled and stretched out his hands towards the dog, his tiny fingers wiggling with anticipation. '*Chien-chien!*'

'He like you dog,' said the young woman, in a heavy accent.

'Then he must stroke her.' Clutching Bébé, Margaret followed the girl carrying the child as they climbed up the stairs.

'*Vous avez le bonne chance,*' said Margaret, as they turned into the Second Class saloon and perched on the edge of a sofa. '*Trouver votre enfant.*'

The girl replied again in broken English. 'No. No my baby. *Orphelin! Orphelin!*'

Margaret heard 'awfully'. She did not understand what the young woman was trying to say. She put Bébé down, and the child crawled across to stroke her.

'What is his name?' asked Margaret, then remembered another French phrase. '*Comment s'appelle l'enfant?*'

'*Je ne sais pas, exactement. Monsieur Hoffman, son père, est mort ; sa maman également.*'

Luckily the girl was talking slowly enough for Margaret to understand.

'*Vous savez du famille?*' she asked, trying hard to be correct in her French, but knowing she must be getting it all frightfully wrong.

The girl was shaking her head. Was this because she didn't understand or because she didn't know the family?

Margaret had pretty much exhausted any French she knew, so sat silently for some time watching the baby play happily with her dog.

She was aware that the engines had stopped.

A shock of horror shot through her.

No!

They weren't going to have to go through all that again?

Someone was out on deck clanging bells.

The baby started to shriek.

Margaret jumped to her feet.

'Oh God!' she cried. 'Are we sinking?'

A hand went down on her shoulder. She turned to find it was Gilbert.

'Ssshhhh, Margaret! Ssshhhh!' He held a finger to his lips. 'It's a call to deck for the funerals of the really unlucky survivors… The ones who didn't make it in the end.'

After dinner, when Margaret had slumped in her dining chair, despite trying so hard to stay awake, one of the *Carpathia*'s passengers had steered her down to her own cabin.

Late in the evening the ship was enveloped by a thick fog, and was now moving very, very slowly. Every five minutes the sombre muffled sound of its horn blew into the impenetrable night.

Margaret begged not to get undressed. She needed to be ready, she explained. Ready for the next time.

The lady obeyed, and left Margaret fully dressed on the bed, still wearing her damp shoes.

She was so full of fear she dared not sleep, but her body had taken over and, despite all her efforts, her eyes closed, dragging her down into a deep dream. All night long she kept waking, certain that the *Carpathia* was sinking, that the angle of the floor was slipping away, that somewhere in the fog lurked another berg, waiting to tear into the ship's hull. But Margaret knew she wouldn't be able to wake in time to get into a lifeboat. In her dreams she was running along corridors, knee-deep in water, searching for her husband, though Margaret knew that she had never had one.

She was very glad to wake up properly and find Gilbert perched at the end of the bed, playing with Bébé.

'Where am I?' she asked.

'Some rather sweet lady in the First Class offered you the use of her cabin. They're all being so awfully nice to us.'

'Where did you sleep?'

'Oh, I'm all right.' Gilbert shrugged.

'I didn't ask how you were, Gilbert, I asked you where you slept?'

'If you must know, in a very comfortable enamel bath on bridge deck. Delightfully situated, in its own stunning grounds, enjoying an elevated position commanding the most splendid views of the basin and WC, all mod cons, running hot—'

'Can you please stop joking about everything?'

'Anyway…' Gilbert shuffled uncomfortably and got to his feet. 'I knew you were out of it, old girl, so this morning I took the wee lass up for walkies. But now that I know you're back among the living—'

'I didn't die, Gilbert.' Margaret was indignant that he wasn't taking her seriously. 'I was just asleep.'

'I meant we were all convinced you were going down with some bug – pneumonia or something. You were in quite a state, you know. Anyhow, I'll leave you to get dressed. Even though I can see that you are already dressed. Erm. Anyway. You've missed breakfast, so I pinched a roll and some butter and marmalade and left it there for you, on the dresser. If you'd like some hot tea or coffee, I'll rush up…'

He was standing by the door, very near her head. She reached out and caught his hand. 'No. Gilbert. Please don't go.'

'Right ho, old darling.' He shrugged and remained there, one hand on the handle. 'Whatever you like.'

'I want to ask you to do something for me.'

'Fire away. Your wish, et cetera…'

'I want you to take Bébé.'

'I've already taken her once.'

'No. I mean *take* her. Forever. Make her your dog.'

'Erm, I—'

'I mean it, Gilbert. I can't look at her now without feeling terribly guilty.' Margaret hauled herself up and sat on the side of the bed. 'So… If you'd like to take her off, now, then you can start making friends with her right away, and then, before we have to get off, you'll be well and truly in love.' She pushed her hair back from her face and stood up. 'Right. Now that that's sorted, let's go. I have much to do.'

'All right...' Gilbert was squinting at her out of the side of his eye. 'I'll take the little ball of fun. For now—'

'No!' Margaret raised her voice. 'I mean forever, Gilbert. You must take her to Albany with you. To live with you. Forever.' Without touching the food Gilbert had brought for her, Margaret pushed past him and out into the corridor. 'Now come on.'

Bébé trotted faithfully behind Gilbert, who trotted faithfully behind Margaret. She marched along the corridor, turned and marched back along the parallel one. After about an hour exploring different corridors, Gilbert asked Margaret what was her goal, exactly.

'I'm looking for something.'

Gilbert pulled out his watch. 'Well, I don't want to bother you, honey, but I really don't want to miss lunch. Especially as there is a big meeting this afternoon.'

'What meeting?'

'Oh, it's about... you know... what happened. Everyone from *that other ship* is going. That loud woman, Mrs Brown, has organised it. We cannot be absent. Nor can we sit there with our stomachs growling like lions in the savannah at sunset.'

'I wish I knew what you were talking about.' Margaret had stopped outside a cabin door and had her ear pressed against the wood, listening. 'Do you think it might be this one?'

The clanging of a distant gong.

'That's the last call for lunch. We really have to—'

'I'm not hungry.'

Gilbert thrust himself in front of her and grabbed her hands. 'Well I am, Margaret. And so should you be. Whether you like it or not, you are coming with me to eat.'

Margaret tried to break free but he kept his tight grip.

'Look, Margaret. You have to come to this meeting, otherwise you will look like someone who is ungrateful—'

'Me? Ungrateful?'

'Ungrateful...' Gilbert pressed on '...both to Captain Rostron and the crew of this wonderful ship, and for your own life... And the rescue of all of us who are so, so very, very lucky to be here.' He looked down at his feet. 'Especially when so many others are not.'

Margaret sat with Gilbert and Olive, about two-thirds back from the dais. Lily was sitting on the end of the row, in the aisle seat. On Margaret's other side was a stranger, a woman in her nightgown and coat. She felt oddly trapped.

She scanned the other faces in the saloon. She saw the young pregnant Mrs Astor and Eleanor Widener. They both looked stunned. But this time Margaret wasn't meaning to spot celebrities. She was searching for just one face. Why hadn't she taken more interest in her earlier, because now that so many women were sitting huddled up in this room, she wasn't sure she would recognise the girl again.

But Margaret had to find her.

She twisted around to look at the women who had arrived too late to get a seat and were leaning against the walls.

Some man was up on the dais, droning on and on and on.

Suddenly everyone in the room applauded, shocking Margaret out of her quest.

'Now we'll have a show of hands, please,' said the gentleman speaker. 'All those for the proposal, please raise your hand now.'

Practically every hand in the room shot up.

Though she had no idea what she was voting for, Margaret didn't want to stand out, so she raised hers too.

'Yes, we must thank the Cunard Line for rescuing us,' a strident American female voice rang out. 'But I'd like to know what the White Star Line are doing to help? Are any representatives in contact with this ship?'

'Mr Ismay is onboard...'

A rumble went around the assembly.

'Then get him up here,' yelled one woman.

'He is not well and cannot leave his cabin.'

More discontented grumbling, before the people onstage continued.

'I saw him, you know. Mr Ismay.' The woman next to Margaret started whispering in her ear. 'He came straight from the life-boat, demanded to be fed and given a bed in the captain's cabin. He's not the pleasant, assiduous man we met onboard the... the... other ship.'

Margaret wasn't really listening, but the woman wittered on.

'I lost my husband. He drowned. Isn't it awful?' She said it in the same tone as if she had lost her hairbrush. 'My steward tells me there is a sign on Mr Ismay's cabin which reads DO NOT DISTURB. One of the Irish stokers ripped it off and kicked the door so hard the wooden panel is cracked.' She laughed at this. A tiny tinkling laugh. 'How I wish I was an Irish stoker, then I would find that monster, tie a millstone round his neck and throw him overboard.' She smiled wistfully then turned back to listen to the speakers.

Margaret was still trying to scan all the faces.

Then she saw the girl.

She was standing near the door on the other side of the room, leaning forward concentrating hard on the speakers.

Margaret spent the rest of the meeting staring at her, hoping to get her attention.

Once the gathering broke up, Margaret leapt to her feet and hastily shoved her way through the crowd.

But the girl had gone.

Margaret was about to follow through the door when Olive grabbed her arm.

'Come along, Meg. We're going down to help the staff in the restaurant.'

'But I have to—'

'Poor things,' Olive continued. 'They have to lay twice as many places, and as they spent yesterday looking after us, and gave up their beds for us, they're all done in. So Mother offered our services, while they take the rest of the afternoon off. Come along. Or don't you want to help?'

Margaret dragged back. They didn't understand. She had to find the girl.

But Lillian and Gilbert both had hold of her and steered her out of the saloon and down the stairs to the dining room.

'This is how we can make ourselves useful, you see, Margaret,' said Lily, laying down a knife and fork from her boxful. 'This is the way we can do something constructive.'

'Oh no!' Margaret looked at Gilbert. 'Where's Bébé? Where have you put her?'

'Calm down!' Gilbert looked up from the table where he was busy folding napkins. 'I lent the furry little ball to an eager bellboy who wanted to take her for a walk up on deck.'

'But I asked you to keep her—'

'Margaret.' Lily Potter spoke firmly. 'Dogs aren't allowed in dining areas.'

Margaret relaxed. She knew that this was true.

She forgave him.

But how she hated being trapped downstairs.

'Right! Wine glasses,' said Olive, entering from the kitchens bearing a tray. 'Then I think we're done.

Gilbert grabbed a stack of water glasses from a sideboard and, balancing them as though he was performing in a circus, started laying them down, one by one, till his stack was almost gone and he was near enough to Margaret to whisper to her.

'What's wrong, honey? Come on. Chin up. We're all in the same boat, so to speak.' He hunched his shoulders and pulled a face. 'We're the lucky ones, remember?'

But this time it did not make Margaret smile.

She just wished they'd all leave her alone to finish her important business.

'May I go now?' she asked.

'Of course.' Margaret couldn't miss the look of concern that flitted between Lillian and her daughter.

But they didn't know.

How could they?

Taking off the apron that Olive had tied on her, Margaret ran out of the room and up the stairs.

As she bounded up, two steps at a time, she collided with a cabin steward.

'All right there, miss?' he asked.

'I'm looking for a French girl of about seventeen. Quite large. She had a baby with her. An orphan. French too.'

'I don't know about the girl,' said the steward. 'But I do know there is a rescued French orphan onboard. He is rather poorly, I'm afraid. Currently in the care of one of our passengers, a Miss Danforth.'

'Thank you!' Margaret ran up to the purser's office, where she knew there was a book containing the list of passengers, hanging from a string on the noticeboard.

'There's a wind coming up,' said the man behind the desk. 'Hope you've got your sea legs. Looks like we'll be in for a rocky night.'

'I'll be fine.' Margaret turned and flicked quickly through the passengers' handbook.

Danforth, Eleanor. From Maine, USA, travelling to Naples, Italy. Cabin 23.

Margaret ran down the stairs again, and along a network of corridors until she arrived, panting, at the door of Cabin 23.

She knocked gently.

'Come in!' A female voice.

Margaret opened the door, and slipped inside.

'Miss Danforth?'

The American girl had to be around her own age.

Margaret's eyes flicked straight to the bed, where blankets were bundled up. The pillow only showed a headful of black curls.

'I'd like to help you with the baby.'

'Baby?' Eleanor Danforth looked puzzled. 'He's no baby. But I certainly could do with a little help, if there's some on offer.'

Margaret felt crestfallen.

But now that she had offered her help, she knew that she couldn't withdraw.

'Well... Here I am.'

'He got awful seasick when he was in the lifeboat.' Eleanor looked down at the curly hair. 'Doctors rehydrated him and gave him to me so he could have a bed. I've just got him feeling better, but, look, the ship's only started rolling again. So I presume the little blighter will be throwing up all night. Perhaps you'll keep me company holding the bowl.'

Margaret really wished there was a way out.

She could sense the ship start to roll and pitch. And, unlike on the last ship, on *Carpathia* you really could feel it.

She had not found that baby. But sacrificing herself in here for another sick child must count for something.

Eleanor began asking Margaret questions about the wreck, and strangely she thought that talking about it, describing it all, made it feel a little better.

She must have been in the cabin around two hours when another knock interrupted her description of the dawn and the first sighting of *Carpathia*.

'Sorry to stop you,' said Eleanor. 'This'll be Gladys come to visit. She's one of you lot.'

Once Gladys had arrived, perhaps Margaret would have an escape, so that she could get out of here and continue her search.

'Come on in, Gladys, dear. Draw up a seat. This is our new friend Margaret.'

Margaret stood and held out her hand ready to shake with the visitor.

But Gladys was in no position to shake hands, for in her arms was the baby Margaret had been so desperate to find.

CHAPTER 35

Tuesday 16th–Wednesday 17 April 1912, onboard RMS Carpathia
By morning Margaret had discovered many things.

The children looked so like one another, and were clearly so attached to each other, that everyone deduced they had to be brothers.

'At first we thought they were too numb from cold to tell us their names,' said Eleanor, at supper the night before.

'Then we realised they were foreign,' added Gladys, 'and didn't understand a single word we were saying.'

'Next that homely French girl, Bertha, appeared on the scene. She recognised them right off – she'd spent time looking after them, you see. The children had been travelling in the Second Class, where she had encountered their father.'

Gladys lowered her voice. 'And she told us how the poor little mites' mother died last month, very tragically, and very young.'

'According to Bertha,' Eleanor also assumed a low confidential tone, 'their father was a Mr Louis Hoffman, a solitary type.'

'Dressed them up like tailor's dummies, she said.'

'Pity he didn't do the same before throwing them into the lifeboat!' said Gladys. 'As the boat slipped off into the ocean, my friends remembered two men throwing the children in. They were practically naked. The children, that is, not the men... or my friends.'

Everybody laughed.

'As the father spoke French,' Eleanor said, 'Bertha presumes he was a Frenchman and that like her he had boarded at Cherbourg.'

'I came aboard at Cherbourg too,' said Margaret.

'Remember, Bertha also believes that the children bore the Christian names Lolo and Lump Which,' Gladys added dryly, 'seems highly unlikely to me. Especially if they're from a Roman Catholic country, like France. They'd have to have saints' names. I'm no hagiographer but I've never heard of Saint Lump, have you?'

'Once we arrive in New York, what will happen to them?' asked Margaret, never taking her eyes off the little babe on Gladys's lap.

'The Children's Aid Society will try to find a relative. And then, if they're unlucky, they will pack them off to an orphanage.'

'No!' said Margaret emphatically. 'Not an orphanage. That cannot happen.'

'I can't see how you could prevent it,' said Gladys. 'It's how things are done in America.'

'Not on my watch,' replied Margaret. 'I am going to take them in. They are coming to stay with me and my family in West End Avenue, as my guests.'

As a result of this late-night conversation, on Wednesday morning at breakfast, Margaret told Lillian and Olive of her plan. They seemed appalled. Margaret had deliberately chosen to tell them when Gilbert was elsewhere.

In fact, for some reason or other, Gilbert was late down to breakfast. Margaret suspected he was larking around, entertaining the troops, up in the smoking room.

'But what will your mother say?'

'And your father?' Lillian Potter appeared horrified. 'He's a busy man.'

'It's nothing to do with them.' Margaret noticed the glance which the do-gooding mother exchanged with her bespectacled daughter, so added brightly, 'They will be delighted. They, like you, adore doing charitable work.'

'I telegraphed to your father that you were safe,' said Lily. 'But I didn't warn him that you were bringing home two foreign orphans from the Second Class.'

'Oh, do look at the time!' Margaret wasn't going to listen to this stuff. She took a last bite of toast and polished off her cup of coffee, only then glancing down at her watch. 'I have to go and do my duty. See you ladies later!'

Margaret, inflamed with joy in her new role, ran down the stairs, taking them two by two.

The ship had at last stopped rolling, but, once again, the foghorn was roaring away every few minutes.

Despite sleeping in her new little personal space, on a mattress in a corner of the library floor, today Margaret was full of beans.

It seemed rather rude to be bursting with delight, especially when so many around her were weeping. But the heavens were constantly showing her signs. In the dawn light, she had lain awake, staring at the spines of books a foot away from her face. Those titles included: *The Boy Castaways of Black Lake Island*, *Two of Them* and *Whom God Hath Joined*.

You see! It was all meant. She knew it. This was her destiny.

She knocked on the door of Cabin 23.

A bleary-eyed Eleanor Danforth answered.

'Oh, it's you. They're not here any more.' She kept the door open a mere inch. 'Gladys and I realised we were both flat on the floor with tiredness so we surrendered our charges. Enough is enough. You know, I'm meant to be on holiday.'

Margaret was filled with panic.

'But where are they?'

'Some rather helpful women took them off.'

'Which women?'

'No idea. They're somewhere on the steamer. You'll have to look around.'

The door closed in Margaret's face.

Totally despondent, she sloped away. It might not be 'the Big Ship' but the *Carpathia* was still large enough to make looking for two children like looking for a pair of needles in a haystack.

She went up to the promenade deck and stood gazing at nothing at all, for the fog was so thick it was like staring at a white sheet on a washing line.

The horn blew out again, making Margaret jump with shock.

Why was she so nervy? Her heart beat so she could hardly breathe.

Gripping the rails, she took a few deep breaths.

Somewhere ahead lay New York. Someone had said that, God willing, they should arrive at the Cunard pier in Manhattan tomorrow.

She'd been away four months, but it felt more like four years. She wondered if she would recognise her parents. Would they come to meet her? How would they know where to go, which pier? Mrs Potter had told her that she'd cabled ahead, but Margaret had heard people saying that the captain wasn't allowing passengers to send private cables, as they were still transmitting more important information, like the names of survivors. Perhaps back home they had no idea she had been saved.

Would she have to limp along to the taxi stand and get home in a cab?

But how? She didn't have a penny on her. Not a cent. All her money had gone down with the ship. Would a taxi take her all the way up to West 83rd Street for nothing but pity? Margaret presumed that by now people in New York must know that their mighty deluxe steamer had gone down to the depths of the ocean.

Then Margaret wondered, had she ever told her parents about the change of plan? Maybe they thought she was still merrily touring all those ancient boring ruins, and had no idea she had been aboard… *that ship*.

Somewhere amid the blank white that surrounded her, she suddenly heard a child sobbing. Her ears, like antennae, focused on the space the sound had come from. The muffled quality of the fog made it very hard to be precise, but Margaret sensed that it came from the prow.

Stepping around the *Titanic*'s lifeboats, which were now strapped to the deck, Margaret made her way, cautiously, trying not to slip on the damp boards. The howls were getting louder.

Eventually she pulled open a door and stepped inside.

There was a stairwell. The cries came from the bottom.

She ran down and found a large dining room, full of poorly dressed women, some wearing shawls, others in woollen knitted caps, all talking to each other in hushed tones. The anxiety of the room chilled her.

But the cries had stopped and she couldn't see any children here at all.

She scanned the faces.

Some she recognised from before, others not. But everybody looked so old, their eyes haunted.

A long bout of sobbing which sounded almost like hiccups.

Margaret swung round.

How disappointing.

The cries were coming from a little girl of around six or seven. A woman with her arm around the child saw Margaret staring at them and beckoned her over.

'She's lost her doll. She left it behind on... You know...'

The woman crooked her finger, asking Margaret to come even closer.

'I don't have the heart to tell her...' The woman herself sobbed now. 'We sold our house in England, you see, and brought the money with us. Not only all our money in the world, but her dear father, my beloved husband, lies on the ocean bed. How can I tell her now, when she misses her doll so?'

'I'll look for some toys. I promise.'

The woman told her the cabin number and Margaret moved out of this room of sorrow.

She asked at the purser's office first, hoping there might be some toys somewhere onboard. But the purser told her that the supply was totally exhausted, so many children had needed cheering.

'Is there anything else I could help you with?'

Margaret paused, then decided not to ask him about formal procedures regarding taking the French orphans home, as he might give her some reasons why she couldn't and then he'd call the authorities and have them taken away, where they would grow up in some hateful Dickensian institution. Better she just feigned ignorance and took matters into her own hands.

She went in search of Olive and Lillian.

Peering out on to the deck, she saw that the fog had been dispersed and replaced by driving rain. The visibility wasn't that much better, but at least with rain you got a feeling of movement.

There was much laughter coming from the saloon, a strange sound on this tragic vessel of widows.

Margaret stood in the doorway, saw the cause, and her heart leapt with joy.

Gilbert was in there, making Bébé walk on her hind legs.

The laughter was coming from the little French baby and his bigger brother.

Both children were decked out in new suits, sewn from blankets, with baggy trousers and cross-braces. They looked just like the painted blue Dutch boys on her father's table china.

Margaret quietly crossed the room and, not wanting to interrupt the intoxicating sound of children's laughter, stood some yards behind them.

Gilbert noticed her come in and swiftly finished his piece of canine theatre, leaving the children to pet the dog.

'I didn't know how to get hold of you,' he said. 'But I thought it only fair to give those two ladies a break. And as luck would have it, the older child is now recovered from his *mal de mer*, so the kids are doubly delighted at being together again *and* playing with *chien-chien*.'

'Do they speak to one another?' asked Margaret.

'Oh, emphatically. But, as it's in Froggy, old girl, I only catch the odd word, like "Papa" and "hotel".'

'I wonder how we can find out their names?'

'No idea, old darling. The little one does say Lolo a lot. Perhaps Lolo is the name of the big one?'

'Lolo?' she called. The older boy turned towards her.

'Problem solved.' Gilbert held up a finger. 'He's called Lolo.'

'But that's not a real name, Gilbert. Think of real names which Lolo could come from.'

'Lorelei?' suggested Gilbert. 'Lorenzo? Low-level? Lo and Behold?'

'Oh, Gilbert, please stop being glib and think! Perhaps Louis. That's a French name. Lots of kings were called Louis. Their father was called Louis, apparently.'

'I suppose I don't understand why you are so bothered about it.'

'For one, it would be nice to be able to address them by their names. Then there will be all those forms to fill in when we arrive in New York. You know how we Americans are about red tape and immigration. They'll want the lot. Names, ages, address of relatives, date of birth, height, weight, colour of eyes, et cetera.'

'Oh, Margaret, dear.' Gilbert winced. 'You're certainly not going to get all that stuff now, are you?'

'I know that, Gilbert. I can make most of it up. But as long as we know their names, the rest will be so much easier. We know that the surname is Hoffman. Now let's find the Christian names.'

'I don't know, Meg, honey. Sounds like a wild goose chase to me.'

'I've got it!' Margaret knocked her forehead. 'How dim can a girl be? There are at least two Frenchmen aboard. They were in our life-boat, Gilbert, don't you remember?'

'Not that obnoxious baron, I hope.'

'No. One was talking about stage scenery. The other rowed wearing his monocle. So that's what you have to bring me next, Gilbert. A man in a monocle.'

'But I… Other people wear monocles. I wear a monocle! How will I know it's the right one?'

'Don't be silly. He'll wear a monocle *and* speak French. That's how you'll know. I think his name was Marshall. Something like that.' She glared at Gilbert. 'Well? What are you waiting for? Chop-chop!'

'Oh. I see. *I* am the one to do the search.'

'That's right, Gilbert. Come on. We have less than twenty-four hours.'

Gilbert loped off, leaving Margaret contentedly playing with the children and the dog.

'*Je m'appelle Margaret,*' she said.

'*Bonjour,*' said the bigger child.

'*Bonjour,*' echoed his little brother. 'Lump!'

Silence.

There was one useless try.

'*Vous appelle Louis?*' She tried to say it as though it was a question but they looked at her with much the same puzzled expression as when she spoke to them in English.

'Lump,' said the younger.

'*Votre chien est très chouette,*' said the elder boy. '*Très drôle, aussi.*'

Within the hour, Gilbert arrived back with Monsieur Maréchal.

The man approached the children gingerly.

'*Bonjour,*' he said with a little bow.

'*Bonjour,*' they replied in unison.

Monsieur Maréchal then jabbered away really fast. Margaret caught only one word in ten. Why on earth, she wondered, didn't he give them time to reply?

The boys did seem rapt by whatever he was saying.

Then the monocle man put both arms out and said something very proudly.

Suddenly all hell broke out.

The elder boy put his hands to his ears and jumped up and down. He started howling, then ran into the corner and crawled beneath the grand piano. His brother followed him, step by step.

Margaret had no idea what had happened.

She turned to Monsieur Maréchal, only to see that he looked as puzzled as she was. 'I didn't ask you here to scare them to death, but to get their names.'

'I know that,' said the Frenchman. 'They have an odd accent. But I tried to entice them in a manner which always works with little boys.'

'It didn't work today, though. Why is that?'

'I have no idea. It is most unusual.'

Margaret was livid. Now, thanks to this idiot, rather than getting their names or their addresses or anything, she had two terrified children, frightened out of their wits.

'What did you actually tell them?' Margaret tried to ask this in a reasonable tone, but it came out in a furious frenzy. 'That you are the Coney Island child-catcher come to eat them for dinner?'

'No, mademoiselle.' The Frenchman answered slowly and deliberately. 'I told them something about myself. Something which always, until now, ravishes the listener, whatever their age. I explained to them that in France I am very famous and told them my occupation.'

Margaret could imagine what job he had. Mass murderer? Orphanage keeper? Guillotine operator?

'I told them, Mademoiselle Hays, that I am a man of the skies. I am an aviator.'

CHAPTER 36

Thursday 18 April 1912, onboard RMS Carpathia

Just after teatime on Thursday afternoon, bellboys walked about the ship telling people that they had passed the Fire Island lightship and would soon be entering New York harbour.

The ship would dock, they told the passengers, in about four hours.

Margaret's first thought was that she should go to her cabin and pack. Then she remembered she had no cabin, no luggage and nothing to pack.

All she had were the clothes she stood in.

And the two children.

She sat quietly with them and Gilbert, who gripped Bébé in his arms.

The sun was shining. Margaret decided that that was another good omen.

Barely had the thought run through her head than a black cloud obscured the sun and the ship was plunged into darkness.

'Is there going to be an eclipse or something?' asked Gilbert. 'It's too dark to be true. There's something odd going on.'

Margaret went to the window.

Hallelujah!

Through the murk she could see land.

'We're surrounded by tugs, Gilbert!' There were scores of them, and they appeared to be heading from every direction. 'You wouldn't think a ship this size needed such an escort.' She moved away from the window and sat down. 'I hope Daddy is waiting there, and Mummy too,' she said, wondering whether there would be room for all of them inside the car.

'Now… Margaret. Sorry to have to say this, but I'll have to be pushing off, I'm afraid.' Gilbert patted her leg. 'With any luck I've just time to nab the last train up to Albany. Don't want to have to run to a hotel. Not if I don't need to. No money. You know the problem.'

Margaret felt a sudden pang.

'You could stay with us, Gilbert.'

'Really, Margaret, I couldn't. After all, you're bringing home quite a bit of company already with these two!'

Desolation swept through her.

Much as the voyage had been a trip through hell, she couldn't bear the thought of separating from all the people who had shared it with her. How would anyone else ever be able to understand?

Olive and Lily would be heading straight down to Philadelphia. No doubt a car would be waiting at the pier.

And she didn't know what to do about Bébé. Would it be best if she went off with Gilbert, to keep him company? Or should she keep her in West 83rd Street, to amuse the children?

She glanced up at Gilbert.

Poor boy.

He looked as forlorn as she felt.

'Promise me, Gilbert, that if you miss that train, you won't go to a hotel. You'll come along and stay with me on West 83rd. Right?'

'Right ho. Promise.'

A sudden shudder and the boat rocked.

Margaret gripped the sides of her chair. 'What was that?'

'A wave, I think.' Gilbert had gone pale. 'Perhaps it's something to do with those tugboats.'

Please, please do not let us sink now, prayed Margaret. Not when we are so near home. Not after all we've been through.

A deafening crash and an instantaneous blinding flash.

Margaret, along with many people in the saloon, flung herself down on to the floor.

'What is going on, Gilbert?'

The children started crying. Margaret and Gilbert held them tight.

'It couldn't happen again. Really, Margaret. That would be too, too unfair.'

Rain was thundering on the roof. Or was it hail? The noise was so loud that it sounded as though each drop could batter through the metal.

The sky kept growing darker and darker.

'It's too dark. It shouldn't be so dark.'

'It'll be night falling, old girl. Don't worry... That and the storm.'

They sat up, huddled together on the floor.

Another crack of lightning lit the room.

The smaller boy buried his face into Margaret's side.

A long roll of thunder followed.

'What a homecoming!' Gilbert whispered. 'It feels as though this journey will never end.'

Margaret hugged the sobbing children and dared not respond.

Eventually, as the hailstorm calmed a little, Gilbert clambered to his feet and walked to the windows.

'I say, Margaret, look at these little boats. They're holding up signs for us.'

'Welcoming us home?' Margaret stood up; then, taking the hand of the older boy and scooping the smaller one into her arms, joined Gilbert.

'Not exactly.' Gilbert turned to face her, looking glum. 'See for yourself! The *New York Herald*, the *Tribune*, the *Sun*, *Evening World*...'

'They want our stories,' said Margaret, watching the flotilla.

'No, Margaret.' Gilbert put his arm around her waist. 'They want to drink our blood.'

In spite of the lightning and driving rain, men were standing up on the tiny boats, leaning against the guardrails, yelling up through loudhailers.

'We will pay for your story!' hollered one. 'Good money for exclusives.'

All over the black water, lights were popping. But these flashes were from their cameras, not the sky.

'Do you know Mrs Astor?'

'How is Mrs Widener doing, having lost her whole family?'

Margaret turned away, trying to think of something else.

She wished that it was not so dark outside.

She would have liked to show the boys the New York skyline and point out the Statue of Liberty, the pride of America. Then she remembered that Lady Liberty was as French as they were.

But the boats were bobbing all around them, jostling against their hull, tooting horns and yelling messages.

'Did you glimpse the iceberg?'

'How long did the *Titanic* take to sink?'

'How many bodies did you see in the water?'

Margaret moved to the other side of the room and looked out towards the shore which was growing nearer and nearer.

Then, as the ship slowly turned into the pier, Margaret saw the crowds. Under the steely lights of the dockside, thousands and thousands of people lined the quay. They stood quite still, eerily silent, looking up at them with lined, grey faces. Some held large banners with names on them – Drew, Fortune, Gregson, Barkworth.

How would she ever find her parents in that crush?

The ringing of a handbell led them to turn. The captain had arrived.

He spoke quietly to all the passengers gathered in the saloon. He told them that, when they were further upriver, he had prevented journalists boarding. And how he now hoped that, after all their terrible tribulations, they would have a peaceful debarkation and a happy life.

He left the room to go and talk to the other passengers elsewhere. A steward then informed them of the details of the disembarkation procedure.

At 9.35 p.m., after all the *Carpathia*'s passengers had left the ship, Margaret strode down the gangplank, holding the baby in her arms. She was followed by Gilbert, who gripped Lolo's hand and had Bébé at the end of a leash.

Olive and Lily walked ahead of them.

As Margaret stepped on to the dockside, safe at last, the crowd surged forward and she was cut off from the others.

'Tell us your story!'

'What was the lifeboat like?'

She tried to shove through but couldn't get anywhere, particularly as she was trying to protect the howling child in her arms.

'Did you see the ship go down?'

Gilbert was a few yards in front of her. She could see his hat.

'What was the worst moment in the lifeboats?'

Margaret couldn't think. Every moment in the lifeboat had been awful beyond words.

'What's your name?'

'Margaret. Margaret Hays.'

A flashbulb went off nearby, making her temporarily blind.

'Which lifeboat were you on, Miss Hays?'

The child in her arms clung tightly to her, squashing his face into her chest.

'Number 7.' Margaret had been hoping that perhaps if she replied they might get out of her way. 'One of the first ones off.'

'Did you see Captain Smith on the deck?'; 'How many friends or family did you lose?'; 'Did you see Mr Astor?'

'Yes. His wife was about to get on—'

The journalists pressed more closely around her.

'Is that your child? How did she feel in the lifeboat?'

'He's French. He's just a baby.'

Margaret feared that if these men crushed in any tighter she wouldn't be able to breathe.

'There are two. I'm looking after them.'

Lily Potter's hat was now also visible. Margaret stood on her tiptoes. Where was Gilbert?

'What's his name?'

And Olive… If only she could see.

'And the other one?'

'Lolo.'

'Short for Louis?'

'Come on, old gal.' Gilbert appeared at her side, with Lolo in his arms. Grabbing Margaret's waist, he thrust them forward, through the shouts of journalists. Lolo was clutching Bébé's leash.

Both children were now crying.

Bébé was barking.

'They're orphans, don't you understand? We need to give them space. They have lost their family.'

Suddenly Margaret saw her mother and father.

'Mama!' she yelled, waving her free hand high above her head. 'Mother!'

The journalists parted and, seeing a more juicy target, ran back to interview a tall bespectacled Englishman.

Too late to be of real use, a line of policemen created a pathway for Margaret, Gilbert and their entourage.

Margaret's mother rushed forward and was about to hug her. Then she saw the child in her arms.

'I saved them, Mummy,' said Margaret. 'This little boy and his brother. I saved them from the shipwreck.'

Gilbert presented Lolo.

'*Bonjour*,' said the child, holding out his hand to be shaken.

'You'll all need a hot bath,' said her mother. 'After that ordeal.'

'It was days ago, Mummy.' Margaret had snapped at her mother, who only meant well. But she didn't want to live the rest of her life wrapped in cotton wool.

'This is Gilbert. We met in Naples.'

Gilbert smiled, lifted his hat and explained that he needed to rush off.

Lily and Olive were chatting to Margaret's father. They too hastily made their excuses – the car was waiting, the poor driver had been sitting here for hours, they had a long drive ahead… And were gone.

Alone now with her family, Margaret climbed into the car and squeezed up against her parents. The two children sat on Margaret's lap, quietly babbling to each other.

'My poor darling girl. You can't imagine how awful it is for a mother, not knowing. I was near to nervous collapse.'

Margaret turned away.

'I don't want to talk about it.' She clutched the baby and looked into Lolo's mournful dark eyes. They knew. They might be only children, but they knew that the whole *Titanic* saga didn't belong to anyone but them.

'Gilbert seemed a nice boy,' said her father, in an attempt to lighten the atmosphere.

'Yes,' replied Margaret.

She didn't even want to talk about Gilbert or the ship or the life-boats or the rescue or anything to do with it with anyone who didn't understand, who *couldn't* understand.

'It must feel very good to be home,' said her mother. 'I've had Cook make some supper and your room is all lovely, waiting for you.'

Margaret grunted. How she had longed to come home. How many nights had she dreamed of seeing New York? But now she was here it all felt bewildering and wrong. Why had Gilbert, Lily and Olive gone off and left her? She wanted only to be with people like that. People who had been there. People who *knew*. Not these strangers, her parents, who asked questions Margaret could not answer.

'It was all awful. We had a terrible time. And we don't want to talk about it. Don't you understand *anything*?'

After that Margaret's parents were silent.

'Welcome to New York, *mes chéries*.' Margaret clasped Lolo's hand and simultaneously bent forward and kissed the baby on the head. '*Bienvenu à votre nouveau vie*. Welcome to your new life.'

Inside the family home Margaret felt like a ghost. The house was exactly the same as when she had left, but now it seemed like a house from a dream.

More perplexing was that, although she had been to hell and back, Margaret felt as though she had never been away.

The only tangible thing which made it different was that now these two little strangers were with her.

Her father had disappeared straight into his office, but her mother was fussing around, staring at her, touching her, stroking her cheek.

'Please stop, Mummy,' Margaret shouted. She knew her tone was brusque, but she meant it to be. 'I told you, I don't want any fuss.'

'You may not want any fuss, Margaret, but I have so many questions. Not least…' she lowered her voice '…what do we do with these… urchins?'

Urchins! Urchins? They weren't living in some Charles Dickens novel. This was modern-day New York.

'They're orphans. Orphans! Don't you understand, Mother? They have no one to help them right now. No one in the whole world but me.'

Margaret glanced down at the children, standing beside her in the hallway, looking around slightly fearfully, and wondered now what she had done bringing them with her.

Yes, those people on *Carpathia* had hurt her by implying that she cared more about Bébé than she did about the poor souls who had drowned. But where were those critical women now? They couldn't see that she had made it all better.

'*S'il vous plaît, mademoiselle?*' Lolo pulled at Margaret's skirts. '*Mon frère veut faire dodo.*'

Margaret hadn't a clue what the child wanted. She presumed food, so she led them through to the kitchen, where Annie, the cook, had prepared a little supper of hot chocolate and biscuits.

'I don't know what you were thinking,' her mother hissed into her ear as the children sat at the table. 'You know that there are public services for these type of things?'

'They're not things, Mother, they're children.' Margaret stood between her mother and the boys who were eating hungrily, pulling their cups right up to their faces, leaving brown smiles on their cheeks. 'Anyway, you have no idea what it was like out there. I couldn't just leave them. Not after what we'd been through.'

'There must have been other women who could have—'

Margaret spun round. 'Every other woman there had lost somebody: their husband, their children, their parents, their friends. I still had everything. My friends. You. Money. Clothes. Jewellery. Life. *Everything.* You don't appear to understand how *lucky* I was.'

Then, with a bonk, the smaller child laid his head on the table and fell instantly asleep.

'Look how fragile they are. We have to protect them.' Margaret moved forward and scooped the baby into her arms. 'And now they need to go to bed.'

'So do you, darling.' Mary Hays pulled at Margaret's elbow. 'You look done in.'

'I'm wide awake, Mummy. I don't want to sleep.'

Margaret knew that Hannah, the maid, was upstairs, hastily preparing one of the guest rooms for the children, making up a double bed for them to share.

'*Allons, Lolo,*' she said. '*Dormir maintenant.*'

The boy stood up and politely bowed towards Annie. '*Merci, madame. Bonne soirée.*' As he left the room he lifted his hand and waved.

Lolo trotting at her side, Margaret carried the baby up the stairs. Her mother followed.

'Let me help, at least, Margaret. You might not know it, but you are exhausted.'

They went through to the guest bedroom together. In silence the two women stripped the boys.

'What dreadful clothing.' Mary Hays held up the makeshift trousers. 'They must have been travelling steerage.'

'Don't be ridiculous. This clothing was made for them out of ship's blankets by very kind passengers on the *Carpathia*.'

'They have no nightclothes?'

'They have nothing, Mother. *Nothing*. Don't you understand anything I have been saying? They'd already lost their mother, then the ship took their father. The only person they had in the world went down with the *Titanic*. They were thrown all but naked into the very last lifeboat. So you see, nightclothes are the least of their problems. Nightclothes we can buy.'

Lolo climbed up into the bed.

Margaret laid the baby beside him and pulled up the covers.

'*Bonne nuit, garçons,*' Margaret whispered.

'*Bonne nuit, mademoiselle,*' replied Lolo.

Mary Hays stepped back and sighed. 'In the morning we'll have to take them shopping for clothes. We can't have them wandering around here looking like two little Ellis Island immigrants straight from the potato fields of Romania.'

Margaret looked at her mother. Everything had changed between them. Life could never be the same again.

Down in the drawing room, Margaret's father stood in the bay window. The curtains were drawn.

'We have to talk,' he said, moving behind his large mahogany desk.

Margaret remained standing, while her mother sat.

'I have called and left messages at the French Consulate, and with the Children's Aid Society.'

'But, Daddy…'

Why were her parents making her feel as though she had committed some hideous and heinous crime? She had helped. Helped, during a tragedy which they could never comprehend.

'And I have also phoned a friend at the *New York Tribune*, and given him all the details we know about the children, so that we can start the search for their relatives.'

'I'm sorry, Daddy, but—'

'You have been under tremendous strain, Margaret. I think now you should go to bed and rest.'

'I lived through a tragedy, Daddy. I survived. And I would hope that you and Mother will stop patronising me.'

There was a fierce rapping on the front door.

'Hell.' Frank Hays stood. 'Who can that be at this hour?'

Margaret prayed that it was Gilbert, having missed his train to Albany. How wonderful to have somebody here who could help her explain. She ran out and, beating the maid to it, pulled open the door, ready to welcome him.

'Miss Hays!'

A crowd of men wearing homburgs and derbies, wielding notebooks and pencils, pushed forward.

'Miss Hays! How is Louis?'

Margaret tried to close the door but there was a foot in the way.

'Miss Hays, Miss Hays! Tell us about the *Titanic* orphans.'

CHAPTER 37

Friday 19 April 1912, New York City
Margaret and her mother walked the children through the clothing
section of Franklin Simon department store on Fifth Avenue.

'Should we dress them both the same?' asked Margaret, approaching a display of trousers and shorts.

The two boys stood together, holding hands, occasionally murmuring into one another's ears.

'They're not twins, dear. And the small one is little more than
a baby.' Mrs Hays was flicking through a rail of children's coats.
'Matching clothes would not be suitable.'

Margaret was already holding four pairs of leggings and some
pants for the boys.

'Ladies, may I help at all?' One of the floorwalkers hovered.
'Perhaps I could carry your items. Are they for these little ones?'

'They are.' Mary Hays nodded. 'My daughter saved them from
the *Titanic* catastrophe. Poor things, washed up without a stitch of
clothing.'

Another, younger girl behind the counter looked up from her
bookkeeping. 'Oh! Good lord! You must be Miss Margaret Hays!'
The girl came round to greet her. 'I must shake your hand, Miss Hays.'

'How did you know my...?'

'Why, it's all over the papers. Everyone in the staffroom has been
talking about it all morning. "The lost waifs of the *Titanic*!"' The girl
beckoned some other shop assistants in the adjacent shoe department. 'Look – here! The *Titanic* orphans!'

From all directions members of staff and customers formed a
circle, billing and cooing around the boys.

The floorwalker glanced at the scene, excused herself and rushed away.

'Ladies!' Mary Hays put her hands up. 'Thank you so much for your interest, but really we must be allowed to get on with finding clothing for the little mites.'

But barely had the crowd dispersed than the manager of the store arrived at their side.

'Mrs Hays, Miss Hays!' He grovelled before both women, then stooped low to greet the boys. '*Messieurs.*'

'*Bonjour, monsieur.*'

Both boys held out their hands to be shaken.

The manager obliged.

'*Bonjour, monsieur,*' echoed Monmon.

'Yes, indeed. *Bonjour, mes enfants.*' The manager rose and addressed Mrs Hays. 'If you wouldn't be offended, I would like very much to contribute a little something to this noble cause. And so, on behalf of Franklin Simon, I should like to supply the boys with complete outfits: underwear, shoes, outer garments, everything they need.'

'That's all very well,' Mrs Hays looked sternly at him, 'but that is exactly what we've been trying to do for the last half hour.'

'Ah, Mrs Hays, I do believe I may have expressed myself less than clearly. Franklin Simon would like to *give* you these pieces of apparel, free and gratis, a gift of the shop.'

After the children were dressed in new outfits, the remaining clothing was packed up by smiling assistants.

The manager then escorted the party up to the toy department, where the store's photographer was waiting.

'Now the youngsters must choose whatever they like. One toy each.'

Margaret could remember this word in French. '*Choisir,*' she said to the boys. '*Choisir un jouet.*'

Hesitantly, the children stepped forward to the shelves of toys.

Both went directly to the same shelf, and each picked the same toy, but painted in different colours.

'Do you think that's quite right?' asked Mrs Hays under her breath.

'Don't look at me,' replied Margaret. 'It's what they chose.'

'How lovely, and how fitting!' The manager stepped forward to arrange the children for their photograph. 'Little tin boats.'

When they arrived back at West 83rd in a taxi crammed with boxes of clothing, more journalists were waiting on the steps.

'Miss Hays! Mrs Hays! Any more idea of who their family might be?'

'Passengers from the *Carpathia* say that they are the sons of a Monsieur Louis Hoffman.'

'Were you friends with Mr Hoffman?'

'Did Hoffman give them to you to take care of?'

Holding both children tight, Margaret pushed forward trying to reach the front door and get inside. Her mother was close behind, muttering.

None of this had been part of Margaret's plan. She simply wanted to be left alone, to be on her own with the children, playing skittles or something on her bedroom floor.

'I didn't know Monsieur Hoffman.'

Margaret had managed to get to the top step. She reached out to pull the bell, but a large man in tweeds blocked her way.

'Was he alone or with a mistress?'

'They tell me alone. But, frankly, I don't understand how two such small children could be cared for by a man on his own without their mother or some kind of a nanny with them,' she replied. 'Now could you please let me inside my home?'

'So you're saying that they came from low stock?'

Margaret turned on the wiry little man who had made this insinuation.

'Absolutely the contrary. Their manners are so perfect they must have come from a *very good* home.'

'Is that their table manners?'

'Everything about them,' replied Margaret, stretching a hand out and jangling the bell. 'They have been perfectly brought up. In fact, the first thing they asked on rising this morning was whether they could please have a bath.'

Why was nobody answering the door? Margaret pulled the bell again.

'How are the kiddies shaping up after their ordeal?'

'They're very happy.' Margaret banged her gloved fists on the door panels. 'Not at all homesick.'

Someone inside finally opened up.

Margaret ushered the children into the hall, then put her arm around her mother and steered her inside too. Once safely in, she slammed the door and leaned against it.

'I don't think I can stand much more of this,' said Mary, pulling off her hat and striding away up the staircase.

'Oh good. You're back.' Frank Hays stepped out of the drawing room. 'I have a visitor for our little guests.'

Margaret panicked. Surely no one could have come to claim them so soon.

As though noticing their new surroundings for the first time, the baby looked around the hall, turned to Lolo and asked, '*Où est Papa?*'

Lolo took his brother's hand.

'*Papa est parti,*' he said.

Margaret knew what they had said. Papa is gone. She dared not speak.

'Come along!' Mr Hays held the door open and beckoned Margaret and the children in.

'May I present His Excellency, the Consul General of France, Monsieur Étienne Lanel.'

After the initial pleasantries and getting a few more details from Margaret, at his own insistence, Monsieur Lanel asked to be left alone with the children.

Margaret sat on the stairs in the hall.

She had done her best to get information out of them, hadn't she? She feared that they would be in there now with him spilling the beans and she would look a fool. The man would come out and lecture her for taking the children, and interfering where she had no business. Margaret waited for over an hour until the consul emerged, alone.

Hearing the click of the door, Frank Hays came out of his office. He called for the cook, who bustled into the hall and hurried the children off to the kitchen for lunch.

The consul stepped forward. 'I am sorry, Mr Hays, but I seem to have drawn a blank. You see they really are such nice children. They appeared worried about disobliging me, and, as a result, to everything I asked they simply replied "*oui*".'

'And their names?' asked Margaret. 'Did you discover their names?'

She dreaded that the ambassador would have succeeded where she had failed.

'Oh yes, Mademoiselle Hays. According to my enquiries they are called "*Oui, monsieur*" and "*Oui, monsieur*".' Monsieur Lanel laughed. 'Although it seems that I did make quite a significant breakthrough when asking for the names of their parents.'

Margaret felt crushed.

Her father leaned forward in excitement.

'I asked them both, one after the other, what was the name of their mother, and they replied concisely, without any hesitation on either part.'

'Well?'

'When I asked, "What is the name of your mother?" they replied... "Mama".'

'And their father?'

'"Papa" of course.' The consul chuckled at his little joke. 'However, there was one thing. I did notice that they had no reaction whatsoever to the name Hoffman. Are you absolutely sure that Hoffman was the man accompanying them onboard the RMS *Titanic*?'

'I only heard about it from a woman onboard *Carpathia*. You see, Monsieur Lanel, I was travelling in the First Class, while the boys and their father were travelling in the Second Class. We never had the opportunity to mingle.'

How awful it must sound, thought Margaret. But it was simply a fact.

'The woman – well, a girl really, called Bertha – had also made the crossing in Second Class and it was she who told me that the father's name was Hoffman, and that, apart from that, she knew nothing about him. She said he spoke to no one. He was very protective of the children. The only thing she remarked upon was that they were always so well dressed.'

'So, all in all, Monsieur Lanel,' Frank Hays appeared disconcerted by the failure of the consul to discover anything which they did not already know, 'this visit has been a total waste of time.'

'Not exactly.' The consul bristled at the implication. 'I also asked the boys where they lived. Of course they replied "*oui*". But I left them for a few moments to talk between themselves and, from that chatter, one thing is clear. They speak in a very striking accent. I myself have heard this accent before. It is a particular type of patois, from southern France.'

'Marseille?'

'No, no, no. The Marseillaise speak with a much more guttural sound. Their accent is gentle. I would make a guess that these children come from the area around a very beautiful town called Nice.'

'I went to Nice!' Margaret had loved the city: the curve of its bay, the turquoise water, the terracotta houses with their brightly coloured shutters. But the Potters' very charged itinerary meant that they spent only one day there before moving on to Italy. 'The Bay des Anges!'

Margaret had hoped to grab a sandwich, but barely minutes after the consul had gone, Mr R. D. Neill of the Children's Aid Society arrived and presented his visiting card.

He was invited in.

For around fifteen minutes, Mr Neill bombarded Margaret and her father with the same questions that everyone else had asked. He then demanded to meet the children, so, despite their being in the middle of enjoying pudding – ice cream and strawberry sauce – they were summoned to the drawing room.

Making no allowance for their age, Mr Neill spoke sternly to them, barking questions in a loud voice. Naturally he spoke entirely in English, believing that volume conquered all language barriers. It was obvious that he also thought not being able to understand the English language was a sign of mental retardation.

Before him, the children cowered.

When the baby started crying, Margaret stepped in.

'I'm sorry, Mr Neill,' she said. 'This isn't right. They are just babies. Babies who, in the last weeks, have gone through enormous suffering.'

'Miss Hays, you do not need to tell me how to handle children. It is, after all, what I am paid for. And, from years of experience, I have found that a little strictness can only improve a child's character.'

'Their characters, Mr Neill, are impeccable.'

'But, with respect, Miss Hays, you are spoiling them with ice cream and toys, allowing them to lead you a merry dance. I also believe that that French envoy chappie of yours was absolutely wrong. There is a reason he couldn't get a word out of them, and that reason is quite simple. These children are playing you, Miss Hays. And from what I have heard of their speech, they are not French at all. I agree that they are of foreign birth, but I will not be at all surprised when it is eventually discovered that they are in fact Polish.'

Margaret wanted to hit the man.

He must know that, here in New York, Poles were considered the lowest of the low.

While the children played on the floor of the guest room, Margaret lay on the bed, watching them sailing their little boats across the carpet.

It was obvious that they did not equate these toys with the huge floating palace from which they had been rescued.

It was funny: when Margaret walked across the room she swayed from side to side. After eight days at sea and only one on dry land, she had developed whatever was the opposite of sea legs. Land legs? Even sleeping in her bed last night here in West End Avenue, she felt the gentle sway of the waves.

How long would it take to go back to normal? She glanced down at the children. Did they also feel as though they were at sea? As they played, so self-sufficient and placid, Margaret questioned whether it might have been better to have let them be, and to have kept Bébé.

A rap on the door.

It was Hannah.

'Sorry to disturb, miss, but there's an awful lot of letters come for you. I thought as you would like to be starting on them, right away.'

'That's fine, Hannah. Just hand them to me.'

'It's not quite so simple as that, miss.'

Hannah stepped back to reveal the mail boy standing on the landing. Together the pair of them hauled in a huge sack and emptied it on to the bed.

Margaret spent the afternoon opening and reading the letters, one by one.

Letter after letter, from people either desperate or mad, all wanting the same thing: to possess her two orphans.

The begging letters, and the ones who simply wanted gossip about the shipwreck, Margaret put straight into the waste-paper basket.

After about an hour, her father came in and joined her, sorting the letters and cables into neat piles.

'All those years of my youth, working as an insurance agent,' said Mr Hays, tossing another scrawled missive into the bin, 'gives me a remarkably clear eye on a fraud when I see one.'

By nightfall Margaret and her father had reduced the sack to a pile of about thirty hopefuls – people who were willing to come from all over the United States to pick up 'their' children.

Over two hundred letters were in the bin. About fifty more to go.

'Oh, and, Margaret dear, I haven't told you yet, that we've had telephone calls from Mayor Gaynor. He is also offering you his help.'

'What can Mayor Gaynor do?'

'I've no idea. But maybe when the time comes he will be useful.'

It was with mixed feelings that Margaret read a letter signed by a man called Franck Lefebvre from Mystic, Iowa. He said that he was writing to her father too. 'The man of the house' is how he put it. His children, he wrote, had boarded *Titanic*. He'd not seen their names in the lists. Perhaps he should not lose hope.

Margaret knew that it would be lovely indeed to reunite the children with their real family.

But... then she would lose them.

They would remember her, surely, and feel love towards her for helping them mend their lives.

Wouldn't they?

She looked down at the pile of mail. Not many letters left. She read on.

Some of them were mighty strange – tales of children kidnapped and young runaways. Few of the writers seemed to take into account the fact that the children did not speak English, were much too young to be runaways, and had arrived from Europe, not Nebraska or Texas.

Margaret tried to imagine little Lump running away. He'd be lucky if he got to the end of the bedroom carpet without falling over.

Another jangle from the front door.

Every time this happened Margaret's heart broke a little.

What if it was an aunt or big brother arrived out of nowhere to pick up their dear ones?

But it was only a Miss Greeley-Smith, some lady journalist from the *Evening World*. Margaret's father had invited her for an exclusive 'intimate interview'. A way of putting their side of the story, after today's bombardment of headlines. As she was female, Frank said, she would have a different take on it all. She would be more compassionate.

Margaret greeted her in the hall, a short plump woman with a centre parting through dark hair which seemed slightly windswept.

'Oh! How do you manage with all those hounds at your door?' She threw Margaret a sympathetic glance. 'And you must be brave little Margaret.' Margaret blushed. At last someone had recognised what she had managed to do.

'This way, Miss Greeley-Smith.' Frank Hays ushered them both through to the drawing room.

'Call me Nixola,' Miss Greeley-Smith murmured quietly, as she caught sight of the children playing on the carpet beside a large armchair.

'We really want to put the story straight,' said Frank. 'There has been so much rubbish written over the last twenty-four hours.'

'Of course, Mr Hays.' Nixola Greeley-Smith nodded and smiled graciously. 'I couldn't agree more. Some of my male colleagues are quite brutish with the truth. As long as they get a good story, they don't really mind about whether or not they get it right. Whereas I really *do* mind. Have you noticed any misapprehensions, Mr Hays?'

'Oh yes, we have. For instance, there is the story that the children were in the same lifeboat with my daughter and that they clung to her instinctively. This is absolutely wrong. They were in quite separate lifeboats and my daughter only met the children once safely aboard the *Carpathia*.'

'Then she saw them and took them over?'

'No!' said Margaret. 'That wasn't what happened at all—'

But her father continued over her, 'As my daughter was the only woman on the *Carpathia* ladies' committee who had not suffered some personal loss, it was felt that she was in a unique position to take care of them and she gladly did so. These children found themselves on that ship, as it were, all alone in the world. Look at the size of them! They needed someone to look after them and my daughter did her womanly duty.'

Lolo was pressed against the skirting board, racing his tin boat along the rug, the baby on all fours in hot pursuit.

'But, Mr Hays, they are no longer on that ship.' Miss Greeley-Smith gave him a hard stare. 'So why are they here in this luxurious townhouse and not under the care of the Children's Aid Society or indeed the Travellers' Aid Society?'

'My daughter felt that they would be more comfortable with us.'

Margaret noticed the sly look Miss Greeley-Smith gave her.

'Once we locate a bona fide relative, we will of course give them back, as it were,' Frank Hays continued. 'We have no intention of keeping them.'

'But, Daddy—'

Mr Hays again spoke over his daughter, preventing Margaret from interrupting.

'We are doing all we can to locate somebody who knows these children.'

'Really? What are you doing? Exactly?' Miss Greeley-Smith glanced up from her notepad. '*How* are you going about finding relatives?'

'We are working with the authorities both in New York and all around the world. Mayor Gaynor, for instance, told me this morning that Scotland Yard in London is assisting in the search.'

'You have no idea whatsoever who the children are, do you, Mr Hays? You don't even know their names!'

'No, Miss Greeley-Smith—'

'Nixola!'

'They are called Lolo and Lump.'

Miss Greeley-Smith's high-pitched laugh was enough to make both children look up from their game.

'In other words you know nothing about them.'

Margaret wished she could stop the blush rising on her cheeks. She noticed that her father's knuckles showed white as he gripped the arms of his chair.

'That's not quite correct, Miss Greeley-Smith—'

'Nixola.'

'My daughter was told that the children had travelled on the *Titanic* in the Second Class under the care of a man called Hoffman. We have shared this information with all the authorities. We have invited—'

'But I thought the shipping companies exact personal details, addresses, et cetera, from all purchasers of steamship tickets.' Miss Greeley-Smith gave Margaret and her father an ingratiating smile. 'So, why has it not been possible to get some information from the office where this man, Hoffman, bought his ticket for the ill-fated steamship?'

Margaret noted that the woman said the word Hoffman as though she and her father had invented it, some kind of subterfuge to cheat the world.

'I'm sure I can't say,' Mr Hays replied, shortly. 'I have never travelled Second Class or steerage, so I don't know anything about such matters.'

Nixola Greeley-Smith smiled and put away her pad and pencil.

CHAPTER 38

Sunday 21 April–Monday 22 April 1912, New York City
It had been the weekend from hell.

The journalists were still stationed on their doorstep. Ridiculous articles continued to appear in the press. The constant string of visitors to the house had frayed everyone's tempers and tired them out.

Mary Hays had packed a suitcase and stood in the hall, threatening to leave them all to it. She was going to escape to her parents' home in Piscataway Township, she told them.

'When will you come back?' asked Frank, as his wife called the maid to help get her luggage downstairs and into a taxi.

'Isn't it obvious?' snapped Mary. 'When the brats are gone and all this brouhaha has died away.'

In order to calm her parents, Margaret said that she should be the one to go, taking 'the brats' with her.

'But, Margaret,' wailed her father. 'Where will you go to?'

'Anywhere. Anywhere willing to take me and give these dear children the chance in life that they deserve.'

'While we're at it, why don't I leave too?' said Frank, with a stamp of the foot. 'Then everyone can have a bit of peace and quiet.'

They were interrupted by another sharp rap on the front door.

Margaret stepped out of the way as Hannah rushed past to answer it.

'It's Mr Lefebvre,' Hannah announced. 'To claim his children.'

'Damn,' snapped Frank. 'He's one of those letter-writers. I spoke to him on the telephone. I didn't think he'd come in person.'

Hannah pulled the door open and a dirty-looking man stepped inside.

'I am come to collect my kids,' he said, wringing a flat cap between his hands. 'Please can you bring them to me.'

Mary put a handkerchief to her nose and took a step back, then disappeared again up the stairs.

'Should I bring in the children?' asked Hannah. 'I believe they are in the kitchen with Cook.'

'Yes, yes. Whatever you like.' Frank stepped forward. He slightly raised his hand to shake, then changed his mind and slipped it back inside his trouser pocket. 'The little boys will be brought straight out, Mr, erm, Lefevrier.'

'Boys?' Mr Lefebvre dropped his cap on the doormat. 'But I am searching for three little girls and one boy.'

Margaret wondered if the man could have read any of the newspaper accounts at all before he wrote in. The one and only thing they had always got right was that it was two boys.

Hannah emerged from the kitchen, pushing the boys ahead.

The children wiped their mouths and bowed.

'*Bonjour, monsieur.*'

'No! No!' Mr Lefebvre took a step back, bumping into the door. 'And I have come all the way from Iowa.' With a loud sob he collapsed into tears.

'Wallet. Desk,' Frank mumbled to Margaret, who rushed through and fetched her father's wallet. Mr Hays pulled out a ten-dollar bill and squeezed it into Mr Lefebvre's grimy hand.

'I'm very sorry that you wasted your time.'

But as Mr Lefebvre left, Margaret was again filled with joy... until her mother loomed at the top of the staircase.

'Did you see the filth under that man's nails?' she cried. 'Frank Hays! Enough of this preposterous carnival of lunatics.' She glared down at Margaret. 'And I am particularly thinking of you.'

As Mary Hays swept down the staircase and out of the front door, Hannah quietly turned the boys around and took them back to finish their ice cream – or rather, as it now was, warm cream.

The rest of the day was a stream of similar cases. The worst, in Margaret's eyes, was a frightfully well-to-do matron from Upper Fifth Avenue ('Millionaires' Row', as the woman kept reminding them) who wanted *to buy* the boys. 'Oh, my dears, they would look *so cute*, dressed up in Ver-sails pageboy costumes and talking in their sweet little accents, standing beside me at my famous Mary Antoinette soirées. I can just picture them in those fluffy cravats and wearing neat little white wigs with pigtails.'

There were weird predatory-looking men who arrived at the Hays' door, wanting to spend a bit of 'private time with the kiddies', followed by woeful middle-aged women who, unable to have children of their own, needed heirs to inherit their fortunes.

Then a tall man in spectacles appeared in the drawing room, telling Margaret that he was a science teacher from some London school with a name which sounded like Dullish College. Margaret thought that, if he was anything to go by, the school was aptly named. He told them solemnly that the children were definitely onboard the *Titanic*, in Second Class, and that they had travelled down from London to Southampton in the same railway compartment as him. They were accompanied by their father, a man called Mr Hoffman.

As if she didn't know all that already!

Just when Margaret thought she had seen the end of the claimants, and flopped back in an armchair for a moment's peace, her mother arrived in the drawing room with some lumpish young woman in tow.

'This is a nanny,' she said brusquely, presenting the girl to Margaret. 'She is come to look after the children.'

'But Mummy—' Margaret jumped up.

'Her name is Miss Utley. I picked her up from the Children's Aid Society.' Mrs Hays swept past her daughter, steering Miss Utley into the kitchen. 'Thank God!'

Margaret barely felt the air in the hall settle when the bell rang again and an envoy from the mayor's office stood in the doorway bearing a telegram addressed to Mayor Gaynor.

'The mayor said to bring it right over,' he said. 'It's from a doctor in East Chippewa Falls, Wisconsin.'

Margaret took the telegram and read it: I WILL ADOPT THE LITTLE HOFFMAN BOYS AND GIVE THEM A GOOD EDUCATION AND RAISE THEM RIGHT AND START THEM IN LIFE WHEN THEY GROW

UP. REFERENCES: EX-GOVERNOR THAD. C. POUND, COLONEL L. J. RUSK. COULD MEET BOYS IN CHICAGO.

As if Margaret was going to pack the children off to some dubious man without even setting eyes on him. She thanked the boy and tipped him, telling him that there was no reply.

Many more people sent in letters of application, both to the Hays' mansion and to the Children's Aid Society, offering, if no relatives could be found, to provide a home for one of them, and only one. Luckily, the single point upon which both Margaret and that horrid little man, Mr R. D. Neill, had agreed was that under no circumstances must the two boys be separated. Once read, these letters too were dispatched to the dustbin.

Margaret was in despair.

This was not how she had thought it would turn out.

She had imagined she would bring the boys to her comfortable home, where the rooms would echo with their infectious laughter and the newspapers would talk of her not as a spoilt brat, but as a kind and generous heroine, who had not only survived the *Titanic* disaster but saved two orphaned children while she was at it.

Instead, they had become commodities, and she their dealer.

Even her friends had lost their minds. They called on Margaret to tell her that she was the most famous person they had ever known.

One even asked her to sign their autograph book, right next to a signed photo of Dorothy Gibson. Margaret was about to tell her friend that she had actually met Miss Gibson, but appreciated that in polite society nobody would want to know that she had loaned a star of the cinematograph her knickers. None of her friends said the one thing she was longing to hear – that she was so thoughtful, saving two children.

She hated them all. First she'd been in trouble for saving Bébé, and now even when she had rescued two orphans she *still* didn't satisfy anyone. What more did they want? She'd had enough. Enough.

The only person Margaret really wanted to contact her was Gilbert. But he had disappeared to Albany in a puff of steam. She wondered if she would ever meet him again. Or see Bébé. Why hadn't she ignored those two women on the *Carpathia*, and kept Bébé?

She awoke early on Monday morning and lay in the dark, realising that exactly one week ago she was soaked to the skin, crammed up against total strangers, in a freezing lifeboat, rowing towards the *Carpathia* and the hope of life.

This time last week she had never set eyes on these children. Now their names were linked in newspaper articles across the world, as far away as Australia.

Two sweet little orphans who had turned her life upside down.

She wanted to cry, but her eyes seemed to be suffering some kind of drought.

If only she could run away with them and go someplace where no one had ever heard of them, and they'd find Gilbert and Bébé, and live together in a farmhouse by a babbling brook, and bake bread and cakes, and play and laugh all day long. And Gilbert would build a swing and hang it from an apple tree outside and each night they would all sit quietly together and watch the sun go down and count fireflies. Then, as the chill drove them in, they would sit around a glorious log fire burning in the grate and—

A knock on the door.

Hannah entered, bearing a tray.

On it rested a cup of coffee, a breakfast roll with butter and marmalade, a handful of letters and the newspaper, turned open at Miss Greeley-Smith's piece.

'Your father says he thinks you should look at it.'

Margaret sat up, sipping coffee, and started to read the article.

After a few sentences, she found it difficult to breathe.

It was a malicious personal attack of the first water. The wretched Miss Greeley-Smith made the boys sound like petulant, spoiled children, which they never were. She implied that Margaret had been cruel in giving them boats to play with (the boys had chosen the boats, for goodness' sake) and that her father was a pretentious, pompous snob, which he was not, and that she herself was a silly little idiot.

The last line was the final straw: *Why, oh, why can I never learn to keep my distance from the aristocracy of West End Avenue...?*

Margaret threw the paper across the room.

The whole world was laughing at her.

And all because she had a tender heart and wanted to help.

She felt as though she might be sick.

A line kept going round and round in her head: *That woman with the lapdog. It would have been better if she'd found babies to cling to…*

For a few minutes she sobbed, though still no tears came. She wished she had Bébé with her to cuddle.

Then she flicked through the letters.

Even from the handwriting, Margaret could recognise that most of them were from cranks, with an ulterior motive. Cranks who were hell-bent on taking the children away from her.

A man wrote from a farm in Montana that he was willing to 'take 'em, and breed 'em up' because he needed young men to work on his farm. The mother of an Oklahoma family of ten would welcome the boys, as she believed 'the more the merrier'. One single man had lost his wife and needed someone to look after him in his old age.

Margaret flung them away.

It was absurd.

The floor was now littered with paper.

The last letter in the pile bore the crest of the New York French Consulate.

Margaret ripped it open.

Monsieur Lanel had heard from some woman claiming to be the children's mother.

Margaret groaned.

Oh really?

Their mother?

A likely tale. Another maniac after publicity.

She read on.

Margaret really could not believe this one!

It was utterly preposterous. The children's mother had died last year. Didn't everyone know that by now?

So this mysterious ghost-mother, come back from the dead, had gone to the American consul in France and got him to write to his French colleague here in New York.

That was it! Enough! Margaret crumpled the letter and tossed it after all the others in the direction of the waste-paper basket, where it belonged.

And as the paper hit the wicker, Margaret made a decision.

She would put an end to this silly hunt for a non-existent family.

It was the only way these poor infants would ever again know peace.

Anyway, there was simply no need to search anywhere else.

Margaret loved the children.

The children loved her.

She had all the money she needed to keep them and give them a good comfortable life and a decent education.

So that was final. Margaret would go downstairs now and put the idea to her father. From this moment on she would end the search.

Tomorrow she would start the legal procedures to adopt Lolo and Lump.

PART THREE

Marcella

CHAPTER 39

ONE DAY EARLIER Sunday 21 April 1912, Nice

Marcella stared down at the tablets spread out on the newspaper.

It couldn't take that many, surely, to put an end to this world – a world in which she had lost her sweet children. A world where her husband had taken them to their deaths and no one seemed to care. Her wicked husband, running from her, hoping that she would cease to exist in his life, had taken them on a fatal journey. A voyage into the cold night, where along with hundreds of others they had all three lost their lives in the icy waters of the Atlantic Ocean.

She closed her eyes, but that made it no better. She pictured her tiny children gasping for breath, swallowing the dark salt water, sinking like stones to the seabed.

A dry sob rose in her and burst out. Then she wailed.

Pulling the brandy bottle close, she raised her head from the table and took a swig. The spirit seared her throat. She slid another four pills towards her.

Her eyes focused on the tablets; then, trying not to think of what she was about to do, fixated on the newsprint beneath her finger.

Little Lolo.

Now her mind was deceiving her.

She blinked.

But she could still see the words there.

Little Lolo.

It must be the drink.

Little Lolo.

She bent to look more closely.

Yes.

Little Louis and Little Lolo, who are respectively three and a half and two years old, have been gathered up from the shipwreck by Miss Hays of New York.

Spitting out the tablets, Marcella pulled up the page from *Le Figaro* and read back from the top of the article, a long way beneath the major one, THE TITANIC CATASTROPHE, which bore a small sub-headline: SEVERAL LAST-MINUTE DETAILS.

The Daily Chronicle *reports that seven babies younger than two years old debarked from RMS* Carpathia. *No one knows who their parents were. They were thrown into the lifeboats. Two French infants who don't know anything but their forenames, 'Little Louis' and 'Little Lolo', respectively three and a half and two years old, have been gathered up from the shipwreck by Miss Hays of New York, another survivor. It is believed that the children had been accompanied by a Second Class passenger named Hoffman.*

Marcella rushed to the sink and rinsed her mouth, getting rid of all remnants of the pills.

She swilled back the cold coffee left on the draining board; then, tearing off the piece of newspaper and cramming it into her pocket, she ran out into the street to join Henry and Thérèse at the lawyer's office.

CHAPTER 40

Wednesday 8 May 1912, Cherbourg

Marcella carried her small valise towards the queue for the SS *Nomadic* which would take her from the dockside station and out into the harbour where she would board the big steamer bound for New York.

'Welcome, Madame Navratil.' An official from the White Star Line handed her a ticket for RMS *Oceanic*. 'The cabin is in the Second Class and the return portion is for the departure three days after you dock in New York. That is all the time you'll need to sort out this matter... one way or another.' He stood back as Marcella stepped on to the gangplank. 'I wish you luck, madame. But it will be sad, not to mention rather an expensive trip for us, if, after all the fuss you've made, you come back having found that the children weren't yours at all.'

For two-and-a-half weeks Marcella had been in a battle with the authorities. She wondered how much longer it could possibly go on. It had been a roundabout of seeing Theodore Moriez at his office in Place Masséna, the English Consulate at the far end of Rue de France, and the Consulate of the United States of America in Boulevard Victor Hugo.

At every meeting, Marcella had to repeat her story again from the start.

As each new, dubious person arrived on the scene, she had been asked to explain why she truly believed that she was the mother of the now famous 'waifs of the *Titanic*'.

And with every repetition Marcella knew that what she was saying sounded more and more absurd, and it was beginning to fill her own mind with doubt.

She had nothing to prove that the 'orphans' were her own missing children.

For every reason she gave, there came back an indication of distrust.

Her husband had disappeared with them a few days before the *Titanic* sailed. 'But there was no Michael Navratil aboard *Titanic*.'

He borrowed another man's name.

'Can you prove that?'

Marcella marched Louis Hoffman into Theodore Moriez's office. He signed a statement explaining that his passport was missing, along with approximately 30,000 French francs from Navratil's tailoring business, of which he was a partner.

The White Star Line agreed that a man going by the name Louis Hoffman had some weeks ago purchased a ticket for F26, a Second Class cabin, for himself and two children, in the Monte Carlo office of Thomas Cook. They also confirmed that, among the names of those missing after the sinking of RMS *Titanic*, was one Louis Hoffman. No body had been retrieved, but at this stage they were certain that Louis Hoffman had not made it on to the *Carpathia* – the only ship which had picked up survivors. But, they pointed out, Louis Hoffman was not an uncommon name. Marcella's lawyer having found a Louis Hoffman in Nice didn't mean it was the same Louis Hoffman who had boarded the *Titanic*. A policeman was dispatched to Thomas Cook's in Monte Carlo with a photograph of Michael. The young man behind the counter agreed that the photograph looked a lot like the person who had bought tickets under the name Louis Hoffman.

Marcella thought they can't argue with that. Now to move on to more important things like finding out if they were her missing children. But—

'So what?' said Harry Lyons, the American deputy consul. 'That proves nothing. I look a lot like Lionel Barrymore; that doesn't mean I'm going onstage tonight to play *Hamlet*.'

Louis and Marcella brought Stefan before Theodore Moriez. Stefan affirmed under oath that he had helped Michael board the train from Nice for London, and that he had since been in contact with Michael, even receiving a telegram from him sent from onboard the *Titanic*. But, no. He could not produce the telegram as the agreement between them was to destroy all communications immediately after reading.

He confessed that he himself had taken Louis Hoffman's passport from a desk in Louis's mother's house in Cimiez and handed it to Michael in the taxi on the way to the railway station.

'But that is simply your word, Monsieur Kozak,' came back the reply. 'And you have already confessed that you are a liar.'

'Why would I make up a story like this?' Marcella repeated over and over, feeling more and more anxious that they were wasting time when they could have been finding out about the children.

'To make yourself famous, madam,' replied the man from the White Star Line. 'We have asked around, and it appears for quite a few years your sole ambition was to be famous. You wanted to be a singer, didn't you? The *TITANIC* WAIFS are headline news all around the world. What could be an easier route to instant fame? Hundreds, before you, have claimed the children, each one of them trying the same game.'

At the British Consulate, Marcella sat for hours trying to prove that she was the boys' mother. 'Everything you claim – it's all in the newspaper, Madame Navratil,' sneered John Taylor, the deputy consul. 'Small... Well, of course they're small, given their age. Dark-haired, dark-eyed... So is every other child in this town. Telling us that your own children went missing a few days before these ones were discovered is no indication that these particular children belong to you. Especially as when they first went missing you didn't even report their disappearance.'

'But I did!'

How many times had she been to the Commissariat of Police? How many times had they laughed her out of the door?

John Taylor smirked. 'We have checked with Commissaire Guillaume. There is absolutely no record of you reporting your children missing. Though he also tells me you recently took out a lawsuit for divorce against your husband. Perhaps this episode is another way of punishing the poor man even further?'

Marcella's desperation to find her children was battered down by it all. She hated the powerlessness of having to do all this through intermediaries.

'It's all in the public domain,' sneered the American consul, William Dulaney Hunter. 'And, as you have frequently reminded us, Madame Navratil, you came forward only after you yourself read an account about the children in *Le Figaro*.'

'But I...' Marcella wanted to scream now. Why could no one see?

'I need intimate details, Madame Navratil.' Hunter banged the palm of his hand on the desk. 'Proof that you really are their mother.'

Marcella tried: 'Michel Marcel, aged three and a half, loves toy boats but hates aviators and aeroplanes. Edmond Roger, being just two, has few words, one of which is "Lump".'

'But, Madame Navratil, you don't even have the right names for them. These children are called Lolo and Louis.'

The more these officials implied that she was a fake, the more Marcella wondered whether she might have got it all wrong. She wanted so much for these children to be her own... like all the other claimants. Maybe they were simply two lost children, and not her darlings at all.

'Perhaps, Madame Navratil, you could give me something which only the children might know?' suggested Lionel Wookey, the English consul. 'Something, perhaps, which happened the last time you saw them? Something which only they and you know?'

Marcella had a sudden idea. 'Ask them what gift they got on Easter Sunday.'

The White Star man, sitting next to her in the consulate, gave a smug little laugh. 'If you're going to tell me they got a chocolate egg, I can inform you now, Madame Navratil, that it just won't wash. Which child on this planet didn't?'

She told them about the chicken.

'Chicken! Egg!' replied the White Star man.

'It seems quite a long shot.' The consul gave a weary sigh and pushed her folder away. 'Nonetheless, I will telegraph my colleagues and see that your question is put to the children. Perhaps you will write down on this notepad an exact description of this "chicken".'

He pronounced the very word as though Marcella had made it up.

With her lawyer beside her, Marcella sat down and described the chicken with the pull-down tail, the undercarriage which opened dropping little chocolate eggs on to the nest below for the children to retrieve. She listed the colours and the textures, the feathers and the paint.

The consul interrupted her writing, telling her that, considering the children's age and the limits of their language skills, she had proffered more information than was strictly required for the purpose.

She caught the look of exasperation he exchanged with the White Star man when he informed her that her interview was at an end.

'You might have to wait a day or two for a reply,' he added.

Marcella was now at the end of her tether. Why were these men so lackadaisical about something which was so serious, was in fact her very life? She asked why the enquiry could not be made immediately.

'For one thing – time difference. It may be eleven in the morning here in Nice, but New Yorkers are still tucked up, asleep in their beds. And you have to understand that my American colleague and the French consul in New York are both exceedingly busy men. They have a mountain of work on their hands, trying to trace relatives of so many French passengers both surviving and missing who boarded the steamer at Cherbourg.' He gave a final sigh and said, 'They *also* have many time-wasters to deal with.'

Marcella was quite aware of the implication.

One morning a few days later, when she had almost given up hope, Monsieur Moriez sent a runner to Marcella's flat to let her know that the French consul to New York had visited the children, asked them her question and that they had vividly described the chicken.

The panting boy continued, 'Monsieur Moriez says that if you're to arrive in Cherbourg in time to catch the next ship to New York, you must leave immediately for Paris.'

'But I—'

'Don't worry. Ship tickets and so forth will be waiting for you on your arrival at Cherbourg. You'd better get going, madame. Best of luck!'

In Paris, a nervous-looking man was waiting for her on the platform.

'Madame Navratil? Hi there! I'm Warren from the US Embassy. A problem has arisen,' he said, bundling Marcella into a taxi. 'His Excellency, Mr Herrick, sent me here to bring you to see him.'

Marcella's first thought was that someone else had come forward and recognised the children and claimed them as their own.

'No, no, nothing like that, madame,' said the ambassador, as she was ushered into his office. 'But... Well... News has reached us that, since your claim has been accepted by the English consul to Nice, the French Embassy in New York and the White Star Line, Mr Frank K. Hays, who currently has care of the infants, has decided to relinquish them.'

'He's throwing them out into the street?'

'No, no, madame, nothing like that,' said the ambassador. 'Well, not quite. For the time being, they will be put into a home, run by the Children's Aid Society.'

'What is that?' asked Marcella.

'It's, well, in a word – an orphanage. And to be honest, Madame Navratil, no orphanage, even an American one, is a very pretty place, particularly for children as tender and young as these two babes.'

'But what can I do to stop that, Mr Herrick? It's a week until I can get to New York.'

'Nothing much, apart from hope that Mr Hays is slow putting his plan into action,' replied the ambassador. 'Unless by some miracle you can come up with a relative who could be in New York before you arrive...'

They had parted so badly, Marcella wasn't sure that she dared. But...

'Rosa Bruno,' she said.

'And who is Rosa Bruno?' asked the ambassador.

'The children's aunt.'

'They would recognise her?'

'They've not seen her in two years. And when she left they were so young, Edmond was just weeks old…'

'She lives in New York?'

'America.'

'America's a big place. Which town?'

'Philadelphia.'

'Oh, that's not too far. I was praying you weren't going to say Emerald Creek, Idaho or some cow-town with no other transportation but the local mule. I'll let Warren take down the details of this Rosa woman. Then we'll have to rush you up to Gare Saint-Lazare so that you don't miss that boat train.'

'Do you have an address?' asked Warren. 'Somewhere my colleagues could contact Rosa Bruno?'

'Georgian Terrace.'

Warren scribbled.

'What number Georgian Terrace?'

'There is no number. It's the name of a house in somewhere called Elkins Park.'

'Elkins Park?' Warren laid down his pencil. 'That's not a joke in very good taste, madame.'

'It's not a joke.'

'Are you playing us, madame? Elkins Park is the home of one of the most famous victims of the *Titanic*.' The ambassador stood over her. 'Elkins Park belongs to Mrs Eleanor Widener. Poor woman lost both her husband and son in the catastrophe, and is now at home there, recovering from her own terrible ordeal in the lifeboat. She is in deep mourning.' He bent down and barked into her face, 'Did you read about Mrs Widener in the newspapers too, Madame Navratil?'

Marcella could see that, in mentioning Rosa, she had made a terrible mistake, and that now, once again, no one believed her. 'My cousin works in Elkins Park. She is a governess there.'

'And who is your cousin?'

'I told you, ambassador. Rosa. Rosa Bruno.'

'But didn't you just tell me that she is your children's aunt?'

'Italian families are never quite straightforward.' Marcella looked to Warren, whom she hoped would help her, but he would not meet her eye. 'As I said, Mr Herrick, Rosa is a governess to the Tylers.'

'The Tylers of Elkins Park? George and Stella Tyler?'

'That's right. And their young son, Sidney.'

As Marcella's taxi was about to leave the embassy for the Gare Saint-Lazare, Warren leaned in and whispered, 'I know there is a high likelihood that these children *are* yours, madame. But there is a much higher chance that they are not. The shipwreck has created an abundance of misinformation. Every day the evidence changes. You must be prepared for the worst.'

'But you will try to find Rosa for me, won't you?' Marcella called as the taxi pulled away, panicked at the thought of her two darling boys trying to survive in the bleakness of an orphanage. 'You will try to get them in a nice home not that orphanage?'

Warren shrugged.

'Excuse me, Madame Navratil?' asked a woman in a red flat hat who stood near Marcella as the SS *Nomadic* drew alongside the RMS *Oceanic*, ready to embark the passengers on to the larger ship. 'I just heard that official call out your name. Aren't you the lady with the stolen children?'

Marcella nodded.

'How terrible of that friend of your husband's to purloin your children and carry them away on the *Titanic*! Using a fake name too! What a bounder!'

Marcella looked down.

She could not even begin to explain.

'How exciting, though, to have you on the ship! You'll have to join me one night for a drink and tell me the whole story.' The woman looked around the crowded buffet bar, where the passengers were lining up to leave SS *Nomadic* and board the steamer. 'Hey, everybody! This is the lady who lost those *Titanic* waifs.'

Everyone turned to stare at Marcella.

'I'll buy you a glass of champagne to celebrate finding them again!' shouted a man at the back of the queue.

Why were they presuming in this way? It was such bad luck. Superstition dogged Marcella. Until she reached New York, she could not be certain whether or not the children were her own.

'Between you and me, Madame Navratil,' the red-hatted woman snuggled nearer, 'I know we're going to be *great* friends. I adore meeting famous people.'

As Marcella walked across the gangplank and on to the *Oceanic*, she made the decision to stay in her cabin and keep to herself.

She dreaded being quizzed by other passengers. The more everyone made of it, the more scared she became that this would be a wasted journey.

Naturally she would have to go up to the dining room every day to eat, and would take a daily blow-round on the deck, but she did not want to avail herself of the public rooms: the salons, smoking room or library.

However, remaining in her cabin had its disadvantages.

Too much time alone, too many thoughts.

While cooped up in the cabin, a new worry came into her head. Once there, it obsessed her. What if the children in New York *were* her children but, after all they'd been through these last five weeks, they didn't remember who she was? Having met so many other new people, maybe they wouldn't recognise her. What if they told the authorities that she was not their mother?

For three days after the ship passed through the Celtic Sea and into the ocean, the voyage had been so rough that passengers were forbidden from going up to the outer decks. Many people were sick. The inner rooms and corridors stank of vomit and disinfectant. Marcella couldn't bear the rank atmosphere inside so, now that the deck was open again, went up to the top to get some air and clear her head.

The sun was shining; the sea calm now, a deep navy blue with white caps. She chose a bench where the view was bad – surrounded by nautical equipment and lifeboats. That way she was sure no one else would be likely to sit nearby. Marcella wore a hooded cloak, to defend herself from prying eyes as much as from the sun.

More and more her thoughts had started turning to Michael. Anger. Fury. Loathing. Disgust. Michael had lied and cheated. Michael had stolen money. Michael had abducted her children.

But Michael was dead.

Dead.

In her preoccupation with the loss of the children, she had not mourned him. She tried to pray for the rest of his soul, but every time she knelt and crossed herself she was overcome by a desire to call him back from his watery grave and kill him all over again.

She wondered what had become of that woman he had been seeing. Did she know he was gone? Did she weep for him at night? Had she been onboard the ill-fated ship? Or had she perhaps gone on ahead to meet him at the other side?

Last night, down in the restaurant, the ship's orchestra had played that tune of his, 'Amoureuse'. When it struck up Marcella had been in the middle of a bite of bread roll. Her mouth had gone quite dry and she had been unable to swallow.

This morning, over coffee, they were playing the wonderful melody 'The Dream of Autumn', with its majestic sombre chords. She could never hear it without thinking of the romantic nights when Michael held her in his arms and whirled her around the living room of Avenue Shakespeare, whispering sweet words into her eager ears.

She had loved him.

But she was also certain that he could not have loved her as intensely as he hated her.

Michael knew that the best way to hurt her would be to take those children away. He had always been jealous of the place they had in her heart.

He had never forgiven her for loving them.

'AHOY!' a voice called from the crow's nest immediately above her.

Then someone started feverishly clanging a bell.

Marcella peered up.

She could see the watch, binoculars to his eyes, pointing out to sea, while his partner continued ringing the bell. Nearby, sailors burst through the doors and ran to the rails, where they started pulling levers and rolling the handles of the winches.

The *Oceanic*'s engines had stopped. The ship was gently rocking.

Marcella stood up.

The sailors had started launching one of the lifeboats.

An officer, still putting on his cap, ran past her and climbed in.

Marcella crossed herself. Please God, after all this, don't let this ship sink. Not now that she was almost there. Not if her boys might still be alive.

Four sailors followed the officer, jumping into the lifeboat as it disappeared down the ship's side.

With the lifeboat gone, Marcella now had a clear view. She moved across to the rails.

On the deck below, a crowd had gathered. People were pointing out to sea.

Marcella peered towards the misty horizon.

The lifeboat splashed into the water. The sailors started rowing out towards something indistinguishable, bobbing about in the distance.

'That's a lifeboat!' a woman passenger shouted. 'Isn't it?'

'There are people in it. Can't you see?' said the man with her, watching as the *Oceanic*'s lifeboat pulled alongside it. 'Three of them.'

Two more officers rushed out of the door behind Marcella and stood further along, gripping the rail.

One lifted a megaphone and called out, 'Do we know which line it's from?'

'It'll be from the *Titanic*, Lieutenant.' The other said this so quietly that Marcella barely caught the words.

'No, Jim. We're too far south. Two hundred miles or so. Anyway, all their lifeboats were accounted for.'

Marcella watched a wave wash over the partially submerged boat.

'Did you see that?' whispered another woman a few feet away. 'Nobody inside it moved.'

One of the sailors had caught the stray lifeboat with his boathook and was tying it fast. Another jumped across. He bent to inspect the uniform of one of the men lying stretched out on the benches, motionless.

'White Star Line!' he yelled back to the ship.

'Damn!' The officer let the megaphone dangle, murmuring, 'Then it *has* to be the *Titanic*.'

Marcella caught her breath.

Was one of those bodies Michael?

Never taking her eyes from the lifeboats, which were drifting nearer and nearer to the *Oceanic*, Marcella gripped the handrail till her knuckles were white and her fingers numb.

'They must be dead,' said the woman beside her. 'See how their hair has been bleached by the sun.'

'Two crew members, in uniform,' yelled the sailor standing astride the benches in the stray lifeboat. 'One passenger in evening dress and overcoat. All dead.'

Marcella was finding it hard to stay upright, her legs shaking, suddenly too weak to support her.

Another lifeboat along the deck from her was being prepared for launch. Among those climbing inside were the ship's priest and a sailor bearing Union Jack flags and sacks.

They are going to bury them at sea, thought Marcella. Those three stranded souls, those one-time survivors from the most celebrated shipwreck in the world. They would wrap them in weighted sacking, the priest would read prayers over their bodies and one by one they would slip overboard, to sink down to the bottom of the ocean.

But what if that man was Michael?

Should she not at least say goodbye before they buried him? Should she not, as his widow, the mother of his children, go out in the lifeboat to be there at his funeral?

'Excuse me, sir?' Marcella addressed the officer holding the megaphone. 'Please can you find out the identity of that man on the lifeboat.'

He did not reply, just looked at her as though she was some taste-less thrill-seeking ghoul.

'I am Madame Navratil,' she added. 'My husband was lost in the sinking of *Titanic*.'

She saw understanding dawn in the officer's eyes. He darted across the deck, making signals to the men launching the second boat to wait.

He whispered to them, then raced back and stood beside Marcella, holding her arm.

Her heart was thundering.

Marcella could see in his eyes that he also thought it could be Michael lying dead in the lifeboat.

The trouble was that, if it was him, she wanted both to kiss and to kick him.

During so many sleepless nights she had wanted to find him, batter him, kill him.

But it was also true that once she had loved him.

Perhaps, deep inside, she still did. Through all the hurt.

After an interminable wait, the first lifeboat returned to the *Oceanic*'s side, and one of the sailors shimmied up a rope ladder now hanging from the promenade deck.

He came straight up to the officer beside Marcella and whispered.

The officer turned to her and said quietly, 'Madame Navratil. We have retrieved sufficient identification to know that it is not your husband.'

He then ordered the sailor to accompany Marcella to her stateroom and to organise a glass of brandy to be sent to her.

Marcella sat alone on her bed. Twenty-two years old, feeling about a hundred and twenty. In the saloon above, the band struck up. The music floated down. 'Amoureuse'.

She knocked back the brandy, lay flat and let the tears roll down the sides of her face.

CHAPTER 41

Thursday 16 May 1912, New York City
RMS *Oceanic* docked at Pier 54 at dawn.

No passengers were allowed to disembark before the crew had offloaded the remains of the *Titanic's* salvaged lifeboat, Collapsible A.

Marcella hung around in her cabin, waiting until the very last moment. However much she wanted to go and see whether these children were her own, she couldn't bear any more conversations with well-meaning strangers.

For what felt like hours, she sat and stared at the walls she had gazed at for a week. Finally an officer came to accompany her down the gangway.

The morning was damp and dreary. As she stepped on to solid ground, a portly stranger standing in the cold glare of the dockside lights moved towards her.

'Mrs Navratil?' He stretched out his hand in a gesture of bonhomie. 'I am Superintendent Walsh of the Children's Aid Society of New York City.' He grabbed her by the arm and tugged her along a line of people waiting to greet her. Marcella had not expected a welcoming committee.

'This is Miss Utley, the nanny we sent along to the Hays's home, at Mrs Hays's request, while we waited for Miss Bruno to arrive.'

As Marcella shook hands, she tried not to imagine how Lolo would react to this stern-looking woman.

'This is Mr Frank Hays, who generously took in the children.'

He had a kind smile. In one glance Marcella saw that he must be extremely rich.

'This is Mr Hays's daughter Margaret. She found the children all alone on the *Carpathia* and took them under her wing.'

Marcella looked at this girl: blonde, thin and sophisticated. She must be her own age. Yet, in Marcella's eyes, she seemed little more than a child.

'And Miss Rosa Bruno.'

Marcella had not seen tall, blonde, beautiful Rosa since she watched her leave the reception after Monmon's baptism. The worst thing was that after watching her being insulted by Michael, Marcella had let her go and made no attempt to run after her. Now she felt ashamed and embarrassed.

They locked eyes.

Rosa stepped forward and opened her arms. Marcella let herself be enfolded in her cousin's wordless welcome.

Rosa *knew* Michael. She had warned her about him. She had always known. But Marcella had not been willing to hear her.

Rosa started to speak. 'The children…' was all she managed to say before Superintendent Walsh took Marcella's arm and walked her away towards the street.

'Right,' said the Superintendent, busily rubbing his hands together. 'I'm sure you want to waste no time, so we will proceed straightaway to the Children's Home.'

Marcella turned to try and see Rosa. They caught eyes. Marcella could only read anxiety there. Had she identified the children? Marcella was still in the dark. She only realised that she was sobbing loudly when Margaret Hays stepped forward to put her arm around her waist.

'*Les enfants sont très beaux,*' whispered Margaret as they all moved towards the taxi rank. The children are very handsome. '*Comme leur mère.*' Like their mother.

How touching all these people were. Marcella raised her gloved hand and wiped the tears from her cheek. She did not want to let them down. But as the party climbed into two waiting taxis, Marcella continued silently to weep.

The superintendent shoved himself in beside her. Margaret Hays joined them.

Marcella wished she could have travelled with Rosa, but was deeply touched by Margaret, struggling to make her comfortable by trying sentences in French.

'*Ils on mange bien,*' she said. '*Bonne santé, maintenant, après le mal de mer de Lolo dans le canot de sauvetage. Guerch!*'

Marcella tried to smile, but felt that her face must be contorted by anxiety.

When Margaret's French ran out, Marcella looked out of the windows at the passing sights of this strange frenetic city. But the very height and immensity of the buildings instilled a feeling of claustrophobia and doom in her. She couldn't look, despite Superintendent Walsh's running commentary on the highlights of the architecture.

Not having anywhere else to rest her gaze, Marcella stared down into the lap of her black dress.

Black for a widow. Black for mourning. Mourning for a husband who had hated her.

She glanced across to the elegant freshness of Margaret's beautifully stitched peach silk dress, then back to her own. Worn patches, loose threads.

They must think me a peasant, she thought.

As the taxi came to a stop at the corner of 23rd and Park Avenue, Marcella leaned over to open the car door, but the superintendent grabbed her hand and pulled it away.

'I should go first,' he said. 'Look ahead! A baying mob of vultures!'

Marcella was blinded by the splash of a flashgun. When her sight returned, she saw that the pavement was crammed with people straining forward, trying to get a glimpse of her.

The superintendent and Miss Hays got out of the taxi and were joined by Frank Hays, Rosa and Miss Utley, all five forming a protective barrier so that Marcella could push through to the entrance.

'How are you feeling, Mrs Navratil?'

'Are you a fake?'

'Shame on you, seeking fame through these poor kids!'

'What if they aren't yours, lady? Will you still take them then?'

As flashguns popped and fizzed around her, Marcella pressed on. She felt as though she was walking to the scaffold.

Finally she reached a dark, cool hall with brown gloss walls.

'This way, this way,' called Superintendent Walsh, overtaking and running towards a great oak staircase.

As she climbed after him, Marcella could see, in the edges of her vision, that every door in the building was open and in each room people were sitting at their desks staring at her as she passed.

'It's on the fifth floor, I'm afraid.' Striding forward, the superintendent turned to the others, bunched around Marcella, all heading upwards.

Marcella was aware of the hollow tread of their feet on each wooden step.

On every landing it was the same, a huddle of people peering silently at her.

At the third landing, the party paused to take a breath, but Marcella wanted to carry on.

Panting, they arrived at the fifth floor and proceeded through a further maze of dark gloss-painted corridors.

Then, by a forest-green door marked NURSE'S PARLOUR, the superintendent and Miss Utley came to a halt.

Marcella felt her heart thumping so hard it might burst through her chest.

But it wasn't the strain of the stairs.

It was the thought of what could be beyond that door.

The party accompanying her fell back, leaving Marcella alone to move forward.

For a few seconds she rested her hand on the knob.

This was it.

The moment of truth.

Happiness or misery.

Life or death.

Taking a deep breath, Marcella turned the handle and stepped inside.

On a window seat sat Lolo, holding up a large illustrated book called *A is for Apple, B is for Boat*.

Crawling about on the lino floor, Monmon, gripping pieces of a wooden jigsaw puzzle, murmured to himself.

Marcella gazed at them.

She could not move.

She didn't want to break the overpowering beauty of the scene.

But, sensing the unusual silence, Lolo glanced up from his book.

Silently, he slipped down from the window and stood staring at Marcella.

He seemed scared.

Monmon now looked up from the floor, then rolled back on his haunches and sat gaping.

Her fear had been realised.

They didn't know her!

Marcella could sense the superintendent and the nanny standing behind her in the open doorway, judging her.

Awkwardly, Monmon clambered around on to all fours.

He knelt back, screwed up his eyes, then rubbed them in mystified bewilderment.

Lolo, wide-eyed, swayed from side to side with confusion.

Suddenly Monmon opened his mouth and let forth a blaring wail. He dragged himself to his feet and half staggered, half crawled towards Marcella.

Instantaneously Lolo darted forward, sobbing.

'*Maman! Maman!*'

'*Maman!*'

And, through the fog of her own tears, Marcella ran to them, scooping both children into her arms.

'*Maman, chérie!*' Seeing his mother's tears, Lolo turned his face away and covered his eyes. '*Oh Maman, oh Maman!*'

'My darlings, my darlings,' Marcella murmured, kissing their tiny heads. 'My precious darlings. My darlings.'

She heard the door behind her click closed.

EPILOGUE

At the press conference, soon after their reunion, Marcella was asked if she had spoken to her children about the shipwreck or their father. She replied, 'I do not want them to think about things like that. From now on, only happiness. No distress.' As the words came out of her mouth, Marcella knew that this truly was the only way forward. She would never tell her children any bad things about their father. Despite everything, she would leave them only with a picture of kindness and of his love for them.

'Do you have any other thoughts about their rescue?' a hack asked her.

Marcella looked across the room to Margaret.

'My gratitude to Margaret Hays could not be put into words,' she replied. And that was the truth. Marcella would never ever forget her.

'And enormous thanks must also go to my dear cousin, Rosa. I was very lucky to have such a true friend living and working in Philadelphia, and that she was allowed to take the children to stay with her while I was at sea.'

'How did Mrs Eleanor Widener take that, having lost her whole family in the *Titanic* wreck? It can't have been fun for her seeing two kids who made it safely here?'

'I know nothing of that, sir.' Marcella could feel that they were edging for a story which wasn't there. 'I can only tell you that my cousin took the children to stay with her in Elkins Park.' Marcella looked over the sea of heads. Rosa was leaning against the wall at the back of the room. 'And that while there they made a new friend in the son of my cousin's employers, Mr and Mrs Tyler. I know that Mrs Widener is the Tylers' aunt and lives in another mansion across the park. That's all. Poor woman.'

Marcella imagined, with a pang, how terrible it must have been for Mrs Widener, to lose a husband whom she loved and her son too, and yet to survive herself.

A flashgun popped in her face, alerting her to the next question.

'How about the Hollywood movie company, Mrs Navratil, which wants to make a feature film of your story?'

'No,' said Marcella firmly. 'I don't want my children to be a spectacle. I want them to have a calm and happy life.'

During her remaining couple of days in New York, Marcella received scores of letters offering to give the children wonderful homes with all the luxuries of an American life, no expense spared. Marcella politely declined all applicants, telling them, 'Nothing can separate us now.'

One proposal came from a man offering Marcella not only a home for her and her children but a job as his maid, and, he added, later on, maybe more. That letter she ignored.

On her last whole day in the city, a French-speaking female representative from the Children's Aid Society took Marcella, Rosa and the two children for a taxi tour of Manhattan. First they went up Fifth Avenue, to admire all the department stores. The taxi then took them through Central Park, where Lolo crowed in delight at the horses with their flowered harnesses and feathered plumes. Privately Marcella knew that, for her, there would never be anywhere as beautiful as Nice's Bay of Angels. Nonetheless, she told her hostess how magnificent she found the city of New York.

Next they went uptown to a very special destination, the Hays's mansion in West End Avenue, where Hannah served tea. While Monmon cuddled up to Marcella, Lolo chose to sit on Margaret's lap.

'I'll bet you're enjoying the scant few days they've given you on dry land,' said Frank. 'Considering everything, I think they've been particularly stingy with you.' He took a mouthful of cake. 'I will be taking action with the White Star Line on my daughter's behalf. I can act for you too.'

'I don't want any more fuss.' Marcella gripped Monmon's tiny hand. After all this, she had no more time for lawyers and court cases. 'I have got the only things I wanted.' She kissed her son's head.

'I still think you shouldn't let those crooks from White Star off the hook.'

Margaret shot her father a look. She understood Marcella.

'*J'adore Nice, Madame Navratil,*' she said. '*Les très belles plages. Le mer bleu.*'

What could she reply? 'Please call me Marcella.' The name Navratil, which even *he* didn't want to take to America with him, weighed heavy on her.

'At school we learned a poem, Madame— Marcella.' Margaret felt nervous but was determined to try. 'It was in French, this poem. Please forgive my accent. Since the day I realised you were the right person and that you were coming here, it's been going round and round in my head:

'Elle est retrouvée.
Quoi ? – L'Eternité.
C'est la mer allée
Avec le soleil.'

'Ah yes,' sighed Marcella. 'Rimbaud. "She is found. What? Eternity. It is the sea running with the sun." We still have a long way to go.'

Marcella was thinking not of the sea journey, but of life. Life which could never be the same.

'You must be looking forward to getting home to Nice.'

Emotion welled up inside Marcella. Thank God for the kindness of this slip of a girl. Marcella looked at her, sitting so erect on the lovely chair, in a powder-blue silk tea-gown, so full of life and hope. She was a strange American reflection of the girl she herself had been, only a few years ago.

'I don't have enough words to thank you for rescuing my darlings.' Marcella could feel tears pricking her eyes. Luckily Monmon was struggling in her arms, so she bent forward to lay him on the floor. 'One day, Miss Hays, you will come back to Nice and visit us, won't you?'

As Marcella left the Hays's mansion, both women hugged and quietly wept.

That night, Rosa sat up with Marcella in the bedroom provided by the Children's Aid Society.

They talked into the small hours, the children sleeping beside them, cuddled together in their bed.

'Thank God you were here.' Marcella stretched out a hand and patted Rosa's knee. She stifled a sob. 'Thank you, dear Rosa. Thank you. I'm not ashamed to admit it. You were right from the start.'

'I don't agree, Marcella. Over the last week, playing with my little cousins, I've had a lot of time to think. And I see now that, without thinking about it, you made better decisions than I did.'

'Don't be silly. Surely you are happy, Rosa? Look at your clothes! You have money, a gorgeous place to live…'

'But you have these two darlings.' Rosa smoothed down the covers on the sleeping children. 'The children who I love are only mine temporarily. I might have their care, but they belong to others.'

'Will you never marry?'

'I don't think so.' Rosa looked Marcella in the eye. 'Would you, again?'

Marcella shook her head. She could not.

Marcella, Rosa and the children came to the pier next morning, at eleven forty. RMS *Oceanic* sailed at noon. Having had quite enough inquisition by journalists, Marcella had deliberately left their arrival until the last minute.

Together the family walked up the gangway. Rosa carried all the gifts which had been showered upon them by well-wishers, while Lolo walked hand in hand with a steward. Monmon snuggled in Marcella's arms and, all the way to their cabin, he whispered secret words into her ear.

Marcella immediately recognised the Second Class cabin she had been allocated. The same one in which she had come to America. The family had barely had time to sit when the door burst open. Inexplicably, the White Star Line had invited a horde of journalists onboard, so, both children clung tightly to her, a multitude of hacks crowded in after them, blocking the exit, asking impertinent questions.

'I am very tired,' said Marcella. 'I want only to rest.'

'Please go,' asked Rosa, rising to face them.

But they had a story to milk, so they would not budge.

'How did you enjoy your stay in our wonderful country?' 'Bet the little fellas will be sorry to leave!' 'After all this they must be quite the little sailor boys!' 'How did you feel when you learned your husband had drowned?' 'Give us a smile, Mrs Navratil…'

The journalists left only when the whistle blew for all visitors to disembark.

Rosa got up with them, hugged Marcella and kissed the children goodbye.

'Give my love to Aunt Thérèse and Aunt Gigi, and to Henry, but above all to my goofy brother, Raphaël.' As she stepped on to the gangway leading down to the dockside, she grabbed Marcella's hand. 'Oh, dear coz, I am so sad not to be coming with you.'

'Me too.'

Marcella waved at Rosa as she walked briskly into the embarkation hall, but Rosa did not turn back.

Once everyone was gone, Marcella returned to her dingy cabin and started organising all the toys the children had been given: a grey wooden horse with tail and mane of real horsehair, a tin duck painted in green and white, a papier mâché dog, many picture books, a furry soft cat and a big red and white ship. Lolo and Monmon were making serious choices – which one they wanted to play with first. Marcella was overwhelmed.

She was about to lie down, when there was a rap on the door. It was a deputation of lady passengers.

'We feel very, very disappointed in your treatment by the White Star Line,' said the leader, an elegant woman in a peacock satin suit.

'Disgusted, to put it mildly!' exclaimed a rotund ruddy-faced woman at her side.

'As a result, we have taken a collection and purchased a more fitting cabin for you and your children.'

Two stewards appeared from behind them and rushed in to start moving Marcella's things.

'The cabin is in the first class,' added the portly woman, as a steward squeezed past her, Marcella's suitcase in one hand, an armful of toys in the other. 'Of course.'

'We all wish you a happy voyage.' The lady in the peacock suit handed Marcella the keys to her new stateroom.

'You've come so far, madame,' she said, leading Marcella and the children past the stewards and into First Class. 'But we realise you've still a way to go.'

The rotund lady called out from behind them, 'What she's trying to tell you, Madame Navratil, is that we promise that for the rest of the journey we will leave you to travel in peace.'

As the peacock lady swung open the door of their luxurious cabin, with its bright wide porthole, plush armchairs and three beds, Marcella thanked them. Lolo ran forward, jumped up on to one bed, laughing.

'Lump!' exclaimed Monmon.

The poem by Rimbaud was now running through her own head.

Elle est retrouvée.
Quoi ? – L'Eternité.
C'est la mer allée
Avec le soleil.

Behind the Scenes
by Fidelis Morgan

One – What Happened Next

Once back in Nice, **Marcella**, using the services of Theodore Moriez and, after he retired, his son Robert, sued the White Star Line for damages. Newspaper accounts from the USA throw doubt on whether she ever actually received any money from it.

Her cause was hindered by the meticulous officials in Nova Scotia, who stubbornly refused to accept that the body they had pulled from the sea was Michael Navratil, since no man bearing that name had ever boarded RMS *Titanic*.

Michael's body had been taken ashore at Halifax, retrieved by the ship CS *Mackay-Bennett*. He was buried in the Jewish cemetery, under a stone bearing the name Louis Hoffman.

Even after demands by Louis Hoffman himself, Thomas Cook's office in Monte Carlo and the Austro-Hungarian Embassy, the team at Nova Scotia refused to confirm that their Louis Hoffman was in fact Michael Navratil.

As a result, Navratil was never declared dead.

Marcella could never receive her final divorce decree, nor become officially his widow. And the bankruptcy case against Michael Navratil went ahead as though he was alive, but absent. His address was recorded as *sans domicile*: 'of no fixed abode'.

Apart from a short article published in the *Evening Star*, Washington DC, when an American journalist discovered Marcella and the boys taking a spa holiday in Bagnères-de-Luchon, south-west France, in October 1913, Marcella herself stayed out of the public eye for the rest of her life, dying in 1974.

Edmond Roger Navratil, Monmon, served in the Second World War, but did not recover very well from that experience and died at Bordeaux on 5 July 1953, aged just forty-three.

Michel Marcel Navratil, Lolo, grew up to be a scholar, earning a doctorate, becoming Professor of Philosophy at the University of Montpellier. He died on 30 January 2001, aged ninety-two, the last surviving male passenger from RMS *Titanic*.

Margaret Hays quickly relinquished Gilbert Tucker (as she had done Bébé), and, on 23 April 1913, exactly one year after she heard the news that a woman was coming from Nice to claim the boys, married Dr Charles Easton of Newport, Rhode Island.

For their first wedding anniversary in April 1914, Margaret and her husband visited Nice, where according to the *Southern Herald of Liberty*, Mississippi, she 'gave away approximately a million kisses without asking her husband's consent'. Those kisses, the article tells us, were bestowed upon Lolo and Louis Navratil (the media *still* got the names wrong). The boys' mother Marcella, the article says, was delighted to see Margaret again.

Her father, Frank Hays, supported Marcella's claim for damages from the White Star Line.

A note from Celia on the names
I have changed the real names of the major characters. So many Ms! This surplus would not have helped the reader, especially as the real names were Michel and Marcelle (sometimes Marcela, even Marcelline) Navratil, who had a child called Michel Marcel. Then came Margaret to add to the M problem. So to make things easier, I opted to call Michel by the anglicised version, Michael. Anglicising was a rage in Nice at the time, so that seemed right. Marcelle I have changed to Marcella as it not only makes it easier but has a slight Italian feel.

Two – on the Trail

How it all began – RMS *Titanic*

Celia and I discovered our own connection with the *Titanic* in 2010, when I accompanied her and her son, Angus, to *Titanic: The Artefact Exhibition* at the O2 in London. Angus was doing a school project.

As we entered and saw the first display – a huge wall which listed the names of all passengers and crew, alongside a chart of the lifeboats in which they had escaped (or not) – I casually mentioned to Celia that I had a relative who was onboard.

She replied, 'So did I.'

I countered, 'Mine survived.'

She answered, 'So did mine!'

We went to the first noticeboard and pointed to our relations' names, then went to the lifeboat section to find how they had disembarked the sinking ship.

It turned out both sets of relations had escaped together, on lifeboat number 1.

My relative, Albert Horswill, was crew – a deck steward. Hers, on her mother's side, were Sir Cosmo and Lady Duff-Gordon, a Scottish landowner, baronet and fencing champion and his fashion-designer wife, who worked under the soubriquet 'Lucile'.

The trouble was that they and their party were the *only* people in the lifeboat. It was later suspected that Celia's lot had given mine money to row away p.d.q.

A terrible story, really, but for us it seemed extremely funny, mainly because of its eerie serendipity.

Another coincidence about our *Titanic* relatives was that the Duff-Gordons had gone onboard the steamer under a fake name.

The name they chose for their alias?

Mr and Mrs Morgan.

But Celia has yet another connection with the *Titanic*, this time on her father's side. One of her great-great-uncles, William Imrie, was a founder member of the White Star Line. Even though William Imrie was dead long before the *Titanic* episode, the surname Imrie is to be seen on items of *Titanic* memorabilia, from tickets to advertising posters.

When, some years later, we heard about the real-life story of 'the orphans of the *Titanic*' we were both intrigued.

As it is a true story, linking RMS *Titanic* (and transatlantic crossings, as in Celia's novel *Sail Away*) with Celia's home town, Nice, France (the setting for her three other novels, *Not Quite Nice*, *Nice Work – If You Can Get It* and *A Nice Cup of Tea*), it seemed a perfect idea for her next novel.

As I am a renowned bloodhound, I was sent off to snuffle out the bones of the story.

Right from the start the primary research revealed amazing facts.

The Navratil wedding

Simply because I happened to be in London, I started with the one episode which took place in Westminster: the wedding of Marcella Caretto to Michael Navratil. I began by ordering the marriage certificate from the General Register Office.

I then set out to track down as much as I could about that ceremony.

All versions of the story gave the same excuse for Michael Navratil having married Marcella Caretto in London, rather than their home town of Nice. They lacked certain papers, everyone said. But, when I looked up the Marriage Acts which were in force in France and in England at that time, I discovered that that could not have been the real reason, because you needed the same papers.

The only real difference between the law pertaining to marriage in the two countries was that in France, for a female under the age of twenty-two to marry, it was necessary to provide official parental consent... preferably by physical presence of the parent. Banns also had to be published twice in the local newspapers, at set periods, before the wedding could take place, so there was no chance of doing it secretly.

In England, banns had simply to be displayed for three weeks outside the establishment where the wedding was due to be held. And for a marriage by banns for a girl under twenty-one, it was not so much that the parent had to give consent; rather that they did not arrive at the ceremony to object.

The postman duly knocked and handed me an envelope containing the official certificate of marriage.

The names of the registrar and superintendent registrar led me, with the help of Cecilia Alvik, Archives and Local Studies Officer at the City of Westminster, to discover the actual wedding venue was a registry office at 48 Poland Street, Soho.

The marriage took place on 16 May 1907.

For their permanent address, the couple gave 10 Marshall Street, Soho, a mere two-minute walk away from the registry office. They were supposed to have lived there for a month.

Michael's profession was entered as ladies' tailor, Marcella's left blank.

Their fathers were both listed as deceased, with Michael's carpenter and Marcella's cabinetmaker (i.e. a superior type of carpenter). Over in France there are, to this day, three types of carpenter: *charpentier*, a person who bangs planks together; a *menuisier* or master carpenter, who makes shelving, wardrobes and suchlike; and an *eboniste*, an expert who creates fine furniture using techniques like marquetry. Marcella's father was the last – to his own ruin.

The witnesses listed on the register were Paul Kühne and Walter Kent.

In the London censuses I discovered Paul Kühne, restaurateur, aged forty-four in 1907, and Walter Kent, waiter, aged seventeen.

In a moment of boredom I googled their names and was surprised to find that the chief witness, Paul Kühne, not only owned 10 Marshall Street, Michael and Marcella's official London address, but, a few years before, had been a witness in a trial at the Old Bailey.

Sidonie Giraud and Jean-Baptiste Sartori

Intrigued, I searched the Old Bailey records and looked out newspaper accounts of the incident, universally described as a 'bloody drama'. It had been reported all over the world.

The principal protagonists of this story too were both ladies' tailors from Nice.

In 1902, a young girl, Sidonie Giraud, had fled from her father's tailor's shop in Rue Saint-Vincent, Old Town Nice. She had been having a secret affair with Jean-Baptiste Sartori, one of the cutters there.

She had discovered that Sartori was married so called it off. But by now he was obsessed with her and made threats to reveal the affair to her religious family. So Sidonie escaped to London to stay with her brother, another tailor called Jean, also from Nice.

Jean-Baptiste Sartori walked out of his job and followed Sidonie to England. He tracked her down. One afternoon, after her brother had gone out, he turned up and challenged her. Hastily scribbling a letter using her rouge, he tried to make Sidonie sign without reading it.

She refused.

Sartori grabbed Sidonie's hand and forced her signature, then took out a gun and shot her.

The letter was a suicide note.

Struggling to get away, Sidonie was shot in the face and part of her left cheek and ear were destroyed. As she ran, Sartori shot again, lodging a bullet in her neck. A third bullet ricocheted then tumbled down inside the back of her dress.

Alerted by the noise, neighbours brought the police in. Sidonie's brother arrived to find his sister slumped on the floor in a pool of blood.

Sartori then tried to shoot himself, but missed completely.

Both were taken to St George's Hospital at Hyde Park Corner, where the surgeon described the wound to Sidonie's cheek as 'dangerous and calculated to destroy life'.

Jean-Baptiste Sartori was found guilty of feloniously wounding with intent to murder, grievous bodily harm and attempted suicide. He was sentenced to fifteen years' penal servitude, with one month's imprisonment (for the suicide indictment) which was to run concurrently.

Jean-Baptiste Sartori had been staying at Paul Kühne's establishment.

I then picked up the trail.

Paul Kühne

A quick search of the London censuses showed that, in both 1901 and 1911, Kühne's address, listed in Kelly's Directory only as a restaurant, was crammed with around twenty 'boarders' from abroad, many in the tailoring business. His 'restaurant' obviously doubled as a kind of flophouse for transient foreigners.

At the time of the Navratil wedding, German-born Kühne was married, with a thirteen-year-old son.

It may well be a coincidence (or a double one, given that Navratil chose Paul Kühne's for his lodging), but Jean-Baptiste Sartori, tailor's cutter, left Nice in 1902, the same year Michael Navratil, tailor's cutter, arrived in the town looking for work.

Then, five years later, Navratil turns up at the same London dive to register his own clandestine marriage.

Harrumph!

A coincidence too far.

In 1914, on the outbreak of the First World War, Paul Kühne was arrested and interned as an enemy alien.

The trail then took me from London to Nice.

The divorce

The archivist in Nice told us it would be impossible to find the Navratil divorce documents without a case number or an exact date. We had neither. However, we do have patience and determination, so I told her that we were prepared to come in and leaf through the books every day until we found them.

We were told we would never find them because each book was handwritten, enormous, and hundreds of pages long. Every volume covered only a couple of months' cases, at most. And the rules of the archive meant that we could order a maximum of three books, but we could only look at one book at a time.

I mentally narrowed down the most likely dates to December 1911 and January 1912, and we ordered those two. One each.

Celia worked back from the end of December, and I worked forward from New Year 1912. After an hour or so Celia did the silent-library equivalent of a very loud 'BINGO!'

We had found the transcript of the Navratil divorce.

The final court hearing took place on 13 December 1911.

We were truly surprised to discover that the case wasn't at all how people had supposed – all accounts imply that Michael had divorced Marcella because she was a nightmare wife.

But the truth is that, aged twenty-one, Marcella Navratil had taken out the plea for divorce against her husband. Her long list of grievances were principally cruelty, both mental and physical.

Michael made her work all hours of the day and night; he tried to keep her away from her children; he followed her everywhere, spying on her – worse, he himself regularly stayed out all night, notably on Christmas and New Year's Eve; he called her vile names in public, or he ignored her; and at home he threw things at her, once breaking a plate.

As a rebuttal Michael had only one charge. He cited one day – interestingly, sometime *after* all the incidents Marcella had charged against him. On 20 October 1911, Michael claimed that he, accompanied by the Police Commissaire Guillaume, had gone to the family flat and found it locked. They had knocked. After a minute or two the door had been opened by a fully dressed "Sieur X'. Michael and the commissaire had rushed through to the bedroom and found Marcella, still in bed, wearing her nightclothes. Later, the commissaire refused to corroborate with the judges that Marcella and "Sieur X' were actually caught *in flagrante*.

The divorce case was due to be finalised six months after Marcella first lodged the petition: therefore towards the end of April 1912.

During the time in between, while the judges pondered who would finally get them, custody of the children was assigned to Madame Magali (*sic*), couturière, of Rue de l'Hôtel des Postes, Nice.

Madame Thérèse Magaïl and the Piano–Bruno family

At first we thought 'Madame Magali' must be some official childminder. The Annuaires, red-bound books similar to the UK's Kelly's Directories, showed that the only couturière listed in Rue de l'Hôtel des Postes that year with a name anything like Magali was Madame Magaïl, who lived and worked at number 11.

Hounding her out was quite tricky.

The Annuaires showed that between 1901 and 1913 Madame Magaïl ran respected shops of her own around Nice: first in Avenue de la Gare (now Avenue Jean Médecin), then in Rue Garnier and later Place Grimaldi, still a chic little leafy square.

Double-checking these addresses against the census gave us her age: thirty years older than Marcella; four years older than Angela, Marcella's mother. It also gave us her Christian name: Thérèse.

I also noticed that based at the same address in Rue de l'Hôtel des Postes was a Raphaël Bruno, Bruno being the maiden name of Marcella's mother, Angela. (This, from Marcella's birth certificate.) The census showed that Raphaël was (fittingly) born in Saint-Raphaël – which is in the Var area, rather than the Alpes Maritimes.

So I tracked Raphaël Bruno in the registers of the Var. His parents were Joseph Bruno (Angela's brother) and Elisa Piano, both of Saint-Raphaël.

I then searched out the Piano family in the Var.

Though hailing from an area around the Piedmontese cities Mondovì and Cuneo (principally Cervere and Bra Domino), by the late nineteenth century the Pianos were based in and around Saint-Raphaël, an hour away from Nice by train.

There was a Thérèse Piano, born in Cervere in 1860. But without further evidence it was a punt too far to *presume* that this was our Thérèse Magaïl. Thérèse was not that uncommon a forename in France.

Then came another 'bingo' moment. I discovered the wedding listing of this same Thérèse Piano to Frederick Magaïl, a cork-maker, in Saint-Raphaël in April 1878. Two years later the Magaïls had a daughter, Valerie Laure, who died, aged two, in 1882. Frederick himself died in Saint-Raphaël in May 1901, aged just forty-seven. According to his death certificate, he had changed profession to truck driver. Thérèse was by then already established working as a couturière in Rue Masséna, Nice.

Thérèse Magaïl continued working in the rag trade until 1915 when she last appears in the Trade Handbooks of Nice. There were no books printed between 1916–18, but in 1919 she is no longer there. During the interim Madame Magaïl may have retired, moved away or died.

Raphaël Bruno
Raphaël Bruno was Thérèse Magaïl's nephew, and also younger brother of Rosa Bruno, who features so largely in all the New York newspaper accounts of the tale of the Navratil 'waifs of the *Titanic*'.

The Nice Annuaires of the period list Raphaël as a painter and decorator.

Raphaël Bruno was called to active service in 1915. Injured in battle, he died in a temporary field hospital on 3 January 1916. He was only twenty-nine.

Rosa Bruno

Born in Saint-Raphaël in 1883, Rosa Bruno moved to Nice to work as a teacher in the early 1900s. In 1906 she was teaching at a large school in Boulevard Victor Hugo.

She took ship to the USA on 31 March 1910 on the SS *Berlin*. The manifest lists her as working as a governess for the Saportas family of Saratoga Springs, New York. The whole Saportas family also travelled on the SS *Berlin*, so presumably Rosa's duties had already started, or would start onboard.

For the rest of her life, Rosa stayed in the US, always employed by very rich families.

To my great surprise, Rosa Bruno was listed in the US immigration records as blonde, blue-eyed and, at five foot eight inches, the tallest woman on the ship. Her next of kin was listed as 'Madame Magaïl, cousin'.

In July 2019 I visited Elkins Park, the Philadelphia estate where Rosa Bruno worked from 1911 onwards, and to which she brought the Navratil children in May 1912 while waiting for Marcella to take the long voyage from Nice to New York.

Amid forty-two acres of grounds, with lakes and bosquets, stables and bakehouses, stand three decaying mansions; once of immense splendour, they are now all empty. Today, nothing but dried leaves dance across their dusty marble ballroom floors. The largest and grandest house, Lynnewood Hall, was in 1912 the home of Eleanor Widener, née Elkins, one of the richest victims of the *Titanic* (she survived but lost both her husband and adult son).

Rosa was nanny to Stella Tyler, née Elkins, and lived in the smallest of the houses, Georgian Terrace. However, when I say 'the smallest' it should be noted that the building was large enough to be used from the 1930s to 2009 as an art college: the Tyler School of Art.

The third mansion in the park, Chelten House, was occupied by Stella's father, George W. Elkins.

The Elkins family – descendants of William Lucas Elkins, a streetcar tycoon, and George W. Elkins Sr, a railroad tycoon – were clearly as intertwined as Rosa's own Piano–Bruno family… The difference being that they had oodles of money.

By 1920 Rosa had moved on to work for another fabulously rich family, the Harris's of Springfield Township, Pennsylvania.

On 5 June 1963, aged eighty, Rosa died in Flourtown, Springfield PA, five miles up the road from the Elkins Park mansion where, in 1912, she had temporarily cared for the Navratil boys.

She never did marry or return from the USA.

Many years after the *Titanic* event, Sidney Tyler, Rosa's charge, who had played with the Navratil boys during their brief stay in Elkins Park, wrote his own account of it all, *A Rainbow, of Time and of Space: Orphans of the Titanic*. Unfortunately the book bears little weight as, when examined closely, it has obviously been lifted practically word for word from accounts published in the *New York Times*.

Michael Navratil

We know from the marriage certificate that by 1907 Michael Navratil's father was dead.

We also know from the letter discovered in the pocket of his coat when he was dredged from the sea by CS *Mackay-Bennett*, written while he was onboard the *Titanic*, asking his mother if she could take the children, that in April 1912 his mother was still alive.

Many versions of this story give Navratil's home town as Szered, which, though now in Slovakia, was, during Michael's lifetime, in Hungary, which itself was part of the Austro-Hungarian Empire.

But it appears that Michael himself was an unreliable witness. In the 1906 Nice census, when 26-year-old Navratil was a lodger in the flat of 56-year-old Madame Marie Papon in Rue Lépante, he gave his birthplace as Presbourg, Hungary, the historic name for the town we now call Bratislava.

By the time Michel Marcel was born in 1908, Navratil was living in an 'hotel meublé' at 8 Avenue Croix de Marbre, (now called Avenue de Suede). In the UK, this would have been called a rooming house.

In 1911, when living with the whole family in Rue Dalpozzo, Michael gave his birthplace as Szered, Hungary.

Michael Navratil was born on 13 August (same birthday as Raphaël Bruno) 1880. He had two brothers, John and Jozsef. John, born in 1879, was married to Anna Holzinger with three children, Henry, Frank and Joseph. John moved to the USA just before the start of the First World War.

Jozsef was younger than Michael, and so was his sister, Maria (born in 1885). Their parents were Michael Navratil and Magdalena Kopeczki.

The ultra-methodical (and revolutionary for the time) recording and annotating of the corpses retrieved after the *Titanic* disaster provides evidence of the things found in Michael Navratil's grey coat (with green lining) when he was fished from the sea. These include:

a pipe in its case

cards from Camilla – Èze, and Stefan Kozal (*sic*)

a silver sovereign purse containing six pounds

a telegram in code, signed M, addressed to E. Stefan, Grand Post Restante, Nice (the post office which was directly in front of Thérèse Magaïl's flat)

two shillings

and a revolver (loaded).

There was also a letter written by Michael to his mother in Hungary asking if his brother or brother-in-law would take the children from him. In it he demanded that under no circumstances should anyone give information regarding his whereabouts to Marcella.

As the letter was in an envelope addressed to George Gurcao, 77 Johseph... Uj... or Tj... Hungary, I wonder if this could be his younger sister Maria's husband.

National service in Hungary consisted of a compulsory three-year conscription, followed by a period of ten years during which a man would have been on reserve. The average age for call-up was twenty. For Michael this would have been around August 1900, so it is highly possible that when Michael arrived in France in 1902 he was still wanted in Hungary. It is also possible that the pistol which was found in his pocket might have been army issue.

That Michael Navratil had been on the run from the Hungarian army was alluded to in various newspapers at the time of his death in 1912.

Navratil's bankruptcy

While searching the local paper, *Le Petit Niçois*, for reports or photos of the missing children, I found on 23 April 1912 – a week after Michael Navratil died – a notice announcing the bankruptcy of 'Michel Navratil, tailor of Rue de France, Nice'.

There are multiple files concerning the Navratil bankruptcy held by the archives at CADAM in Nice.

Due to the interruption of the First World War, the proceedings against Michael Navratil were not wound up till 10 April 1919.

Isaïe Petit, in charge of the proceedings in Nice, wrote to the authorities in Nova Scotia in the hope that 30,000 francs cash which was missing from the company's accounts might be discovered on Navratil's body.

Bailiffs who were sent to the shop a few days after Navratil's disappearance found the till and safe empty. They also found the shop's account book. Navratil had stopped making notes in it on 6 April 1912, the same day he went to Monte Carlo (where there was a branch of Thomas Cook within the Hotel de Paris) and bought a Second Class cabin and passage from Southampton to New York on RMS *Titanic*. While there, he changed some money into English pounds and US dollars.

Isaïe Petit then sent Commissaire Guillaume, of the 4th Arrondissement of Nice, to find out the movements of Michael Navratil from 6 April. The commissaire certified that 'Michael Navratil, businessman, of Rue de France left his shop brusquely on the 8 April without making known any forwarding address'.

This was the same Commissaire Guillaume whom Navratil had dragged round to the flat at 1 Rue Dalpozzo to witness Marcella's 'episode of *flagrante delicto*' but who subsequently, when under oath, refused to verify that it had been exactly that.

The Nice archives hold not only the bankruptcy papers but also the results of the subsequent sales of goods.

And what a read!

Michael Navratil appeared to have rarely paid his bills. By the time of his disappearance, he had run up more than 31,000 francs' worth of debt.

This money was owed to suppliers of sewing machines, threads, fabrics, laces, trimmings, et cetera, none of whom had been paid for many years.

The first to sue for recompense was Perez of Paris, whose bailiff put in a claim for 3,018.50 francs. The same day Beressi, also from Paris, sued for their outstanding account of 1,396.73.

Once the rumours started, more and more creditors piled in: Emile Rodot of Rue Paradis, Nice, *Fournitures Spéciales pour Couturières*, was owed 1,606.20 francs; Bellenger in Paris, 2,253.55. Another Paris shop, Caan and Heurmann, had the largest claim – 6,805.75 – and employed a lawyer, Monsieur Quedeville, to get its money back.

The smallest demand was from Madame Preller, skirt-maker, of 31 Rue Désambrois, Nice, for forty-five francs.

By the end of the three auctions of the shop contents, Monsieur Petit had realised 2,899.30 francs, a pitiful sum compared to the 31,661.18 which Michael Navratil owed when he left town.

The shop in Rue de France

The bankruptcy papers also led to details of the shop's lease, which started a long time after everyone had previously claimed. It was always assumed that Michael Navratil had the shop before marrying Marcella. But no. They didn't open up for business until six months *after* the wedding. Michael's landlady was a young heiress, Alice Baquis, a year older than Marcella. Mademoiselle Baquis owned many properties around Nice, including Villa Baquis, in Avenue Baquis, and had a phone number: 7–91. She appears to have had a formidable team of lawyers, tutors and guardians put in place by her elderly father prior to his death in 1905.

Alice Baquis's lease with Michael Navratil for the shop ran from 7 January 1908 to 30 September 1916, with a rent of 1,250 francs per annum, payable in two instalments on 1 April and 1 October of each year.

Louis Hoffman

A second file relating to the bankruptcy – the list of public auctions – showed who bought everything from Navratil's shop.

Among the buyers was Louis Hoffman, tailor. He bought not only the lease on the shop, but much of the contents, plus the clientele list. The business cost him more than 900 francs.

Hoffman's business card, given to the auctioneer, is still in the file at Nice's archive. It reads: *Louis Hoffman, Tailleur, 38 Chaussée-d'Antin*. In 1912 (as now) the Paris building stands in a small courtyard, a few doors up from the iconic Galeries Lafayette department store, behind the Opéra Garnier.

It would have been, and remains, a very impressive address.

The only people by the name Hoffman listed in Nice Annuaires and censuses of the time were elderly women or men with different forenames and professions. Earlier, in 1906, a man named Hoffman, tailor, had been active in the city. If, after 1908, Louis Hoffman worked at Navratil's shop, his name would have disappeared from those professional registers.

But, from the evidence of the business card, it must mean that at some point between 1906 and 1912 Hoffman had left Nice for Paris.

However, due to his recorded presence in lawyers' offices, at the auctions and the fact that his passport left town with Navratil, it must also mean that Hoffman was back in Nice shortly before Navratil left and stayed for some time afterwards.

It is worth noting that in those days passports had no photos attached.

Being German-born, at the outbreak of the First World War, only two years after the *Titanic* episode, Louis Hoffman was declared an enemy alien and detained under the wartime restrictions. All his goods were seized and put into storage, to be released when hostilities ended.

Unfortunately, the man in charge of caring for Hoffman's professional commodities (which included much of the stuff he had rebought at auction from the Navratil shop) stored it in a dank, mouldy cellar full of moths.

Everything was ruined. At the end of the war, Hoffman made official complaints, to little avail.

Stefan Kozak

Papers in Michael Navratil's pockets, when his body was picked up by the *Mackay-Bennett*, include a card with Stefan's name; also a copy of a coded telegram addressed to E. Stefan. Presumably this was E for Etienne: French for Steven/Stefan.

In something of a turn-up, while looking through records of Nice lawyers, I found that, not long after the *Titanic* episode, Stefan Kozak himself was sued by Alice Baquis, also the landlady of the flat at 1 Rue Dalpozzo, for back rent of that apartment. This was the same flat which, according to the 1910 census, had formerly been occupied by the whole of Marcella's family: Michael, Marcella, the two children, a nurse (Dolinda Gamba) and Marcella's parents, Antonio Frattini and Angela Caretto.

At the request of Mademoiselle Baquis, the contents of the Rue Dalpozzo flat, where Stefan was now the lodger, were put up for auction. The sale lists brand-new ladies' dresses and coats valued at between twenty-six and fifty francs, several rolls of fabric worth from sixteen francs fifty to seventy francs, tailors' dummies, work-tables, irons, shop sofas, mannequins, and three sewing machines worth 310 francs.

Isaïe Petit immediately smelled a rat.

He stepped in, writing to the receiver on behalf of Navratil's creditors. In the letter he describes Kozak (misspelling it Cosaq) as a *prête-nom* or man of straw, a man who was colluding with Navratil to defraud the bankruptcy petition.

But Stefan Kozak was not there to defend himself, as, by July 1912, he had disappeared.

Monsieur Petit then claimed the money from the sale at Rue Dalpozzo for his own creditors.

Apart from the property which had clearly been brought upstairs from the shop below, included in the Kozak sale were: 'item 48 – a box of children's toys', which went for two francs fifty, and 'item 44 – a child's car', which sold for six francs.

Stefan Kozak did come back to Nice after the sale, as Marcella frogmarched him into Theodore Moriez's office to swear the affidavit about his involvement in Navratil's disappearance which was sent to the officials in Nova Scotia, when she was trying to have her husband officially declared dead.

As war was declared in 1914, Stefan, being Austro-Hungarian, was declared an enemy alien.

But when they came to bang him up, Stefan was once more nowhere to be found.

Charles Kirchmann

Perhaps the lack of care shown by the White Star Line towards Marcella was a result of being influenced by the weasel words of the American-German barber, Charles Kirchmann. Kirchmann, who knew about Michael Navratil's *Titanic* voyage, took the trouble of going into White Star's New York offices to enquire about him. While there, Kirchmann told them that he was 'an intimate personal friend' of Michael's. Marcella was a bad mother, he added, whose conduct was not what one would expect from a wife. Michael had caught her *en flagrant délit*, he insisted. He also admitted knowledge of the plot, telling them that Michael 'had made up his mind to get the children away from her'.

The White Star Line then charmingly forwarded this incendiary information to the authorities at Nova Scotia. After that they were far from cooperative with the claimants from Nice, referring to Isaïe Petit as someone who '*claims to be* the Commissioner or Trustee in bankruptcy…'.

Charles Kirchmann, born in Wesel, Germany but a naturalised American, opened his barbershop at 7 Rue Meyerbeer, Nice, in 1910. It was only two minutes' walk from Navratil's shop, and very convenient too for customers from the Promenade des Anglais and all its hotels. The barbershop was right behind the Hotel Westminster – the biggest and most luxurious hotel on the prom before Le Negresco opened its doors in October 1912.

Kirchmann and his American wife, Alice, lived a minute away from the Navratil shop at 47 Rue de France. Alice (sign, perhaps, of what makes a good wife?) did not work.

Although declared an enemy alien at the outbreak of the First World War, Charles Kirchmann was never rounded up by French authorities, as he was safely out of the country.

The Kirchmann barbershop was still going in 1918, but, by the next published trade directory in 1920, had disappeared from the registers. Perhaps after the war, Kirchmann had simply returned to Nice to reclaim his things and shut up shop, wiping his hands of Europe.

Henry Rey di Villarey

Enrico Emerico Emilio Rey di Villarey, known as Henry, was a friend to Marcella. But the only records of any connection come well after the death of her husband, Michael Navratil.

Born in Turin in 1880, Henry was the son of Italian Stanislao Rey di Villarey and Russian Countess Olga Viatcheslavovna Evreïnov.

Contrary to reports that Henry was living in sin with Marcella in Avenue Saint-Lambert from 1912, Henry lived separately from her. In 1912–13 he was renting an apartment at 21 Avenue Malausséna, near the Liberation Market, in the north of the city.

In 1915, once Marcella disappears from records, Henry is listed as proprietor of a flat in the same building as hers in Avenue Saint-Lambert, and that could quite possibly be the same flat as Marcella.

So, from official records, it actually appears that Henry and Marcella came together some years *after* the death of Michael Navratil.

He may or may not have been the "Sieur X' of Michael's divorce accusation. There is no way of knowing.

Neither Henry nor Marcella married – not to each other, nor anyone else...

The building where both Henry and Marcella lived in Avenue Saint-Lambert stands a few doors down from the home of the famed painter and father of the modern poster, Jules Chéret (one of Celia's favourites). I wonder whether their paths ever crossed.

'Nearer, My God, to Thee' – not the music playing at the sinking of RMS *Titanic*

The legend/cliché is that as the ship sank the band suddenly struck up a final song – the hymn 'Nearer, My God, to Thee'.
There are problems with this.

The hymn has three different settings, each one preferred by different denominations of the Protestant Church. If the ship's band really played 'Nearer, My God, to Thee', which tune did they use? American passengers would have known Lowell Mason's tune, 'Bethany'. British Anglicans would have recognised John B. Dyke's version, 'Horbury', while Methodists knew Sir Arthur Sullivan's tune, 'Proprior Deo'. None of these three tunes were included in the book of music issued to White Star Line musicians. The book had 341 songs including sacred music.

The only reports that the band struck up 'Nearer, My God, to Thee' came from two passengers in lifeboats, some way off the ship.

The only people onboard *Titanic* who talked of the band's last tune were Colonel Archibald Gracie and the ship's Marconi-operator, Harold Bride.

First Class passenger Colonel Archibald Gracie jumped the wave which swallowed the *Titanic* and eventually managed to get aboard the overturned lifeboat, Collapsible B. In his book about the tragedy, *The Truth About the Titanic*, he writes: 'It was now that the band began to play, and continued while the boats were being lowered. We considered this a wise provision tending to allay excitement. I did not recognise any of the tunes, but I know they were cheerful and were not hymns. If, as has been reported, "Nearer, My God, to Thee" was one of the selections, I assuredly should have noticed it and regarded it as a tactless warning of immediate death to us all and one likely to create a panic that our special efforts were directed towards avoiding, and which we accomplished to the fullest extent. I know of only two survivors whose names are cited by the newspapers as authority for the statement that this hymn was one of those played. On the other hand, all whom I have questioned or corresponded with, including the best qualified, testified emphatically to the contrary.'

Harold Bride was out on deck, heading towards the men trying to dislodge the last lifeboat, Collapsible A. He told the *New York Times* that the band was playing Archibald Joyce's haunting 'The Dream of Autumn', a great hit of the era – which *is* in the official White Star music book.

'The Dream of Autumn' is written in a minor key, and from a distance, sitting desolate in a lifeboat, could well have been mistaken, by those of a religious persuasion, for Sullivan's setting for 'Nearer, My God, to Thee'.

Of course the notion of the band playing 'Nearer, My God, to Thee' made a better newspaper headline and strapline for memorial brochures than 'The Dream of Autumn'.

Witnesses to the 1906 sinking of SS *Valencia*, which had gone aground only sixty feet from the cliffs of Vancouver Island, reported that the hundred passengers aboard had sung 'Nearer, My God, to Thee'. Possibly the memory of that disaster brought up the potential for a repeat.

But – even though it deprives us of another strange coincidence – I'd come down in favour of 'The Dream of Autumn'.

The coincidence? The Reverend Henry Francis Lyte, the priest who wrote the words to the multi-tuned hymn 'Nearer, My God, to Thee', died in Nice, and was buried at the English Church featured in Chapter 13 of this book.

Collapsible D

Collapsible D was the last lifeboat to leave the *Titanic* in one piece and bearing passengers.

Contrary to the Navratil family's version, based on the evidence of a three-year-old (or was it the reassuring version given later by his mother, Marcella?), all the witnesses from that terrible night in the lifeboats, and later on the *Carpathia*, are united in reporting that the Navratil children were not wrapped up warmly before being placed tenderly in Collapsible D. Michel Marcel was naked but for a shirt, while Edmond was naked beneath a ship's blanket.

Titanic survivors also agree that the children were thrown into the final lifeboat leaving the boat deck of the sinking ship at the last possible minute.

Collapsible A

Another collapsible was swept off the *Titanic*, its sides not pulled up, and as soon as it hit the water was partially submerged. It was seriously overloaded with people who swam to climb in. Most of its passengers were transferred to Collapsible D. Three dead bodies – Canadian passenger Thomson Beattie and two crewmen – remained in the lifeboat, and it was decided to leave it to drift. Collapsible A floated two hundred miles before being picked up, one month later, by RMS *Oceanic*. It was the same voyage on which Marcella was a passenger.

Apart from the three decayed corpses which were buried at sea by the crew of the *Oceanic*, a gold wedding ring was found in the hull of the boat engraved 'Edvard to Gerda', presumably belonging to Swedish Third Class passengers, Edvard and Gerda Lindel.

Children's Aid Society

Considering the hundreds of contemporary newspaper articles linking the CAS with the orphans of the *Titanic*, it is astonishing that its own files show no evidence of its role in the affair.

However, the enormous archives of the CAS New York, held at the New York Historical Society, did turn up one interesting document: a diary written by Mr R. D. Neill, who was named in various news accounts as being in charge of finding homes for the Navratil boys (and other children taken under the wing of the CAS). I quote: 'Presently Mr W spoke. "I think Mr Neill had better do the whipping." "All right," I answered. "I will." And this conference ended. I was feeling a little sore that I, a newcomer to the Society, should be chosen for this disagreeable job, however, I thought it was probably a test case and your brother and Mr Wendell wanted to see how I would acquit myself. I had no qualms and determined in my own mind to make a first class impression all round. In the afternoon Mr R. N. Brace took me aside and said "Don't you know that the Society's rules prohibit corporal punishment, you cannot whip Harry, Mr Kendal was only 'pulling your leg'." "D—n the Society's rules," I ripped out. "Wherever and whenever I meet that boy I will give him the best flogging I have the strength to give him. I will do this not because he has disappointed me, not because I have the slightest feeling of vindictiveness towards him, but simply because I have the conviction that if the boy is not punished severely *now* he is lost."'

I felt free to advise Celia that Mr Neill was not a very nice man.

Margaret Bechstein Hays

Margaret Hays didn't present such a tricky research trail.

She left the *Titanic* on Lifeboat 7, one of the first to be lowered. In her arms was her pet Pomeranian Bébé, which she had some-how acquired in Naples while touring Europe with Olive Earnshaw and Lillian Potter. Lifeboat 7 was loaded up before the 'women and children only' rule started being strictly enforced. Therefore there were quite a few men onboard, including Gilbert Tucker. At the beginning of the disaster, passengers didn't believe that the *Titanic* could sink and were reluctant to climb into little boats, while the ship, as they thought, righted itself. Members of the crew, who knew a bit more about the situation, were anxious to get people into life-boats. Captain Smith, walking by, cried out to those huddled on deck that all newly-weds should get in first. Thus Lifeboat 7 was frequently referred to as 'the honeymoon boat'. The lifeboat also carried some Frenchmen: the aviator Pierre Maréchal, the sculptor Paul Chevré, along with the fake 'baron' (in reality a Belgian-born German, Alfred Nourney, a swindler and fraud who had got an upgrade by using his false identity).

All the passengers in Lifeboat 7 had been travelling First Class.

Margaret's subsequent life, as part of the rich (but not quite rich-est) social scene of New York, is recorded in newspaper columns over the years.

During the weeks which followed the *Carpathia*'s arrival in New York, she was splashed over all the papers, along with her charges, the 'orphans of the *Titanic*'.

The Hays family is also listed in the US censuses of the period.

But for some reason, in 1909, seventeen-year-old Margaret was staying with her mother and maternal grandparents, the Bechsteins, in Piscataway Township, New Jersey, rather than with her father in the family mansion on West End Avenue and 83rd Street, New York. According to the census, her father's house had a live-in staff of two: Annie Dahoney, Cook and Hannah O'Connor, listed oddly as 'Waitress'. Both women were thirty.

Margaret's schoolfriend, Olive Earnshaw, and Olive's mother, Lily Potter, though upright members of society, devoted to charity work and in particular the Red Cross, were slightly lower down the social scale. Lily's late husband Thomas was heir to a linoleum manufacturer, while Olive's husband, Boulton Earnshaw (she was in the process of divorcing him), was a coal merchant, and formerly a gas engineer.

While they were passing through Naples, Margaret also picked up Gilbert Tucker. But pretty soon after they all got back to the States, she dumped him – for, exactly a year later, on 23 April 1913, she married Dr Charles D. Easton.

In a final twist of fate, in August 1956, Margaret Hays, now a widow, died, aged sixty-eight, while on holiday in Buenos Aires – the same town where, sixty-six years earlier, Marcella Caretto-Navratil had been born.

ACKNOWLEDGEMENTS

A titanic thank you to everyone who helped us unearth the details of this extraordinary story:

Cecilia Alvik and Alison Kenney at the City of Westminster Archives – where it all began

The Old Bailey Criminal Archive

The British Library Newspaper Archive

Laurence Sciarri and her colleagues at the Archives Départementales des Alpes Maritimes, CADAM, Nice

Sébastien Ricaud at the church of Saint-Pierre d'Arènes, Nice, and Alfonso Bartolotta of the Sanctuaire du Sacré-Coeur, Nice

Father Peter Jackson, Richard Challoner and the staff of the English American Library at the Holy Trinity English Church of Nice (featured on p. 122)

(We'd like to let everyone know that the staff, of one, at the Archives du Diocèse de Nice was particularly UNHELPFUL; in fact downright obstructive)

Jean-Philippe, Marlène, Garance, Gaëlle, Manon and all the staff at the Alliance Française de Nice, and in particular to Emilie Pardo and Martine Valdiserra for making sure our translation and interpretation of the divorce proceedings and bankruptcy files were a hundred per cent accurate. Also to Paz and the staff at the Alliance Française de Los Angeles, and Adeline and Emmanuel at the Alliance Française de London

Lina Vieira for so many things, including translations from Spanish and Portuguese, also for her kindness every day. *Abraços e beijos.*

To Carsten Hayes for translation of German

To Marcello Alessi for translation of Italian

The chief archivist of the Archives of Mondavi, Italy

The chief archivist of the Archives of the Department of the Var

Paul Smith, the company archivist at Thomas Cook

All the staff of the Belfast Titanic Museum, and especially those onboard SS *Nomadic*, the Cherbourg tender for both *Titanic* and *Oceanic*, which now rests, in all its glory, in dry dock at the museum. It was strange to stand onboard a ship which had carried so many of those *Titanic* passengers including Margaret Hays. Later the *Nomadic* may also have taken Marcella out to the *Oceanic* and carried her back to Cherbourg harbour with the two boys

Thanks to https://www.encyclopedia-titanica.org, the most magnificent source of all things Titanic

The staff of the Caird Library, National Maritime Museum, Greenwich

The staff of the Southampton SeaCity Museum (especially for returning Fidelis's lost scarf!)

William H. Miller for his illuminating talks and books about life aboard Atlantic liners

Garry D. Shutlak of the Nova Scotia Archives, Halifax, Canada

Trisha Biggar, costumière, for advice on ladies' tailoring in the early twentieth century

Erin Weinman and Jill Reichenbach of the New York Historical Society

The two Joes at Havenhurst, for giving me a haven in Hollywood

Philip Nakov, for the gift of 'The Last Night on the Titanic – unsinkable drinks, dining and style'

Radio France Bleu Azur, for keeping my soul in Nice each morning while I'm away

Robert Kirby, Dallas Smith, Sophie Austin, Alexandra Rae, Sarah Roberts, Kate Davie and everyone at United Agents

Shelley Browning at Magnolia

Jared Ceizler

Alexandra Pringle, Grace McNamee, Allegra Le Fanu, Sara Mercurio, Ella Harold, Rachel Wilkie, Angelique Tran Van Sang, Lea Beresford and everyone at Bloomsbury

Alexa Sabberton and Lucia Ravano at Personal PR

Erin Mitchell

The entertainment team at Cunard, in particular Jo Haley and Paul O'Loughlin; all the captains of *Queen Mary 2* – past and present; and our very own Rob Ritchie, alias Robbie Howie. (It is worth noting that Cunard's steamer RMS *Carpathia* is the only ship which comes out of this saga with any honour, and, in fact, glory. Bravo Cunard!)

Brahmin Jalloul (Préfecture de Nice) pour son aide avec les procédures infernales à cause de l'enfer du Brexit

Olivier Leperini – for legal guidance

Daniel, Fabrizio, Florence, Patrick, Agbessi, Amine, Gianni and *tous nos amis aux Jardins du Capitole*

Tous nos amis du Safari and La Civette du Cours: Raymond, Cyril, Charles, Daniel, John, Michel, Gilbert, Anaïs, Loïc, JF, Laetitia and (even though you've moved away) Richard and Sebastien

Cédric *et toute l'équipe de l'Auberge Saint-Antoine*, who kept us going through post-confinement

Marilène Geille et l'équipe du Séjour Café

Laurent, Virginie and Frederic at the Negresco Hotel, which during the setting of this book was a mere building site! (p. 274)

OGC Nice forever. Issa Nissa! (but, remember, Mèfi!)

And *baietas* to the City of Nice: beautiful, moving, elegant and generous. Dear France, thank you for being a refuge from the madness of Covid-19 and Little Britain...

A NOTE ON THE AUTHOR

Celia Imrie is an Olivier Award-winning and Screen Actors Guild-nominated actress. She is known for her film roles in *The Best* and *The Second Best Exotic Marigold Hotels*, *Calendar Girls*, *Nanny McPhee*, *Bridget Jones*, *Absolutely Fabulous*, *Year by the Sea*, *A Cure for Wellness*, *Finding Your Feet* and *Mamma Mia! Here We Go Again*, and for the FX series *Better Things*. Celia Imrie is also the author of her autobiography, *The Happy Hoofer*, and the top ten *Sunday Times* bestselling novels in the Nice Trilogy – *Not Quite Nice*, *Nice Work (If You Can Get It)* and *A Nice Cup of Tea* and *Sail Away*.

@CeliaImrie

Fidelis Morgan is the author of several non-fiction history books, including *The Female Wits*. She has lectured around the world, from Stanford University to the University of Utrecht. In 2014 she was Granada Artist-in-Residence at the University of California. Her four historical murder mysteries have been translated into several languages. Fidelis's acting roles include parts in *Jeeves and Wooster*, *As Time Goes By* and *A Little Chaos*. Her directing credits include *Drama at Inish* and *But It Still Goes On* at the Finborough Theatre, and Celia Imrie's revue *Laughing Matters* at Crazy Coqs and the St James Theatre.

www.fidelismorgan.com